PRAISE FOR *THE VA*

"John Renehan's *The Valley* is both a gripping, tightly wound n
served look at the complex internal politics of the U.S. Army, the deterioration of men tasked with too vague a mission and too little support, and what happens when they trifle with the intricate power structures deep in the mountains of Afghanistan."

—PHIL KLAY, *NEW YORK TIMES* BESTSELLING AUTHOR OF *REDEPLOYMENT*

"*The Valley* is a riveting, gut-wrenching tale destined to take its place alongside Tim O'Brien's *The Things They Carried* and Philip Caputo's *A Rumor of War* as modern warfare classics that paint their word pictures in emotion as much as blood."

—*PROVIDENCE JOURNAL*

"The author served in Iraq but sets his debut novel in deepest and highest Afghanistan, in a premise that prompts comparisons to Joseph Conrad and Francis Ford Coppola. But his story, told with suspense and substance, stands alone."

—*MILITARY TIMES*

More Praise for John Renehan and *The Valley*

"*The Valley* is a puzzling mystery, a relentless action chronicle, a riddling brainteaser—and a book that's hard to put down."

—*The Wall Street Journal*

"*The Valley* is an acid-rock infused thriller, a police procedural camouflaged in a mind job." —*Los Angeles Review of Books*

"A military thriller packed with action and mystery. . . . A must-read if you want a glimpse of the turmoil Americans faced in Afghanistan or if you just want a page-flipping good yarn."

—*Kirkus Reviews*

"Renehan has a fine eye for the etiquette of the Army, as delicate and complex as the rural aristocracy depicted in Jane Austen's novels." —Thomas E. Ricks, *Foreign Policy*

"John Renehan's *The Valley* is an absorbing novel of war that refuses to give easy answers or wallow in sentimental hero-worship. His characters talk the way real soldiers do, and he perfectly captures both the intensity of deployment and the blurred morality that can develop in remote outposts, under fire, far from home and family. *The Valley* belongs among the great novels of America's twenty-first-century wars."

—Kayla Williams, author of *Love My Rifle More Than You*

"For readers who absolutely need a payoff, there's a big reveal at the end that wraps up almost all of the mystery's loose ends. But *The Valley* is really about how our vague mission in Afghanistan affects the men charged with carrying it out. That's what will stay with you." —Military.com's *Under the Radar*

"*The Valley* is rich with detail, compelling, and complex."

—*The Columbus Dispatch*

"A page-turner. . . . *The Valley* gives the best description of the American military base environment (and the post-9/11 Army) that I've ever read, both accurate in the details and evocative in atmosphere."

—*The Weekly Standard*

THE VALLEY

THE VALLEY

JOHN RENEHAN

An imprint of Penguin Random House LLC
375 Hudson Street
New York, New York 10014

Previously published as a Dutton hardcover, 2015

First paperback printing, March 2016

THE LIBRARY OF CONGRESS HAS CATALOGUED THE HARDCOVER EDITION OF THIS BOOK AS FOLLOWS:
Renehan, John, author.
The Valley / John Renehan.
pages cm
ISBN 978-0-525-95486-6 (hardback) 978-0-451-47186-4 (paperback)
1. United States. Army—Fiction. 2. Americans—Afghanistan—Fiction. 3. War stories. I. Title.
PS3618.E5749V35 2015
813'.6—dc23 2014018588

Printed in the United States of America
10 9 8 7 6 5 4 3 2 1

For Susan, with all the rest of it

THE
VALLEY

GHOSTS

In the dream he climbed a narrow foot-trail alone in the sun, on a bare mountainside littered with metal corpses.

At the summit above him the stone building sat framed in light. She stood shadowed in the window, as she always did. He saw no face.

The path ran straight to the door. He pressed higher, pebbles and gravel skittering away beneath his bare feet.

He passed one hulk. The twisted remains of a car. Another was unrecognizable. Strips and shards of metal lay strewn across the trail. He felt one enter the underside of his foot.

A concrete bunker built into the hillside was full of soldiers. They reached their arms through the opening and called wordlessly to him as he pushed on higher.

The path grew steep, his feet slipping with every step now. The shards went into his soles, straight through to the bone, and opened the soft flesh between his toes.

He leaned forward and scrabbled at the ground with his fingers, trying to pull himself higher. He saw metal come through the back of one hand and cleave the fingers of another.

The mountain heaved beneath him. The figure in the window turned away and receded into the little building as one of its walls slid away in a cascade of stone blocks. A voice from below called without words for him to come back down.

His footing gave way as the mountain buckled. He fell forward and met the trail with his face. A shard went through his cheek and into his tongue. The bombs fell in earnest, all around him. He clawed the ground but it disintegrated beneath him as he slid backward into the crater—

He jolted awake, honking the horn with the palms of both hands. The meager little toot cried *4-cylinder economy rental,* but to him it was deafening in the dark and quiet of the sleeping neighborhood.

The center console of the car had some napkins wadded into it, which he pulled out and used to dry his face. He sat with his hands on his legs, eyeing the little house and waiting for his breathing to return to normal.

The second-story windows remained dark. He sat back against the seat and stole a look in the vehicle's mirror. The eyes that met his in the silvered rectangle looked coal-dark and hard, the gray half-circles smudged beneath them hollow and soft. He sighed.

A backpack sat on the passenger seat. From its overstuffed depths he produced a miniature leatherbound book, small enough to fit in the palm of his hand. A taut leather band inside it held a tiny pen.

He drew this out as he flipped through to the inside of the back cover. On the last page of the book he scratched a little hash mark, next to a collection of other hash marks.

Stuffing the book away he reached for the ignition, where the key sat in the OFF position. He turned it to ON and threw an arm over the passenger seat.

Casting a final glance at the house, he craned over his shoulder and rolled the car in neutral down a gravel drive. He waited until it was on the street and pointed downhill before starting the engine and putting it in gear.

Bungalow homes slept on either side. At the end of the block, pulling the wheel to the right, he switched on the lights.

The dim road cut across the broad foothills of a low coastal mountain range. Above and to his right, the forested ridges. Below and to his left, moonlit rooftops spilled down four miles to a black bay spanned by great bridges.

Receding behind him, beyond the houses and above the trees, a soaring gothic building rose like a cathedral against the night. In its shadowed buttresses the hosts and legions, gargoyles and cherubim, crouched and dancing, wept and stood watch. He turned onto the main descending road and made his way down to the edge of the water.

Out over the bridges, across the glassine bay and into the hills. Another hour south to where the highway met the ocean. Then the long moonlit ride along the mountainous California coast.

There were more direct routes to Los Angeles. He took the long way, winding beneath the crags with the waves crashing far below. He rolled the windows down and played no music. The hours turned small.

South of Big Sur he passed beneath a castle built on a mountaintop by a long-dead man who'd made his fortune in newspapers. When the highway turned in from the coast he stopped in a one-street tourist village hidden in a tiny valley.

He remembered its late-night liquor store. Squinting under banks of fluorescents, he purchased a tall can of "energy drink," which tasted like bubble gum dissolved in cleaning fluid.

The road from there skirted the ocean again, past a great rock that loomed invisibly from the dark sea, then continued inland and began to hint at civilization. He rolled up the windows and put on the radio, wincing as he slurped at the can.

The sun was rising when he arrived at Los Angeles International Airport. He dropped his car at a frenzied off-site rental facility crowded with exhausted vacationers, slung his backpack over his shoulder, and went through the motions at the security checkpoint with as little human interaction as he could manage. On the airplane he turned down the flight attendant's offer of a free drink and promptly passed out.

The plane flew east, through the day and the night and into the next day. He woke after a couple of hours and couldn't sleep any longer. They made many stops.

In Ireland, he bought a pint in an airport pub that was inexplicably open in the middle of the night. In the Netherlands he changed his undershirt and socks in the bathroom, pulling fresh ones from his straining pack and tossing the old into a garbage can.

He switched to a private charter and flew on. In Kuwait City he and his fellow passengers milled in a private terminal for an hour or so before climbing back on board and heading east again. He thought: *Wouldn't it have been faster going the other way?*

At its final destination, in the hollow of the night, the plane disgorged its passengers into quietly orchestrated chaos.

A cavernous "terminal" of wood and canvas hummed with the sounds of transit—parties seeking other parties, terse announcements issued on lo-fi speaker boxes, the zip of tightening backpack straps, and the soft thump of duffels released to the floor. There were civilians—reporters, private contractors, people whose occupations he could not identify—and many military.

He followed a group of these outside into the dark. They trudged over gravel paths between tents and temporary buildings, to a large and well-lit shack at the edge of a black airfield. There they checked a dry-erase board that passed for a departures list, and sat down to wait. He watched a slightly built young journalist with quiffed hair and rectangular glasses fiddle with his backpack and press badge.

Throughout the night, in twos and threes, they disappeared. The airfield serviced a steady stream of helicopters and cargo planes, coming and going in the dark. One would arrive, barely audible as it crested the hills, its sound building until the whole shack vibrated.

People would file out into the dark and rush of noise, the plywood door snapping shut behind them. Off they would go to their destinations. Then silence, until the next.

It was a small crew that was scheduled to ride on his flight. Him plus two reporters and ten military. He had some time. He stood outside the shack for a while, watching the flights come and go.

He enjoyed hearing the first comforting sounds of the helicopters beyond the hills, trying to spot them as they approached. With all their lights turned out this was a trick. They could be right above you, deafening pale ghosts in the night, before you spotted them.

And he enjoyed standing in the silence after they left. Watching the blue tarmac lights wink at the empty sky.

Deep in the night his turn grew close. A great cargo plane was to come and take him and a few others to their final stop. A helicopter wouldn't cut it. Their destination was too distant—one of the farthest locales serviced by this particular airfield, and one of the least desired.

Tore up, the young soldier was thinking, *from the floor up.*

He was used to seeing disorganized civilians, sloppy contractors, even people who were in the Air Force. You got 'em all when you came to this place.

Not everybody can be as squared away as us, his sergeant would say if he were there. *It's a grab bag in this place.*

He understood. Still, the kid sort of felt obligated. How old was this guy? Twenty-five? Older? Old enough to know. Besides, he really wanted to wash his hands and get moving before he got yelled at.

He approached and reached out to tap the guy's shoulder.

"Excuse me, sir."

He turned, startled. A soldier, nineteen years old, tops. Standing there waiting for who knows how long.

He came back to himself, noticing for the first time the sound of a large propeller-driven airplane taxiing outside. His flight was here. The soldier was probably desperate to wash his hands and get his bag and get outside before he got chewed out for cutting things close with the plane.

When the time had neared, he'd gone to the modest restroom to wash his face. He'd lingered over the only sink staring into the only mirror, surveying the damage of the last thirty-six hours of travel.

He figured he had slept for about four of those hours. His dark eyes still bore their dark circles, which he'd been pondering when the soldier startled him.

"Sorry," he said.

He stepped aside and turned to go as the soldier started washing.

"No problem, sir."

The kid was clean-scrubbed, eager.

"Um, excuse me—sir?"

He turned back.

"I'm sorry, sir, but your . . ."

By way of explanation the soldier reached up to his right shoulder, pinched his fingers together, and tugged. He came away with a long, green clump of tangled thread, which he held up for inspection.

"I figured you hadn't seen it there, sir," the kid said, suddenly flustered.

He reddened and thanked the young soldier, who gave an embarrassed "No problem, sir," and disappeared.

He turned back to the mirror, regarding himself. A young man eyed him back warily from beneath a dark brow that angled toward a scowl, as though he were always squinting just a bit against a strong light. His hair, the color of deep forest soil, was cropped to an inch or less all round. His eyes, though yet unlined, managed at all times to seem burdened, leaving people with the disconcerting impression that they'd met a much older person who'd been manhandled into a much younger body and then left there to just lump it.

Those eyes traveled down his own person.

C'mon, man.

The laces of one tan boot loose and dangling. One pant leg partly untucked from the other boot. Coat appallingly rumpled, even for a camouflage coat. Turning to inspect his shoulder, he saw that the thread had been hanging loose from just behind where a Velcro American flag patch sat. The patch was crooked.

Which is to say, he was in the Army. He hated the Army.

He tore off the flag and replaced it, carefully. He bent and fixed his laces and pants, straightening to inspect the rest of him.

In black thread on the center of his chest, on a square of Velcro-backed material, was sewn the vertical bar of a first lieutenant. An officer. A low-ranking one.

To one side of the bar was a Velcro strip that read U.S. ARMY. To the other side was a name tape that read BLACK.

He had a first name, though Lieutenant Black knew to a near certainty that for the next six months not a soul he encountered would use it. Few of those people could really be counted as friends. Few, he was fairly sure, even knew what that name was.

He rooted around and found a pair of nail clippers, using them to snip off several other loose threads. When he was done, he extracted a small razor from his backpack.

He turned on the water in the sink, which ran only cold, and proceeded to scrape the wet razor across his face. When he finished he packed it away and gave a last look at the slightly less haggard young man in the mirror.

He shouldered his pack and left.

At the door of the shack he swiped his ID card through a reader mounted in the door frame, presided over by a sleepy soldier reading a book, and went out onto the windy tarmac with the others. Waited to be given the signal. Trudged up the ramp into the darkened cargo hold. Strapped himself in to a seat made of netting, watched the ramp close, listened to the roar of the engines filling the black compartment. Closed his eyes and slept at last as the aircraft went up into the night, up there with the ghosts.

PART ONE

1

Dude, don't do it."

Black startled and turned in his chair to see one of his least favorite people in the Army.

Bradley Derr, twenty-four going on college freshman, slouched behind him with his hands in his uniform pockets, lip fat with dip, peering over Black's shoulder at the memo sitting out in the open on his desk.

Black hadn't heard him approach. Hadn't even noticed as Derr placed the plastic soda bottle he used for his dip spit on the desk right next to Black's arm.

He considered the bottle now as its two inches of dark brown fluid content came to rest. He turned slowly back to Derr and regarded him with a look that he thought was full of significance. It bounced right off Derr's sunburned forehead.

"Damn, Black, you lost in space or something?"

He had been. Before Derr appeared he'd been staring for a long time at the same piece of paper that Derr now gestured to with a flip of his chin.

"Dude, I'm telling you. Don't do it."

Derr was a lieutenant. A junior officer like Black. Unlike Black, he did not work behind a desk in the battalion's paperwork office.

Derr spent most of his time outside the dreary midsize base where Black spent all of his time, stomping through the Afghan backhills with his platoon and shooting at people. It was precisely what Derr had imagined he would be doing when he set out to become an Army officer, and the universe had graciously given him no reason to question his assumptions.

Once every couple of weeks he would come back to the base with his guys and spend a day or so crunching around gravel pathways in his sunglasses and eating at the chow hall. When he had paper-type business he needed help with, he made his way back to Black, to be found reliably behind his desk doing precisely the opposite of what *he* had imagined when he became an Army officer.

Which was where Derr stood now, sunglasses inverted on the back of his head, looking down at Black with mild pity from beneath blond gel spikes.

"What do you need, Derr?"

"I need a hard copy of my pay stub so I can show the bitchwife I ain't holding out on her."

Derr considered himself a laugh riot, in addition to handsome and suave. Apparently some misguided young lady somewhere back in the United States thought so too. Derr was, inexplicably, married.

"Bitchwife" was only one of the fond names by which Black had come to know Derr's beloved. She was also, depending on the day, "fuckslut," "my opinion," or "the 'ho,'" along with other names Black cared to forget. It occurred to him that he did not actually know the unfortunate girl's name.

"Such deep respect," he said blandly as he turned to his computer.

Derr snorted.

"Pfft! You should hear what she makes me call her in bed."

He laughed and sent a fresh muddy slug into his dip bottle. He was proud of his ability to spit shining wads of tobacco phlegm cleanly through a two-centimeter Coke bottle opening, straight to the tidy puddle at the bottom, without leaving the brown residue often seen trickling down the insides of such receptacles. Derr considered this, alone among all aspects of the Army's second-favorite pastime after smoking, to be unsightly.

"You know," he said, "that's funny, Black, because 'Deep Respect' is actually our name for one of our things she makes me do."

He adopted an athletic stance and prepared an expressive tableau.

"I sort of get her by the legs right here, and—"

"Why don't I print your thing."

Derr shrugged.

"Suit yourself, bud. Deep Respect's good stuff, though. Works every time."

Black did not ask and tried not to wonder what "works" meant. He called up Derr's records and printed off his most recent Leave and Earnings Statement. He observed that, as fellow first lieutenants, he and Derr made precisely the same amount of money.

Who should be more offended by that?

"Here's your L.E.S., man."

He handed it over.

"Thanks, Black."

Derr turned to go, then stopped and thumbed at the paper on the desk.

"And I'm telling you, dude. Don't do it."

Black sighed. He finally bit.

"Why not, Derr?"

"Because you think you got hosed. You think the Army fucked you over that thing."

That thing.

Black said nothing.

"Okay, so you need to fuck it back," Derr continued, shrugging as though this were the simplest thing. "Don't sign that paper, and don't take it to the commander. Fuck that shit."

Derr rotated ninety degrees left.

"Am I right, Sergeant Cousins?"

Cousins worked with Black in the "S-1 shop," which was Army-speak for the battalion's administrative office, handling personnel business for the unit's four hundred people and supervising several paperwork soldiers, none of whom were present for some reason. He reclined heavily behind his desk with his feet up and his nose down in a men's magazine.

"Mmm, you got it, sir."

He didn't look up.

Black was searching for something else dry or snide to say to Derr when it occurred to him that, coming from a guy like Derr considered himself to be, to a guy like he believed Black to be, this was pretty generous and friendly advice.

"Thanks, Derr."

"You got it, bud," Derr said graciously.

He wove his way through desks and makeshift workstations toward the makeshift door.

"Take it easy, Sergeant Cousins. Gotta go fight and stuff."

Cousins turned a page. Derr called over his shoulder.

"Don't take no Deep Respect from the Army, Black."

He chuckled at his own wit and fired another clean shot through his spit bottle opening, which while walking was actually a good trick.

"Nothin' but net," he told himself happily as the plywood door clattered shut behind him.

The office was quiet again. Black resumed staring at the paper on his desk. Cousins tossed his magazine aside and turned a balding head and gentle eyes on Black.

"You know, sir, far be it from me to agree with anything that Lieutenant Derr says, but he's kind of right."

Black just stared at the paper.

"I mean, you got your own opinion of things, so don't let the Army tell you what's what. You tell *them*."

"How does not signing this help me tell the Army?"

"Gotta show up to stand up, L.T."

L.T. The Army nickname for lieutenants, the most junior and least experienced of officers.

It came from the way the rank was abbreviated in writing: capital *L*, capital *T*. Some sergeant sometime in prehistory thought it was funny to spell it out loud and address his green platoon leader that way instead of "sir" or "ma'am."

Over the years it evolved. Sometimes it was a term of familiarity or affection, of something approaching respect. Sometimes it was just a way to avoid having to say "sir" to some college kid who had been in the Army for about a fifth of the amount of time you had but was in charge of you because he had been anointed as an officer.

Black was reasonably sure that where Cousins was concerned, it was more or less the former. Cousins considered him a worthy project.

"Thanks, Sergeant Cousins."

"Got your back, sir. Now come on, let's get some chow."

Chow was a frequent topic of conversation in the office. Cousins pushed back and eased himself to his feet.

Black checked his watch and told Cousins he'd meet him there in a minute. Cousins gave a *Suit yourself* shrug and strolled out.

Alone in the office, Black sat with the pen in his hand, hovering over the memo, for a long time before he finally put point to paper and scratched out his name. He put the memo into a manila envelope and sealed it, setting it on the desktop. He looked at it a long moment and left.

Outside, the air was cool. An easy fall breeze cut across the front of the temporary office shack where he and Cousins and the paperwork soldiers spent their days sitting and doing paper and talking about food. He cut left, though he knew Cousins had cut right.

The gravel network weaved its way between shipping containers, little prefab housing units, Porta-Potties, generator trailers, and all the tidy detritus of the American army deployed overseas. Soon he was walking on bare ground, climbing the dirt slope of a man-made hill.

It was probably sixty feet high, standing solitary above the rest of the base. The top had been bulldozered flat and across its surface sprouted a crowded collection of antennas, transmitting dishes, and all manner of electronic communications gear. They called it Radio Hill.

He turned at the top and had a sweeping view of Forward Operating Base Omaha. His "fob." His home.

It was as dreary and flat, aside from the hill he was standing on, as every large FOB in Afghanistan was dreary and flat. Like most others, it had grown in fits and starts as military needs changed over time. From above, its hodgepodge nature was clear to see, with different "neighborhoods" and working areas identifiable by the different types of temporary buildings and construction materials.

He walked around to the far side of the antenna cluster to see what he'd come to see. Radio Hill was close to the edge of the FOB.

One of Afghanistan's great eastern plains spread before him. Brown grass and scrub rolled gently to the horizon. Beyond that rose the great dark mountain massifs of the Nuristan branch of the Hindu Kush.

Black came to Radio Hill nearly every evening to watch the sun go down behind them, watch the shafts cut across their summits and the valley entrances fill with shadow.

The mountains were where most of the fighting that FOB Omaha supported took place. Oh, there were the usual mortar attacks on the base itself from time to time. But those were bands of jokers, paid small change to lob some shells from a safe distance and keep the Americans on their toes.

The real-deal guys, the guys who fondly remembered the brief heady days when the law of an angry god was the law of the land and who wanted to make it so again, the guys with the forces and planning ability and networks to do it—*those* guys were in the mountains. The hills at the edge of the plain were where people like Derr spent their weeks, trading steel barbs.

Other units went deeper, and the fighting got worse. A smaller number of thrill-seeking Americans more or less lived in those mountains, far up the deadly ridges and valleys in tiny outposts at the limits of Omaha's lifelines.

Those soldiers fought every day. Fought for their lives, for the tiny patches of ground they had staked out. They might spend a year in Afghanistan and only see the FOB once or twice.

That's who the antennas on Radio Hill were for talking to.

Not directly, but through a series of retransmission hubs perched strategically on ridges and peaks like signal fires, bringing the signals over the summits and across the valleys until they found the little huddled enclaves of American life. Black would stand and imagine the invisible network, its tenuous threads running from where he stood, out through the air over the plain and beyond the horizon, and wonder what was happening at those outposts at that moment.

One thing he could tell with certainty from atop Radio Hill was that there would be rain in those uplands tonight. Lots of it. A roiling block of thunderheads gathered over the peaks across the whole range. Some soldiers would be having some sucky guard shifts in some sucky mountain locales.

The sun had gone down fully. Black headed back down and trudged a half mile to the "dining facility." The chow hall. He wasn't hungry but figured he needed to eat.

It was one of the largest and newest buildings on the base. Steel exterior beams and stylish aluminum temp-to-perm exterior walls and adornments. A first-time visitor seeing it from the outside could have been forgiven for mistaking it for a college campus athletics center.

Black marveled every time at the bacchanalian foodstravaganza inside. It was run by a major defense contractor, and it would have made the most well-appointed hospital cafeteria in America blush.

Wings and burgers and steaks. Fries nightly. Entrees upon entrees. Buttered vegetables in steam trays. Grill-to-order station. Banks of refrigerator cases stocked with sodas and sports drinks. Sandwich bar. Salad bar. Pasta bar. Ice cream bar with thirty-two flavors. Soft-serve machine. Cookie piles. Selection of cakes. Four times a day, including Midnight Chow, every day. If you lived on the FOB, as Black did, it was now entirely possible to get fat while deployed to war.

"Hey, shitbag."

There it was. He'd been moving through the tray line when he heard it. The voice came from the exit line passing by in the opposite direction a few feet away.

He didn't turn or look up. Didn't have to. He knew the voice—knew most of the individual voices that periodically harassed him as he went about his business on the FOB. He knew which name he would have seen on the uniform next to the lieutenant's or captain's rank had he bothered to look up.

So he didn't look up, and the owner of the voice didn't expect him to. It was more of an obligatory ritual by now. He'd grown used to it in the months since he came to Omaha. Almost numb to it, he told himself.

"That's right, shitbag," said the voice, from behind him now, receding toward the exit. "See you next time."

Black got his food and went to a table in one of the big building's distant corners. He didn't find Cousins and didn't try. He knew Cousins didn't really mind anyway. He sat alone and read a mystery novel about a maladjusted Los Angeles detective named after a Renaissance painter who specialized in scenes of earthly sin and eternal damnation.

He peered over the top of it from time to time, watching the spectacle.

Hordes of soldiers lined the cafeteria tables beneath stark fluorescents, scarfing chow. Sports highlight reels traded places with Department of Defense commercials on plasma screens bolted below the rafters. Wall posters spoke of LEADERSHIP and DETERMINATION, accomplished through rock climbing or catamaran driving, or told 1940s-era recruits that Uncle Sam needed them.

Soon, orange and brown vines of crepe paper would encircle the rafters and the walls would fill up with the paper cutouts of turkeys, pilgrims, and cornucopias that he remembered from Thanksgiving time at elementary school. The feast—four feasts, really—on that day would be unbelievable.

"FOBbits" was the Army term for soldiers who spend their whole deployments living on the FOB, working in air-conditioned little office spaces and eating chow and rarely venturing outside the base. It was a term Black had once used himself, before he became one.

It was dark when he emerged into the cooling night. Passing under an aluminum awning he heard another voice calling him. This one he didn't recognize.

"Excuse me there, sir."

He turned and saw the rank. He stopped, glaring.

Sergeant major is the highest of the enlisted ranks. Sergeants' sergeants, in for life.

A favorite sergeant major project is squaring away young lieutenants, whom they generally view as bumbling embarrassments to the officer corps. Black didn't know this one, but he looked the part. Short, stocky, fiftyish, square chin, mouth a grim line.

"Well, sir, if you don't mind, you're just a little crooked here. . . ."

Black's own hand slapped hard over his own American flag patch at just the instant he heard the tearing sound of the Velcro coming up. The sergeant major's iron finger and thumb were momentarily caught beneath his palm. The man's eyes went wide.

"I do mind, Sergeant Major."

Black turned and stalked off into the dark, leaving the flabbergasted old soldier with his mouth hanging open.

That was dumb.

The guy would find out what unit Black was in. A sergeant major can find out anything. He would tell the story like Black had struck him, which was basically as bad as punching out a general.

"Hey, sir!"

He ignored the voice from behind him. Some other sergeant who saw the thing, no doubt, coming to do a citizen's arrest on a lieutenant who'd violated the cardinal rule of always kissing a sergeant major's ass.

"Hey, sir!"

Heavy hand on his shoulder. He windmilled it off him and spun around in the dark, hands up and ready to shove.

"GET THE FU—"

Cousins. Standing there wide-eyed in the dark, his face confusion.

Black felt himself deflate. He said nothing. Just turned around and walked away.

"Sorry, Sergeant Cousins," he mumbled as he disappeared between a row of generators and shipping containers.

He didn't stop walking until he got back to the S-1 shop, didn't stop to talk to the couple of S-1 soldiers who greeted him along the way—didn't respond to their "evening, L.T." or return their salutes. He didn't stop as he weaved his way through the desks and swept up the manila envelope, already on his way back out the door.

Didn't even stop, really, as he knocked on his commander's door, two temporary buildings over. Didn't wait for the inevitable "Come!" but just strode through as he knocked, envelope clutched in his hand.

Lieutenant Colonel Gayley, the battalion commander, responsible for the lives and welfare of the unit's four hundred soldiers, barely looked up from the papers on his desk. He was busy signing something.

"Oh, Lieutenant Black. Good. Sergeant Cousins found you."

Black blinked.

"Here, have a seat. I've got something for you."

He gestured offhandedly at one of the two chairs permanently stationed before his desk. Every commander in the Army had two chairs before his desk. He rooted among his stacks.

"Okay, here we go."

Gayley located a packet of papers, which he began skimming.

"This is the thing."

"Sir?"

"You're not going to like it."

2

Black had decided a while back that Gayley was not a bad guy, as far as commanders went.

True, the beating bureaucratic heart of the Army had a slobbering crush on officers like Gayley. Somewhere in a lab at West Point his instructors had mixed him in a bowl, whipping into him the precise proportions of accountability, flawless attention to detail, chipper optimism, and bold cooperativeness, folding in a hardy tolerance for paperwork and a relentless professional ambition, with a dash of tanned physical perfection for flavor. They had tried and failed many times before, but when they poured Gayley into the mold and pulled him from the oven, they saw what they'd made and cried, *That's it!* then hugged one another and drank reasonable amounts of sparkling cider to celebrate.

He was a little of everything and a little of nothing. He yelled at the right people, didn't yell at the wrong people, didn't fail in his duties, didn't cause surprises or embarrassments. He was just so.

Despite these attractive qualities, Black felt less of the natural suspicion that someone like Gayley would ordinarily fill him with. Most commanders in Gayley's position, having a lieutenant in Black's position fall into their lap, would have put that lieutenant in the flunkiest officer job in the whole battalion and forgotten all about him.

Which was precisely what Gayley had done. Being assigned involuntarily to the S-1 job was essentially an announcement by the Army that *This officer is not suited for any other task*.

But Gayley had not forgotten about Black entirely, and in his own way he'd made a project of his young lieutenant. Mostly this entailed asking him how things were going from time to time, and on the rare occasions when the two were alone giving well-meaning motivational talks on the themes of Making the Most of Things, Turning Setbacks into Opportunities, and Keeping Your Chin Up, sometimes with a bona fide clap on the shoulder for punctuation.

Black tolerated these with more patience than he ordinarily would, because while most officers in the battalion either ignored him completely or were openly hostile, Gayley was merely insufferably patronizing. That he could work with.

Besides, there were aspects of Gayley that Black genuinely respected. He was not fat, for one.

And Gayley had not, in his methodical hand-over-hand up the Army ladder, lost the ability to be succinct. Somehow, despite being known throughout the battalion as a Dudley Do-Right with golden hair and a six-sided jaw who harangued unsuspecting soldiers at length about the power of positive thinking, Gayley could still get to the point when it came to actual work. True to form, he tossed the packet of papers across the table so Black could see it.

"Fifteen-six officer."

"Sir?"

He picked up the sheaf.

"Fifteen-six, son. It's your turn."

Army Regulation 15-6 governs investigations of misconduct within a military unit. The 15-6 investigation is the commander's initial inquiry into possible wrongdoing. The offense might be significant or trivial, might lead to nothing or to court-martials and ended careers. But it all starts with the 15-6.

The investigation must be conducted by an officer of greater rank to the individual or individuals suspected of the wrongdoing. Because most of the people in the Army are not officers, and because most higher-ranking officers don't want to spend their time serving as amateur internal affairs investigators, most 15-6 investigations can safely be shunted off on lieutenants, the lowest-ranking officers, without violating any rules.

Black remembered how a friend had explained it to him when he drew his first 15-6, involving a break-in at a barracks back in the States.

You are investigating soldiers who don't know you, because the regulations require that the fifteen-six officer be from a different unit from where the misconduct happened. So they see you only as a rat. You get no help from the unit itself, because you are *a rat, and also because you are a lieutenant, and no one respects lieutenants because they haven't proven anything to anyone yet. No one trusts you, you get no help, and the whole thing will suck.*

No sense drawing out the pain. Black began skimming the cover sheet. Gayley said nothing.

He recognized the unit involved. Third Battalion, 44th Infantry Regiment, abbreviated 3/44, had its headquarters and barracks on the far side of FOB Omaha. Black often passed through its neighborhood on foot while walking across the base.

He stopped short when he got to REASON FOR INVESTIGATION. He looked up at Gayley, confused.

"A *warning* shot, sir?"

"Whole new war, Lieutenant."

He was talking about the change.

With the military pushing further and further into the rural backlands, its leadership in Washington had pushed out new "rules of engagement" for when and how American troops would use force. Someone had figured out that it's tough to convince civilians you are there to protect them when you keep shredding cars full of people who didn't realize they had to slow down at the checkpoint, or vaporizing four homes with a five-hundred-pound bomb when you really only wanted to get the one bad guy in the one house.

These stern directives, filtered through ordinary bureaucratic tendencies, predictably resulted in many, many routine 15-6 investigations over largely routine uses of force, even when that force resulted in no harm to people or damage to property.

Black realized he was looking at one of these situations right now.

Some soldiers had fired warning shots near some Afghan civilians in a tense situation in a village a few weeks earlier. Had accidentally killed a local man's goat the night before, apparently, and there had been some kind of confrontation the next morning when they went to make amends. It looked like no one had been harmed and, aside from a broken flower pot or something, there had been no property damage. The situation dissipated, and the man had been paid in cash for his loss.

So now Black would have to trudge across Omaha, corner these soldiers on their free time, and grill them over having, by the looks of it, done the right thing.

"When are they coming in, sir?"

"Huh?"

Gayley seemed confused.

"Their next trip in from the field, sir."

Ordinarily, for an incident occurring away from the FOB, you'd wait and interview the soldiers at their unit during one of their periodic resupply trips back to base. Another plus, then: He'd be interrogating guys during their few precious hours of downtime in the middle of a war.

And they're gonna spend their one rest day answering some strange officer's questions and feeling like criminals and thinking about what a fat lot of good doing the right thing did them.

Gayley shook his head.

"They're not coming back in."

Now Black was confused.

"They're busy fighting a war, Lieutenant," Gayley explained. "They're not coming back for this. You're going to them."

Busy fighting a war.

"Sir, can I ask a question?"

"Shoot."

"I haven't been to the field since I came to Omaha, except to fly out for R&R leave and back again last week."

He cleared his throat.

"Am I the best choice here?"

Gayley didn't blink.

"It's the new selection system," he grumbled. "Integrity in selection or some bullshit. Apparently I can't be trusted to pick my own investigating officers anymore."

He was talking about the other change that had come out along with the new rules of engagement. Now 15-6 officers were to be assigned by computer at the division headquarters, multiple levels above Gayley's office. It was essentially random.

The colonel's face betrayed nothing. But Black had hung around the S-1 shop long enough to know that nearly any regulation like this allowed leeway for a commander to decide that a given officer was not fit for a given duty. Either Gayley thought more of Black than he let on, or he recognized the task for the pointless makework it was and didn't want to spend one of his other lieutenants on it.

Hard to say.

"Where are they located, sir?"

Gayley cleared his throat.

"Combat Outpost Vega."

He did not elaborate. Just looked at Black as though waiting for a reaction.

"I'm not familiar with that location, sir."

Gayley nodded once and picked up a folded map. It was covered with topographic markings and military grid lines. Black saw a lot of green.

Gayley flipped it like a Frisbee. It spun across his desk and straight into Black's lap, startling him.

"You're going up the Valley."

There were many valleys in the mountains of Nuristan, and many were hard places where people died hard deaths. But there was only one Valley. Black didn't even know its proper name. But he knew about the Valley. Everyone at FOB Omaha did.

It was the farthest, and the hardest, and the worst. It lay deeper and higher in the mountains than any other place Americans ventured in

Nuristan, beyond the front range you could see from Radio Hill, and beyond the peaks that lay beyond those. You had to travel through a network of interlinked valleys, past all the other remote American outposts, just to get to its mouth.

From there the Valley wound upward, snaking this way and that through the steep mountainsides and apparently, as Black had heard from tales whispered and retold, terminating at its highest point in a narrow pass that crossed over the ridges and into Pakistan. No one could say, because no American had been that far.

Black knew that there were outposts in the Valley, though he didn't know how many or how far in. Stories circulated back to Omaha periodically, tales of land claimed and fought for, or lost and overrun, new attempts made or turned back, outposts abandoned and retaken.

They were impossible to verify. Everything with the Valley was myth and rumor. No one on the FOB seemed to have met anyone who had been there.

Black would hear the young soldiers in the S-1 shop talking once in a while. *Did you see the Valley guys in the chow hall last night?*

Then skepticism from another soldier, followed by protestations to the contrary, joined by another soldier whose buddy said he talked to them and yes, they *were* Valley guys.

Black concluded that the place was far enough away that any soldiers who went there mostly stayed there—spent most of their tour in the mountains and rarely returned to the FOB. When or if they did, they probably just kept to themselves or slept.

He didn't blame them. The only hard information he had seen were the casualty reports, which came down from Brigade headquarters weekly. 3/44 Infantry regularly had the highest counts. Now, 15-6 paperwork in hand, Black understood why. They had been cursed with the Valley.

Whatever the rest of the truth of the place was, he had only been certain that he would never know.

"It's six hours by ground convoy," Gayley was saying, "and a hell of a lot shorter by air."

Black considered the mess of paperwork now splayed across his lap. Combat Outpost—COP—Vega seemed small. Tiny, really.

A "cop," as the joes said it, typically didn't comprise more than several hasty structures with incomplete barriers around them. COPs were meant to be compact and highly defensible, to the extent a tiny base in the middle of enemy territory could be defended.

Vega looked typical in this regard. It had been built right on the slope of the mountainside, well above the river that ran along the bottom of the valley. It had limited views and was surrounded by high ground on all sides. A nice fat target.

"I don't know how Three-Four-Four's gonna get you there yet," Gayley went on. "Their commander's gonna let me know."

He pointed across the desk at the map draped over Black's knee.

"But I would hope for ground, because helicopters don't stay airborne very long up in that place. Those fuckers get shot down all the time when they fly down below the mountaintops."

Black brought the map up to his face. The outpost was accessible by a road, or a track, or what passed for it. But from the reports in his hands it sounded as though at some points there was no road or trail whatsoever, other than what had been worn by American vehicles, which were not exactly making daily trips up there.

"That's what I've got," Gayley said tersely. "What are your questions?"

It was the line that squared-away Army officers always used at the end of a briefing.

Black rooted in the file and brought out a personnel roster generated by the S-1 shop over at 3/44's headquarters. COP Vega was manned by a single infantry platoon, not at complete strength. Forty-seven guys, unless someone had died since the last report had been generated.

Which was entirely possible. The outpost came under attack, frequently. It had been in place roughly a year, and whoever did not want it there had clearly not given up on the idea of making it go away.

"Why there, sir?" he asked. "Why such a poor tactical location?"

Gayley raised an eyebrow at hearing the word "tactical" cross Black's lips.

Let it go.

"They had to build it there," Gayley explained.

Vega's mission was interdicting the flow of foreign fighters crossing the border from Pakistan, down through the higher parts of the mountains and into the rest of Afghanistan. The Valley was a key route. The express lane.

"Everything funnels through there."

Black nodded.

"What else?" Gayley pressed, ready to get back to his evening.

"That's it, sir."

Gayley nodded once and watched Black wrestle the paper pile together.

"These Vega dudes are no joke, Lieutenant."

Black looked up at the colonel.

"Their world is no joke. They're strung out and they've lost a lot of buddies. They are not going to be happy to see you poking your nose around their outpost."

"Roger, sir."

"Ask your questions, talk to everyone you need to talk to, and write it up straight. Do not be ignored."

"I won't, sir."

"But do not get in their way, and do not fuck up their operations. Do the job, write the fifteen-six, and come back here."

The S-1 shop door was padlocked. Everyone back in their bunks playing Xbox and watching movies on their laptops, or at the FOB gym.

Black turned his key in the padlock and pulled open the door. He wove his way through desk-shaped shadows to his own area, at the rear. The place of honor.

He clicked on the desk lamp. A smart-alecky friend had sent it to him in the mail as a joke, after he'd been given the S-1 desk job. It was a little music box number with a painted lamp shade that rotated when you turned it on, wraparound scenes of glorious south Pacific locales crawling around its surface in tacky Technicolor. He tossed the map into the pool of rainbow-hued light and only at that moment, with a faux island ditty tinkling softly at him, realized that he was still clutching in his other hand the manila envelope he had taken with him to Gayley's office.

He tossed that to the side and bent down over the map.

He'd been in New York City years before. He remembered the feeling when he first stood beneath the Trade Center, his brain processing that this thing he'd read about and imagined was real, enormously, almost frighteningly real. That was how he felt looking at the map of the Valley, seeing this almost mythical place in specificity, in actual topographic representations, in symbols and annotations proving its existence, looking back out at him declaring *I am here.*

It turned this way and that like a serpent as it rose through the mountains. Vega was not the only American presence there.

Down at its mouth lay another outpost. Combat Outpost Arcturus. Some officer was on an astronomy kick, apparently, when the names for the Valley posts were assigned. Somewhere in the sheaf of paperwork Gayley had given him he had seen it noted that soldiers called the place COP Heavenly.

I'll bet.

Vega was a few miles further in beyond Arcturus. There were no other posts on the map. Vega was the limit of the American advance.

The Valley kept winding its way onward and upward, terminating—just as lore had told it—in a narrow pass several miles beyond the outpost. That would be the Pakistani border, roughly. The precise location of the frontier was a little hazy in the Nuristan mountains. No one who lived there, it seemed, had ever really needed to know with precision.

He put the map aside, out of his sight in the shadowed part of his desk, and switched on his computer. While it warmed up he considered the unlikelihood of him being selected for this particular job. About Gayley's admonitions.

His civilian e-mail account came up. He opened a blank message and sat a moment, thinking, before typing in a subject line:

The Final Insult

The recipient was a trusted friend whom Black had known since they were both civilians fighting for slots at the Army's Officer Candidate School. They'd gone through training together, but they never saw each other anymore. He was the one who'd sent the lamp when Black had come to FOB Omaha. It arrived without a return address, as befit a package from someone who was increasingly disappearing into the world of classified military operations.

The friend was a highly intelligent wiseass who liked to be entertained and preferred witty banter to plain speech. This could be wearying, but having few American friends on the FOB, Black was usually happy to oblige. Chances were slim he would get the message in time, but if he did, the guy might have some useful advice.

As you are a connoisseur of bureaucratic inanity you will appreciate this. As a perfect cap-off to a stellar military career, your intrepid correspondent will be leaving Forward Operating Base PastGlory to venture alone into the broad sunlit uplands of neighboring Berzerkistan, where he will be welcomed warmly by the hale lads of the 44th Foot and regaled thereby with tales of ales (drank back home) and males (military-aged) over which and whom they have prevailed; and where he will also put the Fifteen on the Six, having been selected as fit for this singular duty by the great churning motherwheel of Army ~~bullshit~~ human resources efficiency.

If I put in words the triviality of the subject matter, you would cry.

Wherever you are on the Earth's many lands, may you be drunk and insufferable. Or killing bad guys.

Care of

He pulled the map of the Valley over and extracted a grid coordinate.

Oscar Zulu 36119 81534. God save your spleen.

Yours from the Land of Mediocrity,

—Lord of the Files

Good enough. If his friend got it, he might actually be amused enough to reply.

He had just sent it when his desk phone jangled. He picked it up.

Gayley. Calling with word on the transportation situation.

"Sir?"

"Ground convoy. They don't like flying helicopters into that place unless someone's dying, and not even always then."

"Okay, sir. When do I go?"

"Tomorrow night."

He'd wanted more time. But Black knew better than to say nothing, or splutter *sir?* or otherwise register his dismay.

"Roger that, sir."

"I know," Gayley said, reading his thoughts. "Their resupply convoy only makes runs up there once a week on Sundays."

It was Saturday night.

"They leave from Three-Four-Four's headquarters at seventeen hundred. Take tomorrow off and get your gear ready. Be there with your stuff no later than sixteen thirty."

"Roger, sir," Black replied. "Sir, does that mean—"

"Yeah, it does. You're gonna stay out there a week."

This time Black lapsed into silence in spite of himself. Gayley did too. Black wondered if he was reconsidering the decision to send him out there.

It was the colonel who finally cleared his throat and spoke.

"Use this opportunity, Lieutenant. Do this thing right. It may not seem like much of a job, but do it right."

"I will, sir."

"Maybe this can be a first step to feeling good about your service again."

Black had to squeeze his eyes shut to clear the vision of beating Gayley's face in with the telephone receiver.

"Thank you, sir."

He couldn't believe he got the words out.

"And, Lieutenant?"

"Sir."

"Stay low."

Gayley hung up.

Less than twenty-four hours. Black wasn't worried about his gear. His stuff was clean and maintained. But there were a couple people he was probably gonna want to see.

He gathered up the map and the 15-6 paperwork and reached to turn off his computer. He paused.

There was one more e-mail that had been sitting unopened in his inbox since he'd returned from leave. He knew the sender but he hadn't opened it. Its entry sat sandwiched in bold text among the rest of his already-read messages.

Subject: ?

He stared at it only a moment before clicking off the computer and heading out.

He stopped at a nearby Porta-Potty, stuffing the papers under one arm and stepping inside. There was graffiti scratched on the wall, of a type that was scratched on the wall of every portable restroom on every base in Iraq and Afghanistan. Black could just make out today's entry as he stood in the dim light.

CHUCK NORRIS DOESN'T FEEL SORRY FOR YOU.
HE ONLY FEELS SLIGHTLY LESS CONTEMPT AFTER
HE ROUNDHOUSE KICKS YOU IN THE BALLS.

3

Back at his quarters, Black opened the padlock and hasp and pushed through into darkness. He lived in a one-story Afghan building that predated FOB Omaha, constructed villa-style around a large courtyard with doorways running along its inside perimeter, opening onto trees and shade. Upon finding a secluded structure already conveniently divided into small- to moderate-size stone rooms perfect for one or two people to live in, the officers and senior sergeants of Black's unit had immediately taken the place over for themselves.

Rough and hazardous electrical wiring had been run to each room, plywood doors hastily installed where there were none. A fire pit and lawn chairs soon sprawled beneath the trees. It was good living as far as deployments went. The junior enlisted soldiers, who lived in noisy open barracks bays, called it the Senior Dorm.

He switched on the light and checked his watch. It was still early evening. He hauled a rucksack from his black Army-issue trunk and shoved several changes of underclothes and an extra uniform into it. Taking up his rifle and pistol, he disassembled each and gave them a careful once-over. Both were clean inside. He moved quickly and mechanically, oiling the weapons and wiping down his ammunition while his mind traveled.

When he was finished he checked the time again. Still early. He peeled off his fatigues and switched into his "PTs." The physical training uniform. Even in the cooling weather these consisted of simple black shorts and a gray T-shirt with ARMY printed on them in reflective lettering.

Black preferred running at night. He stuck to the edges of the base, where he was farthest from civilization and closest to the dirt berm that ringed the FOB. On a clear night there were many stars to see, and if there was moonlight the hulking shadows of the mountains as well, rising above the barrier. Occasionally, if it was dark and clear enough, he would see a point of light here or there on the lower slopes, and would wonder: *Our guys or theirs?*

He completed a lap of the base and trudged out across a boardwalk made of wooden pallets to the shower trailer behind the Senior Dorm. When he returned he put on jeans, a polo shirt, and a light black coat. Cramming a baseball cap on his head, he headed out into the night.

Wearing civilian clothing on deployment was, of course, a blatant violation of regulations. But Black had realized some time back that if you wear street clothes and act natural, people don't look too closely. They just assume you are one of the vaguely civilian defense contractors—private security forces, weapons systems technicians, other more opaque occupations—who mingled freely among the base's military population. He only did it at night. He wasn't likely to be recognized in the part of the base he was headed to anyway.

He stayed off the main thoroughfares. At night, life on the FOB retreated to the chow hall, the gym, and people's "hootches"—Army-speak for the hasty and improvised spaces that soldiers spruced up and lived in while deployed.

He caught dim glimpses of little makeshift worlds as he passed behind rows of shipping containers, cut across motor pools, and weaved through the hodgepodge of temporary structures and tumbledown Afghan buildings, occupied and rendered haphazardly usable for work or living, that made up the various neighborhoods of the base. It was like traveling through a town using only backyards and alleys.

Here an awning made of tarps, beneath it a wedge of light showing a hootch hung in tapestries and strung in white Christmas lights—an all-season favorite—while the scent of incense and sounds of psychedelic rock drifted out into the night. There the echoes of laughter and video game destruction. Over there the orange points of cigar tips hung in the shadows of a homemade back porch.

He walked a long, meandering route, occasionally passing soldiers in

T-shirts and camouflage pants, smoking and stubbing the ground with boot toes or jamming a finger into an ear while they tried to connect a call on a satellite phone—a rare treasure. After fifteen minutes his sneakers crunched onto a thick layer of gravel and he emerged from between a shipping container and a blast wall into stark light. He was on the far side of the base, at the "market."

A square one hundred feet on a side was lined on all four sides with large white trailers, shoulder-to-shoulder, featuring the usual deployment concessions. Barber trailer, two walk-up fast food stands (Nathan's and McDonald's), sewing shop, standard local schwag store—vendors from Turkey selling vaguely Persian rugs and tapestries for soldiers who felt the urge to go local—and a walk-in Green Beans Coffee trailer. Four portable stadium floodlights bathed the place in halide.

There was another market on Black's side of the FOB, but he avoided that one. Many of the interpreters and other foreign nationals who worked on the base lived on this side of Omaha, which made the crowd more interesting anyway. Black headed for the coffee shop.

It was spacious, as far as these things went. A raised trailer on wheels with a wooden deck built around it by some industrious National Guardsmen. Outside, soldiers and civilian contractors lounged at picnic tables. Inside was a full coffee counter and a side room with another four little tables.

He trudged across the gravel and stumped up the steps, past laughter and cigarette smoke. He wasn't even all the way through the door when a voice sang out, filling the small space.

"Breedman!"

Kourash, the Afghan proprietor, greeting Black as he always did. Fiftyish, hair silvering, animated. Grew up in Kabul and still had his family and kids there, but had chased the good American money to the Nuristan plain. Passed the security clearance and got a job at the Green Beans. They had met when Black first came to Omaha several months before. Black was fairly sure "*breedman*" meant some form of "lieutenant" in Pashto.

Kourash hurried around the counter, pulling him into an embrace.

"As-salamu alaykum, my friend," he said, using the Arabic greeting favored by Muslims worldwide regardless of their native language.

Peace be upon you.

He stepped back and smiled at Black, placing a palm over his heart.

"Alaykum salaam," Black replied, looking down and grinning in spite of himself.

Kourash's brow furrowed and he spoke accusingly.

"My friend, where are you?" he asked. "I am not seeing you since . . . one month! Always I am wondering where are you?"

Black explained that he had been in the United States on leave for a couple weeks.

"Okay, this is good. I am afraid maybe you leave Omaha, maybe to fight in the towns or the hills."

"You know I don't do anything like that."

"Yes, thanks God. So you come in!"

He ushered Black forward and slipped behind the counter.

"Your usual?"

Black's usual was black coffee. The place sold every kind of dandyish drink you could find in an American chain shop, or at least powdered deployment versions of the same. He felt sheepish ordering the cheapest thing on the menu all the time, but he couldn't bring himself to order a Triple Chai Smoothie in a war zone. He nodded.

Kourash plied him with questions and dawdled over fixing the coffee. The place was empty except for a couple of young soldiers slurping confections over a table in the other room.

The older man placed the coffee in front of him and refused his money, as usual. Black tossed it all into the tip jar, as usual. He checked his watch. Still a little too early in the evening to make his stops. He was figuring he would sit and read awhile when a thought occurred to him.

"Can I ask you a question?"

Kourash looked at him as though to say: Of all the questions, that one is the only foolish one to ask.

"What do you know about the Valley?"

The older man looked at him blankly. Black pointed through the windows of the shop, in the direction in which they would have seen the mountains if it had been daylight.

Kourash's brow furrowed again. He made quotation marks with his fingers.

"You mean 'the Valley' the valley?"

He said a name in Pashto that Black did not recognize.

Black nodded.

"Why?"

"I'm going there. I have to take a trip there for a week."

Kourash's face darkened and he peered at Black closely. He turned and hollered something in Pashto at a tiny door that led to a tiny walk-in storage closet, which doubled as the shop's office.

A younger Afghan man emerged and took over the counter. Kourash came out from behind it again and hustled Black into the side room, where the soldiers had just finished their drinks and were slinging rifles over their shoulders to go.

They sat. Kourash leaned in over the table.

"Tell."

Black explained about having to do a short investigation at a very small American base there. Kourash folded his arms and listened intently. When Black finished, Kourash leaned back and blew out a slow breath, looking at his friend and shaking his head slightly.

"What?" Black asked.

"This place, these valleys, this is very . . ."

He trailed off, searching with his hands in the air.

"What is the word when never they are with the world today, everyone is yesterday? Behind?"

"Backwards."

"Yes, this. This place is very backwards. Very old. '*Kafiristan.*' You know this name?"

Black shook his head.

"*Kafir.* 'Unbeliever.' All this place, Nuristan, it is the last part of Afghanistan to accept Islam. Always before they call it Kafiristan. Land of infidels, because the old peoples there, they would not come to Allah."

Black hadn't known any of this.

"Now they come to Allah, a long time before the Taliban. But the Talib, they hate these peoples. They still see them *kafir,* infidels. They do not trust. They want this land very much for the Talib."

Kourash frowned.

"So they fight, and now you are here and fight. Taliban want you to go away."

That much Black knew. There was a knock-down drag-out going on between Americans and Taliban forces, all through those mountains, with the tribal people there fighting the Taliban or fighting the Americans or caught in the middle—more or less. Individual people choose individual sides for individual reasons.

"My brother, if you go here, you do not . . . do not get—"

He stirred the air, murmuring possibilities.

"Into . . ."

"Involved?" Black offered.

"I think. You do not go in this war."

Black made calming hands.

"I'll mostly be sitting around the outpost."

"I pray this. These peoples, these *kafir,* they do . . . the fight. I know this word. Fight the blood."

"Blood feud?"

"Probably this," Kourash said, leaning in and pointing at Black. "The families, the tribes, when they fight with each other, the fight may be a hundred years. Brother to brother fight, and his sons, and his sons. They never forget. They are very old peoples. And they hate the Talib."

He leaned back.

"Too many enemies."

He threw his arms up as though confronted with a puzzle too complicated to solve.

"*Big* mess!"

"Okay."

"My brother. You do not know the enemy, you do not know the friend. You do not go in between these peoples and their enemy."

"Like I said, mostly I should just be on the outpost. I don't think I have to get into any of that."

"Thanks God."

Time to get moving. Black thanked Kourash and assured him again that he would be careful, suffering through another embrace.

Outside the crowd had thinned. It was getting later. He cut across the gravel yard and disappeared through a gap in the trailers. It was time to go see the acquisition specialist. Which sounded like an official military title but wasn't.

4

Every Army unit had a supply sergeant, and every unit had an acquisition specialist. They may or may not be the same guy.

The acquisition specialist was the guy on deployment who could find and get anything. He'd usually been in the Army a lot of years, and he specialized not in working Army supply channels, but in working all the other channels besides those.

He knew how to get anything from the formal system, and he knew how to get anything else the other way. He knew where to go to work trades, and he knew how to reach into the local economy when everything else failed.

He was the reason that commanders who wanted a plasma-screen monitor for their command post had to order two or three just to have one make it all the way from the States. There were acquisition specialists at every stop along the way, and smart commanders eventually figured out that they needed one of their own just to defeat all the others.

Sergeant First Class Maru Toma was the only acquisition specialist Black knew personally on FOB Omaha. He was the master gunner—the senior technical expert—for an artillery battalion on the other side of the post. He had spent years as a forward observer, maneuvering with infantry forces on the ground and calling in air strikes and artillery bombardments to support their operations. Now he was close to retirement and he didn't play nice enough with officers to ever be a sergeant major, so he'd been given the master gunner slot. An on-call consultant, basically.

Black knew Toma played soccer most nights with a bunch of Dominican guys who worked in the main chow hall. Part of his network, no doubt. He swung by the dirt lot where they played, but it was dark and empty. He kept going.

Toma lived in an occupied building encircling a courtyard just like the Senior Dorm layout back at Black's unit. He had the largest room in the joint, of course, and he didn't have to share it with anyone. Black saw Toma's empty camp chair as he came around the corner, sitting outside his door with a still-smoldering butt in it.

In luck. He knocked.

The door swung open immediately. Toma must have been heading back out to finish his smoke. He stood there still in his soccer clothes, a beer bottle and opener in one hand.

He was a beefy Samoan with a good bit of the accent still hanging on. He was about four inches shorter than Black but probably weighed half again as much, most of that weight being muscle.

"What up, cuz?"

He crooked his elbow and put his free hand up for a guy clasp, pulling Black into a chest-bump hug. Black felt the opener and bottle clank against his back as Toma's other hand gave it a perfunctory smack.

All forms of alcohol were strictly forbidden on deployment. Toma being Toma, he didn't bother making the slightest effort to conceal the thing.

"Hey," Black replied. "Got a minute?"

Military customs and courtesies were pretty much not relevant in dealing with someone like Toma. He was outside of all that. The sergeant shrugged and gestured him in with his head. Black followed.

Inside, he had to turn in a circle to take it all in. There were guys who tricked out their deployment living spaces, and then there was Toma. His hootch was spectacular.

Stateside furniture, quality electronics, multiple AC units. The typical minifridge would have been beneath Toma's dignity; Black gawked at a full-size stainless steel unit. Somewhere a command post was lonely without the plasma-screen TV that seemed to take up half a wall.

The place was L-shaped, with a split-level "bedroom" space around the corner, inside which Toma had installed a raised wooden deck to hold an improbably large non-Army bed. A hanging tapestry, currently pulled into tiebacks bolted to the jet-black bedroom walls, served as an entry curtain.

"Beer?"

Toma sent a thumb toward the fridge. Black waved him off. Toma shrugged again and settled into an easy chair, cigarette and lighter in hand.

"Whatcha got?"

Black knew enough to get right to it.

"What do you know about the Valley?"

"Who's asking?"

"Me."

"How come?"

"I'm going up there tomorrow night."

"Bullshit. You don't go nowhere."

It wasn't an insult. Toma was just pointing out the truth.

"I've got a fifteen-six at a COP up there."

"Okay, you got a fifteen-six. So?"

"You've been up there."

"Bullshit."

"Bullshit, 'bullshit.' I know you've been up there."

Black did not actually know Toma had been to the Valley, but he assumed that before he'd taken the master gunner gig on the FOB, a guy with Toma's experience and qualifications had been dropping artillery rounds and calling air strikes all up and down those mountains.

"How you know that?" Toma asked, squinting.

Black put on his best conspiratorial grin.

"I know more about you than you think."

It was a lame and risky thing to say with Toma, but he laughed.

"Bullshit. You're guessing. So what if I was up there?"

Black wasn't really sure what he wanted from Toma. It wasn't like he needed some special piece of gear to hunker down in an outpost and stay out of the way for a week. He didn't have anything Toma needed, and he didn't pretend that he and Toma were friends.

He mostly just wanted to see what Toma had to say. Toma's opinions of junior officers were quick and arbitrary, but for whatever reason he seemed to have decided that Black was one of the okay ones. In the past he'd always been cool.

"I don't know, man. Maybe just if there's anything I need to know."

Toma considered.

"Sucks," he concluded.

"Yeah, I figured. What else?"

Toma considered further.

"What's the fifteen-six on?"

Black gave the ten-second version. Angry crowd-type situation; warning shots. According to his paperwork, somebody in the village had given an earful to an Army Civil Affairs officer—Toma snorted at hearing this—who was passing through town on a goodwill mission. He put the complaint into the system, and the 15-6 came out the other side.

Toma took this all in, sitting staring at the wall for so long that Black almost asked him if he was okay. Finally he spoke.

"What town?"

Black scanned his memory.

"I think it's called Darreh Sin."

"Never been to that one," Toma said tersely. "You gonna see the chief?"

"The who?"

"The chief," Toma said, exasperated. "The town chief. Jesus, cuz, you been on the FOB a long time."

"Why am I seeing the chief?"

"Somebody complained, right? Somebody from the town complained to the Civil Affairs fag. That's the chief."

"How do you know?"

"Civil Affairs dude is gonna be a captain or higher. Town chief is the guy that would make a formal complaint to an American officer."

"Okay."

"But he ain't gonna talk to anyone lower than a captain now," Toma explained. "Beneath his station or whatever."

Black was confused.

"Okay, so the chief complained to some American," he said. "Why do I need to talk to him?"

He'd been picturing your standard interview-the-soldiers-involved-and-write-it-up type of situation, not some kind of summit meeting with an Afghan chieftain.

"You need to talk to him so you can get the fuck out of the Valley."

"I don't get it."

Toma pointed at him.

"I know your boss. Gayley, right?"

"Yeah."

"Asshole Boy Scout."

"So?"

"He ain't gonna accept no write-up with just soldiers' statements. He's gonna expect Afghan statements too."

Black hadn't thought this far out.

"You radio in that you talked to the soldiers and they said everything was cool and tell him you're done," Toma went on, "and see what happens. That motherfucker is gonna keep you out there another week and tell you to do it right. Right?"

Toma was right, of course. Gayley had shown no signs of particular love or sympathy for the Afghan people, but he had a taut and highly refined sense of honor and an extreme concern for procedural niceties. When it came to avoiding at all costs the slightest appearance of impropriety, he was a card-carrying Goody Two-Shoes. Investigating a situation involving Afghan civilians without talking to the civilians themselves definitely would not fly. Gayley would expect him to run the thing all the way to the ground, no matter how trivial and silly.

"Right," Black finally responded.

"So you're fucked. Chief won't talk to you."

"Why?"

Toma pointed at Black's chest.

Right. Lieutenant. Beneath his station.

"Okay, so the chief won't talk to me. I find the guy whose house it was."

"He won't talk to you either."

"Why not?"

"No one in the town is gonna talk to you without the chief's permission, and he ain't gonna give it. The Army sending a lieutenant is an insult to him after he complained to a captain."

He raised his cigarette and lighter.

"No offense."

Black considered all this.

"Okay, so what do I do?"

Toma hauled his bulk out of his chair, leaving his smoke behind.

He slumped over to a padlocked trunk in the corner, opening it with a key he wore on a chain with his dog tags. He came back and tossed a small paper-wrapped package at Black, who caught it with both hands.

It was oblong, five or six inches long, about the thickness of a two-by-four but with more heft. The paper was folded around it but not sealed. Black pulled it open.

Inside was a rectangular object wrapped in something like cellophane. It had a brown hue like wet sand. It looked like compressed clay.

Black had seen pictures before, but he stared at it for probably a full ten seconds before it clicked that he was looking at the real thing in his lap.

"A fucking brick of heroin?"

Toma had eased himself nonchalantly back into his chair.

"What am I supposed to do with this?" Black demanded.

Toma lit up his smoke.

"For the chief."

"What?"

"Straight money."

"I don't get it."

Toma blew a long cloud into the room.

"Chief sees that, he knows you got the juice, even though you're just an L.T. He'll talk to you then."

"What, so I'm supposed to *sell* the chief some heroin?"

"*No,* cuz."

Toma shook his head, exasperated.

"It's a present. Like a tribute. You ain't gonna walk into the chief's house and try to sell him one sorry-ass brick of heroin. He'll laugh his ass off before he shoots you for wasting his fucking time and insulting him."

Black tried to process. Toma continued.

"You go to him and you show him your respect and all that, and do it up good. You give him the brick like a gift, like you're showing you know he's the guy. Then he knows you're for real too, you got access to shit, and you guys can do business."

"I thought the poppies were pretty much gone from these mountains," Black said. "Because of the Taliban."

Toma looked pained and pitying all at once.

"Okay," Black said, relenting. "So I give it to him and he thinks I wanna, what? Help him move heroin?"

"Probably. You think it ain't happened? But don't worry, you won't have to make no deals or nothing."

Toma took a long drag.

"He don't need you for heroin. If he's in the business, which if he lives in the Valley he is, he's got all his poppies up in the hills and wherever. This is just a get-to-know-you. It's a dance, going through the motions. You give him the gift and he figures out where you're coming from. Figures maybe you can help keep the Taliban off his back over the heroin, right? Or just do some good trading for other stuff. Those dudes all want electronics and shit. Anyway, doesn't matter. You play nice and say how you wanna see him again in the near future and all that."

"Okay."

"You won't have to see him because you'll be gone from the Valley by then," Toma went on. "But you flirt with him, right? Then before you go, you say you wanted to talk about one other thing."

"The complaint."

"Right. Then you get his statement about the complaint. Probably he tones it down some because you guys are boys now, and you won't have to investigate any more. Then you go back to Vega and you're good to go. You turn in your paper to Gayley and he's happy."

He drew a smoky-handed flowchart in midair.

"Gayley sends it up to Brigade. Then the Civil Affairs pussy probably goes back out with a wad of cash for the dude with the goat and a wad for the dude with the bullet in his damn mud hut. Civil Affairs bro feels like a big shot. Gayley gets a medal for winning hearts and minds."

He crossed his ankles and leaned back in his chair.

"Circle of life and shit."

Black was shaking his head.

"What if the chief tells the Civil Affairs guy or someone from Vega about the brick?"

Toma looked at him like he was deeply stupid.

"Chief ain't gonna tell on you."

Black realized he was right. What on earth would the chief gain by doing that?

"It's still crazy," he said doubtfully. "I can't go walking around with that kind of contraband on me."

As soon as he remembered who he was saying it to, he felt foolish. Toma just looked annoyed. He pointed at Black.

"When was the last time someone stopped you on the FOB and searched your shit, L.T.?"

Black said nothing.

"When was the last time someone made you open your ruck and your duffel and do a layout like you're a soldier?"

"Okay, I got it."

"Look, cuz, you do what you want. I'm just saying, you can take it with you, like insurance."

He took a pull on his smoke.

"If you puss out and don't use it, just toss it in the river before you come home."

"You don't want it back?" Black asked.

"What the fuck I want a brick of heroin for?"

"I don't know, I just—"

"You think I'm fucking dealing?"

"No, man, I just . . ."

Black changed the subject.

"Where'd you get it anyway?"

"Don't worry about it. But I didn't fucking buy it and I wasn't going to fucking sell it, all right?"

"All right."

He put up his hands. Mercy.

"I just thought you might need it sometime like you're telling me to use it," he said.

"I don't go noplace now, L.T. You know that."

Black wrapped the thing back up and felt its weight in both hands.

Hell with it.

He put it in his jacket pocket and stood up.

"All right. Thanks, Smoke."

He used the artillery honorific for the senior sergeant in a howitzer platoon. Toma hadn't been a platoon sergeant for a lot of years, but the name stuck. The only kind of people who called him Sergeant Toma were straight-arrow commanders who didn't know the difference between a supply sergeant and an acquisition specialist anyway. To anybody who knew him he was Smoke.

"You got it."

Meeting adjourned. Black headed for the door.

"Hey, L.T."

Black stopped.

Toma had come back from his trunk with a second object, which had been sitting in his lap the whole time. He turned in his chair and tossed it over his shoulder to Black.

It was a little black canvas zip case, small enough to fit in the palm of a hand. Black reached for the zipper pull that ran around the outside of it.

"Just take it."

Black slid the case into his jacket pocket, giving Toma a squinty *Okaaayyy* look.

Toma blew another cloud and settled back into his chair, turning away from Black.

"'I know more about you than you think,'" he said in the same mock-conspiratorial tone Black had used on him. "Will."

Black let himself out.

He walked, hand on the brick in his pocket, the Valley and its possibilities forking out before him. He was so distracted he'd gone halfway back across the FOB before he realized he had forgotten his other stop. He checked his watch.

It was getting late, but he knew by then that sleep was not going to come anytime soon. He turned and trudged back the way he'd come.

This one would be a quick stop. He veered off into a sparsely populated flatland of motor pools and maintenance sheds.

He found the hootch he was looking for, behind a shipping container at the end of a squat line of hovels. As always, a scratchy recording of classical strings swelled from within and spilled out across the storage rows and parking areas.

Black banged loud enough to be heard over the music.

"Yeah!" came the voice from inside.

He pulled open the plywood door and looked in at the violinmaker of Gandamak.

"Hey, L.T., whatcha doin'?"

The violinmaker sat behind a worktable facing the door. Her hootch was dark except for the warm pool of light from her work lamp, illuminating her hands and her wood.

"Hey, sorry to bug you."

"No sweat. What's up?"

Black stepped in. A vinyl record player spun in the corner, linked to modern speakers.

The violinmaker was an odd one. The craft had been in her family literally for four or five generations, going back to Italy. Only sons had known it, but she had no brothers and had started learning the trade from her father when she was a teenager.

She'd been in the Army for ten years now, a staff sergeant and a medic. She brought her wood and her tools on every deployment. She had a good situation this time around, working graveyards at "Charlie Med," the base's emergency hospital.

Black knew she worked a couple hours every night before going on shift. She hunched over her table shaving wood in boots, T-shirt, and fatigue pants, hair back into a tight bun, ready to go on shift except for the camouflage coat, which hung on a hook near the door.

He felt bad taking her from her work.

"Hey, I'm just taking a trip and I was hoping to get some new stuff."

"Where you going?"

"Valley."

"Fuckin' A."

"Yeah. Whatta ya got?"

"Whatta ya like?"

"I like this."

A brace of violins pulled a chord across a darkening sky, carrying it to night. Lower strings surged from oceans below. He heard tones of deep orange over black horizons.

"Ralph Vaughan Williams. He was English."

"What is it?"

"*Fantasia on a Theme by Thomas Tallis.*"

"Cool."

"The snobs didn't like him."

"Got it on digits?"

The military required its own slang for many ordinary things. He meant: on your computer?

"Of course."

"I'll take it."

Black pulled a little memory stick from his pocket and tossed it across to her. She caught it and thumbed it into her laptop computer, clicking open her own vast digital music library.

"What else?" she asked.

"How about more like this?"

"Nothing's like this."

"Surprise me. You know my tastes."

"Pedestrian?"

"Har."

A few years before, Black had tossed all of the music he had grown up listening to into the trash and started from scratch. The violinmaker was filling out some of his horizons.

She clicked a number of files and dumped them onto the flash drive.

"I saw you at chow tonight with your book," she said to her computer as she worked. "You shoulda come over."

Army people always assumed if you were reading a book you'd rather have company.

"Next time," Black said, though he knew better than to do that to the violinmaker when she was with her pals. To make her be seen associating with him.

She tossed the flash drive back at Black, who thanked her and stuffed it back in his pocket.

"No sweat. See ya later, L.T."

"You too."

"But not at Charlie Med. Stay low."

Black gave a grim laugh and left her to her work.

Back at his hootch he tossed the memory stick onto his bunk next to a pocket-size music player and headphones. He pulled the brick out of his jacket and set it on a shelf in the corner, on top of a leatherbound book with a title in Latin.

He still hadn't opened the case Toma had given him. He pulled it out and unzipped it, surveying its contents briefly before closing it up again. He considered it for a long moment before tossing it onto his bunk too. He regarded the brick in turn, but left it where it sat and pulled his PTs back on. Ignoring his bed, he pushed through the door and disappeared into the night to run again.

He ran and ran.

5

He woke in midmorning after very little rest, feeling like he'd slept a year. He lay in his bunk and felt stillness. It felt familiar.

There was only one thing he really needed to accomplish, and there was no rush about that.

He took his time showering and walked the short distance to the market on his side of the FOB. He bought a pack of smokes at the little PX—the "post exchange," or FOB store—and shoved them in his pocket without opening them. Afterward he sat for a long time with his book at the unfamiliar Green Beans Coffee stand there.

Late in the afternoon he gathered all his gear and went to the S-1 shop. Sergeant Cousins was there.

Black apologized about the evening before. Cousins was good about it and told him don't sweat it, and be careful. There was nothing else that needed to be said.

Black went straight to his desk and dumped his stuff, pushing out his chair and switching on his computer. While it was warming up he took the manila envelope he'd left there the night before.

With a black marker he scribbled BLACK on the outside, and REFRAD below that. He got up and carried the envelope past all the desks and out the door. He thought he saw Cousins shaking his head slightly as he passed.

Gayley's office was empty, but the door was unlocked. Black pushed it open and went inside, crossing straight to the colonel's tidy desk and tossing the envelope down right in the middle of it. He turned and went.

That evening when Gayley returned he would find a memorandum inside titled REQUEST FOR RELEASE FROM ACTIVE DUTY, with all the appropriate documentation appended. It was Black's quitting-the-Army paperwork.

Back at his desk, Black's computer was ready. He opened his e-mail.

Hesitating only long enough to check that no one in the office was about to walk over, he clicked on the message that had been sitting unread since he'd returned from R&R leave the week before.

> I don't know if you are even near any kind of computer and will get this anytime soon. I hope you do, even though I know you won't respond. I wanted to tell you anyway.
>
> I dreamed about you last night. Dreamed that you were here, in my room, sitting in the window watching me. You came close to me, and then you left.
>
> I'm not being irrational or ridiculous. I know you weren't here. I know you are on the other side of the planet somewhere. But I wanted to tell you about it.
>
> I know you don't want to hear me say that I miss you, but I hope you will accept that I am thinking about you. And I know why you won't respond, and I understand. But you should respond anyway and let me know that you got this, at least. That would be good.
>
> I hope you are safe.

Black clicked open a reply window and typed out a few short sentences. He saved it and opened a menu of options, setting the message to send itself in ten days' time.

He was about to turn the machine off when another came in.

> RE: The Final Insult

It was the wiseass. Close to a computer after all. He opened it.

Mediocrates—

Ah, the warrior-scholar departs for a short walk in the Hindu Kush. I am envious. You might find it more, um, picturesque than you would imagine. Also more explosions. Take your unabridged travel guide and remember: There is no survival of the fittest in the mountains. There are only those creatures Chuck Norris has allowed to live.

You caught me at the oasis, but I am off again. Not drunk, but bearded, which is insufferable. Enjoy your revels at the pleasure dome, Padre. And when you return, you simply MUST come for summer at the ocean house with Bradley and Eliza and, of course, yours truly. Squash! Mother asks after you incessantly.

Semper Ubi Sub Ubi,

—Chaz

Weird. Nothing useful either. He switched off the computer and gathered up his ruck and rifle and helmet.

Cousins had his copy of the convoy manifest waiting for him, courtesy of their counterpart S-1 shop over at 3/44 headquarters. Black took it and feigned surprise.

"What, no helicopter?" he said dryly.

"Funny, sir."

He stuffed it in his pocket.

"Thanks, Sergeant Cousins."

"Stay low, L.T."

"Everyone keeps saying that."

"Do it."

He left.

The Humvees were lined up outside 3/44's headquarters with their engines running when he arrived. Six diesels echoed between the stone buildings. He shucked off his ruck and sat down on a wooden bench outside the command post, waiting to be called on.

Soldiers readied the vehicles, moving with the drab efficiency and lack of drama of a rolling unit that goes outside the wire every day. Black knew this was by far the longest regular trip they took, so everything got a little extra attention.

He watched ammunition cases, extra water, and boxes of MREs—the military's famous meals ready to eat—go into the trucks. Three of them towed open-top trailers whose contents were tied down with tarps. Basic resupply for the outpost, Black figured. Medics appeared and tossed their big black treatment packs onto the seats.

A sergeant approached.

"Black?"

"Yeah."

"I can take your ruck, sir."

He didn't like people offering to carry his gear, but the guy's matter-of-fact tone told him he wasn't doing Black any favors. He probably just didn't want him packing it into the wrong corner of the already overstuffed vehicles.

"Thanks."

"You gotta take a whiz before we go?"

"Yeah."

"Around that corner. There's coffee in the C.P. if you want it."

The command post.

"I'm good."

"Cool. Rolling in ten, sir."

He shouldered Black's ruck and trudged across the gravel to the open back of the lead vehicle.

When Black returned, soldiers were piling into driver's seats and turrets. The sergeant pointed him to the truck where his bag was, and he climbed into the back seat.

The convoy wove its way through the buildings and trailers of the base, radios chirping as vehicle commanders made their perfunctory commo checks with one another. Black looked out the little armored glass windows as the buildings fell behind, replaced by sandbags and blast barriers on either side.

The convoy rolled to a stop at the FOB's east gate, in the exit channel. Electronic jamming equipment was switched on, and the vehicles filled with the clatter of weapons being charged. The manifest was passed to the guards, and the gate was opened.

The convoy rolled forward beneath the guard towers and machine-gun nests and wove left-right-left-right through a serpentine channel designed to slow down car bombs. They cleared the walls and the golden plain opened up before them, mountains rising from the horizon ahead.

Over the next hour of lengthening shadow they grew larger, slowly filling the front windows of the vehicles. General features that Black had seen only from Radio Hill emerged into detail and focus, rising above his eyeline. By the time the ground began noticeably to rise toward the mouth of the first valley, the setting sun was throwing orange haze all across the front of the range.

Black, leaning forward in his seat, craned his head and looked up through the gunner's hatch. Ahead and above the looming peaks, another raft of black cloud was moving in from the east. Rain in the mountains again tonight.

He fished out his headphones and put them in his ears. He closed his eyes and felt the stillness returning. The violinmaker's *Fantasia on a Theme* strings soared across his vision and roiled the black ocean of his thoughts below. As the convoy climbed into the range and the road gave way to wild dirt track, he slept.

This time in the dream she lingered in the window as he fell, never turning away as he slid down and into the depths. He still could not see her face.

PART TWO

6

Thunder woke him, and the spatter of raindrops on his face.

It was pitch-dark outside. The convoy was still moving. There must have been a decent wind because the rain was making it past the gunner standing in the open turret, through the opening, and back to where Black sat in his seat.

He looked at the poor kid's legs, soaked almost down to the knee.

Had he not known to a certainty that no soldier worth a damn would voluntarily give up his post to an officer, he would have offered to take a turn up on the machine gun. He didn't really mind getting rained on. Instead he sat and stared past the kid at the lights of the driver's console and the green displays of the stacked radios.

There was nothing to see out the windshield. The convoy was rolling through the mountains in "blackout" drive, using no headlights and relying instead on night-vision gear.

He drew his little leatherbound book out of a pocket and opened it. He scratched a mark in the red glow of his utility flashlight. He stowed it away again.

More thunder. Distant.

"Hey, sir, you might want to get awake back there," the sergeant called over his shoulder, goggles covering his eyes.

"Yeah, I'm up."

"Roger. We're coming into Heavenly."

Black craned his neck and squinted through the windshield but could see nothing in the darkness ahead.

Good light discipline.

The vehicles, still grinding up a gentle slope, began to slow. Finally a dim amber point of light appeared in the rain not far in front of them.

Dark hulks filled the left and right windows. "Hessco" baskets, eight-foot-tall wire-framed cylinders lined with fabric and filled on the spot with rocks and dirt. The cheapest blast barriers on the planet.

They were entering a channel wide enough for the Humvees and not much wider. From the change in the tire sounds from below, it was lined with a thick layer of gravel.

The amber point resolved into a square, coming up fast on the left. A window, built into the blast barriers—no, a shack or some kind of low structure, sandbagged and incorporated into the walls of the channel.

As the lead vehicle approached the window, a pair of hands raised a windowpane from within. A head and shoulders squeezed out into the rain and wind. Black caught a glimpse of an enormous pair of safety goggles and an Army patrol cap squashed on a head backward.

"Woo!" cried the head and shoulders as they rolled past.

Thunder echoed off the mountain peaks above. The convoy came to a stop on the gravel bed.

"Ten minutes, sir," said the sergeant from up front, pulling off his night-vision goggles and stretching in his seat. "Refueling only. Good time to take a whiz if you need it."

Black pulled the heavy latch and leaned on the armored door. It swung open with all the ease of a bank vault. He stepped out into the rain.

His boots sank an inch into gravel. He bent a leg back until he could grab one foot with a hand and held it in a stretch, his other hand on the hot, rumbling vehicle. He rolled his neck to get the stiffness out and looked around him.

No part of Combat Outpost Arcturus was visible beyond the Hessco baskets forming the channel around their vehicles, and the weak amber light from the control shack. He guessed they weren't really inside the COP's perimeter but in a refuel lane designed to service passing convoys quickly and without having to open the main gate, wherever in the dark that was.

Soldiers and sergeants were climbing out of the vehicles and stretching as the begoggled figure hollered from his window at them.

"Nice night to visit! Thank you very much! Woo!"

He wore only a T-shirt on his top half. He was soaked to the skin. In one hand he clutched a radio handset, straining at the end of a coiled cord. He squeezed the button and spoke into it.

"Go, go! Let's go!"

He tossed the handset back into the window and commenced hollering at no one, his goggles already obscured by water.

"Yes! A Heavenly night! This is the reason I joined the Army!"

The sergeant in charge of the shift. All the guy needed was an aviator's scarf.

Black trudged around the vehicle and looked up and down the lane. The sergeant took one look at his shadowed form, standing there uncertainly in the dark, and figured his rank correctly.

"Pisser's up there, sir," he shouted over the noise of wind and engines.

He pointed up the gravel incline past the front of the convoy.

"Smoke on the other side of the Hesscos."

He thumbed toward the control shack's door a few feet away, next to a handmade sign which read PIT CREW.

"Coffee's in here."

Black raised a hand in thanks and crunched away. Ghostly figures appeared through the rain and streamed past him. Soldiers, carrying heavy plastic jerry cans full of fuel.

None spoke to Black as they passed. Some wore dark rain slickers. Others were bare-armed in T-shirts like their sergeant, who shouted overly chipper encouragements at them as they commenced filling the vehicles.

Just past the end of the channel of blast barriers was a blue plastic Porta-Potty. Black tried the door. Occupied. He shoved his hands in his pockets and waited.

There was a wooden signpost set into the gravel next to the john. It was straight from a war movie. Black could barely make out the series of handwritten crossbars as he stood there, rain stinging the side of his face, waiting his turn.

← KABUL: 138 MILES

The arrow pointed back down the mountains the way they'd come.

← BAGHDAD: YOU WISH

← FALLUJAH: YOU WISH + 40 MILES

← JESSICA ALBA: 7,602 MILES

← YOUR ACTUAL GIRL: HOME BLOWING JODY

↓ HEAVEN: YOU'RE IN IT

→ HELL: 0 MILES

"Jody" went back to the Second World War at least. He's the guy who stays home and steals your girlfriend or wife when you're off at war.

There was one crossbar below "HELL," part of which was broken off. The remaining piece had a line painted through it.

~~↑ XANADU:~~

The door opened and one of the convoy drivers came out. Black caught it before it slammed and let himself in. He locked it, closing out the rain and wind.

It was pitch-dark inside. He had a small red-lens flashlight fixed to the front of his gear. He switched it on. It shone straight ahead onto graffiti:

TODAY IS THE LAST DAY OF THE REST OF YOUR LIFE

He emerged, letting the plastic door smack hard in the wind, and made his way around to the far side of the Hesscos. He didn't need to smoke, but there was little point in him hanging out in the busy channel when the joes were trying to work.

There was less noise on this side, away from the diesel engines. The wind was still gusting down the valley, spitting rain slanting in diagonally. But he could hear himself think.

His eyes were adjusting. He sensed open space. He still couldn't see any other part of the COP through the rain, but he could make out what looked to be an awning, ahead and to his left, running along the back side of the Hesscos and the control shack.

As he made for it he realized that there was a parallel row of blast barriers ten or twenty feet to his right. He was in another channel, this one apparently for foot traffic.

Looking skyward, he could tell that there was probably a partial moon behind the thick cloud layer. He could just make out dark peaks rising high and close on either side of the outpost. It sat at the juncture of two deep, steep valleys.

Those ridges, he figured, were probably a couple thousand feet above the elevation at which he now stood. He craned his head up until the back of his helmet hit the neckpiece on his body armor.

"Twenty-one hundred vertical feet, sir."

The voice startled him. He turned to see a man standing there under the awning in a slicker and floppy-brimmed camouflage rain hat.

He couldn't make out a face, but his chest had a sergeant's rank on it. Under the shadowed brim of his hat glowed the orange point of a cigarette. A paint can filled with sand and stubbed-out butts sat in the gravel nearby.

"To the ridges?"

Black stepped under the handmade cover. The rain and wind were much quieted.

"Yup."

More thunder rolled down from above. As he stood looking up at the sky Black realized that it wasn't thunder he was hearing at all.

Once again the sergeant seemed to read his mind.

"Fixed-wing out of Bagram. Probably F-15s. We got an Air Force guy in the C.P. talking to 'em."

"They're out here for you guys?"

"They're out here for *you* guys," the sergeant corrected. "Gotta come out every time a supply run comes through here."

Black was surprised.

"Even in this weather?"

"Fuck, yeah, in this weather," the sergeant replied. "*Especially* in this weather."

"Taliban hate fighting in the dark and in the rain."

"Not your daddy's Taliban."

Most foreign fighters knew that they couldn't compete against American forces in most nighttime situations because they didn't have the gear. And most just hated fighting when they were uncomfortable. Rain meant they stayed inside.

"These dudes," the sergeant continued, "would sell their freaking daughter for the chance to come out here and rocket the shit out of your convoy while you're sitting here getting refueled."

He took a long drag, the cigarette momentarily illuminating a wide, weary face.

"Rain or no rain."

Black considered this.

"Drones don't see shit in this weather," the sergeant finished, "so this is prime time."

Which explained why the outpost had to be in blackout. Its existence was no secret, but in the rain and without night-vision gear, being invisible made a difference.

Black looked up at the sky beyond the ridges.

"Came on station before you got here," the sergeant said. "And they'll be up there until you go."

"Who's spotting for them?"

"We can't see the tops of the ridges from here, obviously," the sergant replied. "And like I said about the drones, so when it rains we gotta put observers on the ground up there."

The guys who spotted targets and told the jets where to drop bombs.

"We got one team on *those* ridges"—the sergeant pointed—"watching the *other* ridges and the other valley walls, and one team on *those* ridges watching the *other* side."

"That's a long climb."

The sergeant took a smoke and nodded.

"Pain in the ass at this altitude. They start out the night before the convoy comes through, then conceal themselves and camp out up there during the day. After you guys go they'll come back down. Probably break their asses in all this rain."

Black imagined the two small teams, each sitting in a puddle in a hunting blind on a mountainside, looking across through a night-vision scope at the other team and wondering whose puddle was deeper.

"Are they hitting targets or just doing area denial?"

The sergeant shrugged.

"Sometimes they'll just drop some stuff here and there to let anybody on the mountain know to just stay the fuck where they are. Who knows in this weather? Could be blowing up a dude with his goats."

Black didn't know what to say to this. Finally the sergeant laughed.

"Relax, L.T.," he said, shaking his head. "I'm kidding. We ain't savages up here."

He flipped his chin upward to the mountainsides.

"If they see something and can't get a good I.D., they just put munitions close enough to scare the shit out of whoever it is."

He sent a long streamer of smoke from the corner of his mouth up the Valley.

"So tell those Vega dudes we hope they like their chow and happy mail packages from home, 'cause guys got their asses on the line down here so they can do sniff-a-panty up there."

"Will do."

A flash from over the top of a ridgeline caught Black's eye. The light hit the clouds, and the boom came rumbling down the valley walls a few seconds later.

"So what are you, sir, the new platoon leader?"

"Huh?"

"Only seen but one officer go up to Vega, and that's the lieutenant up there."

He appraised Black top to bottom.

"Dude looked more tore up than you."

"Thanks."

"No sweat. So you ain't the new P.L.?"

Black shook his head.

"I'm doing a fifteen-six."

"Shit," the sergeant declared. "This whole valley's a fifteen-six. What's yours?"

"Warning shot in a village, no injuries."

The sergeant said nothing and stood still for so long Black thought his cigarette would go out in the damp. Finally he took a long draw and got it back to life. He exhaled slowly and considered his words carefully.

"Son," he said. "Of a goddamn bitch."

"Yup."

Time to get going.

"See you later, Sergeant."

"Take it easy, L.T.," the sergeant said as Black trudged away. "Don't end up in Xanadu."

Black looked back over his shoulder but the man was bending over stubbing out his cigarette in the can. He turned without looking and disappeared through a low doorway.

Back in the cacophonous refuel lane, soldiers were still finishing up with the vehicles, and their goggle-faced leader was still exhorting them with false or crazed enthusiasm from his little window. Black helped himself to a Styrofoam cup of coffee from the PIT CREW shack.

It was a small hive of radios and laptop computers lit only here and there by little red or amber lamps, to minimize any light spillage into the night. People were busy and left him alone. Radio traffic from the teams up on the ridges crackled down periodically through the rain. He downed the coffee quickly and left quietly.

Back outside people were climbing into vehicles for the last push up the valley. The refuel soldiers had disappeared. Goggle man turned his attention to the departing convoy.

"Have a Heavenly evening!" he cried from his window. "Enjoy your stay! Beware he who would be king!"

Black climbed into his seat and pulled the heavy door behind him, shutting out the strange sentinel's ravings.

He was fairly well soaked by then, but it didn't bother him much. He was mostly glad to be leaving Arcturus behind. It gave him the creeps.

The driver and vehicle sergeant were already in their seats, doing radio checks and getting ready to go.

"What was all that?" he called up to them.

"All what?" the sergeant asked.

"About being king."

"Always says shit like that. Bible or something."

"Freak," offered the driver.

"What's 'Xanadu'?" Black asked.

The sergeant shrugged and went back to his checks.

In two minutes the convoy was rolling, the familiar churn of gravel beneath tires. The end of the refuel channel passed the windows. Their view opened up to the familiar blackness. Gravel gave way to dirt, and the invisible outpost fell away behind them as though it had never existed.

Black settled in. He closed his eyes but didn't sleep this time.

"Vega X-Ray, this is Cyclone Mobile, over."

The sound of the sergeant speaking the name of their destination into the radio roused Black from a near trance.

He pushed the light on his digital watch. It had been another ninety minutes of slogging wet travel. The ride had gotten bumpier and slower the farther they went.

The sergeant keyed the hand mic again. Tried his call again.

Moments passed as the signal made its way up into the dark, dancing among the windswept peaks and stone faces above them. Black wondered how far they were from the outpost, how many mountain passes or switchbacks still lay ahead of them. The vehicles ground on through the muck.

A burst of static from the radio.

"Cyclone Mobile, Vega X-Ray," came a scratchy call back.

"X-Ray" denoted a command post or operations center. The voice on the other end was probably a soldier pulling late-night duty in Vega's radio room.

The sergeant keyed the mic.

"Cyclone Mobile inbound, six vehicles, twenty-five personnel. Checkpoint Grapevine, time now."

"Roger," came the voice through the static and interference.

A checkpoint in the military didn't always mean what it sounded like. In this case it was just a common point of reference on a map, so a headquarters could follow the progress of a convoy.

Black was opening his mouth to ask what *"Grapevine"* referred to when the sergeant hollered up to the gunner in the turret.

"Evans!"

"Sar'nt!" from above.

"Down!"

He dropped down from the turret and flopped into the passenger's seat opposite Black. He was good and soaked.

The sergeant turned to the driver.

"Hit it," he said.

The kid pulled off a glove and reached up to the ceiling, touching something with a bare finger. A square of sky blue illuminated on a tiny MP3 music player. He tapped it.

The vehicle erupted in sound. Black jumped.

The crew had wired speakers into the four corners of the Humvee. Not regulation, but not uncommon. Black hadn't noticed the black boxes until now.

An obviously old rock recording echoed in the darkened crew compartment. A punctuated three-note electric guitar figure repeated itself over and over, starting on a higher pitch each time, layering dissonances as it climbed the scale then falling back down to where it had begun and cycling over again. A string section ducked and wove like a serpent through the guitar. Bass and snare drums circled and thudded on a different track, lining up with the guitar only every few bars.

Black saw a dizzying, endless flight of broad stone steps, bounding upward through vaulted caverns to the dark heavens. He liked this song.

The gunner rooted around and found his seat belt. He buckled it, flipped his night-vision goggles up off his face, and settled back into his seat, eyes closed.

"What's this?" Black shouted.

The soldier opened his eyes and looked at him incredulously.

"Seriously, sir?" he shouted. "'*Kashmir*'?"

Black changed the subject.

"Why 'Grapevine'?"

The kid reached up and unsnapped his goggles, handing them across to Black. He put them on and looked around the compartment.

The soldier, now highlighted in green and white, thumbed toward the left-side window. Black unbuckled his belt and half stood, leaning way over to see beyond him.

Out the side window he saw nothing. He thought he could make out a valley wall a few hundred yards away, but it was tough through the rain. He leaned farther. Then he saw.

The roadbed ended abruptly about four feet to the vehicle's left. Stones and dirt gave way to open space. Beyond it, blackness.

"What?" he asked, pointing.

"River," the gunner said.

Black sat down in his seat, shuddering, and rebuckled his belt. He looked ahead, through the front windows.

They were driving along a mountainside—a cliffside, really—on the narrowest of dirt tracks. The road was barely wide enough to accommodate the trucks. A rock wall rose to the right of them, and empty space fell away to the left. Pulling a trailer behind a vehicle under those conditions was madness.

The gunner read Black's mind.

"Supply truck," he said.

"And a Humvee full'a bubbas," the sergeant called over the din.

"Twice," added the gunner.

"And a helicopter another time," offered the driver, prompting the sergeant to tell him to shut up and watch the road.

They had slowed to a crawl. Ahead, the harrowing track wound upward and left, then further up and right. It looked like it curved around into the night sky itself.

He understood now why the gunner had come down inside. It wasn't to keep him from being thrown under the vehicle in the event of a rollover. There was no rollover here. It was to make it more likely the bodies would all be recovered in one place.

He pulled off the goggles and gave them back to the gunner, who snapped them in the UP position on his helmet. He clearly had no interest in watching the proceedings himself.

Black decided it was probably just as well he'd left his own set of goggles in his pack. The gunner read his mind.

"Better this way, L.T.," he hollered, settling back into his seat and closing his eyes again. His chin bobbed right and left to the cycling music.

"Vega X-Ray, this is Cyclone Mobile, over."

"Cyclone Mobile, Vega X-Ray."

The connection was clearer now.

"Passing Checkpoint Two, time now."

"Proceed."

"Evans!" the sergeant shouted again at the turret.

"Sergeant!"

"Be awake!"

The gunner cycled the big .50-caliber machine gun.

The sergeant called over his shoulder at Black.

"All right, sir. When we pull in to Vega it's gonna be hop-hop. We ain't stopping except to drop the trailers and peel out."

"Okay."

"I'm sayin' you're gonna have to un-ass the truck in a hurry."

"Got it."

Black leaned forward in his seat and squinted past the sergeant and driver. Nothing but dark. The sergeant saw him out of the corner of his eye. Now it was his turn to unhook his night-vision goggles. He handed them back over his shoulder wordlessly.

"Don't crash, Nelson," he said to the driver.

"Roger, Sar'nt."

Black took the goggles and held them up in front of his eyes. The world turned green and bright again.

Hints of a rutted track appeared in front of them. The ground was wider now but they were driving basically cross-country, hand-railing a black area below to their left that must have been the river. To their right the ground rose sharply.

They were running along the right side of the Valley, gently uphill. As they came around a bend, he saw it, ahead and well above them.

Combat Outpost Vega was situated on the hillslope, as high above the level of the track as was feasible before the ground became too steep. Immediately above the collection of squat structures and blast walls, the valley side rose sharply.

The whole site was directly exposed to fire from the hills opposite the river and the steep slopes above. High ground on all sides, with minimal ability to see who or what might be coming down the hillside. All in all, a terrible position.

"Need 'em back, L.T."

Black handed the goggles up. He sat back. There was nothing to do at that point but wait for the word to bail out.

The vehicles slowed and turned, began to grind upward. After several minutes like this, the sergeant took up a different radio handset.

"Fighting Fours X-Ray, this is Cyclone Mobile."

Moments passed.

"Cyclone Mobile, Fighting Fours X-Ray."

The return call from FOB Omaha, from the headquarters of 3/44—the "fighting fours"—was distant and staticky. Black realized they were talking through multiple retransmission towers between the convoy and its home, over all the peaks and across the plain to the antennas on Radio Hill.

"Roger, Cyclone Mobile, R.P. Vega, time now."

"Roger, Cyclone Mobile, copy R.P. Vega, time now."

The sergeant set down the handset.

The ground leveled. Black felt the vehicle accelerate and veer into a sharp left turn that pressed him against the door. He put his hand on his rifle and unbuckled his seat belt. The Humvee decelerated sharply.

"Hit it, sir," called the sergeant.

"Thanks for the ride."

"Hooah," came the bland reply.

The vehicle came to a halt. He grabbed the handle and yanked it up, shouldering the sluggish door open into the dark.

Cool air hit him. His boot squashed into mud. He swung around but before he could push it closed another soldier had shoved past him and climbed into the open door. Someone catching a ride back to Omaha.

Lucky.

He looked around himself in the noise, finding his bearings in the poor light.

He was standing in a courtyard, more or less. Seventy-five or a hundred feet on a side, low structures and Hessco baskets all around the perimeter, save for a single ingress-egress point barely wider than a Humvee. There were no visible lights anywhere.

The first three vehicles of the convoy had pulled a wide U-turn before stopping, arraying themselves in a semicircle facing the exit. The rear vehicles had peeled off and with the smooth precision of an aerial acrobatics squad had arrayed themselves side by side, backing the trailers up against one row of barriers.

Before they'd even stopped, their rear doors had come open and a pair of soldiers jumped from each, stomping to the rear of each vehicle and unhitching the trailer latches. Moments later and they had completed the reverse operation with three empty trailers that were waiting for the convoy. Then back into the trucks, which immediately lurched forward and into formation. The lead vehicles were already rolling toward the exit.

It was an obviously well-rehearsed drill, and had taken no more than ninety seconds total. The convoys must have gotten some heat at the drop-off point in the past.

The last Humvee rolled past him, splashing mud and rumbling toward the exit. Before he had really processed what was happening, he was watching the convoy clear the barriers and disappear into the dark. Only at that moment did he notice that someone from the convoy had extracted his rucksack and dumped it in the mud beside him.

The sound of the trucks faded. Black turned in a slow circle.

The rain had lightened, the whistling wind eased. Moonlight was breaking through the clouds and throwing shadows.

He could make out more detail now in the structures lining the courtyard. Some sort of awning or overhang ran the length of it, creating a breezeway all round. Beneath it, darkened doorways beckoned at intervals.

Elsewhere shadowed pathways opened between gaps in blast barriers, presumably leading to this or that part of the outpost. But he saw not a single light in any direction, and heard not a sound save the whisper of the invisible breezefront sweeping gently down through the tree-covered mountainside above him.

He'd been left alone.

Figures.

He turned in another circle. The courtyard was empty and silent. He hadn't been expecting much of a reception at Vega, but a living person would have been helpful.

Black sighed inwardly.

"Figures," he said out loud, a fraction of a second before the fist struck the right side of his face, sending him reeling and disorienting him enough that he didn't even see the dark body coming at his midsection. The blow knocked his rifle out of his hands, driving him off his feet and into the mud.

The one whom the talibs called Tajumal rose from bed at the sound of the distant bombs, dressed quickly, and stepped before the cracked little shard of mirror hanging on the dirt wall. It had been removed from an American military vehicle.

Tajumal saw the face of a boy, perhaps twelve years old, scarf tied as a headband, looking back from beneath a hooded cloak.

For you, Father. For you, my brother.

Always they rained the bombs on the people of the valley on the nights they came. So easy to know. Their stupidity would lead them to justice. Soon. It was time to go see.

Guide me, Father. Show me what I need to see.

Through the little stone house on tiptoes past where Mother slept. The woolen curtain, covering the door against the rain, barely rustled as Tajumal slipped past it and was gone into the night.

7

H*ARAKAT MAKAWA!"*

The face was close above Black's, screaming something in Pashto, eyes wide. All the weight pinned him on his back, grinding him into the wet ground.

"HARAKAT MAKAWA!"

Spittle stung his eyes. The hard point of a pistol drove into his left temple. A forearm rammed hard against his chin, rooting to get beneath it to his throat. He struggled uselessly, his boot heels driving channels in the mud.

"MUQAAWAMAT MAKAWAYE!"

It was only his panicked attempt to keep his chin down and protect his airway that drew Black's eyes downward below the face. It took him a moment to process what he saw.

An elbow forced his chin upward, and he gargled out the only word that came to mind.

"American!"

The weight still pressed down but the wild eyes came into focus, darted up and down across Black's person.

"Speak!" his attacker cried. "Speak English!"

"American!" Black gasped again. "Get off me!"

Still pressing him down with one hand while moving the pistol roughly to his throat with the other, his attacker leaned back until he was straddling Black. His eyes settled on Black's chest. With his free hand he reached for Black's chin strap, yanking it free and flipping his helmet off into the mud.

The man's legs released their crushing hold around Black's middle. He threw his arms up in total exasperation.

"Jesus *Christ,* Lieutenant! What the hell?"

He planted a boot in the mud and hauled himself up to his feet, holstering the pistol. Black lay on his back, panting.

"Goddamn it! I thought you were one of *these* assholes again."

He jerked a thumb up toward the night, to the mountainside.

The man was not particularly tall but was built like a professional wrestler. His bearing was that of a sergeant, not a junior soldier. He stomped around the prostrate Black and scooped his helmet up from the mud. He offered his free hand, which Black took.

With his body armor, gear, and ammunition, he weighed more than 250 pounds. The sergeant hauled him to his feet with ease. Black stood, teetering, his entire back half coated in mud from head to toe.

"Sorry," he panted.

"Don't apologize to *me,*" the man snapped, agitated. "I was about to put a goddamn bullet in your face."

He wore boots and fatigue pants cinched with a tan equipment belt. Both were now smeared with mud. The requisite tan T-shirt, with dog tags now flung loose from the collar, was tucked into his waist. Black could see the bare-armed muscles massing beneath it.

Black spat a brown mouthful between heavy breaths and thumbed over his shoulder.

"I was with the convoy."

"Yeah, I got that," the man shot back irritably, as though Black thought he was particularly dense. "Nobody told me they were dropping off passengers."

"I'm the only one."

"Gee, sir, are you sure?" the sergeant vented sarcastically. "You sure there aren't any other anonymous wandering lieutenants creeping around my outpost?"

He held his hands up in a question and looked around himself theatrically. Black let it go.

The man looked past him, still annoyed.

"Where'd your rifle go?" he asked gruffly.

Black, his breathing slowing, scanned the wet ground and finally spotted it, a few steps away. He trudged over and gathered it up. It was covered in mud and useless until he could clean it.

"All right, you found it. Now come over under here before you get shot for real."

Black glanced up toward the hillsides. The sergeant scooped up his ruck and carried it underneath an overhang, into the breezeway that ringed the courtyard. Black followed, stepping under the overhang as the man dumped the ruck at his feet.

His host blew out a long breath and seemed to compose himself. The agitation was draining out of him. He surveyed Black from top to bottom.

"So," he said wearily, "who the hell are you, sir?"

"Fifteen-six officer," Black answered.

"Fifteen what?"

"Fifteen-six. I'm the one that got assigned to do the investigation."

The sergeant looked at him blankly.

"What investigation?"

"The shooting in the village."

The sergeant's gaze remained blank for a long moment. When he finally spoke, his tone was hard and accusatory.

"*What* shooting in the village, Lieutenant?"

"The warning shots."

"The warning shots," the sergeant repeated.

"Yeah."

The man was becoming agitated again.

"Um, pardon my being so bold, sir, but what fucking warning shots?"

"On the twenty-third, last month. Dispersing the crowd."

The sergeant's eyes went elsewhere, then clicked back into focus.

"Wait," he said. "What, the thing with the goat? The guy with the bullets in his fucking mud hut?"

"Yeah, that. Someone in the village complained to a Civil Affairs officer."

"Someone complained to a Civil Affairs officer," the sergeant repeated dryly.

"Yes."

"Okayyy . . ?"

"And the Civil Affairs officer told Brigade, and I drew the investigation."

"And you got sent all the way from Omaha to this shithole," the sergeant stated flatly, "to do a fifteen-fucking-six on a bullet hole in a wall."

"Yeah."

There was another long silence during which the sergeant stared at him blankly. He blinked several times, and then it became clear that his face was straining not to smile. His face lost.

"God bless the God damn Army," he chuckled, shaking his head.

"Yup."

"So now," the sergeant said cheerfully, smiling while his eyes hardened, "you're gonna waste my soldiers' time doing your little interviews with your sworn statements and all the bullshit."

"Yeah."

The sergeant nodded thoughtfully.

"Mm-hm. Figures."

He spat in the dirt.

"I mean, no offense or anything, L.T. I know you didn't choose yourself for the fifteen-six, but up here we call it what it is."

"Right."

"Right."

He eyed Black for another few moments before seeming to come to some conclusion in his head.

"Okay," he said, businesslike. "So you're here for, what, till the run next week? Or are they gonna send a helicopter just for you once you're done being Columbo?"

"Here for a week."

The sergeant shook his head again.

"All right," he said, shrugging. "Well, shit."

"Yup."

"Well, you're gonna need someplace to rack out, then."

"If you got one."

The sergeant pulled a walkie-talkie off his belt and thumbed it.

"Corelli."

A scratchy voice came back.

"Here."

"Come to the quad."

"Roger," said the radio. "Miller's in the latrine."

"When he's done."

He hooked the radio back on his belt, put his fists on his hips, and exhaled through pursed lips: What to do, what to do?

He looked at Black and extended a hand.

"Caine."

Black shook it.

"Black."

"I have Second Squad. Don't expect a bunch of saluting here."

"Didn't."

Caine gave a grunted laugh that was unreadable.

"That's good. Get you shot anyway."

He thumbed upward toward the hillsides again.

"Snipers," he said with mock wonder, "seem to think bagging an officer is some great catch, for some reason."

He stumped off toward a homemade wooden bench along the wall a few steps away. He eased down onto it, pulling his camouflage patrol cap off his head and extracting a smoke and lighter from a cargo pocket. He tossed the cap onto the bench next to him.

"Welcome to Vega, sir," he said, cracking the lighter. "May as well take a load off. Miller takes forever in the shitter."

Black walked over and sat in silence while the sergeant lit up. In the orange light he could see a square jaw below full cheeks, and close-cropped sandy hair over an open face that managed to be babyish and manful at the same time. He could have posed for the Burly Army Sergeant pin-ups calendar.

Black figured him for about thirty. Caine offered a smoke from his pack, which Black waved off.

"So, sir," Caine said, blowing a cloud, "how'd *you* get picked for this glorious duty?"

"Luck of the draw."

Caine snorted.

"Gotta love how you officers find new ways to fuck each other over," he said, sending smoke into the breezeway.

"Just my turn."

"Bullshit."

Caine shoved the smokes and lighter back into his pocket and continued.

"I mean, no offense, sir. But someone fucked you, whether you know it or not. You probably cut in front of some colonel at the ice cream line on the FOB."

"I don't eat that stuff."

"Yeah, right," the sergeant snorted. "I'm just messing with you, L.T. I eat the *shit* out of that chow hall when I'm back on the FOB."

"When was the last time you were back?"

"Let's see. Three months? Something like that. Was back there for one whole day to pick up some incoming joes, then back up here to the glory life."

He took another drag on the smoke and took his time letting it out.

"What was that you were yelling at me?" Black asked.

Caine pawed the haze in front of him.

"Just stuff," he said, shrugging. "You pick up stuff. 'Get down,' 'Drop your weapon.' You know."

He filled his lungs again.

"'Suck faster.'"

He chuckled at his own joke and turned to Black.

"How's the face?"

"Hurts."

Black worked his stiffening jaw around. He'd been trying not to rub it in front of Caine.

"Sorry," Caine said, not sounding it. "Like I said, no one told me you were coming. It wouldn'ta been the first time one of those suicide fuckers snuck on board in a U.S. uniform to blow his ass up."

He jerked his chin at the muddy courtyard.

"It was during a convoy stop last time, too. Snuck through the gate while the trucks were doing the drop-off."

"That's weird," Black said. "I thought you guys knew I was coming."

"Maybe they told our fearless leader," Caine muttered. "If so, he didn't tell me shit."

He could only be referring to the young officer in charge, or nominally in charge, of the platoon. Black had seen his name listed in the 15-6 paperwork.

"Lieutenant . . . Pistone?"

"Not 'Pist-OH-nee,'" Caine corrected him. "'Pis-TONE.'"

He exhaled haze.

"Like 'alone.'"

"Oh."

"Anyway, yeah, that's the one."

Caine said it in a tone that told Black everything he needed to know about what he and probably the other sergeants and soldiers in the platoon thought of their lieutenant.

"I should probably link up with him in the morning," Black said.

Gayley had told him Pistone would be his point of contact.

"Ain't here," Caine answered through a cloud.

"What?"

"Left on the convoy. R&R leave, or the commander needed him or some shit."

Black recalled the figure passing him in the dark to climb into the Humvee he was exiting.

"Too bad," Caine deadpanned. "Not sure how we're gonna make it out here a whole week without his guidance and mentorship."

Black was flummoxed. A 15-6 investigation was officer business, and he'd expected to coordinate things through the platoon leader.

"Who's the platoon sergeant?" he asked.

The platoon sergeant was the senior noncommissioned officer in the unit. He would be second only to the lieutenant, though in reality it was often the sergeant and not the officer who ran things.

"Dead."

"Oh."

"You got me, and you got Sergeant Merrick," Caine explained. "He had First Squad, but he just got his E-seven, so he's the acting platoon sergeant."

"E-7" was the administrative designation for a sergeant first class. The stripes on Caine's cap said he was a staff sergeant, one rank below Merrick.

"But we pretty much split the duty," Caine added.

"Okay."

"Merrick is just gonna *love* you and your investigation, sir, by the way."

"I don't doubt it."

Caine tapped his smoke and sent ashes to the stone walkway.

"Anyway, we're it. Us and some E-fives"—buck sergeants—"and a buncha joes, out here flappin'."

Out there flappin'. Army-speak for being left alone to do a thankless or dangerous task with no backup.

"Got it."

Caine looked at him.

"Don't worry, L.T.," he said. "You can do your little investigation. You can talk to the joes you need to talk to, and make all your paper."

"Right."

"But you do it on *our* time and you don't disrupt our operations."

"Don't intend to."

"These joes are wrung out and they got jobs to do and they got buddies dead," Caine went on. "They hardly got any downtime as it is and they don't need to spend it on some chickenshit that some FOBbit officer dreamed up."

He took another drag.

"No offense."

"None taken," Black answered, but the sergeant was already looking past him, scowling.

Black turned at the sound of footsteps jogging down the breezeway toward them.

"'Bout time," Caine said crossly. "Tell Miller to eat a bran muffin."

"Roger, Sar'nt," came the earnest answer.

A soldier stood bolt upright before them, feet apart and hands crossed behind the small of his back, staring at an invisible point in the universe above Black's and Caine's heads. Parade rest—the position a junior soldier assumes when talking to a sergeant of any rank.

His build was slight, his hair short and blond, his complexion pale even in the secondary moonlight. He looked to be about nineteen, tops. He wore a private's rank.

The name tape on his fatigues read CORELLI.

Caine flipped his cigarette to the ground and stubbed it with a boot. He pulled his muscled frame up from the bench. Black stood too.

"This is Lieutenant Black," he began, but before he could go further Corelli's eyes, wide and earnest on a searching face, darted involuntarily from empty space down to the center of Black's chest, registering the bar on the Velcro square.

They clicked forward again as his feet clapped together and he snapped to a salute.

"Put your fucking hand down!" Caine snapped, waving his own hand so aggressively Black thought he was going to reach right up and smack the soldier across the side of his head.

Judging from Corelli's flinch reaction, it looked like he thought so too.

"I told you, Lieutenant Pistone told you, don't fucking salute out here!" Caine harangued him. "You think it's different because there's a different L.T. standing in front of you?"

"No, Sar'nt!" replied the abashed Corelli, who had snapped back to his previous position.

"Annnnnywaaaayy," Caine continued, speaking pointedly and deliberately as though to someone who was very slow. "This, once again, is Lieutenant Black. He is here from FOB Omaha. He will be here for a week. He will be conducting an investigation pursuant to Army Regulation Fifteen-Dash-Six. He needs a bunk."

He pointed at Black's gear.

"Take his ruck, get the master key, and secure his ruck in Lieutenant Pistone's room."

"Master key" was sergeant lingo for a bolt cutter. Everything in the Army got padlocked, but the person with the key wasn't always around when you needed it. Sergeants ended up cutting open a lot of locks.

"Sergeant?"

Corelli's voice registered hesitation.

Black understood. Even a platoon leader who got no respect was still an officer. Corelli wasn't looking forward to being the one to break into an officer's quarters.

"Did I fucking stutter!?" Caine shouted.

Corelli flinched again.

"*He* ain't using it! Now take the lieutenant's shit!"

"Roger, Sar'nt!"

Corelli scrambled to grab up Black's ruck and sling it over his shoulder. Black didn't need or want anyone to carry his bag, but decided it wasn't the time to say so.

"Here, take his rifle too," Caine said, extending his open hand out toward Black.

He saw Black hesitating this time.

"Ain't no use to you filled with mud, sir. You've still got your sidearm."

He gestured down at the holster on Black's hip, which somehow had remained fairly clean.

Black's rifle was almost certainly nonfunctional at this point. He handed it to Caine, who handed it to Corelli.

"Secure that in the room with his ruck," Caine told the soldier.

Corelli turned to go.

"Actually," Caine said as though the thought had just occurred to him, "take it to the armory and clean it first. Then secure it."

"Roger, Sar—"

"I'll clean it," Black said flatly.

Only the dirtbaggiest of dirtbag officers would have ever consented to a soldier cleaning his weapon for him.

"All right," Caine said to Corelli, eyeing Black. "The lieutenant likes to clean his own weapon."

He leaned back against the wall.

"Secure his muddy weapon in the room."

Corelli "roger"d again, apparently relieved to be dismissed. He sent a last glance toward Black and hustled off down the darkened corridor.

Caine turned to Black.

"Resident choirboy," he explained. "Super religious. Good soldier, though. Put him in charge of the armory because he can actually count. Unlike some of these bubbas."

Black nodded.

"Anyway, figured it makes sense to stick you in the L.T.'s room. One of the only private racks we got."

Black was not going to complain about that.

"Well, shit, sir," said Caine, stretching. "May as well give you the grand tour."

Tajumal watched the two Americans disappear into the bowels of their outpost, then backcrawled into the bushes and sat back against the cold hillside. There was much to consider.

Why did they fight?

This one was easy. The one American had shouted at the other. Not in Tajumal's language. In the trade language of the cities, which Tajumal understood.

He thought the other was one of us, even though he wore American soldier clothes.

The Americans were ready for this tactic. Tajumal swelled with satisfaction.

Just as I told Qadir.

Stupid Qadir, who was probably squatting high above right now, somewhere on the opposite hillside, looking down at the wrong side of the American base with his rifle. Hotheaded Qadir, full of brash ideas and recycled schemes, who thought the talibs would respect him if he shot enough Americans who were foolish enough to walk about in the open, or blew himself up like the dumbest Arab *mujahideen.*

Why would they care about a teenage boy who can kill only the stupidest and most worthless of the Americans?

Qadir, who treated Tajumal like an idiot and a child because he was a whole five years older. Who knew where to find the Americans' base but knew nothing more. Whose highest achievement would be to end his life in meat chunks on the mountainside. Who probably wouldn't even manage to take any Americans with him because they would see him coming a mile away.

Qadir does not know what I can do. Does not know who I am. He only knows a useless little boy he sees creeping around the mountains, which he thinks are his *mountains. But he will know. And the talibs will know, and the Americans will know.*

Qadir had some use. He had certain information Tajumal had needed to know. But Qadir didn't know what to *do* with that information.

I do.

With the Americans, the real fight was the battle of brains.

Which is why I watch, and I watch again, until I find the knowledge I need. Tonight I have found it. Once again, Father, you have guided me true. May you be proud in paradise. And may Sourabh, God's blessings upon him, play happily at your feet, and may you rub your fingers in his hair as you used to rub them in mine, and may he gaze up at you with all his love, forever.

Only Tajumal had been close enough to hear the shouting, to know that Qadir's latest plan was pointless. Only Tajumal had held firm, not fled at the commotion as Qadir would have done. And only Tajumal had seen the thing that was much more important, the thing Qadir could not have seen as he cowered up there on the wrong side of the valley in the dark.

The salute.

Only Tajumal knew what the others could not know. What would bring hope to all.

The officer has returned.

Praise to Father. Praise God.

8

It was bigger than he'd expected, and there seemed to be no open air anywhere.

He'd imagined the usual arrangement for one of these remote bases. Individual structures and outbuildings and fortifications scattered across a small area of open land, with the whole thing bounded around by a berm or maybe concertina wire. But wending their way through the various wings of the sprawling outpost, nearly everywhere Black and Caine traveled was underneath some kind of roof or overhead cover. A lot of it was fully indoors.

It had started the way most COPs did, Caine explained as they walked. Before Americans came, there was an existing structure, high on the hillside—a large and well-constructed Taliban chief's house. A sprawling mansion that doubled as a sort of meeting center.

When the first Army unit had come, Caine had been with it.

"That was a year and a month ago," he said, walking alongside Black, their footsteps echoing off rough tile and stone walls. "We were livin' the high life back at Omaha like you."

Black held his tongue.

"Then they rousted us out of there and sent us up the Valley," Caine went on. "No one had been this far. We were looking for a good site for a COP to run interdiction on the routes these crazy jihadis use to come across from Pakistan."

He pointed through the walls and downward as they walked.

"There's a town a little ways down below here, and here we are coming up the Valley and we get to the town and ask 'em, Where's the H.T.I.C.?"

Head Taliban In Charge.

"And they point up the hill. So we take a squad up the hill and we find this dude's house, just sitting up here on the side of the mountain behind a wall with nothing else around it. Like, a regular villa."

He shook his head.

"Splendid isolation or whatever."

They were walking now up a plywood hallway with fluorescent lights strung high at the seam of the wall and ceiling, which was itself made of plywood. Somewhere on the other side of a wall, a generator hummed peacefully in the night, its noise rising and fading as they passed.

"Anyway, he must not've been expecting us because he only had like two or three bodyguards in the place when we came. They made it easy too, because they started shooting at us, so we didn't even have to call it in and ask, Do we capture the guy or what? We just killed the bodyguards, and we killed the Taliban's ass because he was shooting at us too."

"He didn't run?"

"Hell, no. Kinda surprised us, 'cause we figured as soon as we showed up and started layin' it on he'd just wanna, you know, un-ass the villa. But he freaking stayed put. Rifle in one hand, pistol in the other. Went down in a blaze of asshole."

He chuckled at his own joke as they turned a corner, leaving the plywood behind. Their feet struck concrete. The walls in this corridor were hard and cold. A breeze found its way through a crack somewhere and whistled at them as they passed through.

"So afterwards we call it in to our command and tell 'em we found this big house. And when I say 'house' I mean, like, brick and cement and tile."

He bumped a fist along the wall as he walked. Black now noticed it was clean cinder block.

"Properly made," Caine continued. "Not even a lot of stone in it like most of the crap construction they have here. And so we say we found this house and what do you want us to do? And command comes back: Hold the house."

They stumped up two plywood steps between split-level corridors.

"And we're like, for how long? And they say: Until relieved."

"Which was?"

"Two weeks," Caine answered scornfully. "Two fucking weeks of holding this place on the fly. We weren't even a full platoon, even counting the squad that was down in the town, which was Sergeant Merrick's squad. He was here too."

"What did you do?"

"We called Merrick's squad on the radio and we said get your asses up here, which they did, and we fucking hunkered down for the night, scared shitless. And we didn't sleep one wink because we had the joes out all night building machine-gun positions and setting Claymores and all that shit."

"Wow," Black said flatly, and meant it.

The modern military had a low tolerance for sending its soldiers into the kind of unplanned, uncontrolled, outnumbered, seat-of-the-pants situations that featured more prominently in older and more desperate wars. Nowadays that was a good way for senior officers to get relieved of duty and prosecuted for negligence.

They had stopped at a low concrete doorway with "C.P." stenciled on it in black spray paint. Caine nudged the plywood door open with a boot and had to duck his head slightly to stick it through the entrance. Black followed suit. The hum of a box fan and the twinkling of electronic lights greeted him.

The command post. A radio room, essentially. Square, cinderblock walls, maybe ten feet side to side, no windows. Its floor was set a couple steps below the level of the passageway. Large topographic maps of the countryside lined the walls. An industrial desk sat in the middle of the room, making an L with a table containing multiple stacks of military radio equipment. From here whoever was on duty could talk to everyone inside the COP, from the guard towers to the aid station, and anyone outside it on patrol, as well as keep contact with 3/44's headquarters back on Omaha.

The only light came from a lamp on the desk and the winking green displays on the radio sets. The rest of the room was bathed in shadow and mostly empty, save for a rack with portable radios against the back wall and a cot in a dim corner to Black's right. Two guys could share a long overnight shift and split time sleeping.

A soldier in camouflaged pants and tan T-shirt slumped on his elbows at the radio desk, bleary-eyed, reading a paperback novel with spacecraft crossing trackless heavens on its cover.

"Hey, highspeed," said Caine blandly.

Highspeed. The timeless Army descriptor for a squared-away go-getter. *That is one highspeed soldier.* It could be used sincerely, or sarcastically, which is how Caine used it now, eyeing the schlubby sentinel.

"This is Lieutenant Black."

One eyeball came off the page, registered Black's presence, and rejoined its colleague. The rest of the soldier remained still. Probably, Black figured, he was wondering when his buddy was gonna get back from the latrine or chow or wherever so he could rack out on that cot.

"Hooah," the kid mumbled.

Caine pulled his head out and let the door shut. He continued trooping down the hall.

"'Wow' is right," he said, picking up their conversation where it had left off. "That was some fucking real-deal, old-school Vietnam firebase style, dump-your-ass-in-the-middle-of-nowhere-and-hope-for-the-best bullshit right there."

"Out there flappin'," Black offered.

"Out. There. Flapping."

Caine drew a long sniffle and spat in the dirt. They were passing through a brief open-air passageway walled by head-high blast barriers on either side. It served as a channel between one structure and another. Black could smell the trees and the dry air.

"Dudes that night were praying and shit," he said as they ducked into the next part of the complex. "Writing their freaking *I'm sorry* notes on the backs of M.R.E. boxes and all that."

The air was close again, more humid. Every corridor in the place seemed to be made from a different combination of materials than the last. Ammunition cans of various types, Black noted, were stacked in corners at regular intervals throughout the labyrinth.

"And don't think we didn't get attacked that very same night and every fucking day after," Caine continued. "Two weeks, seven K.I.A.s, and pretty much everyone got hit at least once."

Black imagined the desperation of the situation. Caine was right; it was like something out of another time.

"They had to send birds to drop ammo and M.R.E.s and water for us, every day. But we held that shit. And after two weeks the engineers got here, on a fucking helo . . ."

He spat again, with contempt.

". . . and checked out the house."

Army engineers specialized in building temporary roads, bridges, and barricades, and fortifying existing structures on the fly.

"What'd they say?" Black asked.

Caine snorted.

"They looked around and stroked their chins and made smart faces and said, 'Hmm, solid masonry. Hmm, load-bearing members. A good core.' And all the shit I could've told them over the radio on day one. And then the bird came back and they got back on it and left, and our command said this is gonna be the COP. And we held it another five days until the engineer assets started getting here."

Caine explained how the engineers started with the house, building around the big stone-and-cement structure as the core. They fortified it first and built off its existing sheds and outbuildings, then incorporated the masonry wall that surrounded it. They sandbagged up all its windows and emplaced portable "crow's nest" guard towers on the rooftop corners.

Then came generators, shipping containers for supplies, blast walls around the mortar pit, and all the usual stuff. By the end they had built a standard little outpost, a series of structures centered on the chief's house, all perched on the shelf of level ground against the steep hillslope.

It hadn't been enough. There was too much high ground all around it. The place was attacked constantly from the mountainsides.

Over the course of the past year, most anything that was not covered had gotten covered. Fortified pass-throughs were built between structures, outdoor areas were turned into indoor areas, rooftops were sandbagged, blast walls were set down everywhere.

Some of the work, the heavy stuff, had been performed by engineers after repeated insistence by Vega's sergeants and their headquarters. The rest had been done piecemeal by the soldiers themselves.

Now the place had grown to a sprawling, patchwork complex of passageways and chambers, a Russian dollhouse of buildings within buildings, additions atop combinations. A compound.

Black found the place fascinating. You never knew as you turned a corner whether you would still be in the same structure or someplace totally new, grafted together on the fly. He guessed that you would be hard-pressed, looking at it from the outside, to identify the original house which sat at its core.

Caine pointed out to Black that they were at that moment passing through what had formerly been a front hall and sitting area where the chief would receive guests. Black looked down and saw broad, ornate floor tiles.

"Why'd they call it Vega?" he asked.

"Who knows?" Caine replied blandly. "Naming stuff is officer business."

Fair enough.

"C'mon, sir. I'll show you the roof."

They had passed from the front hall and turned a corner into a darkened passageway. It was lit only with green glow stick "chem lights" placed in what looked to be soup cans that had been attached at intervals to the wall. The fancy tile was gone and the flooring was rougher here. Black felt the temperature drop as they walked.

They reached the base of a stone stairwell, leading up into darkness. Caine stopped and turned to Black.

"Hey, L.T., I see you've got your flashlight hooked to your gear there," he said, pointing at Black's chest. "I'm sure I don't need to tell you not to turn that thing on past the top of these steps."

Black just stared at him.

Caine shrugged.

"Hey, sir, you'd be surprised."

He turned and clumped up the dark steps. Black followed.

After several steps the stairs turned right. Another chem light marked the corner. Black felt a slight breeze coming down the well from above.

When he peered up the stairwell he saw a dim blue glow hanging in the dark above them.

They reached a tiny landing where the steps turned again. The glow was right in front of them, at about chest level. Black now saw that it was coming from behind some sort of sheet or curtain strung across an opening in the wall. Caine yanked a corner of it back.

"What's happening, Oswalt?"

The curtain had been drawn across a recessed area set into the wall about four feet off the floor. Inside was the tiniest hootch Black had ever seen—a stone cavity maybe seven feet long by four feet high by four feet deep.

Hooks and masonry nails had been driven into fissures in the bare stone sides, from which a toiletry kit and various personal comfort items hung in little mesh bags. Some kind of mattress or bedroll was wedged into the space and draped crookedly across the uneven stone surface.

On it, reclining against a couple pillows, was a soldier in long-sleeved PT gear watching an action movie that Black didn't recognize on a portable DVD player. Registering his visitors, he pulled a pair of enormous headphones off his ears, releasing a cacophony of tinny car-chase sounds into the stairwell.

"Oh, hey, Sergeant Caine."

He had wide eyes and a young face, though he was not a small soldier and looked to be past twenty. His hands were large and strong and his hair buzzed down nearly to the skin, and his face carried a look of mild surprise that seemed to be a permanent expression. His deep voice echoed as from a hollow log lined with moss.

He didn't seem fazed by, or even to take note of, Black's presence.

"Hey, Oswalt," Caine answered. "Whatcha watchin'?"

"*Transporter 2.* Hubbard gave me the DVD."

"Is it as awesome as the first one?"

"Sure is, Sergeant."

"All right, then."

Caine turned to go. Black followed.

"Have a good night, Oswalt."

"Good night, Sergeant," Oswalt answered, pulling his headphones back up. "Good night, sir."

Surprised, Black mumbled a "good night" over his shoulder as he and Caine trudged upward again. Caine didn't speak, so Black just came out with it.

"There was no weapon in his hootch."

Soldiers' weapons rarely left their sides on deployment, whether they were on duty or eating or sleeping.

"Hey, we got Columbo after all," snorted Caine. "Guess you'll be a good investigating officer, sir."

Black waited.

"We let him secure it in the arms room when he's not on duty," the sergeant offered.

They walked further.

"Oswalt is special," Caine said finally.

Black considered this.

"Head injury, or just special?"

"Just special," Caine replied tersely. "Don't ask me how he got through basic training, but he did."

Black dimly saw another turn in the stairwell ahead. He smelled pine.

"Army takes all kinds, I guess," Caine mused.

"Got it."

"Don't get me wrong. He's a good soldier. Work as hard as you want him to work. No attitude. Not a bad shot either."

He shrugged.

"Nice kid. Just slow in certain areas."

"He lives in the stairwell?"

"Hey, different strokes. He likes living there. But he does not go on the roof."

"Never?"

"No," Caine answered flatly, pointing at his head. "Doesn't pack the gearbox. Too easy to get shot up there, or shoot the wrong thing while you're by yourself on guard duty for six hours."

"What *does* he do?"

"This and that. Fixes up a weapon pretty good. Let him listen to the radio sometimes when nothing's goin' on."

He shrugged.

"Ya know. Earns his keep."

Caine had stopped at the turn in the stairway.

"All right, sir, you're just gonna need to walk kinda fast when we're up there."

"Will do."

Caine turned and started up. Black followed him around the corner. At the top of the stairwell a rectangle of gray light loomed. The stairs ended in an opening cut flush into the roof. The two ascended.

After spending the past couple minutes in darkened hallways lit only by chem lights, Black's eyes had adjusted to the dark. The stairwell fell away beneath him and he felt a tingle of vertigo as he stepped up into the vast open space.

To one side, beyond the edge of the roof, a forested mountainside rose before him. In the other three directions, empty air. The outpost was perched on an outcropping of ground set on the steep valley slope. It was probably close to a mile across to the opposite side. Above them, the ridges were a thousand feet up or more. Beyond that, the clouds had broken further to reveal broad patches of crystalline starlight. The breeze that moved them carried down past the mountaintops and gently touched his face. It smelled like deep fall.

He hesitated only a moment before hearing Caine's "All right, then, sir," as he trudged away briskly across the roof. Black followed.

The roof was wide and flat. Planked pathways had been created by laying wood pallets end to end, making walkways that forked out in three directions ahead of them. Caine took the middle one, heading for the hulking shape of a guard post squatting at one corner of the roof.

The thing looked like a haystack made of dark green sandbags. As they approached, Black could see many of them were split and spilling sand from where they had taken fire. From the haphazard pattern in which they lay, it looked like fresh ones had been laid down over old more than once.

Black looked left and right as they tromped across the wobbly planking, the racket of their steps sounding loud enough in the vast silence to reach the high ridges. He could see at least two other haystacks at far corners of the roof.

Their path led straight to the dark opening at the rear of the guard post. Caine stepped through without pausing. Black stepped in after him.

The roof inside was low. The interior of the guard shack itself was only a few feet on a side. Two rectangular openings faced out over the corner of the roof, one to the left and one to the right, with wide views of the moonlit Valley. Machine guns sat mounted in each window, and behind each one sat a soldier on a four-legged stool.

One had been speaking to the other in low tones, about what sounded like girl problems, as he looked out into the night beyond his gun. The other sat sideways on his stool, his back against the wall of the post, the window to his right, facing his friend.

"Goddamn it, Bosch," said Caine. "You think you might want to watch your fucking sector?"

The soldier said nothing but cast an appraising look at Black and rotated lazily until he, like his friend, was facing out over his weapon.

"All right, sir," Caine said, sounding bored.

At the "*sir,*" the first soldier cast a glance over his shoulder at Black.

"So down there you've got the river."

He pointed down the carpeted slopes and descending ridges. Black could not see water but could identify the gap in the trees several hundred feet below them where the course of the river must run.

Caine pointed to the right, a little higher.

"And if you go downhill that way, not quite as far as the river but around that bend in the hills there, you get to a little side valley. That's the village I was telling you about."

"Darreh Sin."

"Yep. Shithole."

"Is that what it means in Afghani, Sergeant?" said the first soldier, chuckling.

"Shut up," said Caine mildly. "So that's the town I was telling you about, sir, where we first found out about this place."

He pointed farther to the right and higher.

"And if you go *up,* there's a trail—more than one trail, probably, but there's a trail that goes all the way up the Valley and gets you to Pakistan."

"How far?"

"By foot?" Caine shrugged. "Who knows? Never been. Ain't allowed to go. Probably seven or eight miles, except nobody fucking knows where the border is. It's all disputed lands and shit up there."

He stuck his hands in his pockets.

"But we know the trails go all the way because the local Valley dudes move heroin to Pakistan and the Taliban moves fighters from goddamn everywhere all the way down through here"—he swept his hand across the panorama like a cleansing wave rushing through the mountain passes—"and out to the rest of this outstanding country."

"You guys interdict?" Black asked.

"Fighters? Yeah, technically that's part of the mission. Right after 'Stay alive and don't fucking get overrun.'"

The first soldier gave an approving nod.

"We keep pretty busy on part one," Caine went on. "So we don't get a lot of spare time to chase incoming jihadi tourists all up and down through the hills. We mostly try to just kill 'em when they try to kill us."

"What about drugs?"

Caine shrugged again.

"That, we don't really worry about so much," he said. "I'm sure there's poppy fields in the mountains on this side of the border too, but like I said, we don't really know 'cause nobody's ever been."

He looked up through the hillsides.

"I'm sure they take care of their business up there," he said, "and we take care of our business down here."

Black took this all in, following Caine's gaze up the slopes. The forest seemed surprisingly noisy this time of night, between the light breeze and the frequent sound of animals snapping twigs and brushing through trees.

"How often you guys go down to Darreh Sin?"

Caine nodded as though expecting the question.

"We take a patrol down there about once a week or so."

"Goodwill, or catching bad guys?"

Caine's head jogged left and right: This and that.

"In Darreh Sin," he said, "more goodwill. We gotta take pictures of this water collection system they're building, that the U.S. paid for. Like, get the water from the mountain streams down to the crops and stuff more efficiently."

He shook his head.

"Me, I'd figure it'd mostly piss off dudes in the next town over that this town gets cash and gets the better water. But what the fuck do I know? I'm not a Civil Affairs officer. I'm just a dumb sergeant. Anyway, gotta get pictures and show progress and shit."

Black nodded.

"Fog's coming in," interjected the first soldier from behind his machine gun.

Caine leaned forward and peered downward.

"Yup."

Black leaned forward and looked. Wisps of mist were creeping about the hillsides at the bottom of the slopes where the river ran.

"Gonna fill up the whole valley," Caine said to Black.

"I hate that shit," said the first soldier.

"I love that shit," said his friend, Bosch, speaking for the first time.

Caine turned to face Black, hands still in his pockets.

"So, sir, unless you've got more questions for this stop on the deluxe tour, I can take you down and show you your rack."

Black indicated that he didn't.

They turned to go.

"Have a good one, sir," said the first soldier over his shoulder.

"Yup."

They creaked across the rackety planking again and back down through the stairwell, past the curtains of Oswalt's hootch, which was still filled with blue light from the DVD player. They wound through fresh passageways Black hadn't yet seen, until they arrived at a series of three or four wooden steps.

A plywood door was set into the wall on the right. In large stenciled letters it read:

THE SHIT

Someone had taken a marker and added WELCOME TO above it.

Caine yanked open the door to reveal a sort of indoor-outdoor closet containing a Porta-Potty shed. It sat on wood planking and was completely enclosed in blast walls and plywood roofing. Black assumed there were layers of sandbags piled on top, on the outside of it. The little built-in plastic chimney rose up from the shed and disappeared through the fortified roof.

"Here's the nearest latrine, sir. Like our indoor plumbing?"

"Impressive."

Back at his unit in the States, Black had known a sergeant who figured out how to convert a little utility closet in their headquarters into a stand-up shower, complete with a tile floor and fully waterproof. Great for showers after morning PT. Once people in other units found out, everyone wanted him to build one for their headquarters. This potty closet rivaled that in its ingenuity. It was a nice piece of construction.

"We kind of had to build it this way," said Caine with a little pride. "A kid died in the shitter last year when a mortar hit one of the Porta-Johns."

"Yuck."

"Yeah," Caine drawled. "What a way to go, and so forth. Anyway, all of 'em are enclosed now."

He turned and headed up the steps, into a low-ceilinged plywood hallway strung with fluorescents. Several doors sat at intervals along the left wall. All but one were padlocked shut.

Caine stopped at the one which wasn't and pulled the door open.

"Home sweet home, L.T."

He held the door.

Black stepped through into a windowless room with concrete walls and a fluorescent light blaring from the ceiling. Lieutenant Pistone's hootch.

It looked well kept and orderly. Black's ruck, courtesy of Private Corelli, slouched in the middle of the floor.

He turned to Caine.

"Thanks."

"Hey, gotta give you someplace to rack out," Caine shrugged. "*He* ain't using it."

"Right."

Caine lingered in the door. He shoved his hands in his pockets, hesitating.

"Listen, sir," he said. "I know right now you're thinking 'Is this dude gonna be a pain in my ass?'"

Black didn't bother denying it.

"Look," Caine went on. "I know you have a job to do, even if it *is* pointless and stupid."

Black said nothing. Caine sighed.

"I'm not gonna make life difficult, all right, sir?"

"All right."

Caine looked at Black searchingly.

"But I told you how we got here," he said. "I told you how we got this place, and now you know. Now you know why I call it 'my' outpost. I figure after what we went through here we kind of own it at this point, right? There's more of our goddamn blood on the floor of this house than the other side's. You know what I mean?"

"I do."

"So I'm just saying, be respectful of that when you're investigating my guys, okay?"

"I will."

"I know how things start sounding," Caine went on, "when you put it on paper and send it up to Brigade headquarters. How some simple thing like the mob and the warning shots starts sounding like some goddamn massacre or like we're terrorizing the town or some shit."

"I know."

"That's not my soldiers," Caine said, looking him in the eye. "They got friends dead and they gotta worry about not getting themselves dead. I don't want them thinking they fucked up and are in trouble for doing their jobs."

Black nodded.

"They go through enough shit out here," Caine finished, "and they don't need that too."

"Not my speed."

"Right," Caine said dryly.

He looked Black up and down and shook his head. He laughed again.

"Shit, sorry about all the mud and the face, L.T."

"Don't sweat it."

"Anyway, so you saw where the latrine is, and anybody can point you to the chow hall. Just find me when you're up in the morning, and I can get you what you need."

"Will do."

"Better yet," Caine said, looking at the dark circles under Black's eyes, "you should probably sleep in. You look like you haven't slept in a week."

"Sounds good."

Black thought Caine was finally going to go. Instead he just stood there, looking at Black silently.

He was about to ask the sergeant if there was anything else he could help him with when Caine sighed, as though saddened by something. Before Black knew what was happening the sergeant's hand shot out, straight toward his chest.

He yanked the Velcro rank patch, with the lieutenant's bar, from the center of Black's uniform. He clutched it in his fist and stepped in until his face was close, looking up at Black's. His eyes had gone dark.

"You go wandering around bumping into shit and fucking up our operations," he said in a hushed voice, "and I *will* fucking shoot you, officer or no officer."

He paused the merest moment, took one step back, and slapped the rank patch, crooked, back onto Black's uniform. He turned on a heel and strode off down the hallway, calling a cheery "Good night, sir!" over his shoulder.

Black just stood there, his heart rate returning to normal. Colonel Gayley's words returned to him.

They're strung out and they've lost a lot of buddies. They are not going to be happy to see you poking your nose around their outpost.

He closed the door.

9

The room was sparsely appointed. Bunk, wooden chair, wooden rod with uniforms hanging from it, little homemade set of shelves with socks and underclothes folded, little homemade nightstand. Not much else.

Black was used to hootches wallpapered with posters or swimsuit calendars, strung with Christmas lights, littered with knickknacks from home. The closest thing to decoration here was a little framed picture on top of the shelves and what appeared to be a leatherbound journal sitting on the nightstand.

He bent and looked at the picture. The top half of a young man, his bare arm crooked round the neck of the top half of a girl.

She was small and sprite-like with a frizzy blond mane, caught in mid-laugh as she squinted happily at the camera. He wore spectacles, and his own hair was buzzed nearly down to the skin. His narrow face was almost babyish. He looked into the lens with a pursed smile and pinched eyes that seemed to be trying hard to project confidence. The couple stood beneath palm trees somewhere fabulous, on a hill or a cliff with the ocean behind them.

Lieutenant Pistone, presumably. And his girl.

The setting, the pose, the exuberant pixie of a girlfriend, the selection of *this* photo as the one you bring to the Valley. Black was a quick study of the various sorts of people who are attracted to the military. There were a lot of different ones, but he felt he could peg Pistone pretty quickly. Geek made good.

He had known the type before. The brainy guy who was never good with the girls, never got picked for the team, spent an ineffectual childhood probably getting picked on a little bit, developed a nice put-upon complex. Then discovered the military somehow and learned that even if you are all those things you can still get to do *this*. That your military life can stand as a triumphant ongoing *Fuck You* to all the guys who'd always been cooler.

He became your squared-away supersoldier, in his own way. Fastidiously organized, diligent about physical training. Not necessarily a good leader.

He walked around with the sound track of his freshly awesome life playing in his head. He tended to forget that succeeding in the military was not so much about his own cosmic journey to heroism as it was about how good he was at dealing with people, handling people, taking care of people. Sooner or later, the Army turned on him, left him friendless there as in life.

Quick to judge.

He stepped over to the nightstand and ran his fingers across the cover of the journal, which was embossed with Celtic scrollwork. It was a fancy leather job with a strap tie and everything, your standard overpriced impulse buy in an economically nonviable specialty store hawking wind chimes on the quiet main street of a tourist town you visit with your pixie girlfriend.

Diary?

He looked around and only then noticed a small footlocker under the bunk. He let that be. He unslung his rifle and sat down in the wooden chair, feeling keenly aware that not only was he making himself at home in another man's space, but that that man had no idea when he left it that his home would be intruded upon while he was gone. It was weird.

Shaking off the feeling of being a burglar, he rose and opened his ruck. He pulled out a fresh uniform and stripped off his muddy one, hanging it on a spare hanger from the wooden rod. He dressed and pulled his weapons cleaning kit from the ruck, sitting in the middle of the floor with his dirty rifle in front of him. He disassembled the weapon, stripping it down to the extractor, and spent the next hour working in silence, the pieces spread on the floor around him.

Weapon assembled again, he set it on the crisply made bunk and sat down next to it. He stared at the door and realized that sleep would not come quickly if he lay down. He thought of Caine's warning, but only briefly, as he rose and stepped out into the hallway.

"Good way to get shot by mistake, sir."

The soldier cocked one eye over a shoulder from behind his machine gun as Black ducked his head and stepped into the guard post. Other than that, he and his friend had hardly acknowledged Black's arrival at all.

He had nearly lost his way getting back to the roof, turning back once or twice before finding himself in the chem light passageway. Quietly up the breezy stairwell and past Oswalt's little wall hootch, which was finally dark inside and emitting beefy snores. Then up and out across the planks.

Caine had not been exaggerating about the fog. From the higher parts of the Valley, down the river run, it had flowed and swelled until it filled every available space. Then it rose. A silent gray sea lay before them, stretching across the Valley, its near shore only a couple hundred feet below the outpost.

Black stood with his hands in his pockets, mesmerized. Finally the first soldier spoke.

"Probably clear out Sniper Town at least."

"What's that?"

The soldier pointed upward, indicating the hillslopes above Vega.

"Watch our asses all the time. But they hate this crap. Usually go home when it comes out."

Black said nothing.

"Their own goddamn valley and it even creeps *them* out," the soldier said, shaking his head. "Superstitious about it. You know what they call it, sir?"

"What?"

"'Devil fog.'"

"What's that mean?"

"You know, sir," the kid said, making disdainful quotes in the air. "'Folklore' and stuff."

"Like what?"

The soldier shrugged.

"You know, like, the bogeyman," he said. "Got all kinds of stories about it. Like, the Devil walks in the fog and steals your babies and shit."

"Oh."

"Which is hilarious, 'cause what they should be scared of is themselves," the soldier continued. "All these fucking tribes with their chiefs always assassinating each other and raping each other's daughters 'cause somebody took your goat a hundred years ago and all that bullshit."

The kid shook his head.

"Jackasses," he concluded.

The other soldier, the one called Bosch, was leaning back against the wall again and regarded Black idly from behind dark, unimpressed eyes.

"I see you found the laundry service, sir," he said dryly, eyeing Black's fresh uniform.

In response, Black rooted in his pockets and pulled out a pack of smokes and a lighter. He mouthed one and offered the pack to the first soldier, who frowned at the lighter.

"Light discipline, sir."

Black shrugged.

"We're under cover. You said the snipers are going home anyway."

The soldier said nothing. Black held the pack out to his friend instead. He recognized a kid who broke rules just to prove something when he saw one.

Bosch looked at it a moment and then took one. They lit up. Black inhaled slowly.

Don't cough like an amateur.

After a minute or two of first-puff haze, the first soldier spoke up.

"So, sir, can I ask a dumb question?"

Black gave a *What's that?* flick of his head as he blew a streamer out past the machine guns.

"Um, what are you doing here, sir?"

"Wanted to see the fog."

The soldier frowned.

"No, sir. I mean, what are you doing at Vega? We haven't seen any other officer here besides the L.T. in, like, never."

Black blew out a streamer of smoke and shrugged nonchalantly.

"Gotta take care of some bullshit."

The soldier nodded gravely as though that were as thorough and forthcoming an explanation as anyone ever needed to give for anything in the Army.

"Roger that, sir."

They shot the breeze.

The first one had a girl who he'd been having problems with since he deployed, which was nothing new for soldiers. He was round-faced and freckled, jaded in a mellow Midwestern way. Most of his high school friends were home doing meth.

The other soldier, Bosch, didn't say a lot, but he seemed like a cynic with principle, which Black approved of. An observer. Black felt his skeptical eyes on him even when he was talking to the other soldier.

He was smallish but solidly constructed, not short enough to be called short, but just short enough to be called not tall. His hair pushed the limits of Army regulations and looked as though it would flourish into dark curls had it been allowed to grow any longer. He wore a permanent *Yeah, what about it?* scowl, and a thick mustache straight from the '70s.

Black reminded himself to ask about his funny name if the kid ever opened up a little. He guessed Bosch had kicked more than one bigger kid's ass over it.

"Where you from, sir?" the first soldier asked him.

"In the Army, or the world?"

The soldier shrugged.

"Either one, I guess."

"Long story."

"Army or world, sir?"

"Both."

The Army was full of people who took a lot of long roads to wherever they were standing at that moment. Some of them didn't like talking about those roads. The soldier was unoffended and unfazed.

"Cool."

They smoked and watched the Valley fill up with fog.

"How often do you guys get hit?" Black asked.

They told him. It ran the gamut. In the outpost and out on patrol, large ambushes, small ambushes, solo snipers, heavy weapons and light, anyplace and anytime.

Except in the past two weeks. Things had been quiet, except when they left the COP on foot for patrols. No real attacks on Vega to speak of. Hardly any sniper activity even.

"Which just means they're gonna hit us again," the first soldier said. "Hard."

He drummed his hands on his legs.

"Always do. They're just watching our asses out there. Just figuring shit out."

Drum, drum.

"Who's watching you?" Black asked.

"Shit, you tell me, sir," the soldier spat. "Half the time we don't even know who the hell it is attacking us. Supposedly the Valley tribes hate the Taliban and stuff, but then we know for a *fact* that it ain't always Taliban dudes that are coming at us. We'll get in a firefight and find dead bodies of fuckers we just saw in the village the day before, so we *know* Valley guys are mixed in there too."

He shook his head.

"Smile at our asses in town and then try to kill us on the mountain."

"Why?"

"Fuck if I know, sir. These Valley assholes got so much shit going on with all their alliances and breaking alliances and drugs and feuds and changing sides every day, who the hell knows how the Taliban fits in with it all? The shit's so complicated you may as well ask why you got kicked off yearbook staff."

I miss joes, thought Black.

"Fuckin' Taliban," the soldier muttered. "Fuckin' Valley dudes."

He turned to Black.

"Gimme one of those— I mean, sir. If it's all right."

He pointed at the pack of cigarettes, which Black had left sitting on the window ledge. Black made a *Be my guest* motion. The soldier grabbed one, peeked over his shoulder toward the stairwell, and lit up.

"This place," he announced sagely, "is fucked."

That pretty well summarized in four words all the intelligence that had ever come across Black's desk concerning the Valley. He said as much. The kid laughed.

"Yeah, well, welcome to it in three-D, sir!"

He swept his hand across the panorama before them.

"Hope you get a good show before you gotta go."

"Pass," said Black dryly.

The soldier chuckled.

"When's your next patrol down to the town?" Black asked.

"Day after tomorrow, I think."

The three of them lapsed into silence and stared at the gray ocean rising toward them. Its blanket seemed to silence everything in the Valley. Through the open windows Black heard not a single noise of night.

He thought back to his days as a trainee at Officer Candidate School—OCS—back at Fort Benning, deep in the mountainous woods of western Georgia. The instructors would send the candidates, as they were called, out into the wilds to test their land-navigation skills.

You'd get a topographic map and a compass and a sheet of paper with a set of grid coordinates. The grid coordinates were your "points." Each point on the map represented an actual little signpost planted in the woods somewhere.

A point might be on top of a mountain or in the bottom of a ravine. Wherever. Each trainee got his own sheet of paper with his own set of points. Each point had a hole punch with a unique imprint hanging from it. You traveled alone, and you had a certain amount of time to find a certain number of points and punch your paper at each of them.

It was a pain. The training course was a few miles on a side. It had some of just about every kind of woodland topography you could think of inside it. Swamps, mountains, rivers, forest so dense you could barely squeeze between trees, sticky vines that cut your face, tempting logging trails that looked like dirt but turned out to be made of Benning's famous orange clay and became ultraslick mud-butter in the rain. Trainees regularly came out of the course soaked to the skin, bruised, faces lacerated.

But "Land Nav" training got you out of the school's main complex where the instructors screamed at you all day and woke you up all night, and into the woods where you finally had some peace and quiet. If you were fast enough finding your points, you could even lie down and take a nap, and not a soul on Fort Benning would know where you were. Everyone loved Land Nav. At least the daytime sessions.

The night sessions were different. You had animal sounds and invisible gullies to fall into and your own overactive imagination to deal with. There were trainees who took their sheet of points and just walked fifty meters out into the woods and sat down against a tree for three hours, thinking about the vastness of the black course before them. At the end of the session they came back to camp and said, *Sorry, I couldn't find any of my points tonight.*

Most hated the nighttime runs. Black loved them. He loved the challenge of finding a way through the dark. Loved the mental discipline involved. Being alone in the woods at night scared the hell out of him.

Some trainees were shooting the breeze after a session one night, warming up around a burn barrel. One of the guys told the others how he had been at the bottom of a shallow valley looking for one of his points. He'd been blundering around in circles where the infernal signpost was supposed to be, not finding it, losing momentum, starting to feel the woods close in.

He looked up and in the dim light he saw a fog bank at the top of the rise. A real fog bank, like in a movie, coming slowly down the slope toward him. It was like a living thing.

He turned around and ran. Literally ran away from it. He saw it coming and his response was so instant and visceral he forgot all about finding his point and just bailed out, tripping over logs and branches, to get away from the thing. When he told the story he didn't even bother trying to pretend that he hadn't nearly peed himself.

He took some ribbing over that. But now, staring out at the ghostly layer before them, Black knew exactly what the guy had been talking about. He realized he'd have run too.

The closer the fog layer got, the quieter the Valley sounds seemed to get. Even the animals seemed to retreat from it. Black crossed his arms against the cooling air. No wonder the people who lived in the Valley were scared of it.

"You're right about the fog," Black said finally. "It's creepy as hell."

"Yeah, right, sir?" said the soldier. "Sick of looking at this shit."

He blew out a long jet of smoke.

"What time is it?" Black asked.

"Oh-dark-thirty," the first soldier muttered without looking at his watch.

Oh-dark-thirty. From the way military times were stated. Oh-four-hundred. Oh-six-hundred. Oh-dark-thirty was a time of night that was obnoxious even by Army standards.

Oh-dark-thirty was what it had been the very first morning at OCS. They'd all been up until the wee hours the night before, slogging through inprocessing stations, scribbling out paperwork hunched over in one-piece desks ripped off from an elementary school, standing in sleepy lines to get needles in the arm. Finally to their bunks for what seemed like fifteen minutes. Then metal trash cans clamoring down the hallways in the dark. Their instructors, saying good morning in the middle of the night.

Off into the January woods. A "terrain run," the instructors called it. Streams to slosh through. An obstacle course tucked away in a lonely glade, sodium lamp atop a pole casting orange shadows on their struggling forms. Sprints up and down a paved hill overlooking a sprawling airfield. Hand-to-hand fighting in icy puddles. Then back into the black trees.

Hours later, they emerged exhausted onto a dewy field in the morning half-light. A mile-long running track awaited them. The instructors' final joke on their charges. Everyone twice around for time, fast as you can go. Miss the standard and you're out, "recycled," to wait around for weeks and hope to make it into the next class.

He ran. The first half mile, his shins burned and pains shot from his back down through his legs. The next half mile he decided to quit. In the last mile his body limbered and he ran like the wind.

He stumbled through the scrum of trainees huffing beyond the finish line and found his friend. The wiseass who would one day send him novelty lamps and witty e-mails. He stomped up to Black and they threw a spontaneous arm around each other's shoulders: *We're actually here*. It was one of only two times Black could remember when his friend had dropped his wry, cultivated façade and allowed himself to be seen.

"Well, anyway," Black said, stubbing out his cigarette. "Probably get going."

"Take it easy, L.T."

"Yup."

He was turning to go when Bosch spoke up.

"Hey, L.T.," he said. "So why the fuck are you really here?"

Black told them about the 15-6.

"Wow, sir, you weren't lying," said the first soldier. "That is *some* bullshit."

"Like I said."

The soldier appeared to be thinking about something.

"Well, then I guess it's lucky me and Bosch weren't in Darreh Sin that day, right, sir?"

"Why's that?"

"Well, 'cause if you're the fifteen-six officer, then we're not supposed to be shooting the shit like this, right?"

Black stuck his hands in his pockets and shrugged.

"Damn, sir," the kid said. "You really don't give a fuck, do you?"

He made for the stairwell, moving briskly across the pallets. He was almost there when he caught the movement.

Just a shadow moving against a shadow. He stopped and squinted.

A man squatted in a parapeted corner of the roof, back to Black, working intently at something. Black fell to a crouch, fingering his pistol, before he was able to make out that the man was wearing American camouflage fatigues.

"Who's that?" he called in a stage whisper, feeling mildly foolish.

The man whirled around, startled, and had to put a hand out to keep himself from toppling over.

"Danny! Danny!" he whisper-called back, holding his palms high in the dark. "Chill, man!"

His voice was heavily accented. Black trotted in a crouch over to where he was, squatting next to him just below the top of the roof-wall.

The man shrank back, eyeing him uncertainly. He was slender and olive-skinned, deep ochre eyes set in a narrow and inquisitive face topped by scrubby black hair. Black guessed him at about thirty. His slight frame struggled to fill the fatigues, which were blank except for a tape over his left breast that said U.S. ARMY, and another over his right that said DANNY.

"You're the 'terp," Black stated.

Any platoon having regular contact with Afghan people would have an interpreter—a 'terp—embedded in it. Most were Afghan guys who risked a great deal for the good pay that came with working as a contractor for the Americans.

Most used a false name, usually a Western one. It wasn't so much courtesy as self-protection. Didn't want Americans accidentally spitting out a real name in front of some dude who might come back later and slit the 'terp's throat and his family's too if he found out who the guy was and where he was from.

The guy nodded and stuck out his hand.

"Danny," he said, stating the obvious.

Black shook it, seeing Danny examining his own rank and name tapes.

"I'm Black," he offered.

Danny furrowed his brow. He clearly knew enough about the Army to know that there wasn't room in one platoon for two lieutenants.

"You are the new L.T.?" he asked.

Black shook his head.

"I'm just here a week."

"Okay, man," Danny said, nodding again. "Cool."

'Terps were generally pretty traditional guys. Danny didn't pry further than what was offered.

Black looked past him. A metal radio antenna rod had been fixed in place in the corner, extending up into the air above the edge of the wall.

At its top was a wire lattice antenna that looked like the kind of thing you'd see on the roofs of houses in old pictures from the sixties and seventies. A cable ran from its base down through a crack in the roof's stonework. To Danny's room, Black presumed.

"What're you trying to pick up?" he asked.

Danny turned and scowled at the antenna.

"Radio," he grumbled. "Nothing, man."

"Can't you just get some music from the guys here?"

Danny shook his head.

"I try to get my music," he said. "Afghanistan music."

He jerked a thumb over his shoulder.

"I buy this from guy in Valley who says we got little radio up here. I put it here, I move it over there, I . . ."

He searched for the word while wringing the neck of an invisible antenna stand.

". . . adjust it every day."

"You get anything?"

Danny threw his hands up.

"Nothing!" he nearly shouted, then caught himself and ducked down, glancing up at the hillsides and smiling sheepishly.

"I didn't mean to scare you before," Black offered apologetically.

"Heh," Danny chuckled, waving him off. "I thought you shoot me."

There was a mirth to his voice when he spoke. A mischief.

"Sorry," Black said.

"Don't worry, man."

"Well," Black said. "I guess I'll see you."

"Okay, L.T.," Danny replied. "You need anything, I help."

Black nodded.

"Thanks."

He trotted back across the roof and into the stairwell, leaving Danny to wrestle with his antenna.

Down the hillside, rocks skittering away underfoot. Into the fog. Sandals finding the trail. A young boy's form, invisible in the white night, gliding fluidly amidst the hazy shapes of trees and bushes. Left here, around that one, duck low there. Greeting them like old friends.

Cowardly Qadir and his rifle probably ran away an hour ago. Probably took the high trail, up and over the long way, just to avoid the silly mist. He may as well take his clothes off and run around on top of the mountain so the Americans' silent plane can blow him up.

Palms on sandstone, up and over a familiar boulder. Bounding into the gray, feet finding purchase, moving efficiently downhill.

Qadir and his devils and demons. He is as foolish as the farthest and highest of the mountain people, clinging to their superstitions and blasphemies from a thousand years ago. He should just go live with them and stop bothering me.

The noise of the river coming into hearing.

How can I fear fogs and nonsense, Father, when I walk by your side with every step? When I share your true faith?

The sound of water rippling over stones.

When I know the true devil?

Fifteen minutes walking blind on the river trail, then up the slope a ways and over the draw, down into the gentle depression in the land.

Qadir and his stupid boasting. Slitting throats and widows wailing and all his silliness. He knows nothing of strength. He knows nothing of me. He would be too stupid to understand if he did. I will show him strength.

Sandals wet on the mountain grass. Dirt and pebbles at the threshold. Through the curtain, past Mother's room, blanket in hand and back out the door. Hands on the cold stone, up and over the edge onto the roof.

I sleep closest to you, Father. No false devil troubles my sleep.

Tajumal lay back on the thatched roof under the threadbare blanket, basking in the enveloping mist, and dreamed warm dreams of cruel vengeance.

10

Aw, *FUCK,* Caine!"

The man who had just been introduced as Sergeant First Class Merrick threw his little green government-issue hardcover notebook down on the table. It landed square on the surface with a nice clean smack. Soldiers' curious heads rose and swiveled across the tiny plywood-walled chow hall.

Merrick was tall and lean, a straight line with angular mantis limbs. His face matched the rest of him, long and taut, fur-brown hair shorn close in a stark-cornered frame around it, hard brows angled over a pair of examining, intelligent, nearly black eyes. He exuded scowling competence.

He'd been standing among a gaggle of soldiers and junior sergeants, dishing out instructions for the day. He was not pleased to meet Black.

"Why didn't you tell me about this bullshit?" he was demanding of Caine.

"What do you mean, tell you?" Caine shot back defensively. "I didn't know! Nobody knew except Lieutenant Pistone, and he didn't tell me shit."

"Well, then where the fuck is *he?* He should be nearly awake by now."

He didn't mean it in a flattering way.

"At Omaha. Remember? Left on last night's run."

Merrick threw up his hands.

"Well, no problem!" he said sarcastically. "Now we've got a whole new lieutenant already!"

He stubbed a thumb at Black, without looking at him, and continued raving.

"Who the fuck sent him up here?"

"Your battalion commander," interjected Black, who was wearying of being talked about in the third person.

Merrick ignored him.

"I'm not doing this," he said to Caine, pointing a finger at his chest. "I'm not wasting one hour of one fucking soldier's day on it."

"Sergeant," Caine said placatingly, using Merrick's rank as a nod to the pecking order. "He got *assigned* the fifteen-six. He doesn't have any more choice in it than we do."

"Well, hooray for him," Merrick shot back, speaking quickly and precisely. "I don't have time for a bullshit investigation of my soldiers *in the fucking field* while they have jobs to do. He can talk to them all he wants when they get back to the FOB, if we ever get back to the fucking FOB."

"Look," said Caine, lowering his voice. "The L.T. and I talked last night. He just wants to knock it out and do what he has to do and get it done."

He turned to Black.

"Right, sir?"

"I don't give a fuck how he *feels* about it," Merrick snapped, and finally turned his sharp gaze to Black.

"Look, sir," he said. "I appreciate that you don't *want* to take up my joes' time with a stupid investigation, and I appreciate that you didn't *assign yourself* the fifteen-six. But I don't care. I'm sure you've noticed since your arrival that we are busy up here staying alive."

Let him huff and puff, Black figured.

He knew a lot of it was for the benefit of Merrick's soldiers, several of whom were now watching intently from their tables. Merrick was a senior sergeant who'd been in the Army a minimum of twelve to fifteen years. He had to know he was obligated to assist an investigating officer. Or else he knew it but didn't care because he was confident that he was untouchable up here in the Valley, that he could do whatever he wanted and deal with it another day.

Either way, Black figured he may as well find out now. If it was the latter then he could go sit in Lieutenant Pistone's hootch for the rest of the week and go home and tell Gayley he'd been obstructed. Then some major would get assigned the 15-6 and it wouldn't be his problem anymore.

Merrick continued venting, stepping in closer to Black.

"Do you know when my last K.I.A. was, sir?"

"No, I don't."

"Five fucking days ago. You know when was the last one before that? Three days earlier. And I will probably have either more casualties or another goddamn K.I.A. to deal with by tomorrow. So I'm sorry, *sir,* but I don't have time for bullshit."

Black knew from enough experiences with enough aggressive sergeants that the *You don't speak to me that way!* approach would be a loser in this situation. He also knew that to back down completely would be death.

"Neither do I," he said evenly.

Merrick's eyes hardened and he spoke slowly.

"What does *that* mean, sir?"

The two men stared at one another. The joes stared at both of them.

Let him backtrack.

"It means," Black answered calmly, "that I've got better things to do than schlep up here and waste my time and waste your time. But that's what I got told to do, and *I'm sure you've noticed* I'm in the Army, so here I am."

Black raised his palms in a *So what are we gonna do here?* gesture.

Merrick scowled at him for about a solid ten seconds. Finally he turned to Caine, who was looking at the two of them doubtfully.

"Wow," he said in an utterly unimpressed voice. "A lieutenant with balls."

He leaned slightly to one side and spoke past Caine toward the gaggled soldiers at their tables.

"Get out."

The soldiers leaped to their feet and beat it.

Merrick turned back to Black and stared at him some more for good measure while the joes were filing out. At last the room was empty.

"Hey, sir," he said. "So was Sergeant Caine right when he said you are planning to knock this thing out with a minimum of bullshit and get out of my hair?"

"Only what I have to do," Black answered blandly.

"Well, hooray," Merrick said dryly, turning to Caine. "He's only gonna do what he has to do."

He had capitulated. He didn't like it, but Black could see that he knew his responsibilities. He had just been trying to feel out whether he could scare Black off. Standard for senior sergeants who disliked officers snooping around their business.

Merrick turned back to Black and swept his arm through the air, indicating the entire outpost.

"Then please, sir," he said sarcastically. "Be my guest. My house is your house."

"I won't steal anything," said Black, sarcasm-ing him right back.

Merrick just stared at him blankly.

"So what first, sir?" he said in an *Okay, fine, YOU tell ME, then* tone of voice.

"I want to go to Darreh Sin," Black said flatly.

Merrick's features froze. He eyed Black as though Black had made him a bargain and then cheated him out of all his money. His gaze darkened.

"Darreh Sin," he said, looking at Black through hard eyes.

Black just shrugged.

"Talk to the chief," he said as though it were the most obvious thing in the world.

"What's the chief got to do with anything?" asked Caine.

"Can't talk to the dude with the bullet hole in his house until I talk to the chief, right?"

Merrick's eyes visibly narrowed. Despite his volatile manner, he seemed like the more well-schooled and people-savvy of the two sergeants. He looked at Black as though he were trying to figure out just who he was dealing with.

"Sir," he said, his own voice low and controlled. "We just finished having a conversation about how you're going to conduct your trivial chickenshit business in the least disruptive manner possible. What makes you think I am going to gear up a special patrol and put my guys on the line just to walk you down to the town to talk to someone who's not even an American about something that didn't even happen to him?"

Black waited for Caine to chime in. Caine said nothing and looked at the floor.

"You don't have to send a special patrol," Black said breezily. "You guys go down there every week, right?"

Merrick looked at him closely.

"Who," he said slowly, "gave you information about troop movements?"

Troop movements. Merrick had used the big-boy term favored by senior officers who gave Operations Security briefings. "Disclosing troop movements," even inadvertently, was your classic Army security violation. The kind of thing that got soldiers court-martialed and journalists tossed out of country.

Black ignored the question and tried to look confused.

"It's not a secret around your outpost," he said.

Caine kept staring at the floor.

"What's the problem?" Black asked innocently. "You guys are scheduled to go down there tomorrow, right?"

He saw Caine's head jerk toward him in surprise. His mouth opened, then closed.

Merrick very slowly turned his clenched and reddening face toward Caine. Caine looked like he had wanted to blurt out *I didn't tell him about tomorrow!* but thought better of it.

Merrick, unhappy but stuck, stepped in very close to Black.

"Lieutenant," he said quietly. "Don't make me regret not telling you to go fuck yourself and your investigation."

"It's not my investigation," Black said tiredly. "It's the Army's investigation."

"Oh," said Merrick, looking into his eyes. "Then go fuck yourself, Army."

"I'll pass on the message."

Caine took that as his cue.

"Hey, sir, why don't we get moving?"

"Good idea," Black said breezily, looking at both him and Merrick. "I want to talk to your guys today anyway, before we go out to the town tomorrow."

Before a rapidly reddening Merrick could say anything in response or otherwise burst a blood vessel, Caine cut in and put a hand on Black's shoulder.

"All right, then, sir," he said, gently steering him toward the door. "C'mon, we'll sort that out."

Black stepped in front of him and led the way out into the hallway, where curious soldiers lingered, waiting for the chow hall to open up again. The plywood door smacked shut behind Caine. The joes pretended not to look at him and Black as they passed.

"Wow, L.T.," Caine said sarcastically. "You make friends good."

Black ignored it.

"Brydon, Shannon, and Corelli," he said.

"What?"

"Those are the three I want to talk to today."

They kept walking. Caine appeared to be thinking over the names.

Is he smart enough to get it?

"Corelli because he's the shooter," Caine began slowly, as though talking to himself. "Brydon because he's the medic, and Shannon because he was the dude closest to the shooter."

"Yup."

Caine seemed to recognize that this was a bare-minimum request that would cover all the required bases and get the maximum paperwork value out of interviewing the minimum number of soldiers.

"All right, L.T.," he said finally. "Cool."

He thought for a moment.

"All three of those guys are on guard shift until sixteen hundred. You can talk to them at their rooms after that."

Black took note of the fact that Caine knew the three soldiers' schedules from memory and didn't have to pull out a little green notebook or crumply piece of paper with the daily shifts on it. He was on top of what his guys were up to.

"Sounds good," he said.

"Corelli you know from last night," Caine said as they walked. "Seems like a pussy, but he's all right."

"Okay."

"Shannon you won't like, and he won't like you."

"All right."

"Brydon," Caine went on. "That's the Wizard."

Black cocked his head.

"Weird kid," Caine said. "Grumpy, like you. Doesn't talk. But he'll put his ass on the line for any man here. No fear."

Black nodded.

"You ever put your ass on the line for someone, L.T.?"

Black ignored the question.

"The Wizard?" he asked instead.

"You'll see."

Black waited for Caine to ask him who it was that told him the patrol was scheduled for the next day, but Caine said nothing. Maybe he figured he and Black were even, after Black had covered for him back in the chow hall.

They had arrived at his room. Black opened the door.

"I'll be back here at sixteen hundred to get you," Caine said.

Black turned back, standing in the threshold.

"Remember what I told you about being here to do a job and go home, Sergeant?"

"What? Yeah, I . . ."

"Then why don't you spare me the extra bullshit?"

Caine was startled.

"What? What bullsh—"

"You should just thank me," Black interrupted, "for covering for you in front of Big Daddy."

Caine reddened.

"'Big Daddy'?"

Why are you antagonizing this guy?

"And don't think I didn't notice that you set me up to look like a jerk in front of all the joes back there."

"What? Sir, no one set you—"

Black closed the door in his face.

11

He sat down on the bunk, irritated.

Merrick, obviously, was the man around Vega. He was the ranking guy, and despite Caine's talk about he and Merrick "splitting" the duty, Merrick was clearly the dude. Caine worked for him, period. He wondered what Merrick would have thought of the other sergeant's bluster about "my" soldiers.

Black thought he knew Merrick's type. He could recognize a sergeant who was just not going to make his peace with having an officer in his hair, ever. The officer could be the most squared-away guy on the planet, but the sergeant was never going to see it, because at the end of the day that young officer had the authority to tell the old sergeant what to do, and that was just too much.

Merrick was going to be a pain, start to finish, no matter how painless Black tried to make it for everyone.

Great.

Sergeants and their pride. For Caine's part, Black figured he had definitely set up the chow hall encounter that way on purpose, to undermine Black in front of soldiers he might have to question.

Caine knew Merrick, and he knew that Merrick would blow his top when he found out about Black and the 15-6. There was no reason for him to wait until the next morning, in the chow hall, in the presence of both Black and a bunch of joes, for him to drop the bomb on Merrick. In fact it was improper for him to wait so long to tell the senior guy that there was a visiting officer in his post.

Either he was dumb, or he thought Black was dumb, or both.

He set his rifle in the corner and stretched out on the bunk, trying to shake the same uncomfortable feeling of being in someone else's living space. His jaw still hurt from where Caine punched it the night before. He pulled his book out and started reading, pausing periodically to stare at the ceiling.

After a while he realized he hadn't gotten chow when he went to meet Merrick. He was hungry. He rose and gathered up his rifle, slinging it over his back, and headed for the door, happy to get out of Lieutenant Pistone's strange hootch.

He stopped at the funny restroom closet and took note of the vast field of Chuck Norris–themed graffiti scrawled all over the walls inside. In keeping with venerable tradition, most of it drew upon the martial artist's grave reputation (WHEN THE BOOGYMAN GOES TO SLEEP, HE CHECKS UNDER THE BED FOR CHUCK NORRIS), improbable powers (CHUCK NORRIS IS SO FAST HE CAN RUN AROUND THE WORLD AND PUNCH HIMSELF IN THE BACK OF THE HEAD), and fearsome prowess in all things.

Directly in the center, in large print, was what appeared to be the original item.

CHUCK NORRIS SHAT HERE
AND SHIT WAS NEVER THE SAME

He browsed some of the other entries, appreciating soldiers' endless, often vulgar creativity. He was still smiling over a clever one (CHUCK NORRIS CAN LEAVE A MESSAGE BEFORE THE BEEP) as he pushed open the door and nearly ran into two young soldiers walking down the narrow corridor. They had seen him grinning.

"Something funny, there, sir?" asked one.

Black didn't miss a beat.

"Just Chuck."

"Oh, you a fan of Chuck, sir?"

He had the air of the smartass about him.

"Who isn't?"

The kid smirked at his buddy.

"Just thought maybe you officers were too fancy for Chuck, sir."

Black put his hands in his pockets and turned to go.

"'Chuck Norris is so badass,'" he said, making one up on the fly, "'he can even kick the fancy out of an officer.'"

It took the two soldiers a silent, goggle-eyed moment to process just how lame Black's attempt at humor was. But only a moment.

They both erupted in astonished laughter.

"Damn, you all right, L.T.!" called one as Black headed off down the hallway.

"Hooah, sir!" called the other with mock enthusiasm.

Their voices faded behind him, one of them musing aloud about a white officer named Black.

"Take it where you can get it, bro!" he heard the other one laugh.

He made his winding way back to the chow hall, which he'd expected to be empty at this time of day. It wasn't.

Several soldiers around a table looked up as he entered, their conversation immediately lapsing into silence. They stared at him blankly, dark circles under their eyes as they watched him cross to the food station. As had all young soldiers once he'd passed the age of twenty-five, these ones looked like they were fourteen years old.

He said nothing and went about his business. Gradually conversation picked up again, in quieter tones.

He had expected these guys to be living on M.R.E.s pretty much year-round. There were cartons of them stacked in the corner, but at least for a couple days after a supply run it looked like they could scrape together something approaching food. The outpost must have had a minor ability to keep things refrigerated. A generator-powered chest freezer or something somewhere. Not too bad.

The grub wasn't anything to write home about. Cooler cases filled with cold cuts and bags of spongy white bread, with an open box of mustard and mayo packets off to the side.

But it wasn't M.R.E.s. The joes at the table chomped their limp sandwiches greedily.

Black grabbed a paper plate from a stack and started fixing himself a baloney with mustard on Wonder. He heard the door slap shut.

Someone came up next to him and grabbed a plate. He felt himself being examined sidelong.

"Afternoon, L.T."

He looked up long enough to see a soldier he didn't recognize. The kid looked as skinny and haggard as the rest of them.

"Hey."

He looked down and recommenced squeezing half-filled mustard packets onto meat folds. The soldier did the same.

He felt himself being examined again. He raised his head suddenly and looked the kid in the eye.

"What?" he asked sharply.

"Uh, sorry, sir," the soldier said, flustered. "Um, nothing, sir. I was just, um—"

Black gave him an *Out with it, then!* look.

"Sir, sorry if this isn't my business, but . . . weren't you the, uh, the guy that—"

"No."

Black went back to his cold cuts. The soldier realized their brief conversation was done.

"Oh, okay. Uh, sorry, sir."

"No problem."

Black took his plate and sought out the table closest to where the gaggle of joes was chatting. He sat down with his back to them. Their mumbled talk got even quieter.

You're a pain in the ass.

He finished his food quickly and went back to Pistone's spartan quarters. He lay on the bunk and read his book. He made a quiet decision while he did so.

Four o'clock came and went. Caine didn't show.

He didn't mind. He didn't want to bombard guys the minute they came off shift anyway.

At about four forty-five, he finally heard Caine's knock on the door. He rose and grabbed a little green hardcover notebook from the side table, just like the one Merrick had had in the chow hall. Five by eight inches, standard government issue, fits in the cargo pocket of a uniform. Mandatory equipment for officers and senior sergeants. He shoved the thing in his trousers, crossed to the door, and opened it.

Merrick.

Black let his surprise show on his face. Merrick saw.

"Expecting someone, Lieutenant?"

Merrick looked down at him with what Black could only describe as unconcealed contempt.

Annoyed at himself, Black ignored the comment and stepped into the hallway. Merrick set off immediately, forcing Black to step quickly to catch up.

"No, I'm not leaving my second to take you to talk to my soldiers," he said, answering a question Black hadn't asked.

He left a perceptible emphasis on "*my*."

"If you're going to waste their time with bullshit, they hear it from me."

Black again said nothing. They went down a different set of passageways and breezeways and bits of sky than Black had seen the night before. He was increasingly impressed with how much there was to the place.

They turned a corner and made their way down a corridor made of temporary blast walls on one side and an exterior wall of the building on the other, with metal sheeting for a roof. They arrived at a square stone opening fitted with a homemade wooden door. The door read:

BAY TWO

HELLRAISERS

Inside was your classic soldiers' deployment rabbit warren. You started with a large empty room in an occupied building. Some kind of big space, preferably with a high ceiling. You got a whole lot of wood sheets and two-by-fours and turned the soldiers and their sergeants loose on the place with saws, hammers, and nails. Within a couple days it was transformed into dozens of individual living spaces.

None of them had roofs because there'd be no ventilation otherwise. The electricity situation, a creeping-vine chaos of extension cords, power strips, and amateur splices, was an inevitable and ongoing flout to the niceties of the fire code.

But every joe had his own space and his own door. It might be the size of a closet, but it was his. On deployment, that was no small thing.

The bay was lit by a couple of large overhead fixtures set fifteen feet above them in the ceiling. Merrick started briskly down the first narrow passage.

He stopped in front of a door. Many of them were written or painted or stenciled on, but this one was blank. He stopped just past it and turned to face Black.

"Brydon," he said, motioning curtly to the door with his head.

Black stepped up and knocked.

"Yeah," came a gravelly voice from within.

Black pushed the door open and stepped through. Merrick stepped in after him. Black turned around immediately and stepped back out again.

This time he waited, forcing Merrick to step out after him. As soon as he did, Black turned on his heel and took several steps up the passage, away from the open door. He turned and waited for Merrick to catch up.

"What are you doing?" Black asked.

"What do you mean?"

"I talk to the guys alone."

"What the fuck are you talking about?"

"I'm the investigator, and you're their superior," Black said matter-of-factly. "You don't go into the interview."

Merrick shook his head.

"That's not how you do it," he said, angering. "What is this bullshit?"

"Like hell it's not," Black answered coolly. "You ever been around a fifteen-six before?"

Merrick did not like that one bit. He stepped in close and spoke tersely.

"Yeah, *Lieutenant,* I've seen a fucking fifteen-six before. Have *you?* That's not how you fucking do it. I stay with my guys."

In for a penny . . .

"Yeah, well, if you saw a fifteen-six like that," Black shot back, "then you saw someone doing it wrong. You ever read the regulation, *Sergeant?*"

From the look on his face he was pretty sure Merrick would like to hit him. He pressed.

"I go in alone. That's how you do it. You want to stop me, stop me. I'll sit in Lieutenant Pistone's hootch and read my book all week and go home and say I got obstructed, and then you can deal with a field-grade officer up here in your business."

Merrick seethed downward at him.

"Or you can let me do *my* business," Black finished, "and go home and you can forget all about me and this fifteen-six."

He waited. Behind his anger, Merrick appeared to be thinking things through. Given his experience and obvious intelligence, it occurred to Black that he might actually have read the regulation.

The sergeant turned on his heel and stomped down the hall to Brydon's blank door.

"Hey, fuckhead!"

"Yeah," came the same voice in the same even tone.

"The *lieutenant* here has some questions for you," Merrick said in clipped tones into the doorway. "He has come all the way from Colonel Gayley's bullshit unit to conduct a fifteen-six investigation."

"Roger," drawled the voice, sounding bored.

"You will answer his questions accurately. You will *not* fucking speculate on any information that you do not have specific personal knowledge of. If the lieutenant takes more than thirty minutes of your time"—he turned to look at Black—"you will report it to me afterwards."

"Roger."

"And try not to cast any fucking spells on him. He's only a lieutenant."

"Roger."

Merrick turned to Black.

“That is Shannon’s door over there,” he said irritably, pointing down the hallway. “Corelli’s is the last one around the corner.”

He stalked away down the hallway in the direction he’d pointed.

Black watched Merrick knock heavily on the door he’d identified as Shannon’s.

Can’t believe he bought that, he was thinking as he stepped into the Wizard’s room.

12

A picture was coming into focus.

The kid's room was tiny. Maybe eight feet by five feet. The centerpiece of the place, on the wall directly opposite him, was a large and rumpled tapestry of black nylon. An upright five-pointed star sprawled across it in white silk screen, points extending just beyond the arc of a circle, making it look almost but not quite like a pentagram. In front of the star, his back to the viewer, was a man, naked, feet planted defensively, palms raised before him protectively, reeling back against whatever looming power lurked within the giant star.

On another wall was tacked a page torn from a magazine, a fantastical painting of a city perched atop an improbable mountain which tapered inward at its lower latitudes until the whole thing rested on a thin spear of rock. The rest of the wallspace was occupied by hand drawings on pieces of white paper, crowding one another in themed bunches like billslips on a RENT NOW bulletin board. One corner featured beefy creatures thumping huge mallets and lithe elvish archers astride perfect steeds. In another were many pictures of unicorns, in many possible universes. He wasn't a bad artist.

Reclining on the bunk in a tan Army T-shirt beneath the tapestry, eyeing Black over the top of a book with a journeying gaggle of swordsmen and sorcerers on its cover, was Brydon himself. The Wizard.

He was a dumpy sort of kid. Acne scars marked his wide face, and he looked like, but for the physical fitness ensured by his tromping up and down high-altitude mountains all the time, he would be pretty pudgy. He didn't exactly seem sociable.

His eyes were hooded, his hair a scrubby in-between of brown and blond. It was startlingly long even for a deployed soldier deep in the mountains and far from the FOB. There was no skin visible on the sides, and Black figured he probably had two and a half inches on top. A bona fide "shock."

Brydon must've been some kinda good soldier, or some kinda weird, to be allowed to get away with that. Black wondered how many real friends he had in the platoon.

There was a little three-legged half stool in the corner.

"Can I sit?" Black asked.

"Sure."

Brydon was in a half-sitting position against his pillow and didn't move.

Black sat, pulling his little green Army notebook out of his pocket and setting it, closed, on a side table. He leaned back against the plywood wall, noticing for the first time a tattoo on Brydon's right upper arm. A shield with two Latin words inscribed across its front: VAE VICTIS.

He didn't recognize the unit logo. His eyes moved back up to Brydon's face.

"I'm Black," he said, even though the kid could obviously read his name tape. "You know what a fifteen-six is?"

"Not except what Sergeant Merrick said."

Brydon spoke in an uninterested drawl that Black couldn't place. Midwestern Nonspecific.

"Right," Black went on. "So, like he said, it's an investigation that I got assigned to do. It's the lowest-level investigation in the Army."

He put his hands up in a calming sort of gesture.

"I'm not an M.P. or anything, and you're not in trouble."

"Then why am I being investigated?"

This was the part Black hated about doing a 15-6. There was no way to really explain, to the satisfaction of the cynical and reasonably distrustful mind of a soldier, that he was being "investigated" but didn't really have to worry. Soldiers always worried, with good cause. In their immortal motto, learned over and over the hard way: Shit Rolls Downhill.

"It's not you specifically," he explained. "I need to talk to a bunch of guys. I gotta talk to some of the other guys in the platoon, and I have to talk to Sergeant Merrick, and Sergeant Caine . . ."

"So the platoon's being investigated."

"Kind of. Not really. It's not—"

He wanted to say, *It's not an INVESTIGATION-investigation,* but he knew how stupid that sounded.

"It's not the kind of investigation where . . ."

He trailed off.

"Look," he said finally, flustered. "I've had to do these before. I just talk to soldiers and get some facts about something that happened, and write it down and it gets filed and then usually that's the last anybody ever hears from anybody about it. All right?"

He knew a look of total distrust on a soldier's face when he saw it.

"Facts about what that happened?"

Black grabbed his book.

"Why don't we just start at the basic stuff," he said, then caught himself. "Sorry. Do you have any questions before we get going?"

"Like what?"

"Nothing in particular. Just if you wanted to know anything about how it works."

Brydon shook his head. He sat up from his pillows a little bit.

"Sort of figured you'd be a captain or something," he said.

From his two previous 15-6 assignments, Black was used to the usual slights and minor insubordinations of combat soldiers who are both annoyed at being interrogated and scared of being told they'd done something wrong when they were just trying to do stuff right. He ignored it.

"Your full name is Billy Brydon."

"Yeah."

"Specialist."

"Yeah."

It was one rank below the lowest sergeant grade. Some soldiers floated there for years without ever getting their stripes. Some didn't want them.

"You're a medic."

"Yeah."

"How long have you been in Sergeant Merrick's platoon?"

"Who wants to know?"

So the kid was gonna be a pain regardless.

"It's just basic admin data. Just background."

Brydon looked at him skeptically.

"Three months."

"Before that?"

"Stateside. Different unit."

Black asked him all the usual. Where he went to basic training, when his service commitment was up. He could tell the kid's mind wasn't on the answers. He just wanted Black to get to it, so he could find out what he was gonna get rung up for.

Black closed the notebook and set it down on the side table. Whatever Brydon told him he would have to write down later anyway on a standard sworn statement form.

He flipped his chin at Brydon's tattoo.

"What's that?"

Brydon looked down at it involuntarily.

"'Vae Victis,'" he mumbled. "It means—"

"'Woe to the vanquished,'" Black cut in, finishing his sentence for him.

"How'd you know that?" Brydon demanded, startled.

Black shrugged.

"Doesn't matter," he replied. "Where'd you get the tattoo?"

"Doesn't matter," Brydon retorted, still eyeing Black like he thought he was about to get mugged.

Black let it go. Time to get back on track.

"Okay," he said. "So the main thing I need to ask about is something that happened on the twenty-third of last month. It was a Wednesday. . . ."

He could see the kid searching his memory banks but could tell it was useless. Dates and days of the week were pretty pointless in a place like Vega.

Brydon looked at him blankly, shaking his head.

"Don't worry about it. So, from the paperwork I got before I came up here, it sounds like your squad was on a patrol that day."

"Okay."

"And Corelli was there, and Shannon was there, and Sergeant Caine and Lieutenant Pistone."

"Okay."

Brydon was sitting up on his bunk now, arms around his knees, looking at Black intently. He spoke almost defiantly, as though egging Black on. *Go ahead and tell me what the Army says I did.* He was tense. Shit rolls downhill.

"I guess," Black said, "the people in the village were upset."

"All right."

"And it's hard to tell, but it sounds like they were upset because one of the old guys in town had his goat get killed the night before."

There was a long moment while Brydon recalled the day Black was talking about. His face hardened as the memory locked into focus, and he looked at Black incredulously.

"You're here about *that?!*"

"Well, no," Black said, flustered again. "I mean, not really. It's not really the goat. It's about . . ."

You used to be able to talk to joes.

"Look," he went on, recovering. "I know this whole thing seems really dumb. It *is* dumb. But the Army does fifteen-sixes for all kinds of things nowadays, even the smallest stuff. This is just the one I got assigned to do. Like I said, you're not in trouble or anything. It's just getting the basic facts and putting them on paper and then I go on my way."

He had seen enough looks of disgust directed at himself to recognize one now.

"So why don't we just knock it out," Black said. "All right?"

Brydon didn't say anything. He just glared at Black as though he had decided something fundamental and final about Black's worth as a human being.

"So do you know if that's right? If the guy's goat got killed?"

"Yeah," said Brydon, allowing his voice to drip with contempt for the entire exercise. "The guy's goat got killed."

"You were there the night before?"

"Yeah, I was there the night before."

"What happened?"

"Sounds like you already know, L.T.," he said, impatiently.

"Humor me."

"The guy's goat got killed."

Black gave him a *Come on* look.

The kid sighed noisily and shook his head. He spoke in one annoyed spurt.

"We were on a patrol outside the town and it was dark and foggy and somebody's goat was wandering off his property and Miller, who's an idiot, got spooked and thought it was the freaking bogeyman or something and shot it and the goat got killed. Okay?"

"Okay," Black said patiently. "What about the next day?"

Brydon looked at him and shrugged as though the question, or questioner, was dense.

"We took a patrol down to the town to find out whose goat it was."

"And there was a crowd of people there?"

"Yes," he said tersely.

"What were they doing?"

"Standing there being pissed off."

"Why?"

"Sergeant Merrick told me not to speculate on anything I don't have knowledge of, so I don't know."

"I won't write it down, and you don't have to write it down," Black said, trying to be patient. "Just off the record, I'm wondering if you could tell why they were upset."

"Probably because Miller killed the goat, right?" Brydon retorted, as though Black were slow. "Goat equals livelihood, right?"

"Did someone fire a warning shot to disperse the crowd?"

"Yes," Brydon sighed.

"Who?"

"Corelli."

"Did anyone get injured?"

"Not that I know of."

"So you didn't treat anyone for anything on scene?"

Brydon looked at him like he was the world's dumbest dummy.

"I think I just said that, sir."

"Why did Corelli fire the warning shot?"

"You'd have to ask Corelli."

The rest of the interview went like that. Brydon didn't become any less impatient or any less difficult. Black wrapped it up pretty quickly. He figured he could talk to the kid the next day for any more details and a sworn statement.

He closed with his usual lawyerly, open-ended question.

"Okay, that should do it pretty much. Is there anything else you want to add or tell me?"

"Like what?"

Black reminded himself to be patient.

"It's just a standard question to make sure I got everything."

Brydon looked him in the eye.

"It sounds like you are on top of everything, sir."

He leaned back on his pillows, signaling the close of any kind of cooperative interview.

Black thanked him and took his notebook and left the Wizard's room.

Weirdo.

Most soldiers are at least a little bit relieved when the subject matter of a dreaded 15-6 turns out to be some trivial thing that no one's going to get in trouble for. Some are mad at having their time wasted. Brydon mostly seemed annoyed by the pointlessness, the typical mediocre bureaucracy of the whole thing.

Black had to respect that a little.

He headed down the hallway to the door Merrick had told him belonged to Shannon. He knocked. After a very long silence a heavy voice said, "Enter."

He opened.

The room was standard-issue meathead. Heavy-metal posters and jugs of workout powder. An Xbox video game system sat on a shelf beneath a small and beat-up monitor. The place was roughly the same layout as Brydon's room, but on the wall where the strange tapestry had been hanging was instead a large picture of an overlit blonde with oiled balloon breasts reclining naked on the hood of a pickup truck for some reason.

Beneath her, sprawled two-legged in a chair in a straining T-shirt with his feet up on a side table playing the Xbox, was Shannon. His room was as tiny as the Wizard's. He just took up more of it.

He was something comfortably over six feet, broad, blond, iron-jawed, and sunburnt. As with Brydon, a tattoo stretched across the horizon of a bare bicep—a knife bursting through a flaming garland with the letters XLIV on its blade. He didn't look up from the game or pause his playing in the slightest.

"Corporal Shannon?"

Pause.

"Mm," came the low rumble.

"I'm Lieutenant Black."

Nothing.

"Did Sergeant Merrick tell you why I'm here?"

"Yup."

Thumbs working the buttons wildly. Hails of automatic gunfire over the monitor's speakers.

"Can I sit?"

There was a little half stool against the wall like the one in the Wizard's room.

"Whatever."

Something exploded on-screen.

"You want to look at me while I'm talking to you?"

"Not really."

Black sighed inwardly, then took one quick step forward across the tiny room and in a sweeping motion smacked the controller as hard as he could out of Shannon's hands. It ricocheted off the big kid's forehead, which Black hadn't meant to happen, and put a nice divot in the smooth belly of the reclining pickup truck girl on the wall.

Shannon leaped up, hands flailing reflexively about his bruised forehead. Black sat down on the stool.

"WHAT THE FUCK!?"

His yelling voice was a big one.

"Sorry," said Black, not sounding sorry at all.

"You fucking hit a soldier!" the kid shouted, thunderstruck.

Black crossed an ankle over a knee.

"What, you're gonna go tattle?" he said mockingly. "I hadn't figured you for such a wuss."

The kid gawked at him, dumbfounded and spluttering.

"Go ahead," Black said calmly. "Go tattle. Or you can just hit me back and we can both go tattle, and we'll see who gets it worse."

He would not have been surprised at that moment to be seized in Shannon's beefy hands and tossed against the wall. From the look on the big kid's beet-red face, Black could tell he was considering it. But some part of his brain that was not burning all cylinders on pure rage-ahol registered the fact that while the lieutenant would get a stern talking-to for accidentally knocking a game controller into his forehead, he himself would probably get a dishonorable discharge for striking an officer, or at a minimum a trip down to buck private with several months of docked pay and scrubbing toilets in the evenings once he got back to the States.

Instead, Shannon turned angrily and squeezed his frame beneath the side shelves, coming up with the game controller. Its housing had split open. Black wondered whether it was Shannon's head or the wall that did it.

"You fucking cracked it!"

"Sorry," Black said again, still not sounding sorry. "Can we start now?"

He found his notebook on the floor and picked it up.

"Why don't we start with the basics," he said.

The kid loomed over him, brandishing the broken controller.

"You're gonna wanna get the fuck out of here, *sir*."

"Current rank, corporal. Current job, infantry."

He glanced at a page of his notebook.

"Former job . . . forward observer?"

"Did you hear me?"

"Yeah, I heard you," Black answered, sounding bored. "Do you know what a fifteen-six investigation is?"

"Yeah, and I don't care. Go fuck your questions."

"Then you understand you're obligated to talk to me?"

Shannon, still standing, leaned in toward Black.

"I. Don't. Give. A. *FUCK* what I'm 'obligated' to do," he said very loudly, sending spittle onto Black's face.

He tossed the controller aside.

"I already told Sergeant Merrick I'm not talking to you, anyway."

"Why aren't you talking to me?"

A momentary look crossed the soldier's face. Confusion?

"I ain't talking to you 'cause I ain't talking to you."

Black sighed audibly.

"That's not actually an answer."

Shannon sat, dwarfing his bunk, and looked Black in the eye. Heavy brows roiled against one another.

"Okay," he said. "I ain't talking to you because you look like a pussy and I don't wanna answer pussy bullshit questions about me doing my job from a FOBbit that doesn't live in my world and wouldn't know which end of the goddamn rifle shoots the bullet."

He paused for effect.

"Sir."

An orator, then.

"How do you know they are bullshit questions when you don't even know what they're about?"

"Don't have to," Shannon said tersely. "You're bullshit, so they're bullshit."

"Look, Corporal," Black said tiredly, ignoring the fact that the soldier had already said about a half-dozen things that would get him severely punished if he were anyplace but deep in a godforsaken and deadly valley. "You realize you're not in trouble, right? You realize no one's out to get you, and I just have to ask my questions, then I can go away, right? But if you don't answer any questions, then you *are* going to be in trouble."

Shannon sat back against the wall and crossed his arms, angling himself away from Black.

"Hooray."

"So you're invoking your right to counsel?"

It was the only other angle he could think of.

"My what?"

"To a lawyer," Black answered. "If you're refusing to answer my questions, then you're saying that you're claiming your right not to incriminate yourself, and you want a lawyer to defend you. But like I keep saying, there's nothing to defend yourself against. Unless there *is* and you just don't want to tell me."

"What is this, a fucking cop show? I don't need a goddamn lawyer."

"Okay," said Black patiently. "So you don't want a lawyer, and you won't talk to me. So now you're just refusing to cooperate with a fifteen-six investigation, which is a chargeable offense. So now I have to go back to the FOB and tell my commander you wouldn't cooperate, and some major or a colonel is going to come up here and you'll have to deal with him."

"Bullshit," spat Shannon. "Nice try, sir. Ain't no major or colonel ever set foot in this joint since I've been here. I ain't even seen the captain in command of my own goddamn company."

"They won't have a choice," Black countered. "You refuse to answer a few simple questions and then this piddly little fifteen-six gets blown up into a big deal and they have to send it up to Brigade headquarters marked OBSTRUCTED, and then Brigade *has* to send someone *real* to investigate for *real,* instead of sending a flunky lieutenant like myself."

Shannon regarded him with squinted eyes, smiling a carnivorous smile.

"You trying to scare me, L.T.?"

Black held his hands up innocently.

"Nope."

"Yeah, you are. You're trying to scare me."

"I'm just trying to help you get me and every other officer in the Army off your back."

"Bullshit," Shannon said, pleased with himself for figuring out what was going on. "You're gonna come at me with majors and colonels and think I'm gonna get scared and talk to you."

"Not my intention."

"Yeah, it is. I ain't scared of you or your lawyer bullshit."

Black tossed the notebook aside.

"Well, *someone's* scaring you, because you won't talk to me."

Shannon looked at him like he was straight crazy.

"You fucking . . ."

He trailed off, flabbergasted.

"Me what?"

Shannon shook his head as though to clear it. Finally he uncrossed his arms and put his hands on his knees, leaning forward again to look at Black closely.

"All right, *sir,*" he said disdainfully. "You want it?"

"Want what?"

"You want what I have to say?"

"Please."

"You sure?"

"I'm sure."

"Okay, good," Shannon said.

He took his time sitting back on the bunk. He crossed his arms again. He eyeballed Black for a good moment before he spoke. When he did, it was in tones of pure contempt.

"First off," he said. "*Fuck* you, Lieutenant. Fuck you because you're still a pussy and you don't know shit."

"Okay."

"And you go tell my commander that I cursed at you, if you can find him back at the FOB. I don't give a fuck."

"I got the message that you don't like me," Black replied without emotion.

Shannon's brow curled and flexed.

"See that . . . ?" he spluttered, pointing at Black.

He shook his head again, disgusted.

"'*I got the message that you don't like me,*'" he said in a nasal singsong.

"Look at you, sitting there like you know something. Talking about what scares me."

He loudly snorted phlegm from the back of his throat, and for a moment Black thought he was actually going to spit it on him. He must have swallowed it instead.

"You don't know shit," Shannon said. "You don't know my world."

"Then tell me."

"I *am* telling you, you jackass. You want to know what fucking scares me?"

"I do."

"Good, because I'm going to tell you, since you know so much about what's fucking scary in this place."

"Okay."

Shannon pointed a thick finger at the hallway.

"I heard you talking to Sergeant Merrick this morning in the chow hall. I heard him tell you about the last K.I.A. we had."

"I remember."

"That was Parsons," Shannon said. "He was only here six weeks."

"Okay."

"Sergeant Merrick didn't tell you how he died."

"How?"

"He fell back on a patrol."

"Okay."

"No, you don't understand," Shannon pressed. "I don't mean he got lost, or wandered off or fell back a half mile. You know how far he fell back?"

"How far?"

"Ten meters," Shannon said flatly.

He looked at Black a long moment.

"He was the last guy and he fell back ten fucking meters from where he shoulda been in the patrol, and it was dark and a little bit foggy. That's it. Didn't even hear him get grabbed."

"Okay."

"Know what the Taliban does when they capture a soldier?"

"What?"

"They put his ass on a video and they hold him for ransom until we trade some of their own assholes for him. Which we *do,* even though the commander in chief doesn't admit it when he's on TV talking about how great shit's going over here."

"All right."

"That's the Taliban," Shannon said flatly. "Taliban are pussies."

His eyes bore into Black.

"You know what these Valley fuckers did?"

"What?"

"They left him for us."

Black had a sinking feeling.

"What do you mean?"

"They left him on a tree."

"Oh."

"A hundred meters from our wall, across open ground. First tree we would get to if we walked out."

"Okay."

"Tied to the tree, no fucking balls on him, intestines hanging out."

Black didn't say anything.

"Alive."

He watched Black for his reaction before going on.

"Didn't even call out to us for help," Shannon said, a note of reverence entering his voice. "Didn't want us to go get him and get shot. We didn't see him till it got light the next morning. Still alive."

He seemed to forget Black was there.

"God damn kid, eighteen years old, hooah-hooah airborne trooper, one year ago kissing girls on the Ferris wheel back home, ends up tied to a goddamn tree in this goddamn place looking at his buddies looking back at him from the wall. And we can't go get him because every Valley sniper is up that fucking hillside just waiting for his chance."

Black could only think of one thing to say.

"How long?"

"All day, into the night. You know who finally went out to take care of him?"

"Who?"

"Sergeant Merrick."

"Okay."

"Alone. Wouldn't let any of us come with him. Told us he'd fucking shoot us if we tried to follow."

Black considered this.

"That's a great man," Shannon said defiantly, looking past Black. "And he ain't gonna get no goddamn medal for what he did."

"Couldn't save him?" Black asked.

Shannon ignored the question. Instead he leaned forward again and put his hands on his knees, his own eyes turning back to Black's.

"So there is only one thing in this godforsaken place that scares me, Lieutenant," he said, anger rising again. "And it ain't dying. I ain't scared of that, and I definitely ain't scared of your lawyer bullshit."

"Okay."

"I'm scared that when they get me and I get strung up to a tree with my balls off and my guts out I'm not gonna be strong like little Parsons was strong. I'm scared I'm gonna be weak and I'm gonna call out for my buddies to help me, instead of just dying like a fucking pal. And my weakness is gonna make Sergeant Merrick or one of the other great men who serve here come out and get themselves killed trying to help me."

His speech hung in the air.

"That," Shannon said, "is *my* world, and that's why I don't give a fuck."

"Understood."

"Bullshit," Shannon said, sounding weary. "You don't understand shit."

He sat back against the wall, regarding Black. He spoke in a low voice.

"You don't know what this place is."

"What's that mean?"

"It means the Devil is in this valley, sir. And he will get his."

He gestured with his chin toward Black's notebook.

"So you write what you wanna write in your little book, and go back to the FOB and come back with your majors and colonels. They know where to find me if they wanna come here and get me."

He picked up his video game controller.

"I'll be dead anyway, so it won't matter for shit."

Black gathered up his notebook and stood. There wasn't anything else to say.

Shannon started messing with the broken game controller. Black pushed open the door and left, wondering just how much of a needless pain it was going to be to get a couple simple statements and make his paperwork and go home.

He went to the end of the makeshift corridor and hung a right, as Merrick had instructed him. He took several brisk strides to the last door and kicked it open with his boot.

13

The door swung a hundred eighty degrees and smacked sharply against the plywood wall on which it was mounted. Corelli, the straight-arrow kid from the night before, literally leaped from the stool on which he'd been sitting, back partly turned to the door, writing a letter. The stool went tripping into a corner as Corelli launched himself up and backward, turning in midair and smacking into the wall, his face confusion and terror, his arms up protectively.

"Are you gonna break my balls!?" Black shouted at the kid.

Corelli, back to the wall, flinched and jumped, all at once.

"What? No, sir, I—"

Black, planted in the threshold, stalked into the tiny room.

"Because if you're gonna pull the same B.S. these other two did," he said loudly, "just tell me now so I can go back to the FOB and write all three of you up for obstructing and you can explain yourselves to the court-martial."

The kid looked even more frightened at hearing the word *court-martial* than he had at Black bursting into his room like a bomb going off.

"Sir!" he cried, baffled. "No, I'm—I'm not . . . What?"

Black pointed at the upturned stool.

"Sit."

Corelli scurried and stood it up and got his butt in it.

Black sat down on the edge of his bunk, facing him. He pointed at the soldier's chest.

"Are you going to talk to me," he said sternly, "or are you going to waste my time like your buddies?"

"No, sir," Corelli stammered. "I mean, yes, sir, I will talk to you. I'm not going to waste your time."

The kid looked pale. Black squinted at him for a few seconds, marveling at how young the slight soldier looked. The taut skin on his small neck, Black was fairly sure, had never been shaved.

"I met you last night."

"Yes, sir."

"Do you know what a fifteen-six is?"

"Yes, sir, I do."

"Do you know what this one is about?"

"I think so, sir," Corelli said nervously, rubbing his hand through blond stubble atop his head.

"Why do you think so?"

"Because I knew I was gonna get in trouble over that warning shot, sir."

"You're not in trouble."

Corelli looked confused.

"But I'm being investigated, right, sir?"

Black sighed. Soldiers.

"It's not you, specifically. I'm just talking to everyone so we can write down what happened."

"But I was the shooter, sir."

So the kid did want to talk.

"Okay," said Black, cooling. "I mean, why don't we just start at the beginning."

He pulled out his notebook and a pen, taking a moment to look around Corelli's little room.

It was the most spartan of the three. Little bookshelf with a Bible and some paperbacks. Photographs from back home tacked to the wall. Parents, it looked like, and an adoring little sister maybe. Corelli in civilian clothes posing in a line of wholesome-looking teenagers, arms linked across shoulders, waterfall in the background. Camping trip with a church group from the look of it.

A tinny little boom box sat on a top shelf in the corner, emitting some kind of bombastic 1970s-era art rock opus. Gongs and wind chimes mingled with meandering synthesizers and nature sounds. Didn't seem like the kid's speed.

"Michael A. Corelli, right?"

"Yes, sir."

Black sped through the formalities, which even he was losing patience for. He tossed the notebook aside and sat back against the wall.

"Okay," he said to Corelli. "Tell it."

The kid ran it down. It was pretty much just like Brydon had told it, to the extent he had been willing to tell it.

They'd been down in the village to find the chief, after Miller shot the goat in the fog the night before. They wanted him to identify the owner so they could make amends, but while the meeting was still going on inside his house more and more local guys from town started showing up. They weren't happy, and they were yelling stuff at the joes pulling security.

"What were they saying?" Black asked.

"I don't know, sir. Danny was inside the chief's house."

"How long's Danny been with the unit?"

"Long as I've been here, sir."

The gongs and wind chimes on the boom box had given way to pretentiously complex Look-at-me-play electric guitar lines.

"Okay, go ahead."

"Anyway, I couldn't tell what they were saying, but they weren't happy, and they were starting to get in our faces."

"Where were you guys at that point?"

"We were in the middle of the town, sort of in the town square I guess. It's basically just dirt and grass with homes around it. We were spread out, facing outward, pulling security while the others were inside."

"Caine and Merrick were in with the chief?"

"Sergeant Caine was outside supervising us, sir."

"Where was Lieutenant Pistone?"

"He wasn't on that patrol, sir."

Figures.

"It was just Sergeant Merrick in the chief's house, sir," Corelli went on, "and the captain."

"Captain?"

"There was a captain I didn't know along with us that day, sir. We met him at his helicopter down at the river."

The Civil Affairs officer whose report had triggered the 15-6 investigation.

"Okay," Black said.

"So there were a lot of these guys from the town by that point. Some of them were young, and some of them were the older guys."

"All right."

"And there was this group of younger guys that was close to where I was standing. And, like, they sort of started crowding me. Like, they're yelling at me and I don't know what they're saying but they're mad, and I got the feeling that one of them, the guy who was kind of the leader, was about to grab for my weapon."

"What made you think that?"

"I just had that feeling, sir. You know?"

"Okay."

"I mean," said Corelli, "I've been in more than one of these Afghani towns, sir, and you can tell when something is about to go bad."

"I understand."

"And I'm telling you, sir, this was about to go bad. And these guys sort of pressed in on me and I just could tell, I just knew that this guy was about to grab for my weapon."

The drums had fallen in full force alongside the guitar lines, and a "singer" who appeared to know only how to howl and yowl in the highest registers had joined the fray. Something about honeydew and rivers.

"Was your weapon attached to you?"

"Yes, sir. I had it on the D-ring like usual."

"So what then?"

"So right at that moment when I sort of knew that was about to happen, I took about two steps backward to clear myself from the Afghani guys and I raised my weapon over their heads and I put three rounds into the wall of one of the mud houses off the square behind where they were standing."

Black frowned.

"Where was Sergeant Caine at that point?"

"He was on the other side of the square, sir."

"Why didn't you wait for him to tell you what to do?"

Corelli shook his head: Not that kind of situation.

"It was just one of those split-second things, sir," he said. "He was probably seventy-five or a hundred meters away, and I mean, he could see me and I could see him, but I would have had to shout and get his attention just to communicate. Or use my radio, which would have taken even longer. I didn't think I could wait, sir, and I didn't want to shoot the guys."

"Were they aimed shots?"

Corelli nodded vigorously.

"Absolutely, sir. I found the closest solid target behind where they were standing. I've got a magnification sight on my rifle and I could see exactly where the rounds were hitting the wall. I know I didn't put any into the window."

"You ever been in a civilian-type situation like this in Afghanistan before?"

"Yes, sir."

"And you never had to fire warning shots before?"

"Um, no, sir," said Corelli. "Not in any of the previous civilian-type situations I've been in with this platoon."

The interminable song seemed to be reaching some kind of climax. It sounded as though the entire set of drums and gongs and cymbals and wind chimes had been hurled down a stairwell and powderized in a wood chipper at the bottom. The singer wailed like he was being sucked into a black hole. It was awful.

Black tried to focus.

"Uh, why didn't you shoot into the air?"

Corelli looked at him funny for a moment.

"Well, 'cause they'll come down again, sir. I mean, we can't just shoot crazy in the air like Iraqis do after soccer games and stuff."

"Fair enough."

Black felt foolish. He was having a hard time concentrating on his questions. He was distracted by the lyrics to the song, which apparently wasn't done yet after all.

A thousand years have come and gone

He looked at Corelli, who was looking at the floor.

"I guess I was a little jumpy, sir."

"Why were you jumpy?"

"Because the town had been so mad, sir."

Black thought a moment, squeezing his thoughts between the singer's yowling about the sky stopping or something.

"Why did you say you knew you'd be in trouble before?"

Corelli cleared his throat.

"When we got back from the patrol the lieutenant told me I would probably be in trouble if there was ever an investigation."

The guy wouldn't stop about the frozen sky.

"He mentioned an investigation?"

"That was the term he used, sir."

Black quietly congratulated himself on correctly deducing from a mere photograph the sort of petty and ineffectual leader the absent Pistone must have been.

"Why do you think the town guys were so mad?" he asked.

Corelli looked up at Black, hesitating.

"I don't think that's a question I can answer, sir."

Now the singer wanted the world to end.

"Why not?"

Or for morning to come. Hard to say.

"Um," Corelli hesitated. "Sergeant Merrick told me not to, uh, speculate on anything that I don't have direct knowledge of, sir."

"I thought you said that someone's goat had gotten killed the night before."

"Yes, sir," said Corelli. "It did, sir. I just, I mean, I'm not supposed to assume that I know what's in their head at a particular time, sir."

Praying for the light

"All I know about *that* day specifically," Corelli went on, "is that a goat got killed the night before . . ."

Prison of the lost . . .

". . . and the guys in the town were mad when we were there the next day. I can't say what—"

Xanadu.

Black startled to attention.

Xaaaaaaaaaa-naaaaaaaa-dooooooo . . .

"What's this?" he demanded.

"Huh?"

"What's this?" Black asked again.

Corelli looked at him blankly.

"What's what, sir?"

"This."

Black thumbed at the CD player.

"The music?" Corelli asked. "The Wizard gave it to me."

He looked at Black, brow furrowed.

"It's kind of cool, right, sir?"

"What's 'Xanadu'?" Black asked.

"Sir?"

"In the song."

Corelli shook his head.

"It's just the song, I think, sir."

"What do you mean?"

"The Wizard said it's from a poem, I think, sir."

"What poem?"

Corelli shrugged.

"Some Wizard poem, sir. He reads a lot of crazy stuff."

"Huh."

Corelli appeared to remember something.

"He said 'Xanadu is what comes before the end of the world,' whatever that means. I think it's just the song, sir."

Black shook his head and refocused on the interview. The singer, who now seemed depressed, rolled on.

Corelli explained how the warning shots succeeded in backing off the little group of guys that were hassling him, and startled the rest of the crowd. Caine took over at that point, and the chief came out of his house with Merrick and the visiting captain and calmed everybody down.

"What happened then?"

"At that point, we beat feet and went home, sir," explained Corelli. "We especially didn't want to push it with the town that particular day, so we just got out and came back here."

Black thought back over the interview. The singer, who was howling again in anguish over some sort of existential tragedy, made it difficult to do so clearly.

"Okay," he said. "I think that's it. Are you willing to write it all down in a sworn statement later so I can take that back with me to the FOB?"

Corelli looked at him earnestly.

"Anything you ask me about," he said with his strange formality, "is what I can put in a sworn statement, sir."

"Okay," Black said breezily. "Is that it, or is there anything else to add?"

Corelli was still looking at him.

"That is everything I have to say about that day, sir."

Black thanked him for his time and apologized for startling him before.

"I'm okay with surprises, sir."

Odd kid. Black left him to his letter-writing.

The endless art rock song still hadn't exhausted itself. The guitar line was back, circling around on itself over and over as he stepped out into the hallway with relief.

Black poked his head into the guard shack and proffered the pack of smokes.

"And how, sir."

He came in and they all lit up. They shot the breeze and watched the fog come in again.

"You guys got Internet here?" Black asked.

"C'mon, sir," said the first soldier, dragging. "What do you think?"

"I don't know, I figured maybe a satellite connection or something."

The kid just shook his head, exhaling.

"Ain't no satellite to talk to from here, sir," he said.

He thumbed upward, indicating the steep mountainsides rising above them.

"No line of sight."

Black nodded.

"Ain't no M.W.R. ever been up this valley," the soldier declared, "or ever gonna be up this valley, sir."

That stood for Morale, Welfare, and Recreation, which was the Army term for the makeshift little recreation centers you found on every FOB—Ping-Pong, TV, board games, Internet—and for all Army initiatives taken in the name of M, W, and R, like getting satellite uplinks to remote posts so joes could check in back home.

"Who's Danny trying to pick up on his antenna?"

"Danny," the kid scoffed. "Danny's crazy, sir. Freaking 'terp. Thinks he's gonna get his hajji music all the way up here."

He shook his head again.

"No point," he said. "No one to listen to, no one to talk to."

The other one, the mustachioed Bosch, nodded slightly.

"Only way we're ever gonna send an e-mail," the soldier finished, "is for them to hurry and get us the fuck outta this bitch."

"How long you guys got left?" Black asked.

The soldier made a *How the hell am I supposed to know?* gesture.

"Hell, we ain't even supposed to be here now."

"What do you mean?"

"I mean this post ain't even supposed to be here, sir. Supposed to be closed."

"Where'd you hear that?"

"The L.T. told us," the soldier answered.

"Pistone?"

The kid nodded.

"Came back from the FOB one time and said that Battalion told him this place was scheduled to be shut down. COP Heavenly too."

The soldier hocked up a deep wad from his throat and spat it through the window.

"Said it's part of a 'strategic realignment' or some bullshit. I don't remember what he called it, but the point is, we're retreating. Giving up on this fucking valley."

"I didn't know that."

"Yep, sir," the soldier said. "This base is abandoned. We just ain't abandoned it yet."

"Why not?"

"Assets got diverted. They were all ready to move us out and dismantle this place and then at the last minute Brigade said they needed all the engineer equipment and the backhaul trucks and all that for some big fight they were having in another valley. So they said, 'Sit tight, we'll be back for you soon.'"

"How long ago was that?"

"Three months."

"What?!"

"That's right, L.T. Three months and we ain't heard shit."

He spat again.

"Not even 'We haven't forgotten about you.' Fucking radio silence."

One of the worst sins in the Army, Black had always thought, was leaders failing to pass information down to their lowest subordinates. Too many people seemed to think that hoarding information, then doling it out like pieces of Halloween candy, made you a strong leader.

He wondered at what point in the chain of command, from the sergeants who directly supervised these guys all the way up to the colonel in charge of their battalion, the communication had broken down.

"But of course we can't just hunker down like smart people and ride it out," the kid said, agitated. "We gotta 'Keep On With The Mission.' We gotta keep going out on the trail, go on our goddamn patrols, fucking clear out Sniper Town every other day, cruise the town, get *shot* half the time, so . . . what? Maybe someday we interdict some fucking hajji wannabe suicide bomber? Like they don't know any other goddamn way around this valley."

After his speech he seemed to calm himself. He took a long drag, killing the last of the smoke.

"Welcome to the land of the lost, sir. We are a platoon without a purpose."

"When was your unit in Iraq?" Black asked out of nowhere.

The kid looked at him, startled.

"How'd you know that, L.T.?"

"'Hajji,'" Black offered.

It was a holdover term more common to Iraq. In Afghanistan you'd hear "muj," for *mujahideen*. Among other things.

"Oh-three," the soldier answered.

Black nodded.

"Hey, sir," the kid said. "Hajji is hajji, whatever shitty country he lives in. We go there, we go here, we go all around the world and hajji's always the same. He lives in shit and lets it go to shit, and we keep coming around like we're gonna fucking fix it for him."

Bosch watched his friend rant while allowing smoke to fan upward from his mouth.

"Hajji don't surf," he deadpanned.

The first soldier snorted a single laugh and flipped the butt out the window.

"So here we are, sir," he said. "Remember us when they remember us, I guess."

That hung in the air for a bit.

"Heck," the soldier said unconvincingly, "maybe they won't hit us anymore because they know we're leaving."

Black said nothing. Bosch just looked at his friend with something between exasperation and pity.

"How long since you guys got back to the FOB?" Black asked.

"Shit," the first soldier spat. "Whattaya say, Bosch? Like, two months?"

Bosch tipped a jutting chin upward in a barely perceptible nod.

"Even that," the soldier went on, "was bullshit. That wasn't no trip back to the FOB. Kept us locked down in the barracks there, practically. Did laundry, which was a joke 'cause our shit's gonna be all nasty in a week anyway. Took us over to chow in a group. Thought they were gonna march us over there in formation like basic training. Same for the PX and the Internet café. Didn't get to get out or do shit. Then twenty-four hours later, it's 'Back on the trucks' and we came back up here."

"How come?"

"Ask our leadership, sir. Wanted us to 'stay focused' or some bullshit. FOB Omaha may as well be stateside. I couldn't find my way around that place to save my life. Couldn't even tell you what freaking units are there."

The fog was all the way in and slowly rising again.

"What's 'Xanadu'?" Black asked.

"What's what?"

"Xanadu."

The soldier looked at him blankly. Black looked at Bosch, who shook his head.

"Never mind."

Black took a last drag on his cigarette.

"I'm not supposed to be here either," he said.

The soldier seemed confused.

"What, like, here at Vega, sir?"

"No. Up here in this guard post."

"Oh."

Black tossed his smoke out the window and turned to go. Bosch spoke up.

"Guess we got something in common, then, L.T."

He stopped and looked. Bosch had turned back to his weapon.

Black stepped out into the night. Danny was there at the far corner of the roof again, wrestling uselessly with his antenna.

14

In the dark of the morning the soldiers in the courtyard were gray shapes huddled in shadow. They milled close together all around the edges of the muddy square, keeping under the overhangs. Under cover. Silence punctuated by snaps of equipment clips, rustling of uniform fabric as gear was adjusted over it.

Several guys had headphones on, eyes closed, humming and thrumming in their own worlds. Tinny little cacophonies whispered into the quiet around them as they tranced out, beating back thoughts. Others fidgeted and fingered black weapons or rocked from foot to foot. Sergeants, off in corners, spoke in low tones. No one smoked out here.

Black pushed the button on his wristwatch. Amber light told him 0532. The sky hadn't started to turn yet, but soon. The fog lapping at the shores of COP Vega was thinning and ready to recede.

Black saw Corelli standing nearby, ears free, thumbs hooked in his gear, staring off into the night. Shannon lurked further down the breezeway, a small mountain studded with combat equipment, murmuring to his buddies and ignoring Black.

No one, to be sure, appeared to be paying any direct attention to Black. But he had developed a highly sensitive radar for being glanced at and whispered about, and it was pinging loudly. He did not imagine anyone was particularly glad about having this lieutenant's errand grafted onto their already hazardous patrol.

As his eyes adjusted he saw a larger gaggle of people gathered at a far corner of the courtyard. They huddled around someone tall, someone who was not dressed like a soldier. Black turned to a kid who was standing near him, fidgeting.

"Who's that?" he asked quietly.

The soldier shook his head and shrugged and seemed to find a reason to move away and fidget somewhere farther from Black.

"That's the Monk, sir," came a large, quiet voice from behind him.

He turned. Oswalt, the big soldier from the hole in the wall.

"Morning, sir."

Oswalt smiled down on him. He wasn't wearing gear.

"Morning," Black answered quietly. "Who's 'the Monk'?"

"Oh, he's a spooky-spook guy, sir. A snake-eater."

"What he's trying to tell you," murmured Caine, appearing from nowhere, "is that he's special forces."

Black turned. Caine was geared up and ready. Danny stood next to him in the dim light.

Black squinted across the courtyard at this Monk person.

"He looks like a hobo."

"*Speeeecial* forces, sir," answered Caine.

Black nodded. Not your run-of-the-mill green beret.

"Ours?"

He meant: Army superelite, or someone else's superelite. Caine just shrugged.

"We ain't privileged to know. Shows up every now and then to charge batteries or borrow some wet wipes or whatnot, but . . ."

He held his hands up in the *Your guess is as good as mine* gesture.

"C'mon," he said. "Come say hi."

He strode along under the overhang. Black and Danny followed.

"See you, Oswalt," Black said over his shoulder.

"See you, sir. Good luck."

Caine had said nothing so far about Merrick showing up in his place the day before. By Caine's demeanor Black could have forgotten that he'd slammed Pistone's door in the sergeant's face the day before. Maybe Merrick told Caine to cool his jets and let it go, though that hardly seemed likely.

They worked their way around through milling soldiers to the far corner of the courtyard. There, talking to a couple of junior sergeants and a couple of joes, was a man dressed in a traditional Afghan *budzun* cloak, with a loose brown linen scarf wrapped high around his neck and a rolled, woolen Chitrali hat on his head.

He was about Black's age. He was not large, but tall and well muscled, as was apparent even through the cloak. Black could make out no sign of weapons or equipment beneath his garments, though he figured something must be there. The man's hair fell somewhere between dark blond and sandy brown, with a matching "beard" struggling to cover his lower face in scrubby curls. What remained showing, which was most of it, was a sun-browned visage of angular peaks and valleys that would be tough for most people to place—something strikingly, ethnically European, something from a black-and-white photo-scrum of schoolboys from a hundred years before. Probably a mix of a couple of things.

Bosch, from the guard tower the night before, was there. He wasn't geared up for the patrol, probably because he'd been on duty all night. He'd apparently come down after his shift to chat with the Monk.

They were shaking hands as Black and Caine approached. Bosch turned to see them, stuffed his hands in his pockets, and roamed away scowling at the ground.

"Hey, bro," said Caine, walking up. "How's it going?"

"You know," the man said noncommittally.

He extended a hand languidly and they shook.

"This is Black," Caine said, gesturing. "Came up from the FOB for the weekly package deal."

The man turned to Black and locked eyes as he extended his hand. It was an oddly formal gesture—thumb up, palm vertical, chin tilted, arm crooked ninety degrees at the elbow, the rest of him rock-straight like a chipper businessman from a silent movie.

"Lieutenant," he said, a wry grin on his face.

"Pleasure," Black answered slowly, examining his beard.

The Monk nodded with mock significance and clasped his hand. Caine cocked his head at the strange display.

"Anyway, guys," the Monk continued breezily, ignoring Caine's look, "maybe, like, two weeks?"

"Sure," one answered, clearly enamored of the guy.

"All right," he said, nodding. "Guess I'm out, then."

He seemed ready to go, then thought of something. He turned to Black.

"Hey, bud. You're just here a few days, right?"

Black nodded.

The man fished deep in his garments and came out with a tattered-looking Ziploc bag. He peeled it open and produced a wrinkled little envelope. The kind about big enough for an index card or a piece of folded stationery and that's it. He held it out to Black.

"Mind mailing this for me when you go back down?"

Black took the envelope and held it up in front of his face in the dark. A handwritten address in blocky letters crowded the front. Turning it over, he could just make out a series of hand-colored hearts romping across the seal.

"Don't worry, L.T.," the Monk chuckled. "There's no stamp on it, so you're not mishandling mail or whatever."

He flashed a grin at the rest of the guys.

"I know how you officers worry abo—"

He cut himself off.

"Hey, you mind buying me a stamp too?"

He gave a mock-guilty wince.

"Sorry."

"Sure," Black replied, looking at the envelope.

"Cool. Thanks a mil. Been carrying that sucker for weeks."

He looked at the assembled guys and feigned sheepishness.

"My chickie will be so happy."

The Monk stuck his hands in his *budzun* pockets and made to go.

"All right, dudes. Thanks again. Take it easy."

He turned and trudged across the damp ground toward the gate.

"Wow, sir," said Caine dryly, for the benefit of the assembled joes. "Carrying supersecret mail."

The soldiers chuckled, but Black could tell they were actually a bit envious of him being asked to perform a simple task by the mystery warrior, a man so hard and cool he didn't even care if anyone saw him handing off a love note to his girl.

Black pocketed the wilted envelope, and the soldiers wandered off.

"Why's he 'the Monk'?" he asked Caine.

"Just what the bubbas call him. Lives like a monk in the mountains. Nobody knows his name, obviously."

"What's he do?"

Caine shrugged.

"Eats rocks and tries to figure out where the bad guys are coming from and why every last fucker in this valley seems to want to slit every last one of our throats."

"Where's he sleep?"

"Fuck if I know. Up in trees, down by the river. Probably in a lot of shitty shacks."

"How's that work?"

"What I'm saying," Caine said impatiently, "is that he probably does a lot of hookah-smoking with a lot of dumb locals in their crummy little houses and asks them why their cousin hates the infidel so much when there's perfectly good Taliban here to be pissed off at."

"Yeah, I get that," Black said, showing his own annoyance. "I'm saying, he's white."

"You ever see a Nuristani guy, L.T.?"

Black was not happy to admit he hadn't.

"A bunch of 'em look white, or half-white. They aren't the same as regular Afghans, like, ethnically. Got some white-guy Caucasian mixed in there somewhere."

Black had never heard anyone mention this down on FOB Omaha.

"Why do you think I wanted you to speak English when I kicked your ass the other night?"

"Huh," Black said, recalling this. His jaw still hurt.

"Yup," Caine nodded. "That's why some of these Valley guys can shave their faces and slip right inside an American unit before anyone figures out they're wearing our uniforms. And a white dude can do some halfway decent blending in around here once he grows a beard and puts on shitty clothes."

"Well," Black replied, "so what happens when the Monk guy has to actually talk to people?"

"Yeah, they know he's not from here once they talk to him," Caine said. "Shit, the 'terps don't even know all these crazy Valley languages, besides 'hello' and stuff. Just Pashto. But you can still do a lot of traveling without attracting a lot of attention."

"So they know he's military?"

"I doubt it. He's probably got a good cover story, like he's some crazy Euro hiker tourist guy or something. You know, walk across Afghanistan, live with the locals, write a book about it."

"He told you that?"

"Hell, no. He doesn't tell us shit. I just figured. That's probably why he only comes and goes from here in the dark and when it's foggy."

Black took this all in.

"Where do the Caucasian genes come from?"

"Funny you ask," said Caine, happy to be asked. "Lost Roman legion."

"What?"

"What I said. Roman army came here fighting and a whole legion never came back."

Black hadn't heard any of this either.

"Dudes spread their seed," Caine said, sprinklering the Valley with a sweep of his arm, "and now the people are all mixed up."

"Huh," said Black again.

"Yup," Caine said, pleased with himself. "Yeah, I see you looking at dumb ol' Sarge Caine that way, L.T. Ol' Sarge knows a thing or—"

"Caine."

It was Merrick's voice, behind them and a few steps away.

Caine turned. Merrick motioned him over with his head. He registered Black's presence but said nothing.

"Stay here," Caine said to Black and stepped away.

"He means Alexander the Great," came a heavily accented voice from Black's other side.

He turned. It was Danny. He wore the standard, stripped-down linguist's patrol uniform: a set of cast-off fatigues with a U.S. flag but no rank, and a helmet with no camouflage cover, night-vision fittings, or other accoutrements.

He stuck his hand out. Black shook it.

"How's it going?"

"Hey, man, how are you?" said Danny.

"I'm good. What was that about Alexander the Great?"

"When he was talking about the Roman legion," Danny explained, "they never come here. The British, they come here a lot later, but the Romans was never here. He's talking about Alexander the Great."

"He was here?"

"Yeah, man, he fought near here, he fought the *kafiri*."

Black knew this word, from Kourash back on the FOB.

"Unbelievers," he said.

Danny smiled and nodded.

"Yes, L.T. Good. The infidel who do not accept the book."

When Danny said "L.T." it sounded different from the joes. It sounded more like a straight term of respect. He wasn't in the Army, so he wasn't going to say "sir." Apparently "L.T." was as close as it got.

"So Alexander's soldiers married the women here."

Danny weighed a Little of This and a Little of That between his hands.

"Eh, nobody knows. This is theory. Many theories."

So Danny knew a thing or two too.

"You know why I'm here this week?" Black asked him.

Danny stuck his hands in his pockets and nodded.

"Yeah, man, investigation. Cool. Whatever I help, I help."

"I think today's patrol is mostly for me. To talk to the chief in Darreh Sin."

"Mmmm," said Danny appreciatively. "He's big man, good man. Good man to talk to."

"Okay."

Caine reappeared.

"We're going," he said quietly. "You stay with Danny and me, sir. And don't crowd me."

"Got it."

Around the edges of the courtyard, beneath the overhangs, soldiers had clumped into squads, charging weapons and putting headphones away. The murmured chitchat had gone quiet.

Beginning at the end closest to the gate, one soldier at a time stepped out from beneath cover and walked across the wet ground and through the egress point. The next would follow, leaving a good twenty-five or thirty feet between them. In this way the area under the overhangs was steadily emptying. They obviously had the routine down.

The first to go out, Black noted, was Merrick. This was unusual, the senior person on a patrol placing himself at the front of it, where he could be shot first or step on a bomb.

"Where are you from?" Black whispered to Danny as they waited their turn.

"Kabul."

His father, Danny explained quietly, had come from a minor Kabul family to become a big deal in the old Afghan army, before it splintered into squabbling militias. He hated the Taliban but from what Black gathered he had figured out how to make his way in the new Afghanistan. He was a businessman now, and expected his sons to make their own way like he had.

Danny freely confessed that he wasn't a military type and hated business. He'd opted for becoming a 'terp instead, to try to sock away some savings and make his start in life. He knew the risks.

"Maybe I get shot," he said, chuckling, "or maybe I am big success!"

Black thought he caught the scent of the adventurer in Danny. Someone who had just discovered he enjoyed the risks, whether he would admit it or not.

"How long have you been here at Vega?"

"Four months," Danny answered, then shook his head.

"This place," he whispered, "is crazy, man!"

He chuckled as though a thought had just occurred to him.

"Nuristan, that they call this now," he said, grinning slyly. "Do you know what this means?"

Black shook his head.

"Land of light!" Danny cried, sweeping both hands in an arc that encompassed the whole black valley.

Someone nearby shooshed him. He put a hand over his mouth in a mock *Oops!* and giggled. Black smiled. That was something else he hadn't known.

He found that he liked Danny immediately. He had liked many of the 'terps he'd known. Respected them. Respected the risks they frequently took, above and beyond their formal duties. Respected their readily offered loyalty, though all they were being paid for, technically, was a simple service. Respected their knowledge of the land and its people.

Mostly he respected their wise counsel. A 'terp's advice had saved his life once.

Caine stepped away into the dirt. Black turned to Danny, who gave him the *After you* gesture.

He waited a few seconds and followed, feeling the nakedness of open space and the hillsides above him. He resisted the urge to speed up, which would just bunch him up close to Caine. It was the sort of thing drill sergeants spent all of basic training yelling at trainees to stop doing.

He passed between two junior sergeants waiting at either side of the gate, each one counting every person that passed through the egress. It was sound practice. You can know who's in your squad and your platoon, and who is scheduled to be on a patrol, and who showed up for the patrol—but unless you actually physically count every single body as it leaves the gate you don't know to a certainty how many bodies are supposed to come back through it afterward.

"Seventeen," they mouthed in quiet unison as he passed. They looked at him with unreadable expressions on their faces.

15

He stepped out under the crystal-black vault of stars. The dark mountainsides soared above, ridges mingling with sky. Open ground fell away before him.

With dawn coming soon, only about half the guys had pulled their night-vision goggles down as they left Vega. Black preferred his natural eyesight when he could make do with it. He squinted and located Caine to his right, moving away across the hillslope. He kept his spacing and followed.

The patrol headed downslope only a short distance then cut right along a barely visible trail laden with pebbles and slick in places from still-wet ground. They traveled along just above the fringes of the fog, which visibly receded below them as they went.

No one spoke, save for the whispers of traffic he could make out periodically over Caine's radio in the dark ahead of him. Beyond Caine, shadowy soldiers stretched into the distance in a staggered single file.

He looked behind him and saw Danny, ambling along, hands in pockets. He grinned and gave Black a small wave. Behind him more dark shapes, pointy with black weapons.

After a half mile or so skirting the flanks of the mountainside, the trail began to bend downward. The trees gathered closer and the going got slower. They picked their way along steep, lightly wooded ground.

A half hour in, Black looked upward and saw that the sky had started to turn. Not dawn, but the half-light that is neither day nor night. Goggles were coming off and being stowed away in kit bags.

The narrow trail wound around trees and among boulders, steep at first. As they descended it grew more shallow, finally bottoming out and widening into a broad dirt track running through a narrow offshoot of the Valley proper, a sort of tributary ravine with forested walls. To Black it felt like walking on one of the logging roads back at Fort Benning.

The trip down had taken time. Morning was in full flare by then, emerging to a cloudless sky. The ridgeline on their right was closer above them at this point, perhaps a few hundred feet. Sun shafts were cresting it and striking the higher valley slopes opposite.

The patrol moved at a slow but steady pace. Soldiers' heads swiveled this way and that, up and down the slopes, searching the shadows with the practiced routine of a unit that was used to being attacked.

Caine had slowed his pace and fallen back a bit closer to Black.

"Hey, L.T."

He turned and ambled backward as he spoke.

Black gave him an upward nod of the chin: What's up?

Caine thumbed up and over his shoulder, toward the lower ridges on the right.

Black's eyes tracked upward.

"All the way up, sir. Up top."

He saw. Perched along the ridgeline, between two slightly higher crests. An odd box-shaped structure.

"Binos?" Caine asked.

Black shook his head.

Caine came closer. He dug in a pouch and produced a little pair of field glasses. Black took them and craned skyward.

It was the size of a large shack, but made of stone. The brilliant morning light hit it sideways from beyond the ridges and colored one side a blazing orange. He couldn't make out any doors or windows.

"Blockhouse Signal Mountain," he murmured.

"What?" asked Caine.

"Nothing."

He handed the binoculars back to Caine, who was looking at him funny.

"What is it?" he asked the sergeant, nodding his chin up the slopes.

"Some old British shit from a long time ago. They used to be here. Like, their colonies and stuff."

He stepped up his pace a bit and started moving back to his spot.

"Thought you might be interested, L.T."

Black nodded. He squinted back upward, but his angle on the ridge slopes was changing as the patrol traveled and the little structure was already mostly obscured.

"Telegraph," came Danny's quiet voice from behind, startling him.

Black turned. Danny had moved up within a few feet behind him.

"What?"

"This is the . . ."

He cranked his hand in a circle before him, looking for the words.

"Great Britain, she had the telegraph, in the, the . . . network. All world."

Black vaguely recalled reading about this once, about the worldwide telegraph network laid in the second half of the nineteenth century, largely constructed by the British across their many imperial possessions.

"How old?"

"Eighteen, maybe eighteen-seventy? Eighty?"

The time frame made sense. Right when the world was getting connected.

"So what's that thing?" he asked. "Some kind of . . . hub?"

"Yeah, man. Telegraph tower. End the line. End the network. They build, all way, they stop here."

Black didn't understand why there would be any part of that network here in Afghanistan. He said so.

"This, remember, Pakistan is India those days. British."

"Well, yeah, but . . ."

He trailed off before he said it.

Black knew they were close to the border with Pakistan, but not that close. Danny saw him processing the information. His eyes twinkled.

"Lines on map, these come, these go," he said wryly, turning his palms upward in a *Who's to say?* "Yesterday's line, today's line, tomorrow's line. British man draws lines."

He stuck his hands back in his pockets.

"Afghan man, he knows his land."

Danny faded back to his place before he could be shooshed and scolded by Caine.

Black found it fascinating that the British had built telegraph infrastructure all the way to the Afghanistan border, or what was then more or less the border. They must have still had some optimistic hope for further expansion.

The road bent to the right ahead, around the mass of the mountain. The patrol instead continued straight, off into the trees.

Beyond the road the ground sloped slightly upward. Soldiers ahead fanned out to the left and right through the woods, forming a security perimeter. Black followed Caine as he moved straight ahead.

The trees thinned ahead of them, the morning light becoming more brilliant as it filtered through. Looking to his left and right, Black saw that the land sloped downward in each direction. He sensed that they were walking onto a sort of promontory.

Caine stopped after a hundred meters or so. He put a boot up on a felled tree trunk and stretched, looking back over his shoulder and motioning Black forward. Danny came up and joined them.

They were at the edge of the woodline, on a promontory as Black had suspected, looking down on a recessed flank of the valley. Forested slopes ran down to the river, which would soon be catching direct sunlight. A lesser tributary, something more than a creek but less than a river, joined it from a subsidiary valley rising away to the right. Between the river forks and the hills, nestled along the lower slopes in a crook in the land, was a village.

"Darreh Sin," Caine said, handing over the binoculars again.

It was probably a mile and a half away in a straight line, maybe three hundred feet below them. It wasn't much. A few dozen homes, tops, most looking to be the usual hybrid stone-and-log constructions common to the area. Some creeped up the slopes, piled almost one on top of another. He could make out a few people here and there, out and about, mostly moving toward the river.

"It's small," Black said.

Caine shrugged.

"Yeah," he said.

He watched Black peer through the binos.

"This one's 'friendly,'" he said, wagging quotation marks in the air with the hand that wasn't holding his weapon.

"The others farther up the Valley, not so much."

"Huh."

"Everyone's gotta decide how to deal with the Taliban his own way, I guess."

Black watched the little dots heading toward the river. Women, as far as he could tell.

He pointed toward the little tributary valley. It looked like it led to higher ground.

"What's up there?"

"That's the Meadows."

"Meadows?"

"Sort of a flat place up in there," Caine explained. "Lotsa grass, shady trees. Little nook in the mountains. More farms in there. Houses."

"You guys ever go there?"

"Not much," Caine answered. "It all falls under this same chief and the same council. The Meadows is just, like, the suburbs of this town."

Black craned the binos around but couldn't see far up the side valley.

"Anyway," Caine said, "Sergeant Merrick's taking a squad out now. Get some chow if you want."

He pointed as he started digging in his pack. Merrick and a line of soldiers had assembled fifty yards or so to their right.

"Route clearance?"

"Yup."

Probably they had encountered booby traps and snipers along the way in the past. On terrain like they were traveling on, there were only so many different ways to get where you wanted to go. It was easy for an enemy to plan for American forces using a particular route. Merrick probably wanted to shake the trees a bit and rattle whoever might be out there into going away or fighting.

Black heard noise in the brush to his right and turned. A smaller group of four soldiers in heavy camouflage appeared from the trees and spoke briefly to Merrick. When they were done, they trudged back toward the dirt track, where it continued on beyond the bend in the mountainside. Two carried long-barreled sniper rifles.

They would be heading to positions where they could see Merrick and his squad as it made its way across the Valley floor and along the river—and see anyone else who might be watching them. Merrick's group disappeared downslope.

Black wandered back in away from the woodline. Those soldiers who hadn't taken up positions on the perimeter were scattered throughout the area. Some took a knee. All huddled close to trees, looking this way and that into the distance. They rooted in cargo pockets for little packets of M.R.E. crackers and cookies. These they tore open with their teeth and ate with one hand, the other on their weapons. Sergeants moved periodically among them to make sure no one was getting groggy during the lull.

The patrol had left so early that probably no one had eaten much of anything. Black hadn't either, but he'd had the presence of mind to raid an M.R.E. case that was sitting in the courtyard for the purpose. He sat down on a rock and pulled out a tan Spaghetti with Meatballs packet. It was a prize among M.R.E. entrees. He tore it open and ate it cold with the standard-issue plastic spork.

Danny wandered over and situated himself nearby, squatting on his haunches with his back against a tree. They chatted quietly.

An hour passed with little other talking, except when a nearby soldier asked Black to repeat his Chuck Norris joke. It had made its way through the outpost and was now famous in its lameness.

Caine's radio chirped nearby, startling him. The sergeant, sitting on a log, looked like he'd been getting a bit groggy himself. He stood and unclipped the handset from his body armor, walking toward the edge of the wood line to survey the valley below.

He came back a minute later, speaking in low tones into the radio. Soldiers in the woods around them rustled to life and climbed to their feet.

"Time to go, L.T.," he said. "They're gonna meet us down there."

They traveled the same route Merrick had taken. The downhill going was dodgy at first, loose dirt and pebbles slipping away beneath their sliding boots. As they descended, the slope lessened and grass came up underfoot. They emerged into clear sunlight. Soon they were traveling along reedy green flats near the river.

Black was surprised by how lush it was here, compared with the arid terrain of so much of the country. Flowering shade trees overhanging with shrubs springing up around them, everything subsisting on the nearby river water. It was, frankly, beautiful.

A squat building of timber and stone sat ahead among a clustering of trees between the trail and the river. It looked like it had several rooms in it. Black turned back to Danny questioningly.

"This . . ." Danny searched for the word. "Birth house. Babies, momma."

He explained how in Nuristan villages children were born in a special building outside of town where they and their mothers would stay for a few days.

"Medicine is bad," he said. "Many die."

Past the birthing house they found Merrick and his squad. He turned wordlessly and pressed forward. After another hundred yards or so he turned and bore right, uphill. Caine and the rest of the patrol followed. They were now directly downslope of the village, which Black could see above them through the remaining trees.

Two dark-haired women came downhill, heading toward the river. One wore a black garment somewhere between a dress and a robe, which went down to her ankles. The other's was similar but brown. Both wore embroidered blue scarves around their necks in a light fabric, which they loosely curled up and around the backs of their heads. They kept their eyes on the ground as the soldiers passed and moved on toward their business.

The patrol pressed upward and reached the outskirts of the village, passing the first mud homes as they climbed toward the hillslopes. Outside one a boy of about fifteen in a goatskin vest bent to lace a hide boot. He straightened as they passed. Caine gave him a small wave good morning. The boy watched them impassively from behind green, studying eyes.

More homes appeared on each side. Some were more or less huts. Some were made of stone and logs, and others almost entirely of skillfully crafted wood. A couple had more than one story to them. Smoke from morning hearths trickled upward from more than one.

None of them had fences or barriers around them, despite being built in some cases very close to one another. He'd never seen that in Afghanistan.

People came and went on their morning business. Silver-haired men in gray and black cloaks trudged uphill, squat Chitrali hats or checked *keffiyeh* scarves protecting them from the sun. Probably heading toward the slopes where their goats grazed.

Women headed uphill too, veering off in a different direction from the men. Black followed their path with his eyes and saw that the lower hillsides were terraced for crops. The usable land must have been extremely limited in a landscape like the Valley's.

Beyond the immediate buildings, sprightly children tore around corners after one another. Black heard Danny speaking behind him and turned. The linguist had broken off to the side and intercepted one of them, a boy of twelve or so whom he apparently knew.

After a perfunctory embrace he spoke a few words to the child, who nodded once before turning and jogging away uphill, past Black and the rest of the patrol, waving here and there to a soldier he knew. Past Merrick, who trudged on purposefully, straight through the heart of town, making no effort to interact with anyone.

None of the adults seemed to pay them much attention regardless. Caine waved or nodded to people here and there. These overtures were received with what Black could only read as tolerant disinterest, a sort of blankness. The rest of the soldiers seemed to follow Merrick's lead and kept to themselves, scanning the distance and climbing the hill.

Danny had fallen in beside Black, who looked over his shoulder at the line of guys behind him. Corelli was two soldiers back, making his way up. He stared straight ahead as he went, both hands on his rifle, eyes fixed on some invisible point before him.

A scrum of children playing chase came tearing around a close corner and nearly ran smack into Black and Danny. Seeing the soldiers they skidded on the brakes, coming up short. They looked up at the two men wide-eyed.

Danny gave them a smiling wave and greeting in a language that didn't sound like Pashto. The children just stared at him and Black and began backing up toward the houses, nearly tripping over one another.

A girl in a loose head scarf and dark robe with brightly colored, ornate stitching at the cuffs and hem stepped forward from the gaggle and looked up at Black. Her eyes were such a bright blue they almost looked silver. She smiled and reached under her scarf and pulled a red flower from her short-cropped dark hair, offering it to Black. He reached down and had just taken it before an older boy smacked her head and sent her scampering away.

Black poked the flower's stem through the nylon webbing on his body armor. Danny and Caine had been right. The people were striking. He saw red hair and fair skin mingled among the more traditional Afghan types.

They seemed . . . healthy. Hearty. He was used to Afghans who looked like they could use a good meal. They shook your hand like a wisp of willow. There was no doubt these Valley people were deeply impoverished by Western, or even Afghan, standards. But the hard mountain living had done something to them. They held an intense energy within themselves, even when still.

The patrol was nearing the slopes. The houses spread out ahead of them around a patchy clearing of grass and dry dirt.

Black figured this for the center of town that Brydon and Corelli had spoken about. At the far end of it, nestled against the hill, sat what was obviously the chief's house.

It was nothing impressive except by the standards of the town. It had two floors and its walls were smooth, neither stone nor stucco, with heavy woodwork including a wooden balcony on the second story. It too had no fence, and as they entered the clearing Black saw a middle-aged man in a gray robe standing before it. He turned to Danny and raised his eyebrows: *Him?*

Danny shook his head.

Merrick had come to a stop in the middle of the clearing. Soldiers spread out briskly to take up security positions at regular intervals around the fringes. Townspeople here and there cast glances over their shoulders, curious what was going on.

Merrick motioned Caine to him. Black and Danny hung back.

Black could hear little of what was said between them except Merrick saying, "You." Caine turned and waved Black and Danny forward.

They strode across the grass and dirt to where the two sergeants waited.

"Okay, Lieutenant," said Merrick irritably. "We're here."

He gestured about himself as though at a total loss.

"What are your orders?"

It was a war-movie line. No one said *What are your orders?* in the actual Army, unless they were sending the message that Merrick was now obviously sending: *You wanna come here and play investigator? Fine. This whole thing is yours, SIR. Anything that goes wrong is on you.*

Black ignored the provocation.

"You know why we're here," he answered, letting his weariness with the sharp-elbowed sergeant creep into his voice.

"One half hour," Merrick said tersely. "One minute more and you can walk back by yourself."

Black was considering what to say in reply to this when Caine stepped forward and put a hand on his shoulder.

"All right, then, sir," he said, gently turning Black away from Merrick. "I'm sure we'll have plenty of time."

"No, you won't," Merrick said sharply. "Half an hour, Caine."

Caine turned and gave Merrick a look as he ushered Black around the tall sergeant and toward the house.

"Don't worry about it, L.T.," he said as they crossed the clearing away from Merrick.

He stepped into the lead, letting Black and Danny follow him.

The man waiting in front of the chief's house stood rock still and watched them as they approached. His robe was plain, but the flattened little hat was roped in ornate blues and silvers. His face was sun-lined and his short beard showed touches of gray, though Black figured him for early forties, tops. Black slung his rifle over his back and removed his gloves, stuffing them in a pocket.

Caine stepped up to the man and placed a hand over his heart.

"Salaam alaykum."

The man returned the greeting with a blank face and leaned forward for a perfunctory embrace. He looked over Caine's shoulder at Black as he did so. Danny stepped forward next and repeated the ritual, adding a few words in Pashto. Along with Dari, it was the closest thing there was to a *lingua franca* in the province, whose remote valleys hosted five Nuristani languages in many subdialects.

The man shook his head as he responded and waved a hand as though to say *No, no, not a bother.* His face looked like it most certainly was a bother.

Black guessed that Danny was apologizing for asking to meet the chief on such short notice. Probably the first word the chief had gotten was from the boy Danny sent scurrying up the hill.

Danny turned and indicated Black, speaking again to the man in Pashto. The man nodded curtly.

"Salaam."

He turned without another word and walked up a little stone path to the chief's house. They followed.

"Chief's brother," Danny whispered to Black. "Cranky."

The man strode to the door and pulled it open, shouting two words into the threshold. He stood to the side and held it open, frowning. He raised his chin and looked into the distance as they passed.

Caine went first, then Danny, then Black. He was immediately impressed.

The place was deceptively spacious and unexpectedly well appointed. Smooth tan walls rose from a dark tile floor to a lofted second story, leaving a high ceiling over the great room in which they stood. Natural light spilled down from an opening in the second-floor roof. Music filled the room from somewhere—a scratchy monophonic recording of a woman singing joyously in yet another language Black did not recognize.

On the floor before them lay a broad rug in a roughly Persian design. Dark tapestries hung on the walls. A squat, expertly crafted table in pitch-dark wood sat in the middle of the rug. Around it at leisurely intervals were arranged several high-backed chairs in the same wood, with seats of leather cross-strapping. In the tallest of these, facing the doorway, sat the chief. He rose as they entered and spread his hands wide.

He was tall, nearly as tall as Merrick, and impressively built. Beneath his light tan robes stood a man of obvious prowess. He was strapping and vital where his brother seemed clenched and mild, and despite his gray whiskers he looked as though he could jog to the nearest mountaintop on a whim. His eyes shone silver over bladed, wax-brown cheekbones as he extended ropy arms out before him, beaming toothily as though these foreign intruders were his dearest friends.

"Sergeant," he said in deeply accented English, stepping forward to Caine and drawing him into an embrace.

He turned to Danny next and greeted him in Pashto, squeezing him around the middle like a tube of toothpaste. Stepping back, he looked expectantly past the two of them at Black.

Danny spoke a couple of sentences while gesturing toward Black, who heard his name spoken. When he finished, the chief stepped forward.

"Lieutenant," he said in deeply accented English.

"*Salaam,*" Black choked out as he too was crushed in a muscled embrace.

The chief stepped back again and spoke to the three of them, gesturing broadly with his arms as he did so.

"Welcome again, my friends, to my home," Danny translated for him. "And welcome to Lieutenant Black, a new friend through the blessings of God."

Black smiled awkwardly and nodded.

Still looking at Black, the chief inclined his head toward Danny and spoke a couple of sentences, eyes twinkling. Danny chuckled and turned to Black.

"He says the last officer who comes visit him is a captain, and he hopes he has not offended the U.S. Army."

He meant the Civil Affairs guy. Black forced a laugh, which the chief returned.

"Breaking your balls, L.T.," said Caine, grinning.

"I explain," Danny told them, and began speaking to the chief again in Pashto.

The chief's brow furrowed and he asked a question.

"The other lieutenant," Danny said, "he says he has not seen in many days. He asks where he is today? I tell."

Black listened while Danny explained. The chief apparently took great interest in the concept of R&R leave. At the end, he smiled pleasantly and spoke in measured tones, looking at Caine as he did.

Danny registered surprise.

"Um, this is . . ." Danny began, flustered, hands circling.

"This is . . ." He searched for the word. "Nervous?"

He found it.

"Awkward."

"What's up?" Caine asked.

"Um, the chief, he says . . ."

Danny looked at the floor and cleared his throat.

"If you do not mind, Sergeant Caine, he asks if he talks to the lieutenant alone."

Caine's face went blank a moment.

"Uh, yeah," he said, brightening unconvincingly. "Yeah, sure. No problem."

Black looked at Danny, confused. Danny looked at the chief. The chief looked at Black.

16

I like this," said Black to the chief as he sat in the chair.

He motioned with his hand to indicate the music. Danny translated. The chief grinned.

"This is music of my people," Danny relayed. "Very old. Before Islam comes this place."

"Her voice is beautiful."

Black wondered if any American had ever asked the chief about his music. The chief smiled and nodded. He said something to Danny, who nodded and chuckled something in reply.

"He says the young officer has good taste," Danny told an expectant Black. "I tell him you are scholar. Man of history."

A thought struck the chief. He waved Black back out of his seat—*come, come*—and led him around the chairs to a far corner of the room, near a bright window. He gestured proudly to a wooden cabinet in the corner, chest high with a drawer at the bottom, a fabric opening overlaid with wooden scrollwork in the middle front, and an open lid on top. As he approached, Black realized it was a large and clearly very old record player.

It was gorgeous. Rose-stained woodwork with careful piping carved along the rim. A removable crank protruding from a metal notch in the side. A real mechanical phonograph. The amplification horn must have been hidden in the cabinet beneath the turntable. The woman's voice rang out strong and full from behind the fabric opening.

He bent and inspected the metal badge screwed behind the turntable. EDISON, it read. MODEL C200. Black guessed 1920s. What it was doing far up this Nuristani valley in a house on a mountainside he could only guess.

He realized that he had his nose practically to the side of the player. He straightened, embarrassed.

"This is a beautiful piece of equipment," he said to Danny. "Can you ask him where he got it?"

Danny did so. It was obviously what the chief had been waiting for. He beamed, hands on his hips, and spoke a single word.

Even Danny seemed surprised.

"Russians," he said in wonder.

When the Soviets invaded and occupied Afghanistan in the 1970s, the chief explained, his valley and those all around it were the site of a great deal of heavy fighting. Nuristan, he said, had been the first province to mount a successful revolt against the communists and expel them.

"From this fire," Danny translated, "all Afghanistan catch the fire. All Afghan people see people of Nuristan defeat the Russian army. All Afghan people fight Russians."

The chief spoke directly to Black next, his eyes shining.

"All times in history, all peoples love Nuristan land and Nuristan beauty. All peoples want have Nuristan for his own land. Alexander and Greek man, British man, Russian man. All man try."

His gaze bore into Black.

"All man fail."

Black shifted uncomfortably.

"Now Taliban man," the chief went on, through Danny. "He will try. He will fail. Valley belongs only to God. And we keep for him."

Black nodded. The chief brightened.

"The officer forgets his question," came the translation. "Where I get this player? I get this from Russian *big* general."

Black's eyebrows went up in surprise, which the chief clearly loved seeing.

"Fancy H.Q.," he went on. "Far down valley. Food, alcohol, music."

With a sweeping arm he cast all these aside like toys. Then he shrugged.

"I steal in night," he told them matter-of-factly, "and burn H.Q.! I carry player all way to my home, on my back, like a donkey."

The chief laughed heartily at his own exploits. Black and Danny joined in.

"But do not tell Talibs about the record player," he admonished them, flashing mock concern. "Music make them very mad!"

More laughs as he gestured them graciously to their chairs. Black took one of those arrayed before the chief's chair.

Danny sat opposite him, looking uneasy. The chief approached and sat, clapping his hands twice as he did so.

From a rear room appeared a boy of ten or twelve bearing a silver tray. On it were three silver cups filled with something amber. Tea, Black presumed.

The boy, who wore a simple black tunic, offered the tray to the chief first, who directed him to Black. The boy turned his dark eyes to Black and watched his face silently as he took a cup. Black thanked him in Pashto. The boy said nothing and turned away.

Danny was next, followed by the chief. Black sipped at his tea, which was scalding. The boy disappeared without a word.

"My friends," began the chief, through Danny, "I thank you for coming to my home, and I hope I can help you with any problem that you have."

Black looked instinctively at Danny, who had been looking uncomfortable the entire time since Caine had left. He reminded himself that it is bad form to talk to your translator when really you are talking to the other person.

He turned to the chief and cleared his throat.

"*Sardar,*" he began, doing his best to recall from his phrasebook how to address an elder. "Thank you for graciously taking the time to see me in your home. And I apologize for coming to you this morning with so little, uh, notice in advance."

He waited while Danny translated. The chief smiled and nodded tolerantly.

"I hope," Black continued, "that we also can help you with any problem that you might have, whether it is a big problem or a small one."

He realized that he was sweating. The chief was still smiling and nodding. Black sipped his tea and set it down. He cleared his throat.

"And I hope that you will accept this small . . . token of my appreciation for your time today."

His hand was already in the first-aid pouch on his body armor, from which he'd removed the aid kit before leaving on the patrol that morning. In a smooth motion he pulled Smoke Toma's brick of heroin from it and placed it in the center of the tea table before them.

Danny's eyes widened.

Black sat back calmly in his chair. Toma, Black now understood, had been a hundred percent right. The chief clearly found him pleasant enough as far as Americans go, and obviously enjoyed holding court with easily impressed young officers.

But he just as clearly didn't take Black seriously as someone who could help him in any real way with his complaints. The chief surely recognized that if the Army had cared, they wouldn't have sent someone of even lower rank than the captain whom the chief had complained to in the first place. In the chief's eyes, by sending Black they were more or less telling him to go shove his problems. He had politely said as much to Black himself.

The chief wanted to do business, get relief for his frustrated people. Now he would know that he could do business with this young lieutenant after all.

Danny had gone rock-still and pale as a ghost. He tried to stammer something, but it couldn't quite form itself into words.

The chief's gaze too was fixed on the brick, sitting there in the middle of the table between them like a baby elephant. The big man moved slowly from his chair, rising wordlessly to his full height and turning his gaze down on Black.

Goddamn fuck was the sole thought on Sergeant Caine's mind as he stood in the middle of the clearing, scanning the hills and fidgeting. *Fuck fuckity fuck.*

He heard the chief's door clatter shut.

That was fast.

He turned. Danny had emerged, with Lieutenant Black behind him.

Caine was momentarily impressed that Black had been able to finish his business with the chief so quickly. That thought fled when he saw how fast the two were moving.

"Yo, Merrick!" he called over his shoulder, keeping his eyes on the lieutenant and the 'terp hurrying toward him. Both looked pale.

Black pulled up to Caine, with Danny close on his heels.

"We've gotta go," he said.

"What?" asked Caine.

"We have to go *now,*" Black answered, agitated.

Merrick had come jogging up the clearing.

"What are you talking about?" he cut in. "What happened?"

"We'll talk about it back at the COP. We have to go!"

"Bullshit," Merrick shot back. "What the fuck did you do?"

Merrick turned to Danny and began to demand an explanation but stopped when he saw the linguist's ashen face. Danny nodded urgently.

"Fast, Sergeant," he said.

Merrick and Caine looked at one another. Something unreadable passed between them. Merrick hesitated no more.

He turned on a heel and raised a hand in a rallying sign. He moved briskly downhill, head curled down as he spoke into the radio handset that was affixed to his body armor below his collarbone.

Caine wheeled around and whistled to get the attention of those who hadn't seen the signal.

"Go with him," he said tersely to Black, pointing at Merrick.

Danny and Black fell in behind Merrick while Caine lingered behind to roust everyone into action and make sure no one missed the word. Soldiers on the perimeter looked around themselves, confused, then scrambled to their feet as they saw what was happening. The patrol congealed, forming itself up again into a long, staggered line and falling in on Merrick, who had deliberately slowed his pace to something almost nonchalant.

They moved slowly through the middle of town. Heads swiveled right and left and craned upward to the mountainsides. Black could hear soldiers asking one another tensely what the fuck was going on? The plodding pace was unbearable.

They passed the houses on the lower slopes. Women and children watched them go wordlessly.

The lead soldiers reached the riverside and cut left through the grass and shade trees, back the way they'd come. Merrick, still ambling along, hung back at the bottom of the slope. He waited until the rest of the soldiers, one by one, had passed him.

The instant the last man had reached the flats and was out of sight of the town, he broke into a run. He didn't stop.

The rest of the confused patrol followed suit. It was more of a jog, really, but with the amount of gear, ammunition, and weaponry everyone was carrying, it was no joke.

They ran all the way along the riverside to the slope leading up to the promontory. Sergeants hassled and harangued panting soldiers as the patrol scrabbled up the pebble-strewn ground. In the woods at the top, they commenced running again, tripping through the trees to the dirt track.

The sniper team was there, waiting, eyeballs starkly white against green-smeared faces. Merrick peeled off to meet them. After a few hurried words of instruction they turned without a word and began scrambling up the mountainside, straight up from the track. Merrick and the rest of the group continued on around the bend, back toward Vega the way they'd come.

They had made little noise moving steadily down through the hills to the village. Now the patrol was a huffing, shambling clatter of equipment slugging up the track below the funny stone building.

Guys by that point were truly sucking. Those carrying machine guns or other heavy weapons suffered the worst. Boots scuffed the ground; rifles hung downward from dangling limbs. More than one vomited. They were too fatigued even to peel off to the side of the road to do it.

Caine, who alone among them all seemed to take the physical challenge in stride, stayed at the rear to ensure no one fell behind. *Get up the goddamn hill! Get up it!* he screamed at them, issuing a series of encouragements and threats as he deemed necessary. These ranged from conjuring graphic images of the various sexual liberties and favors the soldier in question would have earned from his wife or girlfriend if he made it to the top of the hill to a simple promise to shoot the guy's balls off if he didn't pick up the pace. How Caine kept this up while hauling himself and his gear uphill Black was not sure.

Black himself suffered as much as anyone. He had kept himself in shape, but Vega sat multiple thousands of feet higher than FOB Omaha, and he had not spent the past several months moving through the high mountains carrying loads of fighting gear. He wasn't remotely acclimated.

As he stumbled upward, lungs burning and boot toes stubbing the dirt trail, his thoughts escaped. Circled back to a night at Fort Benning, at OCS. Their final land navigation test. Three hours to find three of five points, out there in the night somewhere. It was "go" or "no-go." Fail the test, fail the school.

Ninety minutes in, near the far western edge of the sprawling course, he found his friend. The smartass, crouched over a rumpled, waterlogged map with his red-lens flashlight. He was sucking.

He had no points. Drew a bad set, scattered far and wide and virtually impossible in the wet February conditions on the course. The only point he'd gotten close to had been underwater.

Black had found only one of his points. They were both gonna get a no-go.

They looked at each other and said: Not gonna happen. They replotted their points and ran. They ran both sets together.

At nineteen minutes to spare, his friend was still short one. They roamed a valley bottom in circles, running out of time. Over a mile of thickly wooded mountainous terrain lay between them and the finish line.

Go, his friend told him. *Get home in time.*

No way, Black replied, and as he turned to argue he saw the signpost, the point, over his friend's shoulder not ten feet away. They punched his paper and they ran.

Ran like madmen, barreling through the pitch-black forest, tripping over roots, bumping into trees, and falling into streams. His friend wore the Army's famously ugly "birth control glasses," and they were so smeared with fog and sweat that he stuffed them in a pocket and ran without them. At one point they climbed over a series of felled logs, one after another, before switching their flashlights on and finding themselves in the middle of a vast clearing filled end-to-end with cut trees. They had to backtrack and go around. They drove on without hope.

They burst from the forest, drenched and muddy, onto a paved road two hundred meters from the finish. They stagger-sprinted the final distance, Black's friend panting at him to keep going while one of the instructors creeped along beside them in a pickup truck, taunting them through a bullhorn that they weren't going to make it.

They made it, with just over a minute to spare. Fellow trainees gawked at the picture of them crossing the line, covered head to toe in mud and secrets. No one asked them what happened. Most of them had their own secrets.

The instructors would have called it cheating. Black and his friend called it taking care of your buddy. Black had considered it one of the most unlikely coincidences of his life, to find his friend that night, out of a hundred other trainees, in the vastness of the dark course, and decided it must have been fate. What happens on the night course stays on the night course.

They never talked about it with each other afterward. Soon after they graduated, Black's friend was tapped by the intelligence community for unspecified and increasingly spooky work which had left Black knowing little of his whereabouts and dependent mostly on the occasional and unpredictable e-mail like the one he'd gotten before leaving FOB Omaha.

But on that night, they had been equal, and equally raw. It was the other occasion Black could remember, when he felt he'd seen his friend as he really was, behind the puckish mask.

This run, Black decided as he hauled himself upward from Darreh Sin, was worse than that night on the course. Worse than any other exorbitant physical punishment dreamed up by the instructors at Fort Benning.

But not the worst one you've done.

It was all he could do not to fall back into the range of Caine's taunts and torments. He refused to do that.

Danny, who was not conditioned as a soldier, struggled mightily. He wheezed and huffed alongside Black, saved only by his slight frame and the fact that he carried no weapons or gear beyond a helmet and stripped-down body armor vest.

After an eternity on the track they began clawing their way up the steep final slopes, tripping along the high trail. More than one guy slipped on its surface and slid down several feet, having to haul himself back up to rejoin the group.

At last the gate to the courtyard came into view up ahead. The lead soldiers were staggering through it.

Merrick and another sergeant stood on either side of the gate, panting and counting as guys came through. His eyes burned into Black as he and Danny stumbled past.

"Eighteen, nineteenDon'tFuckingGoAnywhereLieutenant, twenty . . ."

Inside, soldiers had scattered across to the overhangs around the perimeter, tearing open body armor and gulping for breath. Helmets clattered to the tiled breezeway floor as guys walked in circles, red-faced with hands on hips, or tried to make their trembling hands twist canteens open. Others' legs buckled beneath them and they went to their knees, palms on concrete, heads hanging.

Black made for the nearest overhang, pulling the Velcro open on his vest. Danny, coughing and dry heaving, followed him to the breezeway but didn't stop. Black watched him disappear around a corner, bent at the waist and making horrible gurgling noises.

He turned and saw the last of the soldiers come through the gate, followed by Caine giving a sweaty thumbs-up as he passed Merrick. That would be everyone except the sniper team. Merrick had sent them along the high ridges to provide cover. They would take more time to get home.

The courtyard perimeter was now filled with confused and gasping soldiers, cursing through wheezing breaths and asking one another what was going on. Caine wove his way among them toward Black.

"What the fuck happened?" he demanded. "Where the fuck is Danny?"

"Barfing."

The effort of saying it nearly made Black do it.

Merrick was right behind Caine, sweating profusely and walking fast.

"Clean up this clusterfuck!" he spat in Caine's direction, sweeping his hand across the smatter of indisposed soldiers and hastily off-loaded gear littering the courtyard.

He pointed at Black without slowing.

"Come," he said flatly, stalking past him.

Merrick led the way off the breezeway through a narrow channel formed by blast barriers, then under overhead cover to a doorway. He kicked it open and stomped inside, leaving the door to clatter in Black's face as he stumbled through on fluttering legs.

They were in someone's hootch. Probably one of Merrick's junior sergeants. He wheeled on Black, who was bent at the waist and gasping for breath.

"All right, sir," he said, still winded himself and looking down at the sorry-looking Black like a furious parent demanding answers from a naughty child. "We're back at the COP. What the fuck was that shitshow?"

In the dim of the hootch a shower of bright twinkles washed across Black's vision and he felt the floor tilt dizzily. He ordered himself not to be sick to his stomach in front of Merrick.

"No," he panted.

"What?"

Black pushed through the cramps clenching his abdomen and forced himself upright. Sweat stung his eyes as he stood to his full height and looked up at the sergeant.

"I am not telling you anyth—"

It was at that moment that the first of the mortar rounds crashed to earth on the grounds of COP Vega, filling the hootch with deafening sound and sending everything in it flying off shelves and tables. The sound of automatic weapons fire followed immediately.

"Get back to your hootch!" Merrick shouted at him, wheeling out the door toward the courtyard.

Black followed.

The courtyard was the expected tumult, shouting soldiers scooping up helmets and weapons and stamping off toward the myriad doorways and passageways leading to the various parts of the outpost. Merrick stood in the open courtyard, shouting into a radio about the sniper team that was still outside the wire.

As Black ran down the breezeway another mortar round impacted just outside the gate, heaving earth over the wall into the courtyard and momentarily deafening everyone still in the open. He saw Merrick rise from a protective crouch and stalk toward one of the exits leading back into the innards of the COP.

Black found the right passage and barreled into it. He pounded up steps and around corners, weaving his way through the outpost as explosions shook the walls and the ground beneath him shuddered. Soldiers stomped past in every direction and ignored him. He lost his way and turned around, then lost it again. The place was a maze.

As he circled and circled again amidst the crashing chaos, he heard only the words of the chief of Darreh Sin, over and over, as he had towered over Black and Danny.

You sneak into my valley like a snake at midnight, he had said, slowly, seething.

And you unleash the Devil, and his work.

He was brandishing the brick of heroin in a gnarled, muscled hand. His voice was louder now, his face red.

And you bring his . . . his servant into my town.

Danny kept translating, involuntarily, eyes wide, hands clutching the arms of his chair, as the chief's voice rose to a shout.

I SHOULD KILL YOU ALL NOW!

The brick squashed through the middle in his grasp, but Black and Danny were already out of their upturned chairs and stumbling for the door. There was no more translation as the chief hollered further horrors at them. The brick in its pieces had struck the wall next to the doorway as Black blundered through after Danny, and as the door clattered shut behind him he'd heard one of the chairs shatter against the wall.

The bombardment of Vega continued for fourteen hours, deep into the night.

"Doing some rule-breaking again, there, sir?"

He offered the pack of smokes. They took. He checked his watch, which read 0212. He'd taken four minutes to get from his room to the roof.

It was quiet again. The sky was crystal-clear black and shining with stars. There was no fog in the Valley tonight.

Everyone lit up.

"How's your investigation going, sir?" asked the first soldier.

Black shrugged noncommittally.

"No one wants to talk."

"Huh," the soldier said.

He inhaled and doused the butt of the machine gun in smoke.

"That's weird, sir."

"How come?"

"Well, I mean, just talking to you, you just sort of seem like the kind of person dudes would normally trust to talk to, sir."

"Oh."

The soldier took another long one.

"Like the kind of person dudes would wanna confess all their sins to."

A breeze blew through the window. Black noticed for the first time that without the fog to blanket the sound, he could just hear the river way down below. It must have been moving pretty good in that stretch.

He didn't like the sound. Didn't like the feeling of it being so close to where he slept.

They smoked for a while in silence.

"You're lost in thought, L.T."

He startled. The first soldier was looking at him.

Black cleared his throat.

Don't push it.

"Was just thinking about what it must've been like."

"What what must've been like, sir?"

"When you first came," Black said idly. "I heard it was like this when you guys first took this place."

"Like what?" asked the soldier. "Clear?"

"No. Quiet. Like they just abandoned it and you guys just took it over and set up shop."

The soldier's brow furrowed.

"Who told you that, sir?"

Black hesitated.

"Nobody. Dude back at the FOB."

"Yeah, well, that dude's fucked, sir."

The soldier sent a ribbon of smoke out the side of his mouth. "It most definitely was not abandoned."

"What happened?"

"When the first squad came up here, that fucking chief was waiting for them with his boys and they were locked and loaded. Knock-down drag-out. But they killed his ass. They took the house and held it for, like, two weeks until they brought assets up here and built this place."

Black nodded.

Maybe not.

He smoked for a minute before noticing something in what the soldier had said.

"Chief?" he asked.

"Yeah," said the soldier. "The drug chief guy."

"I thought it was the new Taliban governor or whoever up here."

"No, it was the fucking local drug lord guy. Kingpin and shit."

"You sure?"

"What I'm sayin', sir."

"Huh," Black said noncommittally.

"That's why he fought so hard," the soldier said. "All the fricken' dope he had up here."

"Heroin?"

"Hells yeah, sir. Like, thirty bricks in the house. A Taliban woulda burned that shit in a heartbeat."

"What'd you guys do with it?"

"Burned it!" the soldier exclaimed, laughing. "Ironic, right, sir? Allies with the Taliban."

"Right."

"Like we said. Welcome to the Valley, sir."

Black smiled.

"You guys were both here then?"

"No way," said the soldier. "There's hardly anybody from those dudes left here. Me and Bosch've been here, what, seven months? That all's just how we heard it."

"Heard it from who?"

"Sergeant Merrick."

Black took a pull on the cigarette and sent a cloud out the window. He stared out the window a full minute before speaking.

"What," he asked the joes, "do you guys think of Sergeant Merrick?"

Bosch spoke up for the first time.

"What the fuck do you mean by that, sir?"

Black finished his smoke and left, out across the planks to the stairwell. He paused, just below the roofline, listening. Then he continued on down, past Oswalt's wall hootch. It was pitch-dark inside.

"Evening, sir," came the voice from behind the curtain.

Black jumped and nearly tripped on the stairs.

"Evening, Oswalt."

"Watch your step, sir."

"Roger that," Black said over his shoulder and kept walking.

He had been careful going up, and now he was careful going down. He did not want to encounter anyone.

He had sat alone in Lieutenant Pistone's room for fourteen hours, through the periodic thump of mortar and rocket fire and the constant hail of bullets, coming in and going out. He was smart enough to know not to go running around the outpost trying to help. To know that as long as their attackers, whoever they were, were firing on the place from up in the hillsides and not actually breaching the compound on foot, he needed to stay out of the way and let the soldiers and their sergeants do their jobs.

He did not want to see the wounded, or hear their screams. One had been carried down the hall past his closed door, which was plenty for him.

He had needed to think.

Now he wanted to get back there. Because he knew now that he wasn't going to be making his paperwork and going home. Knew now that he was an idiot. Knew that he knew nothing except that nothing was going to go right for the next five days.

He stopped at the Porta-Closet near his hootch. By now he had read every entry in the scrawled field of graffiti.

Except he hadn't. He was about to turn and leave when one caught his eye. It was way down at the bottom, below the others, on one of the few bare patches of wall remaining.

He bent to see more clearly. It was only two words. It was definitely new since before he had left on the patrol to Darreh Sin.

CHUCK
SEES

This time in the dream it was him looking out the window, at himself, clawing up at the ground to get to himself, and failing. A gentle hand came to rest on his shoulder. He shrugged it off as he pawed at the window frame, trying to climb through.

Lying on Mother's roof, Tajumal was confused. Much of this made little sense.

But one thing was clear. It had been the right call, not following the bearded one as he left the American compound before dawn that morning.

I was tempted, Father.

But what could be learned that was not already known? That the man was an American warrior who roamed the valleys trying to turn the peoples against one another, to sow discord and doubt? That was nothing new.

That he came and went from the American compound like a jackal in the night? That he stowed away gear and radios in strange places? No one knew these things but Tajumal.

And I will see to that.

No, the wiser course had been to wait and see what else emerged from the Americans' base. To rush straight to town afterward, to be waiting for the chief when he woke. To tell him that the real prize approaches.

The chief was a boisterous weakling, unwilling to lead his people to the true faith, to the true guardians of the valley.

Even Qadir, who sucks up to him, can see that. Even Qadir knows where to keep his true loyalties.

It was no surprise that the chief did nothing, that he let the prey escape.

Yet now he attacks the Americans at their fortress afterward, all day and all night. There was no reason in this. But there was, at least, an explanation.

You wish it to be me who is your vessel, Father. My fragile form to do your work.

Tajumal was to take the prize. The true devil.

And now I have seen you.

PART THREE

17

Heavy pounding on the door startled him awake.

He sat up in the pitch-dark and pushed the light on his watch. 0812. He'd slept for several hours.

Pounding again. The door rattled against the hasp, slim shafts of light flashing in from the hallway. He stared at it a few moments, reminding himself that he was prepared for this.

His bare feet found the pair of flip-flops on the concrete floor and slid themselves in. He rose from bed in his PT uniform and crossed the black room as the pounding continued. He found the latch with his fingers and cracked the door, which pushed itself the rest of the way open forcefully.

"Where is he?!"

Caine. Shouting.

Black squinted at him, bleary.

"What?"

"What did you do to him!?" Caine cried, agitated.

This was not the person or the question Black was expecting.

"What?" he repeated dumbly.

"Danny!"

Black shook his head to clear it.

"What are you talking about?"

"Where the fuck is Danny?"

"What are you talking about?" he repeated.

"Danny the fucking 'terp! Where is he?"

"You can't find him?"

"No, we can't fucking find him! *Where is he?*"

None of this made sense to Black.

"How would I know? Where'd you see him last?"

"With you!"

"He hasn't been with me—" he began, then realized what Caine was talking about.

"You mean when we came back from the patrol?" he asked.

"Yeah, when we came back from the patrol!" shouted Caine.

"That was almost twenty-four hours ago!"

"No shit, sir!"

Black wheeled around and crossed to his sneakers, which were sitting, laced, near his ruck on the floor. He grabbed them and began yanking them on over his bare feet, standing on one leg in an inverted trapezoid of light from the hallway.

"What are you doing?"

"I need to see Sergeant Merrick," Black declared as he jerked the second shoe on. "Where is he?"

"Sir, he's gonna ask you the same quest—"

"Excuse me," Black said, pushing past him. He let the door swing shut behind him and stalked off down the hallway, leaving Caine at his doorway calling after him.

He accosted the first soldier he saw and demanded to know where Merrick was. The kid directed him to the chow hall. Black stalked past, weaving his way right and left through the slapdash compound, reeling.

Merrick saw Black as he pushed through the door to the chow hall.

"Where's Danny?" he demanded.

"What do you mean Danny's gone?" Black demanded simultaneously.

"What?" they both replied at once.

"Where. Is. Danny?" Merrick repeated.

He stood amidst a gaggle of soldiers, where he'd been giving his morning instructions again.

"I don't know where he is!" Black shot back. "Is it true that no one's seen him since we came back from the patrol?"

"No one but you, Lieutenant."

"I didn't see him!"

"Actually, sir, you said you saw him off barfing someplace, so if you'd tell us where that is we'd really appreciate it."

"I didn't see where he went! How can you not have accountability of him?"

An audible sucking in of breath from among the soldiers.

"*Excuse* me?" Merrick said sharply.

"Have you checked the entire outpost?"

"Have I *checked the entire outpost?*"

"Yeah!"

Merrick looked at Black like this was the most outrageous question he'd ever been asked.

"Yes, *sir,*" he replied contemptuously. "While you were asleep in your rack I did in fact *check my entire outpost.*"

A couple of the soldiers hazarded snorky little giggles. Black persisted.

"Did you search his room?"

"I don't root through a man's things, sir," Merrick said disdainfully. "I opened his room. He's not in there."

"Well, how did he get out?"

Merrick gave the soldiers a *Can you believe this guy?* look.

"He disapparated like Harry fucking Potter!"

More snorks.

"There's no force field, sir," Merrick went on, exasperated. "If he wanted to leave he could've gone over a wall without anyone seeing him."

Black didn't like the sound of that.

"Why would he want to leave?"

Merrick looked at him pointedly.

"You tell me, sir."

Black ignored this. He kept thinking of Danny alone in the mountains.

"Have you reported him missing?" he asked Merrick.

He felt foolish as soon as he'd said it.

"Have I reported—"

Merrick turned bright red. Soldiers shifted uncomfortably.

"Yes, *Lieutenant,* I have reported to my chain of command that my

Department of Defense *civilian contractor linguist* has gone *missing in Afghanistan!*"

No one chuckled that time.

"And I am sure, *sir,*" Merrick went on, "that they will be interested in talking to you in the course of their *own* investigation into what happened to him."

Black's thoughts raced. Something occurred to him.

"What if he got grabbed?"

"If he got what?"

"Grabbed. Sergeant Caine said guys have made it onto the COP before in U.S. uniforms."

That one gave Merrick pause. Things had been chaotic for many hours, including deep into the darkness. Danny had last been seen close to the gate, and no one knew where he had been after that.

Merrick's theatrical façade of contempt seemed to fall away a bit, for just a moment.

"Unlikely but not impossible," he conceded tersely.

"So who would want to come onto the COP and grab him?"

Up went the façade again.

"Once again, sir," he said pointedly, "you tell me."

Everyone looked at Black in silence.

Stop dodging.

He cleared his throat.

"Give us the room," he said to the empty air, suddenly aware of how difficult it is to appear authoritative while wearing shorts and a T-shirt with sockless sneakers.

A couple of the younger soldiers started haltingly for the door. The rest looked to their platoon sergeant, who was still looking at Black.

"Go," Merrick said.

They scampered out.

Merrick watched them go. When the door closed behind them he turned back to Black.

"No more bullshit, sir," he said. "Let's have it."

Black swallowed.

"No."

"What?"

"I'm not divulging confidential communications from my investigation."

"What?"

"You need to tell me what's going on."

"What are you talking about?"

"You need to tell me," Black repeated quietly, "what's going on."

Merrick's brow furrowed in confusion.

"Uh, what's going on, sir, is that the soldiers are gone now, so you can tell me what happened with you and Danny in Darreh Sin, so maybe I can figure out why he left my outpost and where the hell he is."

"That's not what I'm talking about."

Merrick looked at him like he was a crazy person.

"Okayyyy," he said, losing patience. "Then what *are* you talking about, sir?"

"Sergeant . . ." Black said, shaking his head.

"Sir," Merrick shot back, mimicking his tone.

"I'm talking about the Valley."

"The Valley."

"You need to tell me what's going on with your platoon and this valley."

"My platoon and this valley," Merrick repeated blankly.

"Yes."

"*I* need to tell you."

"Yes."

Merrick stared at him in silence. Black stared back, waiting.

Finally Merrick stepped around him and went to the door. There was a hasp on the interior of it so that the door could be locked from within. He flipped the hasp around shut and turned the eyebolt so no soldier wandering by could get in.

He turned around and strode back to Black, his mouth pinched in rising anger.

"All, right, sir," he said. "I'm going to tell you the situation with the Valley. Are you ready?"

"I'm ready."

"*You* are the situation in the Valley, sir."

Black said nothing.

"You are here and you're in over your head."

"Sergeant . . ."

"And you are *fucking* up!" Merrick spat. "You have been at my outpost less than seventy-two hours. You have disrupted my operations and placed my entire platoon in danger. You have directly caused four casualties, including two on my sniper team, which nearly didn't make it home."

"Sergeant . . ."

"And you are *lucky,*" Merrick drove on, "that those injuries were minor, which is a goddamned miracle, and you are *lucky* that I have not confined you to Lieutenant Pistone's quarters under *guard* for the duration of your stay here to keep you from getting any of my soldiers killed."

"None of that is—"

"Now," Merrick said, cutting him off, "you've obviously got some idea in your head that you're on to some kind of deep mystery here, because you are talking a bunch of cryptic talk about this valley and how 'something's going on.'"

He spoke quickly, eyes flashing contempt.

"I don't *know* what you are talking about, sir, and honestly I don't *care,* because you are a lieutenant, and lieutenants always think that they know something that the rest of the world doesn't know and needs their help to figure out."

Black took a breath to respond but Merrick kept talking.

"Now you can tell me what that big idea in your head is, or don't tell me. Like I said, I don't care, because I don't pretend to know what goes on in officers' heads. What I *do* care about, and what I *will* do, is fulfill my responsibilities."

He let that hang in the air a moment.

"So now it's time for *you* to listen to *me,* sir. Are you listening?"

"I am listening."

Merrick stepped in very close to Black.

"This is what's going to happen," he said, in clipped, barely restrained tones. "You are going to stop playing whatever games you are playing and recognize exactly the situation you are in, which is that you are an inexperienced junior officer operating outside your level of tactical competence and endangering the lives of soldiers. *Your* only responsibility *as* an officer now is to give me all the information I need to *un*fuck what you have *fucked* up. So now, *sir,* it's time to open your mouth, and there's not going to be any dicking around, and you are going to tell me *exactly* why that shitshow happened back there so I can figure out how to *fix* it."

Merrick waited, seething. Black swallowed again. He didn't break away from Merrick's gaze.

"You're bluffing," he said.

"What?"

"You're trying to change the subject and scare me off."

Merrick's eyes went wide.

"I'm doing *what?!*"

"This isn't about what happened in the town and you know it," Black said.

Merrick appeared to be speechless.

"That's a 'friendly' town?" Black went on, gathering momentum. "How come there were no males between fifteen and fifty? Why were the children looking at us like we were the bogeyman?"

"Now, that's not—"

"That's not a normal town," Black said, feeling his face flush. "And it's not because of a goat. Don't tell me this is about some damned goat!"

"It's *not* about a goat!" Merrick shot back, finding his voice. "It's about whatever you did to get us bombed for half the night!"

"Bullshit!" Black heard himself shout in the sergeant's face. "This isn't on me!"

Yes it is.

"Something happened in that town," Black said angrily, "or happened in this valley, and *you* know what it is! *You* sent me and Danny in there! *You* had the obligation to tell *me* what I needed to know, so don't talk about *my* responsibilities!"

"Nothing happened in that town except you!"

"Stop bullshitting me!"

"No one's bullshitting you! You're making stuff up to cover your ass for fucking up!"

He's right. Tell him.

Black took a step backward from the sergeant.

"This," he said, finding himself suddenly calm, "is all on you."

No it's not.

Merrick lost it.

"FUCK you, Lieutenant!" he hurled at Black, red-faced and shaking. "You tell me what you did!"

He was more or less screaming now.

"You're going to *tell* me what you did, and then you're going to go back to your quarters and sit there and you're not going to do one more FUCKING THING until you leave MY FUCKING OUTPOST!"

"Why," Black asked in a quiet voice, "are you directing soldiers to lie to me about how long they've been at COP Vega?"

Merrick stopped short.

"What?"

"Why are you telling soldiers to lie to me about how long they've been here?"

"Why am I *what?!*"

"Just tell me what's happening, Sergeant."

Merrick's enraged mouth hung open, his face inflamed, flabbergasted.

"You're not going to lock me up," Black continued coolly, "because you're a sergeant first class and you know what obstructing an investigation would do to your career."

"Sir," Merrick seethed, "you need to get out of this room *now.*"

"Just tell me before I find out on my own."

Merrick screamed so hard his eyes squinted shut.

"GET OUT!"

Black turned and went.

The door slapped shut behind him. He stomped down the hallway, unsure where he was headed, his mind circling.

Danny. Gone.

What did you do?

Around the corner a metal wastebasket sat against the wall. He kicked it as hard as he could. It spun down the corridor, pinwheeling paper waste.

Tajumal scampered down the rocks and boulders of the steep ridgeline, making an easy silhouette against the dark skyline but not caring. Giddy.

I knew you would lead me to no harm tonight, Father.

This had been another tough choice, whether to follow the blasphemer as he fled the Americans' base during the fighting, or to take the chance and continue as planned. Tajumal had continued as planned.

And you did not let me fail, Father. You carried me in your blessed arms.

It had been a difficult task, as expected. It had almost seemed impossible, the prospect of getting all the way to the mountaintop, and back again, before daylight. Before Mother awoke.

The peoples of the valleys were born climbers. Goat blood in their veins. But this had been the hardest, fastest climb of Tajumal's young life. And there had been no guarantee of success at the mountaintop.

But you always called me clever, Father. And so I am.

It had been simple, really. Almost as simple as dealing with the equipment of the bearded one, the American warrior who scavenged the mountains for the souls of the people.

This was larger, but presented little problem. Unscrew some cables from what was obviously a very large battery package and throw them off the mountainside.

Once again, with no weapons or explosives, Tajumal had accomplished what Qadir and his rifle and his blustering ideas could not do.

And now the most important part rested safely in Tajumal's pocket. A little metal cylinder with points on each end that joined with the ends of the cables, so when they went together they looked like girls' parts fitting together with boys' parts, as ridiculous an idea as that seemed.

That piece was proof.

Now the talibs will know.

The Americans would come and fix their equipment. But that would take time. Enough time for Tajumal.

And soon the officer will know.

18

"Private Corelli."

The voice made Corelli jump, again. He turned to his right and saw Lieutenant Black step from the shadows. The taciturn young officer's face wore the same taut, furrowed expression, almost a slight scowl, that seemed to be a permanent feature even when he wasn't actually scowling.

"Sir!" he exclaimed, snapping to attention.

He'd been on his way from the latrine back to the CP to finish out his shift and go to bed. Black had emerged from between two abandoned lockers that had been placed against the wall in the breezeway. Corelli wondered how long the gloomy lieutenant must have been standing there lurking in the dark waiting for him.

Black waved off his formalities and made no small talk.

"You're the armorer, right?"

"Yes, sir," Corelli answered, moving his feet apart and placing his hands behind the small of his back.

The lieutenant bore into Corelli with his dark, searching eyes and spoke tersely.

"As fifteen-six investigating officer I am lawfully ordering you to support my investigative efforts."

"Sir?" Corelli said hesitantly, not sure what was going on. Had the lieutenant thought he'd been untruthful?

"It means you have to help me and you can't say no."

"Sir, I . . ."

"Well," Black said, without malice, "you can say no, but you'd face charges for refusing a lawful order."

"Sir," Corelli stammered. "No! I mean, of course, yes, I will help you, sir."

"When is your shift over?"

"Twenty-one hundred, sir."

"Where's the armory?"

Corelli told him. The lieutenant seemed to understand his directions. He was finding his way around.

"Meet me there when your shift is done."

"Roger, sir."

The lieutenant turned to go, then stopped and looked at Corelli again with those eyes.

"Don't tell anyone you're meeting me there."

"Yes, sir," said Corelli.

He hadn't been planning to.

The lieutenant turned and strode away into the night. Corelli watched him go, repeating in his head the promise he'd made to himself.

Black found the door to the armory unlocked. Corelli was already in there waiting for him.

It was one of the most basic Army rules: Every weapon of any kind is to be in someone's actual physical possession, or locked away in a secure place, at all times. There were always extras, so every outpost needed a designated armory to store weapons, scopes, and night-vision gear that weren't in use.

They'd picked a good room for the purpose. One of the thicker wooden doors in the place; windowless cement walls lined with lockers and weapons racks.

A folding table sat in the middle with a folding chair on either side of it. A metal desk lamp provided the only illumination. Corelli hadn't turned on the fluorescents, leaving most of the room in shadow. No light, Black had noted, escaped from beneath the door as he approached.

Corelli was in the chair behind the table. He rose when Black entered. Black waved him down, pulled the door shut behind him, and took the other chair for himself.

"Did you tell anyone you were coming here?" he asked Corelli.

"No, sir. Just like you said."

"Did anyone see you come here?"

Corelli looked at him questioningly.

"I don't think so, sir."

"How long have you been the armorer?"

"Just about the whole time I've been here, sir."

"Which is how long?"

"Um, like I said before, just about four months, sir."

"What happened to the last armorer?"

"He got wounded right after I got here, sir, and got shipped out."

"Why did you get made the armorer?"

"Um, Sergeant Merrick said he could tell I was smart, sir. Mostly I don't think anyone else wanted the job."

Both those things were probably true. The armorer was responsible for keeping track of a lot of identical pieces of equipment. He needed a tolerance for paperwork, the patience to do a lot of counting and a lot of reading and writing of names and serial numbers, and the attention to detail to not screw it up.

Mostly he had to be diligent. Corelli struck Black as diligence personified.

"You have records of all weapons assigned to all personnel in this outpost?"

"Yes, sir."

"And you keep records of all sign-outs and turn-ins."

"Yes, sir."

"Are your records accurate?"

"*Yes,* sir," answered Corelli with what sounded like a touch of wounded pride at even being asked such a question.

That was a good sign.

"Okay," said Black, producing a stapled pair of pages. "You are going to help me verify this roster against your records."

"Sir?"

"I want to know every last soldier that is stationed at this outpost and what his job is," Black told him. "Besides you and Brydon and Shannon, obviously."

In the small sheaf of materials that Gayley had provided Black before he left Omaha was a computer printout from 3/44's headquarters. It purported to be a roster of everyone stationed at COP Vega, including arrival dates and the dates people came and went on leave.

Black had no idea how accurate it was, but knowing what he knew about Army units' slipshod recordkeeping habits, and knowing how violent and fluid the situation was in the Valley, he had reasons to be skeptical.

That's where Corelli came in. The armorer kept track of all the weapons, which meant the armorer kept track of all the people.

Corelli nodded.

"Too easy, sir."

It was Black's favorite piece of Army slang. Everyone picked it up at basic training from the drill sergeants who harangued them as they learned and mastered basic soldier tasks. *You cannot screw this up, privates,* they would say as they showed the trainees how to seal a gas mask or find the north star. *It is Too. Easy.*

"All right," he told Corelli. "Let's run it down."

Corelli grabbed his roster.

"Derek Chen," Black began.

They ran it down. Black would read a name. Corelli would confirm that that soldier was in fact stationed at Vega and would tell whatever he knew about the guy's job in the platoon, where his guard shifts were, and which bay he slept in.

Several, he explained, were out on weeklong patrols in the mountains and only came back to refit briefly before heading out again. They would be tricky to link up with before the week was out, but Black decided to worry about that later.

After each name he would have Corelli cross that person off his armorer's roster, so that when they reached the end Black would know if anyone had been left off of his own printout. After that he would have a complete list of every man he was going to find, face-to-face, and where he could find him.

Seven names in they hit the first discrepancy.

"Robert Dale," Black read.

"Um, he's K.I.A., sir."

"Oh."

Black drew a line through the name on his roster.

Several more names down was another soldier who had been killed since Black's roster was last updated. As they ran through the list there were several more guys wounded seriously enough to be evacuated from COP Vega more or less permanently. Black lined them out.

"Jason Traynor."

They were just a few from the bottom.

"Who, sir?"

"Traynor."

Corelli shook his head.

"No, sir."

"Huh?"

"That's no one here, sir."

"What do you mean?"

"There's no one at Vega named Traynor, sir."

Black looked at the name on his roster, brow furrowed.

"Probably your roster is just really outdated, sir," Corelli offered. "That could be a guy who was here before I ever came to Vega, so I never knew him."

That didn't make sense to Black.

"Well, yeah," he countered, doubtfully. "But you'd have heard guys talking about him."

Corelli looked pained.

"Kind of depends on the guy, sir. Maybe he was a new replacement who got killed before he really got, uh, settled into the platoon."

Black stared at the entry, picturing a young man with no friends, dying among strangers in the mountains of Afghanistan.

His eye drifted across the row. His finger followed.

"Negative," he said flatly.

"Sir?"

"He went on leave."

"What?"

Black fingered the end of the row, where there were two columns titled R&R OUT and R&R RETURN.

Corelli leaned over, looking confused.

"When, sir?"

"Six weeks ago."

He turned the page so Corelli could see.

"Returned from the States a month ago," Black said, pointing out the entry.

Corelli shook his head.

"Can't be right, sir. I was here before that, and there's never been any Traynor here since I've been here."

That didn't make sense. Black knew how these printouts were generated. The unit's administrative office back on Omaha kept master records of every soldier in the battalion and where he was assigned. That office was the last word on who was assigned where, and any changes or reassignments. It was their business, the kind of thing they spent their days keeping track of.

Even if there were an error, when a soldier left FOB Omaha to go on R&R leave it would be caught. Soldiers waited for their flights in a little departure shack next to the airfield. The last thing a soldier did before stepping through the doorway and onto the tarmac to get on the helicopter was to show his or her ID and swipe it through an electronic reader that sat next to the doorframe.

That information was recorded electronically and transmitted back to the administrative office of each unit, where it was used to populate the date fields on the roster. It was a final, official record of who came and went from FOB Omaha. Once the card is swiped, the soldier is in the custody of the aircrew, and once he's dropped off at his next stop he's on his own until he signs back in from leave.

Those rosters were used daily for all manner of purposes, and each company had to verify them monthly. No error could last more than a couple weeks. If the roster said that Jason Traynor was in the unit, someone named Jason Traynor was in the unit.

Black clutched the sheet in his hand and held it in the air before Corelli, who shrank from it.

"This roster is generated by your battalion's S-1 shop," he said sternly. "Are you trying to tell me that the S-1 doesn't know who is in your company?"

Corelli opened his mouth but nothing came out.

"You can't B.S. me on this, Corelli."

"Sir, I'm not—"

"Who's Traynor?"

Corelli looked back at him, eyes wide.

"I don't know, sir!" he protested.

"Corelli!"

"Sir!"

Corelli shook his head, hands up. Black looked at him closely. Corelli squirmed and looked elsewhere.

Black slapped the sheet back down on the table.

"Run down the rest," he ordered.

They finished the last few names without discrepancies.

"Now count," Black demanded. "I need to know how many guys are here, right now, today, besides you."

Corelli ran down his roster.

"Forty-six, sir."

Black counted his own, top to bottom.

"And I get forty-seven," he said irritably, shoving the paper away from him.

He sat back in his chair and looked at Corelli.

"Which accounts for Traynor," he said, casting an eye at the young soldier. "Whoever the hell Traynor is."

Corelli looked here and there helplessly.

"Private," Black said, staring at him closely. "It is very important that you tell me the truth here."

Corelli caught Black's gaze and returned it.

"Sir," he said, without flinching this time, "I would not tell you anything that was untrue."

Black looked him up and down. He sighed.

"No," he said quietly, "I don't think you would."

Corelli seemed to relax a little.

"Sir," he said, "can I ask a question?"

"What is it?"

"Why do you need to know every person who's here?"

"So I can be sure I have talked to every soldier on this outpost."

Corelli stared at his lap.

"Oh."

He said no more.

Black's gaze roamed the shadowy armory, along the weapons racks and lockers. There was a set of metal shelves along one wall. An Army-issue brown towel was spread across one, with small spare parts laid out across it. Firing pins, recoil springs. In the middle sat a bulkier item, cylindrical and made of black metal. Black recognized it as the bolt carrier from a rifle. The primary mechanism required to make the thing fire.

He pointed at it.

"Is that Oswalt's?"

"Sir?"

Corelli looked surprised.

"C'mon, Corelli," he said patiently. "I know Oswalt's special."

It was not all that uncommon, back on the FOB, for leaders to remove the bolt from or otherwise disable the rifle of a soldier known to have mental health issues or suspected of being suicidal. Lessened the chances of him hurting himself, or someone else, and it was less humiliating than taking his rifle away entirely. Until his buddies found out, of course, which they always did.

"Yes, sir," Corelli answered. "That one belongs to Oswalt."

Black hadn't heard of taking the bolt from a soldier out in the field, which would seem to defeat the purpose of him being in the field at all. But it didn't sound like Oswalt was allowed to go out on patrols anyway.

"How long?" he asked.

"For Oswalt, since I've been here, sir."

Black nodded. He gathered up his roster and began to stand up. He stopped.

"What did you mean, 'that' bolt?"

Corelli hesitated.

"Corelli," Black pressed. "Who else's is in here?"

Corelli swallowed hard.

"The Wizard's, sir."

Now it was Black's turn to look surprised.

"Where?"

Corelli pointed.

"In that locker, sir."

"He goes outside the wire!"

"He's a medic, sir. Doesn't really need to be shooting people anyway."

"Is his pistol disabled too?"

"Yes, sir."

Black chewed on all this.

"How long?"

"Just the last few weeks, sir."

"Why?"

"I wasn't told, sir."

Black took his roster and walked to the door. He paused there.

"Thank you, Corelli."

"Nothing to thank me for, sir."

"Just your duty, right?"

"Yes, sir."

His earnestness was painful.

"But you're not going to tell me anything that I don't ask you myself, are you?"

Corelli looked down at his lap.

"Don't be seen leaving here if you can help it."

Corelli looked up, his face pale.

"Roger that, sir."

Don't press him any more.

"Corelli."

"Sir."

"Who didn't tell you why?"

"Sir?"

"Who brought you the Wizard's bolt?"

Black thought he saw Corelli wince.

"Sergeant Caine, sir."

Black turned and left Corelli sitting alone at his little table with his paperwork in the pale pool of light.

19

He pushed open the door to the thrumming command post.

The box fan whirred in the corner. Lights winked on radio stacks. The occasional crackle of static echoed down from the dark mountains and found voice in the speaker boxes.

The soldier with the sci-fi novel sat with his elbows on the table, whiling away his usual shift. He was the one Black had hoped would be there. The bored, distracted one.

"L.T.," he mumbled without interest as he saw Black enter.

Black found it unlikely to the point of near-impossibility that a soldier's name could sit accidentally on the wrong company's roster for months on end. But he decided he was obligated to rule out that possibility definitively, and he knew only one way to do it.

A folding chair sat against one wall next to the empty cot. He took it and plunked it down facing him, across the desk from the soldier. He straddled it, placing his forearms on the seatback.

The kid lowered the paperback an inch or two and looked over it, obviously confused but too cool to show it.

"Evening, sir," he said with a hint of a smirk.

Black saw deep red in his close-cropped hair. The sun had left a flay of dots across the ridges of his cheekbones beneath crinkled, mocking eyes. Black guessed that more than one smaller kid had lain on his back in a playground somewhere and contemplated the patterns of those freckles up close, tasting blood between pummelings.

He reached across and gently removed the novel from the soldier's hands. He set it facedown and open on the desk. The kid followed it with his eyes.

"Do you know why I am here?"

"Um, here in the C.P. or here at COP Vega, sir?"

"COP Vega."

"Uh-uh."

"Then how would you know why I was in the C.P.?" Black asked, annoyed.

The kid shrugged, feigning confusion.

"Just wanting to be clear, sir."

There was the smirk.

"I'm conducting a fifteen-six investigation. Do you know what that is?"

"Nope," the kid announced triumphantly.

"Well here's all you need to know," Black said. "It means I am here on business that supersedes anything your chain of command tells you to do or not to do, and I'm about to give you a lawful order."

The soldier nodded slowly.

"'Supersedes' . . ." he said thoughtfully.

"Yeah, and I can tell you know what that means, so spare me. You are ordered not to tell your chain of command that I have been here in this room tonight, or what I did here."

The kid had nothing to say about that for once. He sat thinking while pretending not to be thinking.

"You can decide whether to follow that lawful order or to violate it," Black went on, businesslike. "But be aware that if you violate it you will face criminal penalties for doing so."

"So what you're saying, sir, is that shit really does roll downhill."

"Are you done?"

The soldier put up his hands in mock surrender.

"Hey, sir, why would I 'do so'?" he asked. "I'm just a dumb grunt. Officers rule."

"I need the radio," Black said.

"Sir?"

"The radio."

"Uh, which radio, sir?"

"The long-range. I'm calling your battalion headquarters to talk to your S-1."

The smirk was back.

"Um, no can do, sir."

"What?"

"Long-range is a no-go."

"Why?"

The soldier thumbed upward, through the roof to the mountain peaks.

"Retrans tower is down, sir. We can't talk to nobody back on Omaha for shit."

"What do you mean it's down?"

"Hajji knocked it out, probably."

"That's impossible," Black countered. "Sergeant Merrick used the radio to report to your H.Q. that Danny is missing."

The soldier shook his head, insufferably pleased at seeing a lieutenant so flustered.

"Couldn't-a done it, L.T. Retrans has been down since the attack yesterday."

All the hair on Black's neck and scalp stood on end. Stars appeared briefly around the edges of his vision. He stared at the kid. The kid stared back.

"I mean, be my guest, sir, if you wanna give it a try," he said, gesturing with both palms at the long-range radio.

Black stood, feeling a wave of dizziness wash over him. On impulse he reached across the desk for the handset as his host watched him placidly. He could not have been happier to watch Black key the hand mic and fill the speakers with steady white noise as he tried unsuccessfully to hail 3/44's headquarters.

Knucklehead.

He set the mic back on the radio set.

"When is it gonna get fixed?"

The soldier shrugged.

"Whenever they send a team from Omaha to fly up there and set one up again, so it can get taken out again."

This struck him as pretty darned funny.

"mIRC chat," Black declared.

The Internet Relay Chat system was an encrypted version of online real-time text messaging systems. Its signal bounced off satellites, and it had rapidly become invaluable to remotely located outposts and their parent units. Someone in a headquarters back at Omaha could sit there on a "merk" terminal—no one knew what the *m* stood for; most assumed it meant "military"—and chat all night, getting nongarbled situation updates from various subordinate units, instead of tearing his hair out trying to talk on seven different scratchy radios.

"mIRC's down, sir, but the commo sergeant's on it first thing in the morning. I mean, unless you wanna go wake him up right now."

mIRC also was prone to going offline frequently.

"Sat phone," Black countered.

Most remotely located units kept at least one satellite phone on hand for situations just like this.

The kid blinked at him once.

"Sergeant Merrick does keep a sat phone, sir, but there ain't no satellite for it to talk to way down here."

He seemed most gleeful of all about that one.

"No line of sight, sir," he shrugged happily.

He picked up his walkie-talkie.

"I mean, you can try it yourself if you want to, sir." He held the radio aloft, smiling. "Want me to get him?"

"No."

"Don't worry, L.T.," he said as Black turned to go. "Run silent, run deep, right?"

He crept quietly up the stairs, stopping this time to listen at the corner until he could hear the snoring from Oswalt's wall hootch. He went by on tiptoe.

He lingered at the roofline, looking this way and that to ensure it was deserted. He walked briskly across the planking, toward the hulking shape of the guard post, and poked his head in.

They were there. He reached in his pocket and proffered the pack of smokes. He had a question for them.

Bosch examined him skeptically with his dark eyes and made no move. The other soldier cleared his throat.

"Um, hey there, sir," he said.

"What's up?" Black answered.

"Not much, sir, not much," the soldier said, fingering his machine gun idly.

He looked at his friend, who said nothing, and cleared his throat again.

"Um, listen, sir, I, uh . . ." he rambled.

"Just say it," Black cut in impatiently.

"Um, sir, I think we can't really be talking to you up here right now, sir."

Black's brow furrowed.

"Okayyy."

"Yeah, I mean, you know, sir, we would just get fried for having anyone up here smoking and joking while we're on duty is all."

"All right."

"I mean, you saw how ticked Sergeant Caine was the other night when ol' Bosch here wasn't posted on his weapon. That kind of thing, sir. You know how it is."

Black's eyes narrowed.

"Sure."

"Not that it's just Sergeant Caine, sir," the kid added. "I mean, any of the NCOs would go ballistic on us if they caught us up here talking to, um, a visitor, sir."

"Right."

Black slid the cigarettes back into his pocket, looking at the soldier closely.

"Sorry, sir."

"No worries."

He turned to leave.

"Oh, and hey, L.T.?" said the first soldier.

Black turned back.

"Um, you know how we were telling you about the first night they took this place?"

"Yeah."

"With the drug lord dude and stuff?"

"Yeah."

"Um, sir, if you don't mind, maybe don't mention to Sergeant Merrick that I told you that."

Black looked at him quizzically.

"He doesn't really like to talk about all that old stuff, sir."

"Okay."

"Bad times and all."

"Right."

He turned again to go.

"Um, and maybe not Sergeant Caine neither, sir."

Black nodded his assent.

"If you don't mind."

"Not a problem," Black answered tersely.

Bosch spoke up for the first time since Black had arrived.

"Best if you just didn't come back up here for a little while, Lieutenant," he said bluntly.

Black shot the testy kid a look.

"Yeah," he answered with annoyance. "I got that."

He snuck back down past Oswalt's hootch, stepping quietly on the stone stairs.

He was learning his way around Vega. He knew a couple different routes back to his own room now. One went outdoors a bit. It was a darker, more secluded way to go.

He took that route, lost in thought.

Danny was gone. No one was looking for him.

A soldier heading in the opposite direction startled him, but they passed one another with mumbled greetings and went each on his way.

Danny didn't get snatched. He wasn't dumb enough to leave himself in a position like that.

He had left of his own accord. Something at Vega was more frightening to him than what was out in the Valley.

"You unleash the Devil, and his work."

He crossed briefly through open air, the shadowed mountainslopes soaring up above his head, rushing up to meet the black sky. He passed through an entrance back inside, nearly back to his hootch.

"And you bring his servant into my town."

There were questions that only Danny could answer. One in particular.

"Jesus, L.T., where you been?"

The voice made him jump. He turned.

Caine, lurking in the shadows, much as Black had done while waiting for Corelli. He stepped out into the half-light, wearing no coat, his muscles bulging beneath his tan undershirt.

"Whattaya doing," Caine asked. "Going for a midnight tour?"

"What do you want?" replied Black.

"C'mon with me, sir."

He jerked his chin back over his shoulder, down a connecting corridor.

"What for?"

"Goddamn, L.T., can't you be easy about anything?"

"What for?" Black repeated.

Caine exhaled in exasperation and glanced to his left and right.

"Because I can help you, sir, that's why."

He turned down the darkened corridor.

"Now c'mon," he demanded gruffly.

He strode away. Black watched him for a few steps before following.

20

Caine pulled the heavy door shut on the shipping container, sealing them in darkness. He fished for a flashlight and sent a beam along the floor until he found what he was looking for. He stepped on the power strip with his toe and a thousand Christmas lights winked on.

They hung in icicles from the roof of the container, filling half the airspace above their heads. More strings ran all up and down the wooden interior walls. A klatch of cheap folding lawn chairs huddled around a makeshift card table fashioned low to the ground from M.R.E. boxes and a plywood plank. A mini fridge squatted in the corner with a boom box and a pile of CDs stacked on top of it. More M.R.E. boxes sat piled against one wall, and a case of water bottles next to that.

The walls were dotted with posters and magazine tearouts of women in various stages of undress. At the far end was reserved the place of honor for a large print of an exotic female emerging from the archway of an ivy-lined villa somewhere, a crystal blue pool behind her, wearing only an airy blouse unbuttoned in front, and sheer bikini underpants. Someone had taken a knife and made two small slits in the poster along the string of her panties, through which a dollar bill had been folded and threaded.

Someone's hangout. Probably Caine's, for him and his junior sergeants.

He had led Black down two dark passageways until a patch of moonlight appeared ahead of them. Caine told Black to hang back a moment. He went ahead to the doorway.

"Beat it," Black had heard him tell someone standing out of sight beyond the exit.

"Roger," came a bored-sounding reply.

Caine had waited, watching whoever it was go, then waved Black out into a long, narrow open space that ran between one exterior wall of the house and a high stone wall that marked the property's edge. The area was dotted with shipping containers, generators, and water bottle pallets. COP Vega's backyard, more or less.

They'd made their way along, close to the wall, for about fifty yards. The entrance to the container faced the wall of the house, away from the mountainslopes, with barely enough room to open one of its doors halfway. Someone had stenciled the words TAJ MAHAL next to the door.

Now Caine eased himself into one of the lawn chairs and motioned Black to the other. He sat.

"All right, Lieutenant," he said tersely. "So are you on the level here or what?"

"What do you mean?"

"Are you serious? Are you gonna follow through?"

"Follow through with what?"

"Look, sir," Caine said impatiently. "I know you're making some moves here. I need to know if you're for real."

"What do you mean, making moves?"

Caine sighed in exasperation.

"Sir, can we cut the crap here? I'm coming to you, all right?"

Black said nothing.

"I know you're making moves," Caine said, "and you know you're making moves."

"You want to tell me why you think that?"

Caine crossed his arms.

"No, I don't. You want to tell me who it was that told you we were scheduled to go to Darreh Sin on Tuesday?"

"No."

"So there we go," Caine said. "You don't trust me. That's your job. Now I wanna know if I can trust you here, or if you're just some lieutenant dicking around playing detective and throwing wrenches until he goes home."

"What do you want to trust me with?"

Caine looked at him a long moment.

"With something fucked up."

Black regarded the burly sergeant under the glow of the Christmas lights.

"I'm not dicking around," he answered.

"Yeah, well, we'll see. That's why we're gonna do this one step at a time."

"Do what?"

Caine leaned back in his chair and reached for the mini fridge.

"You want something?"

He pulled it open revealing rows of sodas and energy drinks, which soldiers drank like water, and several cans of beer.

Caine grabbed two beers and offered one to Black, who shook his head.

"Mm-hmm," Caine murmured to himself.

Caine swapped them for sodas.

They cracked and drank. Black waited for Caine to speak.

"Look, sir," he said. "I know I kind of came on like a dick at first."

He took a slug of soda.

"I don't mean just beating your ass, I mean just the way I came off."

Black shrugged.

"Seemed like standard N.C.O. to me," he said, unnecessarily.

Caine shrugged off the insult.

"Yeah, I guess I deserve that," he said. "Listen, sir, you gotta understand the reason for all that. I couldn't really have you hanging around me or be too, like, associated with you right now."

"Why not?"

Caine eyed him over the top of the can.

"Because you're not the only person trying to get to the bottom of something around here, that's why not."

He drank.

"What are you trying to get to the bottom of?"

"Once again, sir," Caine pressed, "I'd really appreciate it if you could tell me who it was that told you about our patrol schedule right after you'd shown up at the COP out of nowhere."

"That's not what you're trying to get to the bottom of."

"No, sir, but I gotta know who here in this unit I can trust and can't trust. Just like you do."

Black eyed him sidelong.

"Why would an innocent comment by a joe mean you can't trust him?"

"That's my business, sir. You've got your business and I've got mine. We're trying to get an arrangement going here."

"I don't even know what the hell we're talking about yet," Black replied impatiently. "And no, I'm not revealing communications made to me in confidence in the course of my investigation. You want an arrangement, then tell me what's going on."

Caine put the can down.

"Sir, you don't get the risk I'm taking just talking to you."

"Risk from who?"

The sergeant shook his head.

"I can help you, L.T. But you gotta help me do it."

"How?"

"Slow your roll, that's how."

"Slow my roll?"

"Just ease up a minute."

"Ease up on what?"

"On all this pressing."

"Pressing?"

"You know what I mean, sir."

Black sat back and considered.

"So you want me to freeze my investigation," he said. "That's convenient."

"Nobody's talking about that," Caine said. "But you gotta do it right. You start moving into the open like you are, and you're gonna drag yourself into that risk too."

"I'm not moving anything into the open."

"Yes, you are, Lieutenant."

Caine looked square in his eyes.

"Wide open."

Black regarded the burly sergeant.

"I think you're B.S.'ing," he said.

"Really?" shot back Caine, finally flashing irritation. "Let me ask you this, sir. Have I asked you word one about what happened back in Dareh Sin?"

"No."

"No. I haven't asked you, even though it is one hundred percent my sole duty right now to find out what happened and why, so I can protect my soldiers from whatever fucking hornet's nest you stirred up out there. I'm violating that duty right now. But I'm not asking you, because there is something more important, okay?"

"You sound like Sergeant Merrick," Black replied.

Caine sighed. When he spoke again the edge was gone.

"I know you don't trust me, sir," he said. "But you gotta try and trust me a little bit. I'll help you get what you want, but you gotta let me take the lead a little."

Black sat in silence.

Careful.

"Why is Sergeant Merrick directing soldiers to lie about how long they've been here at Vega?" he asked.

"What?"

"He's got soldiers who have been here longer than they're admitting."

Caine squinted at him.

"How do you know that?"

"Well, for instance, when I went to talk to Specialist Brydon, Merrick was telling him that—"

"Brydon is a part of this platoon," Caine cut in, "and he's a goddamn good soldier. Now, sir, you know soldiers say crazy things, so if there was—"

"What?" Black cut in.

"What?" Caine repeated.

Black eyed the sergeant.

"I was going to say," he continued, slowly, "that Merrick told Brydon that I was here from Colonel Gayley's unit. But I know that your guys haven't been back to Omaha but once or twice in the last six months, and when they did go it was for about twenty-four hours and you kept them practically under lockdown."

"Yeah, I know," Caine said. "That was for their own good. We started that for a reason. Those guys don't need to get a taste of the FOB life and then come back up here to this hellhole. That fucks with their heads too much."

"Exactly," Black answered. "That's my point. There is no way some joe stationed here at Vega, who's only been in theater a few months, knows the name of the commander of some other unit on the other side of FOB Omaha. Unless he's been stationed here for a lot longer than he says he was, back when guys used to get more R&R time back there and actually knew their way around the place."

Caine shrugged.

"Eh, sounds like you're reading a lot into it."

"Nope. Brydon acknowledged Colonel Gayley's name without questioning who he was."

In the yellow light, Caine's face looked as though it lost a little color. He opened his mouth to speak, then closed it.

"I think," he said finally, "that you are missing the most important thing, there, sir."

"What's that?"

"I never told Sergeant Merrick you were from Colonel Gayley's unit. I never told him *what* unit you were from."

The two men looked at one another.

"Then who?" Black asked.

Caine didn't respond immediately.

"I think, L.T.," he said, speaking slowly, "that this is a good place to call it for tonight."

He stood from his chair, leaving his soda unfinished on the table.

"Who's Traynor?" Black blurted out.

"Who?"

"Traynor. Jason Traynor."

"Who's that?"

"That's what I'm asking you."

Caine looked at him blankly and shook his head.

"Gotta give me more to go on, sir. I don't know no Traynor."

"Never mind."

Caine pressed the air between them with his palms.

"I'll find you, sir. Soon. Just cool it for a minute, okay?"

Black looked at the sergeant.

"I'm not dicking around," he repeated.

"Yeah, I kind of almost believe you, L.T.," he said. "Just cool it, all right?"

"Right."

Caine went to the door.

"Wait three minutes before you come out," he instructed Black. "You don't have to lock it when you go."

"Okay."

Caine toed the switch and sent them into darkness. Black heard the door creak open and saw Caine's silhouette above him in the skinny frame of moonlight.

Don't.

"What's 'Xanadu'?" he asked.

He watched the silhouette turn toward him. He saw it shake its head.

"Oh, sir, just leave that alone."

Caine went.

Black sat for about a minute looking at the doorway before rising and squeezing out the door. He walked briskly and quietly along the wall of the building, then continued swiftly through the passages toward Pistone's hootch. Something Caine had said had stuck in his head.

He pulled the door to his room shut behind him and went straight for his rucksack, pulling from it the sheaf of paperwork he'd brought with him from Omaha. The mystery roster with Traynor's name on it was at the top of the stack.

He ran all the way to the bottom with his finger.

No way.

By the time he pushed back out through the door he'd forgotten his promise to Caine entirely.

21

He'd figured the Wizard for a night owl, and he wasn't wrong.

"What?" came the bored answer to his quiet knock.

Black took that as permission to enter.

The overhead lights in Bay Two were out, leaving the shadows punctuated only by dusty splays of light rising from a few of the plywood enclosures. Looking left and right he noted that the immediately adjoining hootches were all dark. At least one was emitting snores. He pushed open Brydon's door.

He was lying on his bunk, hands behind his head, staring at the darkened ceiling. No book in sight.

Black brandished the roster, creased and wilted in his hand.

"Who are you?" he demanded.

Brydon exhaled heavily but didn't answer.

"Why aren't you on this roster?"

Brydon closed his eyes. He didn't seem surprised by the question.

"Soldier," Black repeated, sternly. "Why are you not on here?"

Brydon sighed.

"'Cause I'm a ghost, sir," he murmured.

"What? What does that mean?"

Brydon didn't open his eyes.

"Means what it means, sir."

"What are you talking about? Who's Traynor?"

Brydon sighed again and shook his head slightly. Black felt his blood pressure rising and had to remind himself to keep his voice down amidst the warren of open-air hootches.

"Brydon, you can't play games with this," he pressed. "I remember what you said. You said you'd been at Vega for three months. That's not true. Who told you to lie?"

Brydon said nothing.

"You know what's going on, and you're not telling me."

Still nothing.

"Why did you say you figured I'd be a captain?" Black asked, urgently. "Why would I be a captain?"

"I think," Brydon finally drawled, "that I'm all done talking to you."

Black shook his head in disbelief.

"Soldier, are you seriously invoking your rights against self-incrimination? Don't do it like this."

Brydon didn't respond.

"Brydon, I'm not after you here," Black said placatingly. "I don't even think you did anything wrong. Don't make it go ugly on you."

Brydon opened his sleepless eyes and turned his head to face Black.

"Lieutenant," he said flatly. "It has been ugly on me for a long time."

"What?"

Brydon closed them again and lay back.

"Good night, sir," he said.

"What does that mean?"

Nothing.

Don't ask.

"What's 'Xanadu'?" Black demanded.

Brydon reacted as though suffering a sudden pain in the abdomen.

"Ohhhhhh . . ." he groaned.

He rolled away from Black, curling on his side like a dog finally released from the beating.

You're getting sloppy.

It was the kind of trivial comedy of errors that got soldiers killed in Afghanistan every day.

All the stuff you used to not screw up.

It was a lapse indeed. Poor attention to detail, and poor communication practice. He'd been so focused on names of all the other soldiers in the unit that he hadn't even noticed, as he went through his roster with Corelli, that Brydon's name wasn't on it.

He'd told Corelli, *I need to know how many guys are here right now, today, besides you,* without realizing that the meticulous soldier would take him literally and subtract one from his count to exclude himself. Black hadn't thought to clarify, hadn't noticed there was anything *to* clarify.

That's why Corelli came up with forty-six guys to Black's forty-seven, when in fact both rosters had forty-seven men on them. Black's roster, straight from 3/44's headquarters, was missing Brydon but included the absent Traynor. Corelli's was the reverse.

He roamed the silent corridors and passageways, moving slowly, more than once absently losing his way and having to turn back, his mind following his unguided path. Questions were piling upon questions now, branching beyond his ability to sort them.

And lies upon lies.

He found himself in front of Lieutenant Pistone's hootch. His watch told him it was almost three A.M. He let himself in and commenced pacing the room.

Why did 3/44's headquarters believe two facts that weren't true?

Who had tipped off Merrick that he was coming to Vega? Had someone down at Omaha radioed ahead to warn him? If so, why did they tell Merrick and not Pistone, the officer in charge of the platoon?

Everything else, he felt sure, started from knowing this.

He slumped down onto the chair against the wall. His eyes roamed the room, pausing at the footlocker, past the picture of Pistone with his girl in the headlock smiling out at Black, and came to rest on the Celtic journal, gathering dust on the end table.

He sighed. The guy obviously had enough on his young plate dealing with sergeants like Merrick and Caine and a crew of soldiers who had no respect for officers. He didn't need one of his own rooting around through his personal effects.

Stop stalling.

He rose and let himself out for the Porta-Closet. He was so distracted he nearly missed that there was new graffiti text added to the old.

CHUCK
SEES YOU
AT THE END OF THE WORLD

On his knees next to the bunk, the picture of Pistone and his girlfriend facedown on the shelf, he tugged Pistone's footlocker out from underneath it.

"Sorry, brother," he murmured as he tried the lock.

The trunk came open. Why would it be locked? Pistone had had no idea a stranger was going to be living in his space for the next week.

He peered inside. At one end sat a softball and glove that looked like they'd seen little use. At the other, a pair of civilian khakis and a polo shirt sat folded neatly atop a pair of well-worn loafers. Usually people kept one set of civilian clothes buried somewhere in their gear, for when they went on their proper two-week leave back home. As long as you had something to change into from your uniform when you got there, you could buy whatever else you needed.

In the middle was a stack of books, CDs, and magazines. Something large and hardbound sat amidst them. He levered it out, spilling CDs among the clothes. A photorealistic painting of a school, done by an inexperienced hand, adorned the cover.

FAIRVIEW HIGH
CLASS OF 2001

Pistone's high school yearbook. Black found it surprising that he would have hauled it all the way up here.

Glory days?

Surprising and kind of sad. He set the yearbook down and milled among discs and magazines, none of which seemed of interest. He stacked everything neatly on the bunk after inspecting each item, until he got to the very bottom of the stack.

There was a book.

He picked it up. It was a thick paperback whose title wasn't familiar to him. He turned it over in his hands. It had seen some use.

He took a last look in the footlocker to confirm there was nothing else in there he hadn't seen, and began fanning through the pages of the book. Poetry.

At some point about halfway through, the feel of the pages shifted as they ran past and it became clear that it had been heavily read in one part.

He flipped it back over to find the crease in the spine and began fanning pages again, carefully this time, to find the spot. When he turned the book back over he saw that the inner edge of the page in question was cracking loose from the glue in the spine. He looked at the text.

"Son of a bitch," he told the empty room.

He commenced reading.

When he finished the section, he went to the beginning of the book and started reading about the author of the poems. It was a half hour before he realized he was still kneeling on the concrete floor. He rose and moved to the chair, sitting hunched over, turning pages.

He sat like that another half hour, then closed the book and sat up. He stared at the wall.

After several minutes, he rose and crossed the room. The door to Pistone's hootch had a hasp on the inside.

He locked it as best he could using the remains of the padlock Corelli had cut on the first night. It wasn't much.

He went back to the book and took it to the bunk, where he commenced rereading the dog-eared portion.

In Xanadu did Kubla Khan

A stately pleasure-dome decree

He didn't leave the room when day came a couple hours later. Nor had he slept when the knock came at the door that evening.

22

He paused at the hasp a long moment before lifting the broken padlock out of it and pulling the door open.

Corporal Shannon. Cradling a machine gun.

Black froze.

Shannon scowled down on him from towering heights.

"Word from Sergeant Merrick, Lieutenant."

Black could see Shannon looking past him at Pistone's room, at the unmade bunk with the yearbook and assorted contents of Pistone's footlocker spread across it. He registered distaste before looking back to Black.

"He says if you want to help find him, now's the time."

"Find who?"

"If you're coming," Shannon said, ignoring him, "you'll want to bring a pack for the night."

"Coming where?"

"To find out what happened to Danny."

Watch out.

Black didn't hesitate.

"Let me get my stuff."

"Be at the bottom of Oswalt's stairwell in twenty minutes," Shannon directed, and turned to go.

Black opened his mouth to speak.

"Yeah, I know you know where the roof is at," Shannon said, striding away.

Black stood in the doorway and watched him go. As soon as Shannon disappeared around the corner he set out walking briskly in the opposite direction.

It took only a minute to locate Caine. A soldier in the CP said he was at the gym, a makeshift little weight room that he and Black had passed on his first night's tour.

He could hear muted drums pounding as he approached. He cracked the door open and the sound sharpened to full assault, distorted guitars thrashing against the singer's distorted growls. This music he recognized as Death Metal. He'd heard other soldiers listening to it back on Omaha and elsewhere. He would rather have tolerated the Wizard's portentous gong rock.

The place was a windowless, sweaty dump, featuring a rusted, mismatched scrap set of the sort of weightlifting gear that found its way up dangerous valleys in Afghanistan and got passed around from unit to unit once there. The stuff looked like it had been reclaimed from Dumpsters and had almost certainly been in Afghanistan longer than any American currently serving there.

Caine was there with three soldiers in camouflage pants and tan undershirts. The uniform of the quick power lift—drop your coat, press iron, return to duty.

The soldiers gave Black only momentary notice as he poked his head around the door. Caine looked at him questioningly.

Black stared back at the sergeant with what he hoped was a nonsuspicious look of significance. He closed the door and headed back the other way, weaving through the outpost's innards and emerging into the darkened backyard.

There was a junior sergeant and two soldiers inside the Taj Mahal when he got there. Damn.

"Beat it," he declared without hesitation, realizing that in all likelihood he was about to be laughed at.

To his surprise all three rose and exited.

"Sir," said the young sergeant, nodding once as he passed.

This, Black recalled, was the nice thing about freshly minted sergeants.

They still remembered what it was to be lowly soldiers who wouldn't dream of giving attitude to an officer, or anyone else for that matter. The hop-to-it instincts were still there.

Black nodded back and watched them go, switching out the lights as soon as they were gone. Caine arrived a minute later.

"Goddamn it, sir," he said irritably, standing in the meager light from the open door. "I thought I *told* you."

He checked behind him and stepped inside the shadowy container, leaving the door open.

"Yeah, I know, you don't want to 'associate' with me right now," Black said. "This is important."

"I'm not talking about that," Caine shot back in a hoarse whisper. "What are you trying to do to yourself here?"

"What?"

"I thought you said you would cool it and stop snooping around for two seconds."

Black was taken aback. He answered testily.

"Well, I've been sitting in my quarters all day long doing nothing, all right? This is important."

"What's important?"

"Merrick wants me to go outside the wire with him."

This brought Caine up short.

"Where outside the wire?" he asked slowly.

He didn't tell him.

"He said we're trying to find Danny."

Caine pursed his lips. He exhaled slowly and shook his head.

"Sir, don't go with him," he said quietly.

"Why?"

"Sir, I know you probably feel responsible for helping find Danny, but I'm telling you, just don't go with him."

"Why not?" Black insisted. "Tell me something I can use!"

"Damn it, sir!" burst out Caine. "Would you just trust me for one damn minute!"

Black felt his blood pressure rising.

Don't.

"This goes all the way back to the beginning!" he blurted out. "Doesn't it?"

Caine shook his head again.

"Sir," he said, "I thought I told you to leave that alone."

"What?" Black demanded. "Leave what alone? I didn't say anything about the beginning before. What are you talking about?"

"Just don't go out there, L.T."

Black peered at the sergeant, trying to read him in the half-light.

"I'm starting to think," he said, "that all of you are full of shit."

He squeezed through the door and disappeared.

"Sir!" he heard Caine call after him, his voice almost pleading.

Black stomped all the way back to his room and jerked the door open. He shoved an extra set of socks and underclothes into a small assault pack. He gathered his body armor and weapons and was ready to go a minute later.

He stood in the middle of the room, motionless.

Just do it.

He checked his watch. He was to meet Shannon in five minutes.

"Oh, damn," he said aloud, shaking his head at himself in disgust.

He tossed his rifle onto the bunk and picked up Pistone's private journal from the side table.

He opened it. A diary, as expected. He went to the end and ran backward through the blank pages until he reached the most recent entries. He read them back for two pages.

"Oh, damn," he said again.

He set the book down with a trembling hand. His watch now told him he had three minutes.

He stared at the wall, silent seconds passing.

"Screw it," he said to no one.

He gathered his rifle off the bunk and pushed his way out the door, leaving the book lying open-faced on the endtable, its second-to-last page showing.

29 October—

Something is up I am still sure of it. I know SFC Merrick's involved but beyond that I know nothing, except how people have been around here.

2 November—

Danny has been acting so shady since the thing. When I asked him about SFC Merrick I thought he was going to jump out of his skin.

A 15-6 investigator is coming next week, probably about whatever all

Shannon was waiting at the bottom of the staircase, patrol gear piled on his huge frame, rifle hanging by his side, scowling at Black in the dim glow of the chem lights. He turned wordlessly and headed off down the corridor, past the stairwell. Black followed. He hadn't been this way before.

There were no chem lights here. Shannon switched on a red-lens flashlight affixed to the front of his gear. Its weak glow revealed a windowless stone passageway.

At a corner he cut right, then stopped at a door. He pulled a key from his pocket and unlocked it. Black followed him inside.

A closet, several feet long. A mop and a thin collection of cleaning supplies huddled in the red light. There was a second door at the far end of the room.

Shannon closed and locked the first door behind them and crossed to the other. This one was unlocked. He switched out his flashlight and opened the door. Black smelled fresh air. They stepped through and were outside.

They stood at one of the corners in the structure, in a very narrow channel between the exterior of the house and the large stone wall which ran around the property. The space was about six feet wide, tops.

Black looked up and saw tree branches in the moonlight. This corner of the outpost abutted the woodline.

There was a short ladder standing against the wall. Shannon latched the door behind them and gestured to it with his chin.

"Friendlies on the other side," he said in a low voice.

Black nodded and slung his rifle. The ladder was just tall enough for him to reach up and sling a leg over the top of the wall. He straddled it briefly, his helmet brushing against pine sprigs.

He swung his leg over toward the outside and shifted his weight to the edge, dropping down and landing heavily on the ground under the weight of all his gear. He bent his knees as he hit. His gloved fingertips touched dirt.

He saw boots. As he straightened he saw Merrick's tall figure looming over him. In the limited light, Black could make out his usual look of disdain.

Black looked around them. Moonshadows slanted through the trees. They had exited the outpost directly into the forest. From where they stood he couldn't see any of the guard posts on the roof, and he assumed they could not see him or Merrick either.

Beyond Merrick stood three other figures. Black squinted. Two were soldiers he did not recognize.

The third was Brydon. He did not look any happier to see Black than Merrick had.

He heard Shannon slide off the wall and land heavily behind him. He appeared to be it. It was a very small patrol group, smaller than regulations would normally allow. Black had no intention of asking why.

Merrick stepped around him and the others, unslinging his rifle and trudging wordlessly into the forest. The others followed suit, spacing themselves into a staggered line behind him.

The forest floor sloped upward and away to their right. It was littered with pine needles. To the left it fell away steeply.

They skirted the mountainside, moving gently uphill as they went. They were running roughly parallel to the path they'd taken two mornings before as they left for Darreh Sin, though that route already sat far below and was quickly being left behind.

Black had fallen in at the back end of the patrol. After about fifteen minutes he stepped up his pace and began passing the other soldiers.

Brydon kept his eyes on the ground as he passed by. Shannon said nothing but kept his eyes on Black.

He arrived at the front and fell in next to Merrick, just as they crossed an opening in the trees that revealed a spectacular moonlit view of the open Valley falling away to their left.

"So do I get to know where we're going?" he asked quietly.

Merrick looked at him.

"To the O.P."

O.P. stood for observation post. Outposts like Vega would often establish a smaller satellite station, manned by a few soldiers, on tactically important ground. These were especially valuable for keeping watch on enemy movements in difficult or mountainous terrain where you otherwise might not see your foe before he was right on top of you.

Black hadn't been told anything about there being an observation post associated with COP Vega. There was nothing like that on his maps.

"The O.P.?"

"Yeah, the O.P."

"What O.P.?"

"O.P. Traynor."

23

It was situated high near the mountaintop where the ground lay close to vertical, among a steep tumble of boulders and thick trees just below the long summit ridge. From its location were wraparound views down two dark faces of the mountain, the Valley and the river curving around its base. Black assumed he could have seen Darreh Sin somewhere beneath them, had he known where to look.

It had taken them a couple hours to get there. Trudging the final steps along an exposed and slippery path high against a steep gravel-strewn slope, Black felt more than anything like he were entering a treehouse.

In among the wooded cover there looked to be at least three or four separate levels to O.P. Traynor. Separate structures, really, one suspended near or above the other amidst rocks and trees set into a slope that ran nearly straight up at that point.

Each level was tiny and constructed mostly of plywood and sandbags. Each was offset laterally from the next, so that none of them touched its neighbor. Some weren't even fully enclosed, resting somewhere between an open-air room and a platform in the trees. A series of homemade steps and ladders ran up and down between them all, with sandbagged fighting positions scattered throughout.

Even in the cool of the night, at that elevation it had been a slog to reach the place. Black didn't care to think about the effort it must have taken to haul all that wood up there. It must have been some crazy good location to justify putting so much effort into building what was by definition a temporary post.

A short series of steps led from the gravelly surface up into the trees. A wooden platform adjoined a storage enclosure. M.R.E. cases and water bottle pallets sat stacked inside.

Merrick passed this by and headed up the next set of steps. Black and the others followed.

At the next level an open deck adjoined a small wooden structure that appeared to be the post's communications and command center. On the outside was hand-painted RADIO SHACK. Soldier humor.

A skinny, toothy-grinned soldier in camouflage trousers and tan T-shirt ambled out of the shack with his hands in his pockets. He surveyed the patrol.

"Sar'nt," he said, nodding to Merrick.

He had hillbilly stamped on him front and back. Even his short-cropped chestnut hair managed to seem messy.

His eyes fell to Black's rank and name tape. His eyebrows went up.

"Sir," he grinned.

He gave the *What's-up?* chin flip to the rest of the patrol.

"Boys."

"Lieutenant Black," Merrick explained, thumbing in his direction.

"Hooah, sir," the soldier said, appraising him. "Special guest. Haven't seen an officer up here in a bit. Besides L.T. Pistone, I mean."

Merrick turned to Shannon and Brydon and the rest.

"Chill out," he said. "I need to talk to the lieutenant."

Soldiers as a rule don't wait to be told twice when instructed to take a break. You don't know when it's gonna end or when the next one's gonna come, so you may as well get to it. They disappeared immediately up the next set of steps, leading further up into the trees and the higher levels.

The toothy soldier fell in behind Shannon and the others.

"Why yes, now that you ask," he said in a mock-sophisticated voice to no one in particular. "Don't mind if I doooo."

"Drink some fucking water," Merrick said to the retreating group.

Brydon broke off wordlessly from the rest and went into the radio shack instead.

"Hey, Doc," came a familiar voice from inside.

It was the first time Black had heard anyone address Brydon with the customary moniker for an Army medic.

"What's up, Billy?" came another voice, also familiar.

Black watched the joes trudge up the steps and disappear into what looked like a cave entrance in the mountainside, or at least a sheltered space beneath two large boulders. Merrick waited until they'd gone.

"All right, sir," he said, turning to Black. "You and me."

"What?"

"Let's play hooky."

"Where are we going?"

"You can water up right there," Merrick said, pointing to a stack of water bottles outside the radio room. "Come or don't come."

He grabbed a couple bottles and started trudging up the steps, stopping and turning back halfway up to see if Black was coming. Black bent and took a couple bottles for himself, shoving them in his cargo pockets.

At the next level up, Merrick led him into a steep, almost vertical chute running up among the rocks. They climbed between boulders and used tree branches to ascend. After about fifty feet they emerged from the brush into open air and moonlight.

Black experienced the same rush of vertigo as when Caine first took him onto Vega's roof. They were on top of the mountain, more or less, standing on the highest ridgeline.

The ground was bare up here, and the view phenomenal. Looking to his right, Black saw the ridgeline rise gently toward a large cluster of trees surrounding the summit. But for that fact, he would have been able to look down in all directions.

Opposing mountain faces loomed, bathed in moonlight and shadow, their peaks at or below the height where Black and Merrick stood. Somewhere beneath them, the river and Darreh Sin. Somewhere behind, COP Vega.

Merrick stopped and motioned Black to him. He poured his bottles into the water pouch Black wore over his back. Black did the same for him. Merrick stomped the empties flat and shoved them into his pack, turning wordlessly and starting down the back side of the mountain, opposite O.P. Traynor.

The way down this side was as dry and spare as the way up the other side had been lush and wooded. Scrub brush, dirt, and crumbled stones made it as inviting as a coral reef compared to the forest through which they'd traveled from Vega. Far below and to their left, the thin silver ribbon of the river glistened in the moonlight.

They descended for about twenty minutes, mostly in silence except where Merrick would point out old Soviet land mines near the trail. As they got lower on the slopes the foliage picked up a bit, finally offering some welcome cover. Black had felt uncomfortably naked on the moonlit mountain face.

They reached a shelf in the land that was well covered with trees and brush. Merrick stopped at the edge of it and knelt behind a fallen log. Black knelt beside him and looked down.

They had descended to just above a long, wide draw which sloped upward to their right. A creek ran down it to their left.

Across the draw, maybe a mile distant, there was a pass making an opening in the opposing mountainslopes. Beyond it Black could dimly make out a lush area of low, flat land nestled in the high hills. Grassy expanses alternated with thick copses of trees.

Black was fairly certain that this was the draw and the creek he had seen rising up from the main river, from Darreh Sin. Which would mean the sheltered land across the draw was . . .

"The Meadows," he said aloud.

Merrick nodded and took off his pack.

"You want your answers, sir?"

Black looked at him uncomprehendingly.

Merrick rooted inside and produced a hefty piece of equipment, which he handed over. It was a high-powered thermal scope. Detached from a weapon, it was a handy nighttime telescope.

Black took it and switched it on. He put it up to his eye and watched the world go green.

Scanning across the flatlands of the Meadows, he could make out many dwellings in and among the trees, or right out in the open grasslands. Goats and livestock glowed warm in the sight, idling or sleeping outside the homes.

The place looked sheltered and inviting. If you had to live in Afghanistan, he thought, this wouldn't be a bad place to do it.

It didn't take him long to identify what it was Merrick wanted him to see.

Figures moved along the far right edge of the land, where the grass gave way to the higher slopes. Terraced growing fields were planted at the margins, and the figures moved among them, bending and squatting. What looked to be goats stood near a shack at the edge of the crops.

Black clicked the scope to its highest magnification and squinted at the men and their crops.

"Poppies," he said finally.

"Correct," Merrick answered.

"Harvesting the latex."

"Yes."

"For opium."

"And morphine and heroin, yes."

Black scanned his memory banks for the briefing materials he'd once received on the heroin trade in Afghanistan.

"I thought they harvested it in the mornings," he said.

"They do."

"Why are they doing it in the middle of the night?"

"I don't know."

Black pulled back from the eyepiece and looked at the sergeant in the dark.

"I *think,*" Merrick said pointedly, "that maybe they don't want the Taliban to see them."

This didn't make sense to Black.

"Well, the Taliban knows there are poppy fields all through here," he said.

"Right," Merrick declared. "Taliban's everywhere in this Valley, even when you don't see 'em. Even when the locals don't see 'em. Make no mistake, and don't forget it."

"So if the Taliban doesn't like them growing for heroin, why don't they come in here and destroy the fields?"

"Who says the Taliban doesn't like them growing for heroin?"

Black looked at him questioningly.

"Yeah, I know, sir," Merrick said. "The Taliban doesn't like drug use. Officially."

"Officially?"

Merrick looked pained.

"It's not simple here, Lieutenant. The Taliban knocked out the poppy harvest in this country for about one year here. One. Before we showed up. And even then I don't believe for a second that there weren't pockets of it, way up in crappy places like this, or higher up still. The Taliban that are left might dream of those old days again, but for now they know they can't do shit about it. They don't have the numbers or the force to knock it all out. So if *someone* is making big cash off this shit, then they want a piece. We never know who is making deals, who is getting shook down or intimidated. We don't know jack."

"Okay."

"Maybe these guys want to clear the fields and move the stuff through the Valley when the Taliban isn't looking, so they don't have to pay their cut."

"Okay."

"I *think*."

There was the pointed phrase again.

"Or maybe these dudes are hiding from one of the other clans in the Valley. Maybe they're being hustled by the tribe over the fucking hill and they're trying to sneak a little out on the side before the official harvest tomorrow."

"Okay."

"Or maybe a hundred other things. Are you getting the point?"

"No."

Merrick looked irritable.

"The *point,* Lieutenant, is I don't fucking know."

"Right."

"And neither do you."

"Right."

"Get it?"

"No."

Merrick sighed impatiently.

"You asked me what is going on in the Valley," he said. "I don't know what the hell is going on. Whether it's drugs or any other thing. That's the point."

He aimed a finger across the draw.

"*This* is what's going on. This and every other goddamn thing that we don't see and we don't understand and never will."

He turned back to Black.

"This is *their* Valley, sir. These are *their* problems and *their* feuds. This is *their* bullshit. We could stay here twenty years and we're not gonna get to the bottom of it. Not even halfway. Get it?"

"I get it."

"Bottom line," Merrick continued, "I don't know and I don't care, sir. The Army makes me deal with this town and these meadows because bad fuckers come through here and because we're supposed to try and see if friendly works better than 'fuck you' up here. Beyond that, I have no interest in this village or the next one or the next one. I care about keeping my soldiers alive. *That's* my job, not worrying about who is stabbing who in the back over heroin or who's gonna get their fair share of free water once we leave, or whose daughter is gonna get married off to which fat fuck for how many goats, or any other goddamn problem they have with each other that we'll never know about."

Black regarded him in the moonlight.

"Is that why you have an O.P. up here that your command doesn't know about and half your platoon doesn't know about?"

Merrick flashed surprise but quickly composed himself.

"What makes you think," he said coolly, "that my command doesn't know about it?"

He looked at Black with an expression that indicated he was going to say nothing more on the subject.

"And now, sir," Merrick said, pointing across the draw at the Meadows, "I am going to go into this place, because even though he is not one of my soldiers, Danny is my responsibility, and some of the people I have unfortunately come to know there might know what happened to him. *Might.* I have no fucking clue if they will or won't, but seeing as how I don't know shit about this place it is the only guess I have."

The façade of theatrical hostility was falling away again, though what replaced it was no less cold or off-putting.

"I am going in there alone, because there is no way in hell that I am going to risk my soldiers again after what you caused in Darreh Sin. But seeing as how I've now shown you everything that I *don't* know, and seeing as how you already put my entire platoon in danger, I would really like it if you gave me one piece of information to help me possibly keep from getting *myself* killed, which is what the fuck happened with the chief?"

Black stared out at the Meadows.

"What happened had nothing to do with Danny," he said quietly.

Why are you lying?

"Sir," said Merrick. "You might have noticed that we are out here alone in the middle of godforsaken nowhere."

Black had slung his rifle over his shoulder when he took up the scope. He now realized at the same time as Merrick did that his hand was sliding slowly in the dark to his pistol butt.

"Oh, for God's sake," Merrick said with disgust. "If I was going to waste you, do you really think I would show you all of this first?"

Black felt his face flush in the dark.

"What I am *saying* is you may have noticed that I have both violated regulations and risked myself and risked my men to bring you all the way out here on a sightseeing tour to convince you that I need to know what you know. Feel free to tell on me when you get back to Omaha and are getting fat in the chow hall with Colonel Gayley. But in the meantime, as long as we're out here together on the ass end of shitty, do you think maybe you could cut the crap and reciprocate a little bit?"

Black fingered the night scope. Merrick waited.

"The chief said that we had brought the Devil into his town," he answered at last, "and brought his servant too."

Merrick was quiet for a long moment.

"You're right," he said at last. "That probably has nothing to do with Danny."

He held out his hand for the scope. Black passed it back.

"I'm assuming *you* can find your way over the mountain and back to the O.P. without a map," Merrick said.

Black cocked his head, catching the odd tone in the sergeant's voice.

"Yeah, I know your situation," Merrick said flatly.

Black's mouth opened, then closed.

"Do you need me to hold your hand?" Merrick asked disdainfully.

"No."

"I would hope not."

He shoved the scope into his pack.

"I'll be back soon."

Merrick stood and shouldered his pack.

"Who was Traynor?" Black asked.

It was not an unnatural question. Outposts were routinely renamed after someone who died there, usually under heroic or tragic circumstances, or both.

Merrick's reaction betrayed nothing out of the ordinary.

"He got killed up here when we first laid in the O.P."

He offered nothing further. Black nodded and turned upslope.

It took him more than twice as long to ascend the steep mountainside as it had coming down. He felt even more naked than before, moving in the moonlight with his back to the Meadows. About halfway up he was able to cut to his left a bit and enter a wooded area that ran all the way to the summit. It was a minor detour, and it made him feel better.

Near the top he cut right, making his way through the trees and down along the gently sloping ridgeline. He emerged into the open and found where he and Merrick had climbed from the wooded chute. He lowered himself between the boulders and made his way back down to the O.P.

Stepping from the rocks onto the system of platforms and steps and ladders, he looked about himself. There was no one in sight. He heard muted laughter above him, which he assumed was Shannon and the others up in their boulder cave.

He trudged down a level to the radio room and stuck his nose in. Brydon was sitting on the floor with his back against the wall, reading a magazine and pretending Black wasn't there.

A very young private Black didn't recognize sat at the radio desk nearby. The kid's name tape read CHEN. Black was trying to figure out how he knew that name when a familiar voice came from his side.

"Uh, hey, sir."

He turned. Seated on a stool in the far corner was the soldier from the guard tower at Vega. His friend Bosch sat next to him. They were the ones he'd heard greeting Brydon before.

Both soldiers looked stunned to see Black. Even the sullen and punchy Bosch registered surprise behind his usual scowl.

Black crooked his head in confusion and raised his hands: What gives? The first soldier cleared his throat, surprise turning to discomfort.

"Uh, yeah, so it turns out we've got an O.P., sir," he said glumly.

Black realized where he had seen Chen's name. The soldiers on the roster that Corelli had said were out on a weeklong patrol.

"Guess you learn something every day," the soldier continued.

Black fought a sinking feeling.

"When did you guys get here?" he asked.

"Just yesterday, sir."

"Why *you* guys?"

"Guess it was just our turn, sir," the first soldier answered moodily.

Bosch, who'd been staring at the floor, raised his head.

"Well, who sent y—" Black began.

He stopped when he saw the look in Bosch's eyes.

Footsteps tromped on the deck outside. The toothy-grinned soldier poked his head in, looking a little glassy-eyed.

"All right, boys," he began, then saw Black. "Oh, hey there, L.T."

Black nodded. Toothy continued.

"Hey, guys, we're just headin' up to the fishbowl for a smoke. Wanna come?"

He doffed an invisible cap toward Black.

"Invites to you too, of course, sir."

The awkwardness in the air caught up to him. He surveyed the glum crew and drove on through.

"C'mon, then, all y'all, let's go."

"What's the fishbowl?" Black asked.

"Aw, sir, it's the best place for a smoke in the whole world. C'mon, ya gotta come."

He waved everyone out.

"All right, fine," said the first soldier, climbing off his stool.

No one looked happy. The cajoling continued.

"C'mon, you too, Doc. Hey, Chen, you chill out here at the radio, all right?"

The kid nodded. Low man on the totem pole. Everyone else roused themselves without enthusiasm.

"That's right. C'mon, Doc. All right, then, sir."

Black followed him out onto the deck.

24

They'd had to climb a series of ladders then squeeze up through a narrow, vertical gap between boulders to get there. But the kid was right.

The fishbowl was a flat slab of rock, a natural ledge maybe twenty-five feet across, surrounded on three sides by granite and on the fourth by open air. The edge of the slab dropped off into nothingness, with the vastness of two mountains looming side by side across the Valley.

Several collapsible camp chairs sat in a semicircle, arrayed around what Black at first thought was a standard cigarette butt can but then realized was a cylindrical metal wood burner. Someone had stacked a pile of miniature log cuts against one of the rock walls. A couple had been tossed into the burner and were now aflame.

Two soldiers were already up there, lounging in chairs before the fire.

"Damn, Hill," said one, seeing their glazed-over tour guide emerge from the boulders.

Hill. A hundred percent hillbilly and his name was actually Hill.

Another name Black remembered from the roster. Another kid out on a "weeklong" patrol.

"You do enough tokin' for one d—"

The soldier stopped when he saw Black.

"What's up, there, sir?"

The kid and his buddy looked very familiar. It took Black a moment to put it together, what with the two not being covered in camouflage face paint.

"You guys are on the sniper team."

He'd last seen them at the trailside above Darreh Sin, during the mad slog back to COP Vega.

"Hooah, sir," said the kid. "In the flesh."

Merrick had said the snipers nearly didn't make it "home." This, apparently, was home.

Everyone sat, Brydon choosing a chair at the far end of the semicircle and placing himself glumly in it. Hill passed around a pack of smokes. They all lit up.

"So whattaya think, L.T.?" said Hill, sweeping their surroundings with his smoke hand.

Black looked out at the dark panorama beyond the rock slab.

"Not to be a downer," he said, looking at the little fire, "but you guys don't think it's a little bit crazy to be lighting that thing up here on the mountaintop?"

"That's the beauty, sir," said Hill through a breeze of smoke.

"What's the beauty?"

Hill gestured out into the night.

"You look out over there, sir," he said. "We're covered on three sides. The only people that can see this fire is someone that's wayyyyyyy—"

He pointed across the chasm toward the other mountains, whose top halves were visible.

"—the heck over there."

"Okay."

"Only a supersniper could make the shot from that mountain, sir."

He took a drag.

"And Afghani dudes with a rifle generally ain't super," he said, exhaling to the nods of the sniper team guys.

Black squinted at the far slopes.

"It ain't like they don't know we're here anyway," Hill went on. "This fire pit must drive 'em crazy, wanting to kill us every night but not being able to get us. Kinda cool, right?"

"Right."

The two guard tower soldiers from Vega eyed the blackness uneasily.

"And if they *did* actually make that shot one day," Hill continued, kissing a narrow cone of smoke across the gulf. "Well, shit, that's just sporting, right? I mean, they almost *deserve* the kill if they can make *that* shot."

He grinned his cigarette-stained grin and drew another cloud into his lungs.

"Makes you feel *alive* up here, sir!"

Bosch spoke up for the first time.

"That's fucked up," he said sullenly.

Hill leaned back in his chair and stretched his legs out in front of him, crossed at the ankles, gazing out at the void.

"Well *this,*" he said quietly, "is where you come to do fucked-up shit."

He looked at Bosch with piercing eyes.

"Right, Bosch?"

Bosch said nothing. The first soldier shook his head.

"You're crazy, Hill."

"Pfft!" Hill scoffed. "Crazy. What's crazy? We're livin' up here like the Swiss Family Robinson on top of a mountain in the middle of no-freakin'-where. *That's* crazy."

He took a drag and exhaled slowly.

"This place ain't even real," he muttered through the haze.

He lingered in his smoky thoughts before turning to Black with his wide-gapped smile.

"You ever wondered what's crazy and what's real, sir?"

Black turned and looked him in the eye.

"Yeah," he answered flatly. "I have."

For a moment Hill seemed taken aback. He shook it off and squinted at Black, nodding his head mock-knowingly.

"So," he said brightly, "whatcha doin' way up here, sir?"

Black glanced at Brydon, who looked at the ground.

"Just got some business with Sergeant Merrick."

The kid nodded conspiratorially.

"Mmmmm, I gotcha, I gotcha, sir. Hooah. Officer business."

He raised his cigarette in a toast.

"Well, welcome to our humble abode."

Black raised his own and dipped his head.

He was content to listen to the soldiers smoke and joke, but no one besides Hill seemed able to relax with him there. The taciturn Bosch said little, as usual, and kept eyeballing Black. His friend from the guard shack stared off into the night awkwardly. Brydon examined the stone slab and seemed to wish to be invisible. The snipers for their part had never met Black before. Soldiers as a rule don't loosen up around officers they don't know.

"How did Traynor die?" he said to no one in particular, but looking straight at Brydon.

The medic looked up, surprised, catching Black's eye briefly before looking away again.

"Aw, sir," said one of the snipers. "You sure you wanna know that one?"

"Hit me."

The sniper shook his head, took a long pull on his smoke, and told it.

"It was when they first took this ground," he said, gesturing at the rock around them. "All this glorious little tidbit of shitty land here that we're sitting on."

"Okay."

Vega, he explained, was still brand-new at that point. No one had gone much past there, and the platoon came under frequent attack whenever it tried to. Word came down from headquarters that they needed to find high ground to lay in an O.P. between Vega and Darreh Sin.

"They needed a squad," the sniper said. "A volunteer squad, to move fast and light and identify a location. Then air assets would come and secure it."

"Traynor's squad."

"You got it, sir."

The sniper looked around at his buddies.

"That was a tight nine guys," he said, shaking his head. "Knew each other's girls and hung out all the time off-duty and all that shit. Kinda weird, honestly."

Somebody chuckled.

"Not, like, gay weird," the sniper continued, "but anyway, you know how it goes with squads. Sooner or later everything kinda breaks down all onesie-twosie, just each dude with his coupla buddies. Not those dudes. They were like nine freaking brothers.

"So Traynor's the junior guy. E-two private, got to the unit, like, three weeks before they deployed, and here he is trying to hold his own with dudes that are practically like family."

They scouted the ridges and passes for a day before they found the site. It was perfect. They made camp for the night.

They hadn't seen a soul up there. But someone had seen them. Someone was ready. As soon as day broke, they were attacked, by a significantly larger force.

"They never even knew who it was," the sniper said. "Taliban, or what? Never knew how they had got seen or how the enemy laid so much heat on 'em so quick."

The situation rapidly became untenable. Nine guys, barely dug in, with only the weapons they could carry up to the heights of the mountains. There was no chance. Too many attackers with too many heavy weapons and rockets, pushing in around and below them. Multiple guys were wounded immediately.

Under heavy fire, the squad managed to climb higher and drag the wounded up to the ridgeline. They called for air support to keep them alive and MEDEVAC—medical evacuation—helicopters for the wounded.

Attackers pressed them from below, now from both sides of the mountain, lobbing rockets and grenades up onto the ridge and resisting all efforts by the Americans to drive them back.

Most of the squad at this point were either incapacitated or already dead. The attacking force, whoever it was, could taste it coming. The complete overrun and annihilation of an American position. That didn't happen every day.

An attack helicopter arrived and did what it could. It was hard to pick out the attackers in the wooded slopes, and the chopper itself kept coming under fire from the trees. The pilot had to keep pulling back. What he did see, he reported later.

He saw a cluster of Americans on the ridgeline. Only one really was moving. But the one guy was racing back and forth frenetically across the mountaintop, from one edge of the ridge to the other. He moved like a madman, sending grenades and machine-gun fire down into the treeline, keeping up as much flash and noise as he could to convince the attackers that there was still a fighting force up there.

"Traynor," said Black.

"You know it, sir."

The MEDEVAC bird arrived. Its pilot was a madman too.

"Dude had the balls to descend," the sniper said, pointing back over his shoulder. "Fucker came down over the summit and flew right down the ridgeline at about twenty-five damn feet. He was so low nobody could get an angle to fire up at him."

Traynor didn't get on the helicopter.

The MEDEVAC pilot didn't know what the other pilot had seen, which was that there was only one person left fighting on the mountaintop. Otherwise his crew would have made Traynor get on. The pilot only knew that the place was hot and they had critical wounded to get out.

Traynor helped the crew drag three wounded on board and watched it go.

Later, after it was all over, the MEDEVAC crew reported that they had asked Traynor how many guys were left on the mountain with him. Standing there in the rotor wash, he just shouted, "We're good," and ran back to the fight.

But the other pilot, the one flying the attack helicopter, could see only one American moving on the mountaintop after the MEDEVAC bird left. Everyone else with him was dead.

Traynor kept racing around the mountaintop, keeping up the fireworks display, raiding his buddies' bodies for ammunition and grenades.

"How'd it end?" Black asked.

"The Apache finally had to bail," the sniper said, "but Sergeant Caine saw what happened next."

"Caine?"

"Yeah. He was coming with the Q.R.F. from Vega."

Quick reaction force. The rescue squad.

"Everyone was broke off from hustling the whole way up the mountain from Vega," he said, thumbing the black air behind him. "Except Sergeant Caine. You know how he is in the mountains. Freaking machine."

Black thought back to the harrowing climb back from Darreh Sin, with Caine seemingly not even winded, haranguing everyone to speed up.

"He climbs ahead of the rest of the Q.R.F., and he's coming down the ridgeline over the summit up there."

He shook his head.

"Thirty seconds too late. Saw the rocket land right under Traynor's freaking feet."

"Oh."

"Vaporized his ass," the sniper said glumly. "Sergeant Caine couldn't even find some damn chunks of him to stick in his coffin."

Everyone was silent. The guard tower soldiers from Vega had been rapt.

"Best part," the sniper told them, "none of those dudes Traynor put on the MEDEVAC bird even made it."

He examined his cigarette, which had nearly died while he'd been telling the story. He sucked it back to life and shook his head.

"Losing Traynor was rough on Sergeant Caine, man. He liked the kid. Kinda took him under his wing."

"If everybody else on the mountain was dead," the first soldier asked, "why didn't Traynor get on the MEDEVAC?"

"Yeah, he coulda been on that bird and outta there," the sniper answered. "He knew he was probably fucked. But he wasn't gonna leave his buddies' bodies to get fucked up and desecrated and shit, and he wasn't gonna take a space on a MEDEVAC from a dude that was still alive, no matter how hurtin' and critical the guy might-a been."

"Damn."

"Damn right. Hardly knew those dudes for two weeks before they deployed, but he laid it down without blinkin'."

The sniper eyed Black.

"That, sir, is loyalty," he said. "Your boys is your boys, even if you just met 'em."

He took a theatrical drag as the other sniper nodded his approval.

"Y'all got that on the officer side of the house?"

Black gave him a look that, to his surprise, made the kid shut his trap. No one else said anything.

Black's mind wandered, out among the mountain spaces. Hill's voice brought him back.

"Lucky Traynor," Hill said quietly.

"What?" asked the first soldier.

"Taliban, or whoever the fuck, done him a favor."

Everyone looked at him like he was nuts.

Hill stubbed his smoke out and got a fresh one. He put out his feet and leaned back in his camp chair, surveying his audience. Making them wait for it.

"Saw a thing on the news, a few years back," he said. "Sixtieth anniversary of Pearl Harbor, right? They're talking about this dude who was the only survivor of one of the ships that got sunk there."

He lit up.

"Wasn't one of the bigger ships, right? Didn't have a whole lot of guys on it, but he was the only one that made it out."

"Okay," said the soldier.

"Dude was thirty at the time. Been in the Navy a little bit. News story was about how he went out to Hawaii on the anniversary, for the first time ever since the war. You know, old codger tour group with the blue hats and shit."

"Right."

"So he goes out to Hawaii with his wife and some of his kids and the other blue hats and all *their* wives and all *their* kids, and they all have a nice little trip, right?"

"Right."

"You know, breakfast in the hotel, ride on their tour buses and totter around on the docks and stuff, looking down in the water and payin' their respects to their old buddies thinkin' 'bout when they were all kids with no wrinkles or nothin', like we all sittin' right up here on this cliff. Nice happy little trip, everyone sheds a tear, do your hugs and get on home."

He paused for a good drag on his cigarette.

"So when the old dude gets back to his hotel, he tells his wife and his kids that when he dies he wants his ashes brought back there to Pearl, and he says put 'em in the water."

"Okay."

"And, you know, his wife is kinda hurt, right? 'Cause she was thinkin' all eternity in the family plot back in Bumfuck, Nowhere, right? Like, side by side forever in the kinda shithole where I live back home."

He chuckled.

"But his kids see it in his eyes, and she sees it, and everyone sees they can't make him change his mind. So they say, 'Hey, you're the boss a' you,' and they all hug on it or whatever, and they all think he's a little crazy, but hey, he survived Pearl Harbor, so he gets to be crazy, right?"

He blew out a long one.

"Died that night," he said flatly. "Didn't make it back to Bumfuck or nowhere else. Didn't get on the plane. Went to sleep in his hotel bed after the Love-You-All dinner they had that night at the Holiday Inn or wherever, and woke up dead."

"Damn."

"So I'm watchin' the news about this, and everyone in the news story that's hearin' about it from the Bumfuck folks is getting all teary and saying, *Oh, that's so sweet, he stayed alive to make it back and honor his friends before he died*, and all that shit. But that's bullshit."

The first soldier looked at him quizzically.

"He didn't live no happy life," said Hill, taking a drag. "He lived a cursed life."

"Whatta you mean?"

Hill turned to the soldier.

"He didn't die in the ship with his buddies like he was supposed-a."

He inhaled and blew out a long jet.

"So he was damned to walk the Earth for sixty years with his buddies haunting his life the whole time. May-a looked like he lived a happy life, but that just made it worse. The more he got in life—kids, a wife, whatever—that was just one more thing he had to chew on that his buddies never got."

"Oh."

"He didn't go back there to pay his respects and honor his buddies, man. He went back there to ask 'em, 'Is sixty goddamn years enough?'"

The guard soldier was watching him like a kid at a campfire.

"And they said, 'We're cool now, bud.'"

He surveyed the group.

"They set him free."

No one said anything. He went on, with mischief in his voice.

"But his buddies ain't even *that* cool after all. Everybody in the news story is all charm-y and saying, *Oh, he wants his ashes to be with his buddies, how nice*, but they got that one wrong too."

"Whatta you mean?"

"His buddies ain't even there in the water," Hill said, shaking his head. "Coupla the big ships are there—*Arizona*, right?—but the littler ships, they ain't at the bottom of Pearl Harbor no more. They all got pulled up and scrapped after the attack."

He chuckled darkly.

"His buddies ain't lyin' in the bottom of the sea. But that's where he's gonna lie. That's the fuckin' deal they made."

A breeze bent the little fire.

"He ain't never gonna leave there. His wife even said it too. After she got back home the little Bumfuck newspaper did a story and came to her house and made her tell the whole story, right? And when she got to the ashes part they asked her, 'How did you feel about the ashes?'"

"Yeah?"

"And she just looked the reporter in the eye and said, 'In some ways I don't think Gerald ever left Pearl Harbor.' And she'd probably been sayin' that to herself her whole life, but it took that whole time for her to realize how true it was. Blew her life on a man who was damned and didn't even figure it out till practically the end."

He blew a cloud of smoke at everyone and let them chew on that.

"What happened to her?" Black asked.

"Funny you ask, L.T.," Hill said, with a wicked little grin. "She was a little younger than he was, right? Turns out her old high school sweetheart was still doddering around Bumfuck too. Married him six months later and called it a day."

He laughed out loud.

"God damn," said the first soldier, hollow-voiced.

Everyone stared at the stone slab, defeated.

"That," said one of the snipers, "is the worst fucking happy ending I've ever heard."

"Yep," said Hill, still amused. "Probably thought about that dude every week her whole life but still stuck by ol' Gerald. Then Gerald says, 'Thank yee very much for the grand life together, but I'll be sleepin' with the fishes if you don't mind.'"

Everyone lapsed into silence again. Hill eyeballed Black.

"You got a girl, there, sir?" he asked. "There someone back home waitin' around loyally on ol' Lieutenant Black?"

Black didn't return his gaze.

"Mmm-hm," Hill said to himself, taking a nice long smoke before speaking again. When he did he addressed the group.

"Never be the last man," he said, looking out at the mountains. "Traynor knew that. Traynor knew what he was doing. After the firefight, when everything was all over, the chief medic on the MEDEVAC bird told the investigators all about it. He said when the helo touched down and he jumped out onto the ground and ran over to where Traynor was at and he saw the poor fuckers that Traynor had dragged to the landing zone, it was just pathetic. It was obvious none of 'em was gonna make it. They were all mostly dead already. Medic grabbed Traynor by the arm and told him, 'These wounds are not survivable, private,' and told him to bring him some other casualties that might have a chance. Traynor told him 'Fuck you' and made him put the casualties on the bird. Told him the rest of the dudes were okay. Told him 'We're good.'"

Hill rose from his camp chair and walked to the edge of the slab. He had a water bottle in his hand.

"So rest in peace, Jason," he said, tipping a quantity over into infinity. "Say hi to the boys."

He came back and sat. Everyone stared at the stone walls or the slab.

Black looked at Brydon, who stared miserably down at the rock.

"And that," said Hill, surveying the newcomers, "is the story of Private Traynor, for all you O.P. Traynor cherries."

He glanced at Black.

"No offense, there, sir."

Black nodded.

"Where's the latrine?" he asked.

"Eh, we got a chem toilet if you need it, sir, but if you gotta take a whiz . . ."

He swept his arm across the vista before them.

". . . the world's yer oyster."

Deciding it would be unclassy to urinate on the memory of Private Traynor, Black rose and squeezed down between the boulders at the entrance to the fishbowl. He looked around himself. From there it was a short scramble up and over a spine of rocks to the back side of the mountain and a wooded area.

He unslung his rifle and went that way, hopping and scrambling from rock to rock, the heavy bulk of the mountain to his right, empty space falling away to his left as he rounded the summit mass. He had just hopped down from the last boulder and landed on the wooded backslope when hands grabbed his shoulders from behind.

"L.T.!" the voice hissed.

25

He ducked and spun, sending up an elbow to shrug his attacker free.

Danny's surprised, sweating face shone wide-eyed in a leafy shaft of moonlight.

Black charged, holding his rifle crosswise before him. His momentum, with all his gear on, drove Danny several tripping steps backward across the slope until they both fell across a log and landed hard on the slanting mountainside.

Black pushed himself up and away from Danny, backing off several feet and raising his rifle.

"No!" Danny gasped, terrified. "L.T.!"

"It's you!" Black hurled at the linguist, squaring on him. "He's you!"

"What?!"

"The servant! You're the servant!"

"L.T.! No! What?"

"Don't bullshit me, Dan—"

A crackle of leaf and twig behind him.

Five meters roughly.

He spun. A dark figure loomed before his rifle. Before any conscious thought, he squeezed the trigger.

Nothing happened but the dull metallic snap of a weapon failing to fire.

He blinked. The Monk stood frozen for a moment, then glided away downslope, through the trees.

Black whirled around again to Danny, who remained motionless on the ground with his hands up. He let his rifle fall, swinging taut from a short strap D-ringed to his gear, and drew his pistol.

"L.T.!"

"Shut up."

He looked around him and moved a few steps further away to where a log lay across the ground. He lay his pistol on its side on the log, pointing in Danny's direction, close where he could grab it. He unhooked his rifle from its strap.

"What did you do here, Danny?"

He cracked open the rifle and began to strip it, keeping one eye on his work and one eye on the frightened 'terp.

"What, did you rape a kid or something? Did you try to cut in on the chief's drug business?"

He pulled the charging handle out, freeing the bolt assembly, while Danny stammered and protested.

"I'm sick of everyone lying to me out here, Danny."

He yanked a patrol cap from his cargo pocket by its bill, snapping it open with a flip of his wrist and setting it upside down like a dish on the log.

"So you need to tell me the truth now or I'm going to shoot you, right here on this mountain. Do you understand?"

Danny's wide eyes widened further.

"What did the chief want to tell me, before he freaked out over the heroin?"

He tossed the charging handle into the upturned patrol cap and got a fingernail underneath the loop of the retaining pin as Danny opened his mouth to respond.

"Why did he want to get me alone?"

He tugged the retaining pin free and pinched it between his teeth.

"L.T.!" Danny exclaimed, harshly. "This is what I tell you! It was not the chief!"

"What?"

He tipped the bolt carrier into his palm and nothing came out.

"It was not the chief who wanted you to talk alone," said Danny. "It was *me,* L.T."

There was no firing pin in his rifle.

He looked up at Danny.

"The chief did not say for Caine to leave," Danny said. "I say that. I wanted you talk to the chief alone."

Black looked at him uncomprehendingly. Danny went on in a gush of words.

"I make it up, L.T. Chief is talking about *Who is young officer, He looks like baby,* and this. I tell him Sergeant Caine makes apologies but has to go, but he can tell any problem to young lieutenant, and young lieutenant will tell his boss and bring help."

Black's mind spun.

"I hope maybe he tell you, L.T. Tell you what happen."

"What do you mean? What happened when?"

"On patrol," Danny said. "Not goat patrol. Before. One week, ten days."

"What patrol?"

Danny shook his head miserably.

"I don't know," he said. "I don't see. I don't go on this one. Night time. They tell me, Danny you stay at Vega. They come back, something is wrong. I know something is wrong. Too much whispers, soldiers are scared."

"Which soldiers?"

"I don't know all, but some the guys you talk to for investigation. Some these guys for sure."

"Shannon?"

"Yeah. And Corelli. These guys on patrol."

"The Wizard?"

"I don't know, man."

"The sergeants?"

"Caine for sure. Merrick he stay at Vega. And lieutenant too, he goes. He looks bad when they come back. Goes to his room—your room—and stays. He knows the bad thing happens."

"He didn't stop the bad thing?"

Danny just looked at him reproachfully and shook his head slightly.

"I don't know what happened, L.T.," Danny said. "But everything is bad since the night. Everybody is scared. Nobody talks nobody. Then you come. I hope you help. I know chief knows story, because he is different too, every time we come to town after. I hope chief tells you the story."

And you screwed that up.

"What are you doing out here?" Black demanded.

"After Darreh Sin, after chief, I cannot stay at Vega. You do the heroin . . ."

His hands churned the air for the word.

"Heroin square, and the chief is so mad, and the attack and the bombs. Sergeant Caine, Sergeant Merrick, they will ask me what happened with chief. I know you will not tell them, because . . ."

He peered at Black in the dark.

Because you screwed up.

"So I go," Danny said with finality. "It is not safe for me staying at Vega. They will ask, and I'm scared if I lie and help you they will know."

He looked at the ground.

"I don't know what they do to get me to answer."

That hung in the air. Black picked up his pistol.

"Are you lying?

"L.T.," Danny said sadly. "I watch you."

Black cracked open the pistol too and began pulling it apart.

"You are man who needs the truth."

It only took a few moments to get the simpler pistol down to its basic parts. It too had been disabled.

Black looked up at Danny wordlessly. He set the useless pistol pieces down. His thoughts circled backward until he understood.

"What else do you know?"

Danny looked at him with dark eyes.

"The valley, it . . ."

He swept his hands toward himself as though trying to contain a cloud of smoke.

". . . gathering, L.T. No one at Vega is safe."

"What do you mean?"

"I hear too much. All valley people says get the Devil out of the valley."

"Are you with the Monk?"

Danny swallowed.

"I go, L.T.," he said. "Please."

"Are you with the Monk?"

Danny stood slowly.

"Please, I go. I help you if I can."

"Wait."

Black sat back on his haunches, his mind spinning.

"What else did the chief say?"

"L.T.?"

"Right when we were running out. He was saying some stuff that you didn't translate."

He saw recognition in Danny's eyes. Danny shook his head.

"You watch out this chief, L.T. He is in a bad . . . place? With his people."

"What was the thing he said?"

Danny nodded.

"I don't understand this part," he said. "I mean, I hear the words, I understand the words. I don't understand what he means."

"What were the words?"

"Well, you hear he say I should kill you all, right?"

"Yeah."

"Then the next he says, this one is no sense. He says I kill all, I kill every man of you to . . ."

He made spheres in the air with his hands.

"Earth . . ?" he said, frowning. "Ball?"

"World?"

"This, I think, L.T.," Danny declared. "I kill every man of you from this place all the way to the . . . to your end of the world."

Black watched Danny head downhill through the trees as he reassembled his useless weapons. When he was done he rooted deep in a cargo pocket and came up with the little heart-strewn envelope the Monk had given him back at Vega. He slumped down, sitting against the hillside, and tore it open.

A single slip of paper lay inside. He read it, then closed his eyes for a few moments, memorizing its contents. He folded it back into the envelope and returned it to his pocket.

He stared downslope a moment in the direction Danny had gone. He pulled a map from his cargo pocket and held it close to his face, squinting under the red light of his flashlight. When he was done he folded it back up and put it away.

He picked his way slowly back to the rocks that would take him up to the fishbowl where the soldiers were waiting. He was already squeezing himself back up through the last boulders before he noticed the extra voices up on the slab.

He emerged and stood. Everyone turned and looked at him.

Shannon and the two soldiers Merrick had brought on the patrol stood off to the right, near the ledge, having a smoke. Hill and the guys from the guard tower were still in their chairs.

"Hey there, sir," came a voice from his left.

Caine sat in a camp chair next to Brydon.

26

Brydon shrank in his seat next to the burly sergeant.

"Hey," Black answered, looking around the group.

The assembled soldiers had lapsed into an uncomfortable silence without being sure exactly why. Guys exchanged awkward glances.

Except Shannon, who wore his habitual sneer, and Caine, who watched Black with a blank expression on his face.

"Everyone beat it," Caine said. "Gotta talk to the L.T."

The soldiers from the guard shack hesitated, then rose to go. Shannon elbowed the two with him, sending them toward the exit. Brydon squirmed in his seat.

"Yeah," Black said, looking at Brydon. "Everyone beat it."

Brydon rose, scowling at the ground, and went with the others. Only Shannon, Caine, and Black remained.

"Pull up a chair, sir," Caine said, his face still blank.

Shannon was standing near the edge of the slab, behind the chair where Black had been sitting before. Beyond him, the night.

Black stepped forward to a chair at the head of the semicircle instead. He sat, keeping his eyes on Caine, with Shannon's towering figure in his peripheral vision. He placed his useless rifle across his knees, pointing to the left, with one hand resting on it, and waited for Caine to speak.

Caine took his time lighting up a smoke for himself.

"I'm glad you told me where you were going, sir," he said through an idle cloud. "I was getting worried down there."

Black watched the sergeant carefully, his mind racing.

Don't do it.

"Yeah, well, I'm fine," he responded. "But I'm glad you came up here."

"Oh yeah?"

You have to.

"Yeah," said Black. "I was hoping you could do me a favor when you go back down to Vega."

Off to his right he thought he saw Shannon smirk. Caine carefully maintained his empty expression.

"What's that?" he asked.

"I was hoping you could check my room for me."

Caine showed confusion in spite of himself.

"Yeah, I must have left it unlocked when I went to talk to Sergeant Merrick about Danny yesterday," Black said, watching Caine's eyes carefully. "Someone was in there."

There it was. See it?

"Maybe you could check and make sure I didn't leave it unlocked again," he went on, glancing at Shannon, who was looking at Caine.

Caine said nothing.

"Anyway," Black said nonchalantly, turning back to Caine. "It's a good thing I checked all my stuff before I came up here."

Caine's cigarette dangled, momentarily forgotten. Shannon looked from Caine to Black and back again.

"Hey, Shannon," Black said, eyes locked with Caine's. "Why don't you beat it too?"

"Yeah," Caine said slowly. "Beat it."

Shannon gave a last look at Caine and stumped off toward the boulders. He worked his hulking frame down through them with effort, and was gone.

There was no one left on the slab but Black and Caine and the untended fire, which was working its way down to embers. The smell made Black think of camping.

Caine took a long, theatrical pull on his smoke and exhaled slowly, his hardened eyes fixed on Black the whole time.

"Wonder if you're lyin'," he said idly, his gaze drifting down to Black's rifle. "Or who gave you the parts if you ain't."

"Cut the crap," Black said. "What's this, your mob boss impersonation?"

Caine shook his head in mock sadness.

"Told you not to come up here, L.T.," he said. "Tryin' to help you out."

"Where's Traynor?"

Caine's eyes rose from Black's rifle to his face.

"Wonder what else you're lyin' about," he said quietly.

"Where's Traynor? Why'd you tell me you didn't know him?"

"There is no Traynor," Caine answered. "He's dead."

"No he's not. He just went on leave and came back a few weeks ago."

Caine couldn't conceal his surprise at that.

"Who," he asked, "told you that, Lieutenant?"

Careful.

Black swallowed.

"I'm an S-1 POG, remember?"

POG—"pogue"—was for Person Other than Grunt, a fighting soldier's term for those who did noncombat jobs.

He pressed the bluff.

"You think we don't have unit rosters down on Omaha?"

Caine's eyes narrowed as the gears turned. Black knew where the sergeant's thoughts were headed.

Stop.

"You lied about Traynor getting killed here," Black said, piling on. "Merrick may believe that bullshit, but I don't. Where is he? What did you do to him?"

Caine looked Black from top to bottom, seething. His bulk filled his chair, rippling forearms draped over the straining fabric arms, and for a moment Black thought he might spring from it.

Instead he flipped his cigarette at the fire, admiring the opposite rock wall.

"You're reaching," he announced with some satisfaction. "You don't know shit."

He turned to Black.

"And you're bluffing," he said, his eyes cold.

"Bullshit," Black spat. "You don't know what I know and don't know."

"Who told you about Traynor?"

Stop.

"You lied about the day you took Vega," Black pressed. "I know *that.* Why'd you leave out the drugs? Why'd you lie about who you were fighting that day? What have you got going on that you don't want me to—"

"I fucking *told* you, Lieutenant!" Caine snapped, nearly shouting. "I *told* you I was trying to help you, and I still a—"

The ledge shook with the sound of an explosion from below. Caine and Black both jumped up from their chairs. Caine went first, practically leaping through the opening in the boulders. Black followed him down through the network of steps and ladders, to the level where the radio shack sat.

Several soldiers were there in the shadows, looking down into the night with goggles and night scopes. Shannon was pounding up the stairs from the level below.

"What happened?" Caine demanded.

Bosch was there, leaning on a wooden rail, peering downward through a rifle scope. He wore only a T-shirt underneath his body armor, ropy arms bare and tensed.

Shannon started to shout something, but Bosch cut in.

"Thought I saw three guys with rifles," he said blandly, scanning left and right.

Shannon looked at him in surprise.

"What guys?" Caine demanded.

"Don't know," replied Bosch in a bored voice, eye to the scope. "Musta been wrong, or they scattered when I tossed the grenade."

He lowered his rifle and turned to the assembled crowd. Shannon peered at him in scowled confusion.

"Or I got 'em," Bosch mused as though pondering the weather.

He scrawled a finger back and forth across his mustache. His eyes briefly met Black's.

"Probably should check it out in the morning," he concluded with a shrug.

Black looked from Bosch to Shannon and back to Bosch, who raised a palm in a mock calming gesture.

"Relax, L.T.," he said. "Ain't the end of the world."

Heavy steps stomped down the stairs above them.

"What the fuck is going on?"

Merrick, sweating from the climb back up and over the mountain, emerged from the darkness above them.

"Who's lobbing grenades?"

"Bosch," said Caine, looking at Bosch skeptically, "said he thought he saw someone down there."

Merrick noted Caine's presence with surprise.

"What the fuck are *you* doing here?" he demanded.

Caine shrugged.

"Came to check on the L.T."

"What?"

Caine was all innocence.

"I knew you had your business to do, and the L.T. don't know his way around up here and we're sorta responsible for him, so I figured I'd come up and look after him."

Merrick looked squinty-eyed at Caine.

"Anyway," Caine went on, "you find anything out about Danny?"

Merrick brushed off the question.

"How did you know the lieutenant was up here?"

Caine looked at Black in the shadowy light. For a moment Black thought he was going to say it.

"Just figured," he said, shrugging again, his eyes locked with Black's. "He wasn't at the COP, and everyone's trying to find Danny, so I just figured."

"Yeah, well don't just figure," Merrick said brusquely. "Get back to Vega where you're supposed to be."

In the dim light Black imagined Caine reddening, being dressed down like that in front of a bunch of joes. Caine opened his mouth to speak, then closed it again. Finally, he put his hands up.

"Hey, no sweat," he said. "Just tryin' to help."

"Yeah, well, go help at the COP where you're supposed to be fucking helping."

That one, Black thought, must've burned.

"Take Brydon and Shannon with you," Merrick directed. "And stop wandering around by yourself."

"Hey, roger that," Caine muttered, turning to the stairs. "You the man."

"Yeah, that's right," Merrick said to his back, grinding it in. "I'm the man."

"I'm coming," said Black out of nowhere.

Caine and Shannon turned. Everyone else did too.

"What?" said Merrick.

He looked at Black with furrowed brow. Black held his eyes for a long moment.

"I'm going with them," he declared, shrugging as though it were the obvious thing to do.

"I need to talk to you, sir."

"Later," Black replied.

He turned back to Caine and Shannon, who regarded him with unconcealed surprise.

Thanks, Bosch.

"Let's go back to Vega," he said.

They walked the entire way down, nearly two hours, in silence. Black walked in the middle of the line, with Shannon's looming figure behind him. Brydon walked ahead of him, and Caine led at the front. The only words came toward the end when Caine radioed ahead to alert Vega they were approaching.

It was still dark when they came in through the gate to the puzzled look of the soldier on duty there. They crossed the courtyard, where Caine turned to Brydon.

"Go check on the wounded from yesterday," he said.

"Roger," Brydon mumbled and went off, stealing a last look at Black.

"Go get some chow or something," Caine said to Shannon.

Shannon paused a moment, regarding Caine, before lumbering away. That left Black and Caine standing in the courtyard facing each other.

"Guess you probably oughtta go see about your business too," Black said to Caine.

Caine said nothing.

"Thanks for the lift back here," Black added.

He stood motionless, staring blankly at the sergeant, who stared back with barely concealed rage. Finally, without a word to Black, Caine turned and stalked off toward the complex.

Black watched him go as he himself ambled nonchalantly toward the passageway which he knew would take him to Bay Two. As soon as Caine had disappeared from sight, he broke into a run.

27

Corelli wasn't at his room. A soldier wandered around the corner. Black grabbed him by his uniform and demanded to know where Corelli was. The startled kid stammered that he thought Corelli had just gotten off shift at the CP and gone to chow.

Black made his way quickly, stopping at each corner to peer around. The chow hall was empty except for a lone soldier chewing on cold cuts.

"Was Corelli here?" he asked, crossing briskly to the stack of M.R.E. cases in the corner.

"Uh, roger, sir. Like, just a couple minutes ago."

The soldier pointed at a paper plate with half-eaten food on it.

"Where?" Black asked, stuffing an M.R.E. into a cargo pocket.

"The armory, I think, sir," the kid answered. "With Shannon."

No.

Black pushed out the door at a run. He pounded clumsily through the corridors, his heavy gear jouncing against its straps.

He slammed through the door of the armory, his rifle upside down in his hands like a club. Corelli leaped up from his table in surprise.

"Where's Shannon?" Black nearly shouted, looking left and right in the shadows of the room.

"Oh, he just left a minute ago, sir," said the jumpy Corelli, gesturing at his paperwork with the pen he was holding. "I was just recording his draw."

"What draw?"

"He was minus one grenade, sir," said Corelli. "He was out on a patrol tonight, I guess."

The world seemed to spin. Bosch had said *he* had thrown the grenade. . . .

Focus.

Black took three long strides around the table and grabbed Corelli by the arm.

"Come with me now," he said, hauling the confused soldier up from his table.

"What? Sir, I—"

"Where's your weapon?"

"There, sir," Corelli answered, pointing to his rifle and body armor leaning in the corner.

"Get it all."

He shoved Corelli toward his gear and turned to the spare parts shelf where Brydon's rifle bolt still sat. There were several rifle firing pins. He grabbed one and pocketed it.

"Have you got a pistol slide assembly?"

"One down, sir," stammered Corelli, pointing at a lower shelf. "Sir, what's going on?"

"Where's your map?"

"Here, sir," answered Corelli, pointing at a pouch on his body armor.

"Have you got water in here?"

Corelli pointed to a case near the door. Black pocketed the pistol part and went to the case, grabbing two bottles and waving Corelli to him.

"What about your sidearm?"

Corelli patted his pistol holster.

"Come on, then," he told Corelli urgently as he stuffed one bottle in a cargo pocket. "Hurry."

Corelli, desperately confused but obedient to a fault, complied without further question, hustling over with his rifle in one hand and his body armor in the other.

"Take this and give me yours," Black said, holding out his rifle and an empty hand to Corelli.

Corelli complied wordlessly, giving over his rifle. Black charged it and cracked the door, peeking out into the empty hallway.

In a little over a minute they were passing the foot of Oswalt's stairwell and moving down the darkened corridor beyond it. Three booted kicks and the flimsy closet door burst through its lock. He pushed it shut behind them.

Outside it was still dark, though he knew that would not last. He dragged Corelli to the corner in the wall, where a triangle of moon-shadow provided some limited concealment. He squatted down with his back to the corner, looking left and right down both stretches of wall for anyone approaching. Corelli squatted down next to him.

"Gear up," he told Corelli in a near whisper.

He kept watch as the young soldier began shucking on his body armor.

"Sir, what's going on?" Corelli pleaded.

"You're leaving Vega," he said.

Corelli's eyes widened.

"Don't stop," Black admonished him. "Hurry."

Corelli resumed sealing up his vest.

"You need to get out of here now and hide," he said, speaking quickly. "You're in danger here."

Corelli's face was bewilderment and fear.

"Sir, what do you mean? Why am I in danger?"

Because I lied to save my skin, he wanted to say. *And now Caine thinks it's all on you.*

"Because you gave me rifle parts," he said instead. "And you gave me Traynor."

"*What,* sir?" Corelli stammered helplessly. "But, sir, I only—"

"No time," Black cut in. "Here, turn around."

He commenced to pour both water bottles into the water pouch on Corelli's back. When he was finished, he handed Corelli the M.R.E., which Corelli stuffed in his own cargo pocket. Finally, Black pressed the rifle he was carrying into Corelli's hands and took his own back.

"Can you handle a map?" he asked.

The shaken Corelli nodded weakly.

"Then listen to me, Corelli," Black said, rooting in his cargo pocket. "You will die if you stay here on Vega. You are ordered to leave the COP and hide."

"Hide where, sir?"

Black brought out the Monk's envelope and handed it to him.

"Go here," he said. "Don't stop until you get to these coordinates, and don't leave until the Monk comes and gets you, or I come and get you."

Corelli took the envelope with fumbling hands and started opening it.

"Don't look at it now," Black admonished him. "It'll be light soon. Get over the wall. Go that way."

He pointed cross-slope through the trees. Corelli looked flabbergasted and pale.

Black put his hands on Corelli's shoulders.

"Michael," he said, abandoning protocol. "This is too easy. Get over the wall and get out of sight. Use the map and find your point."

Corelli looked down at the envelope. *Find your point.* Black could see him processing the words. Just like land navigation training.

His hands were shaking visibly. All at once Black saw him as he was, as he was in his prior life just yesterday, and as he was today.

In a man's costume.

He rooted in a cargo pocket and pulled the little zip case that Smoke Toma had given him, pressing it into Corelli's hands.

"Take this too."

Corelli looked down at the case. Black put his hand under Corelli's chin and lifted it.

"He's watching," he told Corelli. "Do it right."

Corelli's eyes came into focus and he nodded, swallowing hard.

"Now go," he urged, pointing at the ladder, which still stood where Shannon had left it. "We'll get to you."

Corelli shoved the envelope and case in his pockets. He climbed the ladder and swung a leg over the top.

"I'm sorry," Black called after him in a whisper.

Corelli gave him one last frightened look and disappeared over the wall.

He repaired his own weapons by the light of his flashlight in the closet. When he was done he holstered and slung everything, then stepped into the hallway, pulling the broken door shut behind him as best he could.

He straightened and walked purposefully around the corner, straight through the heart of COP Vega.

It was getting light outside now. Soldiers were going about morning routines. No one paid him much mind except to note privately how haggard and tore-up the visiting lieutenant looked, and to wonder briefly why he was walking around the outpost in all his gear.

Most figured it had something to do with the periodic gunshots that could be heard outside. Nothing new there.

He entered Bay Two for the second time in the past hour. Brydon was not at his room. As Black suspected, he hadn't bothered to lock it.

Black stepped inside and closed the door behind him. He sat on the bed and waited. Presumably when Brydon was done cleaning and dressing wounds he would be back.

An hour later he gave up. But he had an idea where to look.

On his way, he detoured and passed through the hall where Pistone's hootch was. He pulled open the door of the Porta-Potty and peered inside.

What looked to be another hand had taken a marker and filled in words in all the spaces around the entry, leaving in its place two new and unrelated Chuck jokes.

IF YOU SEE CHUCK,

CHUCK SEES YOU. IF YOU DON'T SEE CHUCK, DUCK.

CHUCK READ THAT THE END OF THE WORLD WAS SCHEDULED FOR 2012 BUT DON'T WORRY, HE CANCELED IT.

28

The Christmas lights were switched on in the Taj Mahal. It felt like nighttime as he pulled the door shut behind him.

At the far end of the container, under the poster of the villa girl, was a raised wooden riser, giving the space a split-level effect. Brydon sat leaning against the rear wall, facing the doorway, elbows crooked over his knees, eyes on an infinite point someplace ahead of him. His gear and weapons sat leaning against the side wall near him.

He had put a CD on the tinny little player. Something Black recognized as disco. A breathy, sprite-voiced woman sang over bass and electric piano.

Black stepped forward, bringing a chair from the poker table. He set it just short of the edge of the riser so that when he sat, he and Brydon were speaking roughly face-to-face.

"Thank you," he told Brydon.

Brydon's eyes didn't leave the point before him.

"I didn't throw the grenade," he mumbled.

"Yeah, but I owe you and Bosch for not saying anything. And Shannon."

Brydon's eyes showed surprise at hearing Shannon's name.

"Yeah," Black said. "I know."

He looked at Brydon's weapons.

"Merrick didn't know about the firing pin and the slide, did he?" he asked. "That was just Caine."

Brydon said nothing.

"Caine brought them to you at the O.P."

Brydon just eyed Black.

"What did he offer you for them?" he asked Brydon. "What did he ask you to do?"

"Wasn't like that," Brydon murmured, looking at the riser.

"Okay," Black replied.

He meant it. He believed Brydon.

"Anyway," Black said. "I think those are from my weapons."

Brydon screwed up his brow at Black as the song on the CD cycled over. A mash of rising keyboard tones that made Black think of someone stretching taffy. Another jumping disco tune, with the same airy woman.

"I have to ask you something," Black said to Brydon.

"Okay."

"It's important, but it's the last question I need to ask."

"Okay."

"What did you mean when you told Corelli that Xanadu is what comes before the end of the world?"

Brydon closed his eyes and shook his hanging head.

"You go there, it'll just take you too, sir."

A weight squeezed on Black's chest and filled his throat. He felt his hand reach out involuntarily, then drop. He looked at the miserable soldier without words.

"What *is* it?" he finally whispered. "Why won't you let anyone help you?"

Brydon spoke softly to the floor.

"None comin' for me," he said flatly.

Black shook his head, uncomprehending.

"What do you mean?" he asked. "No one's getting left behind."

It tasted like a slogan in his mouth. Brydon let out a heaving sigh. He dug in his pocket and brought out something small and white and rectangular. He cupped it in his hands.

The disco woman sang like a fairy giving a full-body massage.

"I wanna ask a question now, sir."

"What?"

Brydon stared at the rectangle, cradling it.

"What were you gonna do with your life?" he said. "Before all this?"

It was the first time anyone had asked him that since his smartass friend, early in their training together.

"I was in seminary."

"What's that?"

"I was going to be a priest."

Brydon let out a single hard laugh, without merriment. It was the closest Black had come to seeing him smile.

"Figures," Brydon said, shaking his head.

He flicked his wrist and sent the white object spinning toward Black. It landed on the edge of the riser. Black retrieved it.

It was a military ID card with a picture of a soldier Black didn't recognize. The name he did recognize.

JASON TRAYNOR

U.S. ARMY

Black turned it over in his hands uncomprehendingly. When he looked up, Brydon was looking at the floor again.

"It's all fucking coming apart," he said quietly.

Black shook his head, confused.

"How did you use this?" he asked. "How'd you go on leave?"

Brydon snorted.

"When was the last time somebody checked the picture against your face, sir?"

Now that he thought about it, no one had ever remotely checked his face against his ID card since the day he presented it as he drove through the main gate of Fort Benning to park his car and get on a plane to Afghanistan with his unit. Once you're in theater, everyone just assumes you are who the name tape on your uniform says you are. Why the hell would someone fake his identity to come to *this* place?

He examined the picture on the card. The kid looked like the favorite son of a small town.

"I can't be that guy, sir," Brydon whispered.

"You're not," Black said. "You're not Jason Traynor."

"No, not *that* guy," Brydon replied dismissively.

"Who?"

"The Pearl Harbor guy."

"What?"

Black watched a tear fall from Brydon's hidden face and strike the riser between his feet.

"*Fuck* Sergeant Caine!" the Wizard spat bitterly. "*Fuck* him for making me do it. Tell him I said, Fuck You, *Sar'nt*."

A sob escaped him. He cupped his forehead in a palm and blew out a long breath.

"Who *are* you?" Black pleaded.

"Told you, sir," Brydon sighed, sounding weary. "I'm a ghost."

"Where's your unit?"

Brydon looked up at him with glistening eyes. When he spoke his voice was clear.

"I *am* my unit."

Black lunged, shouting Brydon's name, but the pistol was too close and Brydon was too fast to it. Black recoiled away at the blast, falling backward off the riser and knocking over his chair.

The floor swayed beneath him as he crashed through the assembled lawn chairs, nearly sending the CD player and the fairy girl flying, arms out before him wildly to find the tilting doorway.

Now that you're near
In Xanadu

Now that I'm here

29

He burst from the container and staggered into sunlight, looking left and right frantically. There was a near passageway to the left.

He pounded through, banging on doors. He didn't know this part of the outpost, which looked to be devoted mostly to storage. It was only from the floor, after tripping over a crate, that he heard the muffled sound of music ahead.

He picked himself up, knee throbbing, and pounded the few steps to the door. He crashed through.

Cheap faux-Persian tapestries of the sort sold on every American FOB covered the walls. The floor was carpeted with a mixture of Army blankets and furniture moving pads. There was room for three cots, each with an open sleeping bag draped across it, and a couple of large heaps of blankets and other padding fashioned amorphously into something between a recliner and a beanbag chair.

The only light came from an old-fashioned Lava Lamp in the corner. An Indian sitar played inside a boom box someplace. A haze of pungent smoke filled the room.

Soldiers in shorts and T-shirts sprawled on two of the three cots and lay draped across both of the amorphous heaps. One of them was Shannon.

He'd removed his gear, which was stacked in a corner with his weapons and boots, and lay barefoot in camouflage pants and T-shirt. A tall contraption Black recognized as a water pipe sat on the padded floor next to him, the end of its hose lying close to his hand.

He looked up at Black foggy-eyed.

“I think,” he mumbled, as the other soldiers hazily registered Black’s presence, “that you’re gonna wanna get out of here, sir.”

Black pushed backward through the door, emerging dazed into the dim hallway.

C.P.

He stumbled off further down the hallway and turned corners without direction until he reached an intersection he recognized. He pounded off toward the command center.

Three soldiers slugged down the hallway in the other direction. Two of them were supporting the third, who was hopping on one leg and grimacing in pain. There was a sizable bloodstain on the lower leg of his trousers.

He burst through the CP door and stood panting in the sudden silence.

It was just as he’d left it. The quiet hum of the fan and the occasional crackle of static. The smart-alecky kid from before was at the desk again. He noted Black’s heaving, sweaty presence with a raised eyebrow and smirk from behind his paperback.

“Perfect timing, there, sir,” he said dryly, before Black could speak. “An officer right on time, whattaya know.”

“What?” stammered Black.

The kid lowered one hand from the book and palmed from the desktop a folded piece of paper, which he held aloft between his index and middle finger.

“For you, sir,” he said in a bored voice. “From Sergeant Merrick.”

Black stepped forward, confused and huffing, and with a trembling hand retrieved the paper.

“When did you get this?” he demanded breathlessly.

“Just a couple minutes ago.”

It took Black’s upturned mind a moment to process this. Merrick was back. This was good. Black looked at the folded slip, quivering in his hand. It was sealed with a strip of tape.

“Been doin’ some P.T., there, sir?” the soldier smirked.

Black turned hurriedly to the door. He stopped and spun back around, grabbing the kid's walkie-talkie off the desktop, over his confused protests.

He rang up the aid station, identifying himself as Vega X-Ray.

"You need a medic at the Taj Mahal," he said flatly into the radio.

He sent the radio bouncing and skittering across the desk between its owner's furtive attempts to capture it, and pushed through the door, tearing open the paper.

> LT. B—
>
> MEET ME ROOF, GUARD SHACK
>
> TIME NOW
>
> SGT. M

He pocketed it and jogged away, cutting left and right through the complex. He passed no one between the CP and Oswalt's stairwell, which he pounded up two at a time. He reached the landing with Oswalt's hootch, whose curtain was open just enough to reveal Oswalt himself reclining inside, playing one of his video games.

He stomped past and started up the final stretch of steps.

"Oh, I wouldn't go there, sir," Oswalt called.

Black paused on the stair.

"What?" he puffed over his shoulder.

"I was sayin' I wouldn't go up to the roof right now, sir."

Black took two steps back down to the landing.

"Why not?" he demanded, chest heaving.

Oswalt didn't take his eyes from the game. Rocket volleys decimated the enemy.

"Oh, there's another sniper out this morning, sir," he said, thumbs working madly. "It ain't safe right now."

"A sniper?"

"Yes, sir. Up on the hill. Already shot Garza in the leg."

The soldier being carried up the hall as Black had left Shannon.

"He's been goin' for anyone who sets foot up there, sir."

Black whirled to face the final length of stairwell, finding his rifle unslung and in his hands. He stepped backward and nearly fell down the flight below. He felt dizzy.

He put a hand out to the wall and slowly backed down the stairs, keeping his rifle trained upward as he did so. Halfway down he realized he was probably pointing it the wrong way.

He turned and faced the way he was traveling. At the bottom of the stairwell he peered around the corner, still breathing heavily, before stepping down into the corridor and jogging away into the dark.

He pushed through the broken closet door and out to the narrow strip of backyard, breaking to his right and running in a crouch. He reached the passageway nearest Lieutenant Pistone's hootch and covered its length quickly, weapon up, heart pounding.

He saw no one all the way back to his room. He let himself in and locked the door behind him, breathing heavily.

Standing in the pitch-dark, his breath slowed. He set his flashlight on an end table and switched it on, pointing it at the wall for usable light. He felt the calmness descending on him again.

He stripped off his gear and changed all his clothing quickly, taking a fresh uniform and relacing his boots. He dug in his ruck and came up with a very small pack with a water bladder in it. There were a few water bottles on a shelf, which he used to fill the drinking bladder, and an M.R.E. case in the corner. He tore one open and crammed its pieces into the tiny pocket on the pack.

When he was done he took the flashlight and retrieved his map from the cargo pocket of his other trousers. He sat on the bunk with his back against the wall. With one hand he set his rifle across his knees, pointing at the door, and disengaged the safety. With the other he arrayed the map and flashlight so he could study it in the dark.

When he was done he folded the map and stuffed it in a cargo pocket. He switched off the flashlight. Then he waited, looking at the door, both hands on his rifle now.

He realized that he had not slept in forty-eight hours. The calm had come over him fully now, but he did not grow drowsy.

Five hours in, he switched on the flashlight and shone it on the stacks of items from Pistone's footlocker, still arrayed next to him on the bed where he'd left them. He pulled the yearbook to him and set the light so the book was illuminated. With one eye on the door he started turning pages.

It was a bleak harvest. The inside cover had two signatures, both of which were just that—signatures, and nothing else.

There were a couple more here and there as he flipped through, with one or two perfunctory "Have a great summer!" and "Good luck in college!" pity notes. Eventually he passed the senior photo of Pistone himself, which looked much like the Pistone in the picture on the side table except with larger eyeglasses and a stark comb-over of a haircut.

There was not a single note that looked to be from an actual friend, and none more than four or five words long, until he got to the inside back cover. It was scribbled in odd writing, as though a rightie had done it with his left hand, and it was a healthy length indeed.

> *Hey Pissed-on you faggot.*
>
> *Yeah you left your yearbook lying in the band room, idiot. Thought you were gonna get some cool notes? Hey I got one for you right here.*
>
> *You know who's writing this so I'm not even going to sign it so you can just narc on me again like a pussy. But you know who this is.*
>
> *I am here to tell you that I know it was you and you may think you got away with it but you aren't going to get away from me. You may think you are graduating and I am stuck here all summer and you'll be safe. But I know where you work and I'm going to be there every day after I leave this shithole. When you leave work I am going to be there. And I am going to kick your twisted little freak ass every night for the whole summer. So get ready asshole.*
>
> *GOOD LUCK IN COLLEGE!*

Black could not imagine a stranger memento to haul all the way to Afghanistan. He closed the yearbook and set it down on top of Pistone's journal, switching out the light and resuming his watch.

Several hours later the amber time on his wrist told him it was fully dark outside. He rose from the bed and switched on his flashlight. He shouldered the small pack and grabbed a camouflage patrol cap, leaving his body armor, helmet, and gear stacked against the wall.

He put his rifle back on SAFE and set it down on the bunk. From his trousers he drew his little leatherbound notebook and scratched a mark in it, shoving it back in his pocket when he had done so. He took a water bottle from the shelf and drank half of it in a long draught, switching off his flashlight when he was done and setting it on the invisible bunk next to his invisible rifle and gear.

He turned to the door, seeing only the dim cracks of light around its frame. He stepped forward and removed the padlock from the hasp, unholstering his pistol as he did so. He closed his eyes and blew out a long breath.

"Coming home," he murmured.

I'll see you soon.

He opened the door and stepped out into the corridor.

The soldier at the gate stared off into the young night, watching the sea of fog creep up the slopes below his feet. His walkie-talkie crackled.

"Gate, this is Minor."

Specialist Minor, the guard knew, was inside cleaning weapons in the grand house's former foyer. He picked up the walkie.

"Minor, Gate."

"Hey, man, be advised, that creepy L.T. is coming your way and he's walking through here with his nine-mil out like he's trippin' or somethin'."

"Roger."

"Just, like, so he doesn't sneak up on you or nothing."

"Roger."

The soldier turned and looked back into the courtyard, rifle in his hands. Within moments, the lieutenant emerged and began crossing the courtyard. His pistol was out, just as Minor had said, though he carried it down at his side. When he saw the soldier he holstered it.

He was an odd picture as he approached. No body armor or rifle, just a small pack and a patrol cap.

"Evenin', sir," the soldier said.

The lieutenant just nodded calmly as he passed and said not a word, breezing through the gate as though he were strolling out onto a city street on an ordinary day.

"Uh, sir, you can't . . ." said the soldier and trailed off.

The lieutenant headed downslope. The soldier called after him.

"Um, sir, going to Darreh Sin would be an extremely bad idea."

"Probably," called the lieutenant as he kept going.

The soldier keyed his radio to call the command post as he watched the strange young officer disappear into the fog.

He walked straight downhill until the mist surrounded him and he was sure he couldn't be seen from the gate anymore. Then he cut right and started climbing, using his hands to feel his way through the trees and his impeccable memory for terrain to guide him to it.

See you at the end of the world.

His feet found the trail, and he picked up a slow, steady run uphill.

PART FOUR

30

You see it now. Clearly.

His bootsoles made little sound as they padded against the soft dirt of the rising trail, one before the other. The land climbed ahead of him, gently. Invisibly.

The fog lay heavy upon the trail and the moon hadn't yet risen. But he felt sure of the route, sure of what lay ahead. He watched for tree branches in the mist and let his feet keep the trail.

Go farther. Farther up.

He would be well beyond the O.P. by now. Somewhere far below and miles behind lay Darreh Sin. He'd gone deeper up the Valley, he was sure, than anyone from 3/44 had ever been. Farther than he'd ever been.

Farther from there.

The trail was broad and flat in parts, close and challenging at other points. The river was not far, below and to his left. At times the trail cut close enough to hear it.

When the route moved away, the rest was silence. Only the quiet sound of his footfalls padding the land, over and over, upward to where he knew he needed to go.

You'll find it.

He'd chosen a pace that he could maintain, steadily, for as many miles as he needed to.

You won't falter.

It had been a trail like this one, that first dark morning at Fort Benning. Slugging through the black woods with the instructors hollering at them, emerging to the shining wet track, finding his friend afterward.

Let's go again, he'd said to the smartass, arms linked around shoulders. He had felt he could hit the track and run forever.

You can. Further.

The cooling mountain air filled his lungs and drove his limbs.

Go into the mountains further.

There'd been no trail the final night on the land navigation course, when the two of them made their mad flight across the mountains. They didn't have a prayer. Too far from the finish line. No time to use the map or the compass, no time to plot a route. Only time to run.

Scrambling and falling across the field of felled logs, he had realized that he didn't care. The task was ludicrous. Impossible. But he didn't care. He'd felt certain they would find the way.

You will. This is what you do.

As they bounded through streams and slashed their faces on vines, he had laughed aloud. In that moment he had never wanted to leave that forest.

You don't have to.

He drove further up the trail.

Three hours in, he found it.

Ahead on his right, just visible in the mist. He felt sure enough of the signature feature that he didn't stop to consult his topographic map.

The narrow draw rose sharply up and away from the path. Ahead, the trail proper narrowed and bent around the rump of the mountain, through perilous cliff's-edge portions he'd seen on the map. He left the trail and began climbing.

A rivulet of water trickled down among the stones and pebbles of the draw. He let it flow over his hands as he worked his way higher. As he rose, his thoughts circled back.

Back to the beginning.

Focus.

To the other climb, up the other mountain.

Stay on this mountain.

He clawed and pulled upward. He guessed he'd climbed about five hundred feet when he came over the top.

There was no fog up here. The stars in the black sky were clear.

"It'll just take you too."

Moonlight shone silver on the mountainsides. The ground opened wide before him.

31

A flat-bottomed valley lay cupped in the highlands. He stood at one narrow end, looking down into it, on the lip of a low pass at the top of the draw he'd just climbed. Steep slopes rose up on either side of him, cradling the lowland all along its length.

He guessed it at about two miles long and a half mile across at its widest, with surprisingly level ground along the middle. The view was as though he had just climbed a dam and were peering over the top at the mountain reservoir behind it.

The travel would be easy through here. Then another short climb through the pass at the far end.

He started down the gentle decline to the low ground, still breathing hard from the climb in the thin air. He hadn't gone more than a few hundred yards before he saw the first blossoms.

The waist-high stems were topped with bulbous capsules the size of fists. Flowers had opened atop some of them. Others stood closed, not yet in bloom.

A field of opium poppies.

Examining the map before leaving Vega, he'd been expecting this little valley to be filled with more mountain grassland like that he'd seen when he peered through the scope at the Meadows. A find like this hadn't occurred to him.

The field was vast. Stems and flowers caught the moonlight as far ahead as he could see, and from left to right, filling the flatland between the slopes. Somebody up here was thriving, whatever the Taliban had to say about it.

He would have to plow through or go around and pick his way along the hillsides just outside the field. Either way would be slow going. Either way would put him at risk of being seen by the field's owners.

He stepped to the edge of the field, bending to look at the nearest stalks. He'd never seen a cultivated poppy field up close before.

The capsules were impressive, alien things, engorged with the ancient drug. He reached out and felt one, running his finger over its smooth surface.

Which wasn't smooth. He leaned in to inspect it. What he saw made him duck down low to the ground.

Each capsule was scored with vertical lines inscribed by a blade. At the bottom of each incision was a growing white globule of latex, seeping from the plant.

The field was being harvested.

Everyone knew basically how it worked. The incisions were made at the end of the day, and the capsules were left to drain overnight. In the morning the dried latex—pure opium—was collected.

If it was to be collected in the morning, then the field would be guarded tonight. A plantation this size would be guarded well.

So twice five miles of fertile ground

He blew out a long breath. Words danced at the edge of his memory.

With walls and towers were girdled round

A hazy remembrance reached out across two nights without sleep. He was hearing voices.

Beware! Beware!

No, he was hearing voices. Squatting, he peered around behind him.

For he on honey-dew hath fed

Two orange cigarette pinpoints, moving lazily along the bottom of the slope toward the edge of the field.

And drunk the milk of Paradise

He turned back to the flowers, got on his hands and knees, and began to crawl.

32

He lay with his cheek in the soil, waiting for the voices to fade.

Stay awake.

It had gone like this the whole way. Crawl, then voices, then down on his belly for five or ten minutes. Voices fading, then more crawling.

He checked his watch. Two hours, he thought, since he'd started across the field.

The plantation went on without end. Whoever controlled this land was well funded and highly motivated. He knew only that it lay far outside the realms of Darreh Sin and its boisterous chief.

The voices moved on again. He pushed his body off the ground with some effort and drove on through the stalks and stems, his mind crawling backward.

He had heard stories about it. The guy in Ranger School who was so exhausted and hungry that he bit his own hand open believing it was a cheeseburger. But Black hadn't really believed you could hallucinate from fatigue or fall asleep standing up until he saw someone do it in front of him.

The instructors had had them on another all-night hike through the mountains. A "ruckmarch," they called it. Seventy-pound packs—rucks—all around, and off we go through the hilly backwoods of Fort Benning.

The guy was big. He'd volunteered to carry the big machine gun. He suffered. About ten miles in, at about two in the morning, someone took pity on him and took a turn with the big gun.

As soon as the guy handed it off and traded it for a regular rifle, he fell asleep. Black watched him do it. He fell asleep while walking but just kept on walking. He promptly veered off the trail into the woods. Black had had to chase him down and smack him awake before he hit a tree or fell into a creek.

Pushing through the vast poppy field, he stopped and listened a moment. Nothing. He rose to his knees and hazarded a peek above the bulbs, across the surface of the sea.

Good progress, he thought, gauging the distance of the surrounding slopes and passes. He ducked below the surface and drove on.

Later during that same night at Fort Benning, Black himself had seen the famous Officer Candidate School archway looming in front of him. The brutal march was finally over. They were back at the barracks.

But they weren't. The archway had faded, leaving only black trees and dirt trail.

The poppy stems were thinning. Unbelievable. Glorious. He stopped at the last row, listening for sounds. He heard nothing and poked his head out from between them.

He looked left and right and saw no one. He began to crawl forward, out of the field, but stopped short when he saw what was before him.

A mountain slope rose up sharply in his path, rising high to the stars. This made no sense to him. There should be flat ground ahead, climbing gently to the far pass, which he would traverse to get back to the trail.

He stayed there on his hands and knees for what seemed a long time before it hit him.

He was at the left edge of the field, not the far end of it as he'd thought. Down among the poppies, with no frame of reference, he hadn't kept a straight course.

Rookie inattentiveness. Now he was way off to one side of the field. The left side, he was sure. Right?

Get it together.

He surveyed the mountain features from one end of the depression to the other. Yes, the left.

Cursing himself, he turned and crawled back into the stems, bearing left toward the end of the plantation and the pass that would take him out of this infernal valley. He reminded himself to check his location against the mountains more frequently this time.

The key, he had learned after that all-night march, was to be cognizant of the possibility of hallucinations under fatigue and stress. To know your own physical and mental limits. This very awareness could extend those limits. He'd learned to push his own envelope to the danger point without pushing it beyond. He'd learned that his own capacities were greater, his own limits further distant, than those of most of his fellow trainees. As long as you knew where they lay, you were good.

His friend had seen the California Raisins dancing in the woods that night at Benning.

He was smiling at the memory of his friend's abashed face confessing it the next morning, when he emerged finally, exhausted, at the end of the poppy field, and saw a mountainside rising sharply up before him.

He stared up the slopes uncomprehending, jaw slung dumb, face upturned to the moonlight.

Shaking his head, he turned back into the stems and plowed on. How long now?

More voices, in front and to his right. Another cut-through pathway probably. He went down on his belly.

The voices didn't seem to be moving. A couple guys standing there having a smoke again.

Ten minutes went by, or so. The smell of the soil was rich and fertile.

He checked his watch. Two hours in, he thought. Right? Surely there was not much more left to the field.

Good thing he knew his limits. Knowing your limits was the main thing. Otherwise you push yourself beyond them and you wake up in a poppy field in Afghanistan with a gun in your face.

"From this place all the way to your end of the world."

A moment's rest would do him good.

33

Wake up.

He startled, his face jerking up from the soil.

He pushed stiffly to his elbows and looked all about him, frantic. It was still dark. The cold soil had him shivering.

He pushed the light on his watch. He couldn't remember what time he'd entered the field. Five hours ago?

Dumb, dumb, dumb.

Had he heard something?

Get out.

Adrenaline coursing generously through him now, he pushed off the ground, abandoning thought, and ran. Stems bent and crashed away before him as he stomped through. The mountains rose to his left and to his right.

Moving target.

After not more than a few seconds his feet struck bare, open ground. He almost stumbled at the sudden lack of anything in his way.

He'd been a hundred feet from the end of the field.

He slowed, going to a squat like a runner on the starting blocks. He looked left and right and unholstered his pistol. At the sound of voices he took off running again, wildly.

Get there. Don't stop.

The voices raised to shouts. He ran flat-out until he could hear them no more, and kept running as he hit the gentle slopes to the far pass.

He climbed as quickly as he could, not stopping until he'd crested the pass to the other side. He flung himself on the ground, heaving and panting. It had been easy going compared to the draw, but the thin air and his own adrenaline had him completely winded.

He checked his watch again. Light would come soon.

No one appeared to be following up the slopes. He took a long drink of water, draining the bladder, and collapsed on his back, allowing himself a minute to recover.

A fresh panorama greeted him on this side of the pass. He had crossed back into the Valley. It was narrower here, the opposing mountains closer and the bottom not so far below.

"Xanadu is what comes before the end of the world."

He descended from the pass quickly, back down into the lingering fog. A full haze had enveloped him by the time he found the trail again. He took up his run and drove further on.

He guessed he'd gone barely another mile when he saw it. He might have missed the telltale markings had it not been for the early gathering light.

The goat track rose up and away from the trail to his right. He followed it, climbing through the dewy haze. As he'd expected, he didn't have to climb far.

The track leveled onto a broad shelf of clear ground against the steeper mountainsides. Sheer rock walls, stained in dark brown, rose up from the site for a hundred feet or more before tapering into the rising slopes. He slowed to a walk and passed along its length. Its edge, where the ground sloped down into forest, was perhaps seventy-five feet from the cliffs at its widest. It couldn't have been more than fifty yards long.

A slight breeze had picked up, beginning to move the fog, breaking it into clouds and wisps. The scene presented itself in pieces as he moved through the half-light.

Burned joists forked up through the shifting mist, reaching for the sky. A command post, maybe, or other temporary wooden construction.

The charred remains of a pair of shipping containers came into view next, their markings obliterated by the fire.

Other shapes were unidentifiable. Blackened debris littered the ground. He saw the scalded, skeletal chassis of a large diesel-powered generator.

You couldn't help him.

At the end of the shelf he paused and turned back, surveying the scene.

"Sorry, Billy," he murmured.

He turned and began climbing down the hillside toward the trail, leaving behind him the earthly remains of Combat Outpost Xanadu.

It was nearly fully light now. The Valley narrowed further as he moved deeper and higher. The hazy shapes of the peaks above were closer, the opposite slopes closing in. Trees crowded the trail and hindered the view ahead.

There were no more river sounds. He'd gotten above the springs and runoff that fed it.

The trail tightened ahead and bent around a hillside out of sight. He slowed to a walk and worked his way between trunks and rock at a narrow spot wide enough for a goat or a man and not much else.

Once clear of the bottleneck there was nothing else obscuring his view. The opposite slopes were barely a couple hundred feet away, and narrowing. The trees opened to scrubby mountain grass. Through the last remnants of mist he saw it ahead.

There was no more Valley left to climb. It was there before him, not a hundred yards away. The End of the World.

He approached in wonder, removing a glove, and touched it.

His heart sank.

34

Standing with his hand pressed cold against it, he understood.

It was an impressive construction. There was no way they got vehicles all the way up here. It must have been heavy-lift helicopters laying in all the pieces and equipment.

A wall of walls. Concrete blast barriers lined up twenty feet high, one against another on the slanting ground, shingled all across the gap, with another layer of shorter walls piled haphazardly atop, and more shoring up the gaps at the bottom. There must have been another complete set of walls built behind the one he could see, because the whole hulking thing had been filled with cement. It had oozed and dried like frosting at the seams, puddling through the gaps at the bottom.

It had been built in a hurry. He thought he knew when.

It was a slapdash arrangement, but the engineers had outdone themselves. At the highest, narrowest point in the land, not a hundred feet across, where all converged on a narrow pass between rising cliffsides, the United States Army had sealed the exit and entrance over the border, rendering this valley useless for any significant transit, of goods, drugs, or fighters.

It was pockmarked with black divots of ineffectual rocket fire. Charring and cracking at the bottom showed where a more serious attempt at breaching with explosives had been made. But the wall had held. Barely flinched, from the look of it.

He was sure some of the hardier locals could scale the steep peaks in a pinch. But for any real traffic of any volume, for anyone who hadn't spent his life scampering up and down among Afghan crags, forget it.

There were no foreign fighters coming in this way from Pakistan, and there were no drugs going out. The Valley was closed.

No wonder the joes at Xanadu had called it the End of the World.

His palms felt the cold concrete. He hung his head and leaned forward until it rested against the wall.

Sorry.

He understood that he'd been right, that it had gone back to the beginning. But he'd been wrong. That was all past.

He thought he knew now who the servant was. And he knew that he would have to go back down. He would have to fix what he could fix.

He closed his eyes and heaved a shuddering breath.

"I'm sorry I didn't listen."

I know.

He turned and slumped against the wall, sliding down until he sat at its foot, legs splayed before him, hands palms-up in the dirt. He rested his head against the reinforced concrete and saw the Valley laid out below him to the horizon. The sun had broken over the peaks and colored its heights and depths in golden haze and shadow.

Tearstreaks ran in the grime smeared on his face.

"When?"

Not now.

He palmed his cap off his head and let it crumple to the dirt beside him.

Soon.

He lay against the wall, watching the Valley fill with light, until the concrete chilled him.

Now go.

He pulled himself to his feet and trudged downhill until he found the outlet of a running spring to fill his water. The first spring of the Valley. He splashed some on his face and climbed back to the trail, where he began the long run down.

See you.

As he ran he thought of the Wizard Billy Brydon, sole survivor of the overrun and obliteration of COP Xanadu. He retraced in his head the terrified path Brydon must have followed all the way back down the Valley as he fled the cauldron that had taken all his friends. All the way to where he knew another American outpost lay. All the way to COP Vega, to where Black was not going.

35

Despite the downhill travel it still took him the entire morning and into the early afternoon. He skipped the poppy field this time, working his way around the mountain on the tight portion of the trail. He was glad he had bypassed its cliffs and precipices in the dark.

When he knew that O.P. Traynor lay behind him, he cut away from the path to Vega and began descending the ridgelines that would take him where he needed to go. The sun shone clear along the mountaintops and he counted on his constant movement to give him a measure of protection in the open.

He could not see it yet but had committed its location to memory and moved confidently down across the heights. He had traveled these many miles unmolested and was grateful for his luck. He knew what he needed to do, and with a bit more luck could get it done.

Emerging from the trees onto a sun-drenched ridgeline, he saw it ahead. It was such an unusual feature, squatting on a mountaintop in a place its builders knew little of.

He approached the stone building slowly, not wanting to cause surprise. When he got within earshot he shouted.

"Corelli?"

Nothing. He approached. The stone construction was fascinating, the style alien to this land.

The thing was built simply. From this side, up on the ridge, he could see a single door and a small window set to one side of it. It was stout enough to have survived a hundred and fifty years of wind and snow and sun, and looked like it could do another hundred and fifty in a walk.

What plans they must have laid.

"Corelli, it's Lieutenant Black," he called as he trotted up to the door.

He peeked inside.

"Hey, Corelli, are you—"

Corelli was there. Black rushed to him.

A deep gash scarred his forehead above his wild eyes. He thrashed against bindings behind his back. His body armor, helmet, and rifle were piled haphazardly in a corner. He jerked his head at Black and tried to speak through his gag, panic in his eyes.

"Hold still," Black told him.

A stone worktable had been built into the corner of the room. Corelli's hands were bound behind him tightly and around one stone leg by a pair of sturdy plastic flex-cuffs. Police used these during riots and other mass-arrest situations. Soldiers routinely kept them hooked on their combat gear, for handling prisoners captured in raids or firefights. Black guessed these had come off of Corelli's person.

On the worktable sat a green military radio set. Its cabinet was smashed, its display shattered. With a rock? A hammer? He turned to Corelli's bindings.

Corelli bucked against the gag, desperate to speak. Black yanked at it until he'd worked it over Corelli's teeth and chin.

"Sir, there's a—"

Black heard the sound and whirled around.

An Afghan girl of ten or eleven stood in the threshold. She wore unusually short-cropped hair and a traditional Nuristani girl's embroidered black dress. Her eyes shone silver-blue. Black recognized her.

He had only time to wonder what had brought her all the way up here from Darreh Sin, raising a hand in greeting and opening his mouth to speak, before she brought Corelli's pistol from behind her back and shot Black with it.

The round struck just inside his left shoulder, spinning him and dropping him to the floor. A cascade of stars washed through his vision as his head struck stone. Corelli kicked and howled.

He lay gasping on his back on the cold floor. The ceiling spun. The room went dark and light.

Adrenaline coursing through him, he ordered himself to rise. He could not rise.

Straining, he bent his neck and brought his echoing head an inch off the floor. He peered past his feet.

Through the blurry doorway, speckled in a thousand dots of light, he saw the girl pick herself up off the ground and look about her. Bending to pick something up, she placed it behind her ear and stepped to the threshold. She stood there, eyes ablaze, surveying the scene.

Corelli bucked against his bindings somewhere, shouting at her from a hundred miles away to *Stay away from him!*

She took two steps and stood over Black. It was a red flower, the thing behind her ear. As she bent down she spoke words he did not understand.

She could not believe her luck.

Truly, Father, you have guided my hand today.

It had been an easy call, following the young soldier from his compound, and greatly interesting that he had come to one of the bearded American's hiding places. Normally he and the other Americans pretended they did not know each other.

When dawn came she'd had to hurry back before Mother missed her. She feared nothing might come of this.

I should not have doubted.

It took all the next night of waiting, until her moment came. Once that was done, dawn again, and again back to Mother. Poor Mother.

She had never slipped away in the daytime. But she had felt certain that this time she must.

You were telling me I must.

Even if it were merely for another prisoner for the talibs it would have been worth it. Worth the risk, though it meant traveling as herself.

But this prize was one she had not anticipated. Not so soon.

The officer.

He lay splayed on the floor before her looking pale and weak, his breathing labored.

The one with the black bar.

The frightened young soldier in the corner heaved and tugged against his bindings and shouted at her in his American tongue. She ignored him and stepped forward, regarding her prey.

The servant. Just as they said he was.

He looked back at her with eyes that kept going unfocused, his rubbered limbs grazing the floor ineffectually like an insect speared to the earth. He looked like he would lose consciousness soon. She had probably shot his heart.

You guided my hand true.

She bent over him.

"Let me be your last living sight, devil."

She reached for his chest, waving aside his feeble efforts at defending himself. She pinched a corner of the fabric square that bore his mark, and pulled.

It came away easily. She straightened and turned to the thrashing soldier in the corner.

"Don't worry," she told him. "You won't be alone for long."

She turned and left, heading downhill for home.

Now the talibs will know. There will be no question. They will know who defends this land.

She pocketed the square with the black bar on it. The black bar she had seen in the darkness, cowering in the doorframe of Mother's home, in the flash of light that took Sourabh to paradise, to wait there for Father.

I hope you were not frightened, Sourabh, while you were alone.

She could see no face that night. Only the bar. Qadir had told her what the bar meant. The officer.

Qadir had told her things she needed to know. Told Tajumal. But there was no more need for Tajumal now.

She was the avenger. Not Qadir, not the young men who hurled themselves uselessly at the Americans. Only her. The bar would be her proof.

They will know who is faithful.

She hurried down over rocks and grasses, planning her explanations for Mother.

Rest, Sourabh. Rest with Father.

As she ran she felt tears run on her face, and she realized they were for joy.

In the dream he saw it clearly. Saw that he'd been wrong again. But she told him that was okay, and he was pleased with himself for seeing it now.

He lay on his back looking up at the stone window, and she stood over him. It was not her, but her. She reached and put a hand on his face, and told him not to worry. She told him to rest, there on the soft stone floor. She said he wouldn't be alone for long.

36

He lay in the black depths but could not rest because his head felt as though he were being kicked in it. The floor hardened beneath him.

The muted sounds resolved into a voice, and it came to him that he was in fact being kicked in the head.

"Please, sir. You gotta get awake now."

By Corelli.

"Come on, sir. Wake up now."

Kick.

The kid was using the side of his boot, but come on.

"Stop," he croaked.

His mouth tasted like sand.

"Sorry, sir," he heard Corelli answer. "Can't have you going into shock right now, sir."

He couldn't bring himself to open his eyes yet.

"How long?" he whispered.

"Not more than fifteen minutes, sir. You just gotta stay awake for me, okay, sir?"

"Yeah," Black managed.

His mouth was dry, and his head pounded horribly from where it had struck the floor. Something was on fire in the left side of his chest. Something was wet behind his back.

He cracked his eyelids open and immediately closed them. Much too bright.

I am in bad shape.

"I'm still awake," he mumbled.

"Okay, sir. Good, sir."

Corelli blew out a breath and seemed to go all to pieces.

"Ohhhhh, sir, I'm sorry, sir. I screwed up."

Not now, Corelli.

"I'm gonna need a minute," Black wheezed.

He took a minute. Above all else in the world, he wanted to lie perfectly still. Finally, he cleared his throat.

"What happened?"

"I slept, sir!" Corelli cried miserably. "I'm sorry I slept! I screwed up!"

He stamped the stone wall with the flat of his boot.

"I came here just like you said, sir. I found it and I waited here all day, but I couldn't call the frequency on the paper you gave me because the radio was smashed when I got here."

Oh, damn.

"And then I waited all night," Corelli went on in a gush of words. "And I just laid down to sleep for an hour before it got light. She got my weapon and hit me on the head with a rock or something while I was sleeping, sir. She had my pistol and my knife and my flex-cuffs and everything. She kept screaming at me and pointing until I sat here in the corner, and I was so out of it, sir, from where she had hit me with the rock, everything was just spinning, and she had my pistol and she kept hitting me on the head from behind with the pistol butt while she put the cuffs on. Ohhh, sir, my head hurts."

Black twisted his head toward the sound of Corelli's voice and hazarded another glance. The soldier's face was ashen and the bleeding gash on his head looked ugly.

"I'll get help," Black said immediately, starting to push himself up from the floor.

He didn't get halfway upright before the world spun upside down and he felt himself skewered on a hot poker which pierced him from the inside of his shoulder down through his hip. He collapsed back onto the floor, feeling a wave of nausea wash over him.

"Oh, sir, you just stay there. You're hurt too bad. Have you got a knife, sir?"

Knife. His knife.

With his armor and rifle and gear in Pistone's hootch.

"No."

"Oh."

You idiot.

"Okay. That's okay, sir. I'll figure something out here."

He lay there in silence, waiting for the nausea to pass, while Corelli figured something out. After a full five minutes in which no plan was forthcoming, he realized that there was nothing to figure out. They were stuck.

I just need a minute.

The room's spinning slowed. As long as he lay still, he could think more or less clearly. But he was clearly no use to anyone for the moment. He could really have used some water.

He craned his head and looked at Corelli, who looked pale and forlorn.

"What did your platoon do to that girl's family?" he asked the young soldier.

Corelli looked at him in surprise before casting his eyes to the stone floor. His head followed, until Black could no longer see his face. A great heaving breath came out of him.

"Oh, sir," he said wretchedly. "This is all my fault."

"What did he threaten to do if you told me about it?"

Corelli shook his hanging head.

"Not him, sir. Sergeant Caine."

"That's who I meant."

"What, sir?"

Something in what Corelli was saying didn't make sense to Black, but it wouldn't come into focus through the fresh dizziness. He couldn't crane his head and look backward and upside down at Corelli like that.

He lay on his back and stared at the stone ceiling, breathing deeply and painfully.

"He said he'd kill me, sir."

Black, eyes closed against the dizziness, thought back to Corelli's guarded, meticulously composed answers to his questions that first day at Vega.

"You told me everything you could tell me while you were under threat," he said. "It's not your fault."

Corelli's answer was barely a whisper.

"Yes it is, sir."

Black risked a glance at the top of the soldier's head.

"What did you do, Michael?" he asked quietly.

Corelli's voice broke slightly as he answered.

"*Nothing,* sir."

"Tell me."

Corelli sighed a long sigh. Then he told.

"It was a few nights before the thing with the goat," he began, speaking slowly to the floor. "Sergeant Caine said that someone had spotted a fire above the Meadows, and we were going to take a patrol to check it out. Which was weird already, sir, because the Meadows is on the other side of the mountain and as far as I knew we didn't have anybody out that night that could've seen the fire."

The guys at the O.P.

"Sergeant Caine was real agitated when we were leaving, sir, and he just got worse when we got close. I mean, when he saw it he kind of flipped out. You could see the fire going on the hillsides. It was one of the poppy fields— you know, where the Afghan guys grow the flowers for the drugs. But it wasn't like it was any danger to Vega, so I didn't understand what he was so worked up about."

I think I do, Black said to himself.

"And he went off to the side and was talking all heated with Lieutenant Pistone, like maybe they were arguing but I couldn't really tell, and when he came back he said we were going to raid this guy's house in the Meadows who owns the field. Which was weird, too, because we didn't have Danny along."

"Why not?"

"I don't know, sir. Danny was gonna come along on the patrol like usual. I saw him getting ready. But Sergeant Caine told him to stay back at Vega. I thought that was weird, but I'd only been here a couple months and I'm a private, sir, so, I mean, what did I know? I just kept my mouth shut and came on the patrol."

"Where was Sergeant Merrick?"

"He let Sergeant Caine take that one, sir. They didn't always both go on the same patrols."

"Okay."

"So we headed down to the Meadows, but it all just felt *off* from the beginning, sir. I mean, Sergeant Caine was just real agitated, like I said, and he wouldn't say why we were gonna raid this guy's place."

Black could venture a guess.

"We got there to the house and it was probably a little after midnight, and all the homes in the Meadows were dark, and Sergeant Caine, he goes and he's whispering to the lieutenant again, and then he grabs Shannon, who's there on the patrol with us, and they don't even do the knock-first or anything like we're supposed to do in the friendly towns."

"Okay."

"And Sergeant Caine just kicks the door in and they go in there with the lights turned on on their rifles, and everyone is shouting inside, and I can hear Sergeant Caine shouting back with a couple of his Pashto phrases. You know, 'get down' and all that. And there was a man in there yelling something back at him, sounding real scared, and you can hear a woman in there too, and children, and you can tell it's just chaos in there, sir."

He inhaled and let out a deep breath.

"And after a couple minutes Sergeant Caine comes back out," he said, his voice quavering. "And he's got a *kid,* sir."

"What?!"

"He's got a boy, sir. Like, a small boy, maybe seven or eight years old. And he's got him by his *clothes,* sir, just dragging him like you'd pull a puppy by the back of the neck. And the kid is wailing and crying and he doesn't know what's going on."

Black closed his eyes.

"And then Shannon comes out behind him, sir. And *he's* got the kid's dad. And no one in the patrol knows what's going on. I don't think Shannon even knew what was going on. Sergeant Caine is saying, 'Hold him there,' and Shannon's just standing there holding the kid's dad and watching Sergeant Caine."

A dark chasm opened in Black's stomach.

"And Sergeant Caine just starts screaming at the dad. And he's got his pistol out and he's waving it around, and waving it at the guy's *son,* sir! He just keeps yelling the same thing at the guy."

"Yelling what?"

"I didn't understand it, sir. Sergeant Caine knows a bunch of Pashto phrases and stuff. But I memorized the main part of it and when we got back to the COP I tried to look it up on my phrase card, and it was something like 'Where?' or 'Where is it?' Something like that, sir."

"Okay."

"And the dad is shouting back, freaking out, and he keeps saying something that I didn't understand except that I could hear him saying something about the Talib, over and over, like he was talking about the Taliban."

His voice began to break.

"And he's just *pleading,* sir! He's just begging them to stop, and Sergeant Caine's got his son and he won't stop screaming at him."

He swallowed hard.

"And the guys in the patrol are really starting to freak out, because it's all so *out* there, sir. Like, everyone is scared and just wants Caine to let the kid go and get out of there."

"What did Lieutenant Pistone do?"

He felt foolish asking the question. It required no answer.

He stood by and did nothing.

"What, sir?"

Corelli's voice was tinted with confusion.

"Why didn't he stop it?" Black asked.

Corelli twisted his anguished face up to him.

"He's the one who *did* it, sir."

"Did what?"

Corelli burst into tears.

"Shot him, sir!" he cried.

Black opened his eyes and saw stars.

"What? The father?"

"The boy!" Corelli wailed. "He didn't even say anything before he did it!"

His voice wobbled like a child's.

"He came over to where Sergeant Caine had the boy and he had his pistol in his hand and he just did it! Why did the lieutenant *do* that, sir?!"

Corelli sobbed freely. The telegraph station spun around Black, though he'd been lying very still.

"And you bring his servant into my town."

Memories crowded him, jabbed at him.

"All valley people says get the Devil out of the valley."

His mouth was very dry and his head felt as though it were full of pennies and someone were shaking it.

He took a deep breath and thought: I am a fool.

"What happened after?"

Corelli struggled to compose himself.

"Everyone just freaked out, sir," he said miserably, lost in the horror of the memory. "The father was screaming and flailing against Shannon, and you could hear the women inside just screaming too."

He gave a heaving sigh and shook his head.

"Even Sergeant Caine was freaked out, sir. No one thought the lieutenant was gonna do something like that. Sergeant Caine was yelling 'What the fuck, sir!?' And the lieutenant was acting all crazy."

"How?"

"Like, he seemed spaced out, and he was all, like . . . formal, I guess. I mean, the dad is screaming his head off and crying and hitting Shannon with his fists, and the lieutenant is just . . . rambling, sir, in the middle of all this chaos, saying how 'Now they'll all know' over and over, and giving these orders for us to return to the COP."

"What did you guys do?"

"Sergeant Caine went and grabbed the dad from Shannon, and as he's doing it this other kid runs out from the house and runs away into the trees."

"A kid?"

"Yeah, another young kid. We couldn't even tell if it was a boy or girl, but I guess the kid figured they were gonna get shot too, so they made a break for it."

Girl.

"And Sergeant Caine tells Shannon to go after the kid. And Shannon hasn't said anything this whole time, sir, and he just stands there and looks Sergeant Caine in the eye and tells him, 'Go fuck yourself.'"

"What did Sergeant Caine do?"

From the upper corner of his eye he could see Corelli's head come up.

"He was mad, sir. Like, panicky. And he said, 'God fucking damn it,' and then he dragged the father into the trees where none of us could see and he shot him too, sir."

Corelli let that sit before continuing, matter-of-factly.

"Then he came back and he took us all away from the house, and he took us aside in another part of the Meadows, away from Lieutenant Pistone, and he told us that nothing happened that night and we didn't see anything. He said that if we said one word of it to anyone, even Sergeant Merrick, the lieutenant was going to kill us too. Like, he was trying to act like he was behind what Lieutenant Pistone did, sir. He said, 'Now you know the lieutenant does not play.' But I could tell he was scared, sir."

"Okay."

"Then we all went back to the COP."

"Who else was on the patrol?"

"Besides me and Shannon, it was just Hill, sir, and Chen."

From O.P. Traynor.

"What happened after that night?"

"Nothing, sir. Sergeant Caine would remind us every week, remind me at least, what Lieutenant Pistone was gonna do. Nobody talked about it, and Sergeant Caine tried to just keep on like everything was normal."

Black was confused.

"Why'd he let *any* of you guys keep going out on patrols?" he asked. "Why would Caine want to keep going down into Darreh Sin?"

"He *didn't* want to, sir," Corelli said. "But we *had* to go. We had that water project that we had to go down and take pictures of and stuff, once a week. Sergeant Caine couldn't leave just us in the COP all the time, 'cause that would look too suspicious to the rest of the platoon. And he *definitely* couldn't explain to our H.Q. why we couldn't go take the pictures anymore."

Black imagined these patrols.

"Those trips must have been hairy."

"Very hairy, sir. We went two or three times since it happened, before the time we took you down there."

Darreh Sin was making more sense.

"What about the goat thing?"

"The goat thing was just the goat thing, sir. That's all that was. Honest mistake. Sergeant Merrick made us go down to the town the next day to try and make it right."

"I'll bet Sergeant Caine wasn't happy about that one."

"Not even a little bit happy, sir."

"But he couldn't say anything."

"No, sir. I think he was trying to keep Sergeant Merrick as much in the dark as anyone."

"So you went down there, and the vibe was weird."

"*Very* weird, sir," Corelli said, shuddering. "That's when I knew."

"Knew what?"

"Knew that they knew who each of us was, sir. Not just knew what happened. We knew they all knew. But knew each of us specifically that was there, sir."

His voice went distant.

"I could just see it, the way those guys were looking at me."

"That's why you were so jumpy and ended up firing your weapon."

"I guess so, sir."

Black lay still for a moment. He realized he was terribly thirsty.

"When did Hill disappear?"

He saw Corelli start in surprise.

"Uh, how'd you know about Hill, sir?"

"I just do."

"A couple days after that night, sir. Nobody's seen him on the COP since then. Sergeant Caine keeps saying he's out on a 'long patrol,' but he never comes back in again. And then Bosch went away a couple days ago. I thought that, that maybe . . ."

"They're fine," Black said. "I saw them."

"Sir?"

"Don't worry about it. What about Lieutenant Pistone, after that night?"

"He just practically disappeared after that night, sir. I mean, he was around the COP, but nobody saw him. He just hid out in his room, and he definitely didn't go out on any patrols anymore. Sergeant Caine probably told him to lay low, sir. In fact, the morning after the goat thing, right before Sergeant Merrick took us down to Darreh Sin, Sergeant Caine told me I didn't have to worry because the locals were mostly mad at Lieutenant Pistone, and the last time we were down there he had told the mayor or the chief or whoever that the lieutenant had left Vega and he wasn't coming back."

Corelli shook his head.

"I just still don't understand it, sir. I mean, Lieutenant Pistone didn't exactly seem like a *nice* guy, but, I mean, he definitely didn't seem like . . ."

"I know," Black said.

He reread the diary entry in his head.

"He fooled me too."

They sat and lay a moment.

"Was Doc Brydon there that night?" Black asked.

"No, sir, thank God. I think Billy had enough on his plate."

Black peered up at Corelli, but nothing more was offered.

"What do you know about Brydon?" he asked.

"What do you mean, sir?"

"Like where he was from and what his deal was."

Corelli paused.

"Nothing much, really, sir. I like Billy."

"But."

Corelli was wrestling with something.

"Well, I mean, it was weird when he showed up, sir."

"How's that?"

"The night before he got to Vega, sir, this weird thing happened," Corelli said, drifting back into the memory.

"What happened?"

"Well, I was on duty in the C.P., sir, and I was just monitoring the frequencies and reading my book, and I started picking up all this broken-up chatter on the Brigade net."

The frequency for anyone in the entire area of operations, including the Valley, to talk to the Brigade headquarters.

"Firefight chatter," Black said.

"Yeah, firefight chatter, sir. How'd you know that?"

"Don't worry about it."

"Okay, sir. Um, anyway, it was bad, sir. I mean, the firefight was bad. Well, the connection was bad too. Like, real patchy, like we were just getting little bits here and there. But you could tell something was going on somewhere. Somebody was in real trouble, but we had no idea who. I mean, it wasn't Heavenly, and there's nobody farther up the Valley, so we were sitting there wondering if somehow we were getting transmissions from another valley. Like, maybe the weather was doing it or something."

"Okay."

"Sergeant Caine and Shannon went out to go up to higher ground and check it out, sir. Which Sergeant Merrick would never have let him do, just him and another guy by themselves, but he was gone on his R&R leave and Sergeant Caine was running the show. So he and Shannon went up there, sir, and they came back a few hours later and said they didn't find anything."

"Billy showed up the next day."

He could feel Corelli's searching gaze on him.

"Well, yeah, sir. The next day Sergeant Caine brought Billy to me at the armory, and said he was cross-transferred from another unit, and to add him to the roster. Which was weird because I hadn't known there had been a convoy in the middle of the night or anything."

He sighed.

"I don't know, sir. I guess I just figured maybe he was a guy who had had some trouble in his other unit, which is why he got transferred. And I figured maybe it just kind of bothers him, whatever it is. Like, it's hanging over his head."

"He didn't tell you anything else?"

"No, sir. I got the feeling maybe he wanted to tell me something else, but he hasn't told me, so I don't push it. I mean, I figure whatever he's dealing with, it's his business, sir."

He paused.

"I figure maybe that's why Sergeant Caine always arranges for him to go on so much R&R leave all the time."

"What do you mean?"

"Oh, you know, sir. Just trips for a day or two. They'll send a guy if they think he's, you know, if they think he needs a break for real."

He paused.

"It's just, Billy seems to need a lot of breaks, sir."

Black thought he understood something.

"Did you ever tell him about that night in the Meadows?"

"No, sir," he murmured. "I kind of think he might know, though."

"How's that?"

"He's friends with Bosch, and I think maybe Bosch told him. He started kind of being nicer to me all of a sudden, giving me music and stuff. Like he knew something was bothering me too."

Corelli's breathing sounded as though he might start sobbing again.

"I couldn't do it, sir!" he cried wretchedly.

"Do what?"

"I didn't tell him or anyone! No one was talking to anyone about it. Everyone was scared of what was going to happen to us."

"You tried to tell me, and you're telling me now."

Corelli's voice went wispy and blank.

"I was a coward and I'm going to burn for it," he murmured to no one in particular.

"No one's going to burn," Black said. "It's time to get out of here."

Corelli looked at him questioningly.

"The Monk's coming, sir?"

"The Monk's not coming."

Corelli sat in silence a moment.

"Oh, sir," he groaned. "We're screwed, aren't we? We're stuck up here."

"No one's stuck," Black said. "I'm getting you out of here."

"Oh, sir, you're too—"

In one motion Black pushed himself to a sitting position. Pain shot from his shoulder down through his waist, and his head felt like it would burst. The room spun again and for a few moments he was sure he would vomit.

He looked around himself, panting. Only then did he see the pool of blood on the floor where his shoulder had lain. His left arm hung limply at his side.

He was so thirsty.

"Sir," Corelli said matter-of-factly, "you are in no position whatsoever to attempt any kind of rescue."

Black ignored him, instead turning so Corelli could see the back of his shoulder, where the bullet had passed through.

"Is this actively bleeding?"

"Uh, I don't think so, sir, but there's a big pud—"

"Good."

Corelli watched as Black slowly eased himself forward until he was on his hands—hand—and knees, facing the doorway. Webs of pain spidered out across his chest and side.

"Stay here," Black directed.

He realized the ridiculousness of that statement and laughed out loud. Corelli looked at him with concern.

Black managed to plant a foot in front of him and pull himself up on the doorway edge. Everything went a little tilty.

"Sir," Corelli called after him. "Don't tell Billy if he doesn't know already. I want to tell him myself."

"Billy's dead."

He stumbled through the doorway into the light.

The panorama before him was overwhelming. He felt as though he would fall off the mountain into the sky if he didn't hold on.

He waited for the dizziness to subside and focused his eyes on the ground before him. Corelli's pistol lay in the dirt. He let it be.

He placed one foot in front of the other, facing along the ridgeline toward COP Vega. Then the next foot.

He made it about twenty steps before he fell down.

"Walks in the fog and steals your babies and shit."

He picked himself up and started again.

37

As he staggered and fell across the mountains toward COP Vega, Black heard and saw many things, some of which he thought were real and some of which he thought were not real. After what must have been several hours night fell, and he knew he was hallucinating because he saw the smartass next to him, guiding him to his point.

He tasted dirt. At points he thought he was crawling. The air had turned colder overnight, and with it the ground. He was sure he heard thunder echoing off the mountainsides. He needed water so desperately.

He may have lain down to rest, though the yawning horrors that opened beneath his dreams pushed him back up through the dirt and onto his stumbling feet again.

He was sure only that he was on his face now, in the leaves and needles, and that a rough hand was turning him over. He felt his heels dragging through the brush as the same hand hauled him along like a sled, pulling him by the straps on his pack, until finally it released him to slough onto the blessed ground again.

He opened his eyes and saw daylight filtering through tree branches.

And Corporal Shannon, standing over him, brushing off his cruddy hands and working stiff fingers. Turning to see another figure stepping forward.

Merrick. Scowling down on him.

"Jesus Christ, Lieutenant. Can't you take a hint?"

Black's hand went weakly to his hip and managed to unholster his pistol, which felt like it weighed thirty pounds. He waved it limply in Merrick's direction.

"Oh, hell," Merrick said, exasperated, disarming him in a languid motion.

He turned to Shannon.

"Hurry, let's get him out of here."

More thunder in the distance.

Merrick squatted to inspect Black's shoulder.

"I tell you *this* way, and I tell you *that* way," he muttered, tearing fabric open to get a better look. "I *try* to tell you that I've *got* this. I thought you Regiment officers were supposed to be the smart ones. Jesus, did you even *try* to bandage this?"

Black's body tried uselessly to flinch away from Merrick's hands as the sergeant rolled him on his side to examine the back of his shoulder, which Black only then realized was still very damp.

"How'd you get shot, sir?"

"Fuck you," Black whispered, his throat dry as ageless desert wastes.

"You're welcome," Merrick said irritably, rolling Black back more roughly than he needed to and rising to his full height.

Black brought his right hand to his pocket and fished in it clumsily, finally coming up with a crinkled piece of paper. He tossed it weakly in Merrick's direction. It stalled in midair and made a rough landing at his feet.

"Do it," he croaked, "yourself."

The effort of forcing out three words left him panting and exhausted. Merrick picked up the paper and read it without comprehension.

"What the fuck is this? Who gave you this?"

He handed it to Shannon for him to look at.

"You," Black managed.

"What?" Merrick snapped.

He snatched it back from Shannon.

"Bullshit I gave you this. This isn't even my writing."

He wadded it in a hand and tossed it onto Black's chest. It rolled away and fell to the ground unwanted.

"Is this from more of your snooping around playing fucking detective?" Merrick said angrily. "Sir, how many different ways did I have to tell you I had it under control?"

Black did not understand this, but he was finding that he was losing the ability to distrust the tall, contemptuous sergeant. Or perhaps to care whether he was to be trusted. Too much made no sense to sort out inside his careening head.

"Caine . . ." he whispered with effort, looking forward to not talking for a while.

"Yeah, I know. Caine," Merrick snapped. "Who do you think I've been investigating since before you ever came up here to help me out by fucking everything up?"

"He means," said Shannon, pointing to the little crumple of paper on the ground, "Caine."

That stopped Merrick. He shot a look to Black.

"When?"

Oh, another question. Surely Merrick didn't expect him to talk again.

"Sniper," Black wheezed finally.

Merrick looked at him blankly.

"Two days ago," Shannon said. "You were still at the O.P. The sniper that was out there all day, that shot Garza on the roof."

Merrick snatched the paper off the ground and read it again, processing.

"Shit," he said finally.

Thunder again in the mountains. Merrick peered up through the trees at the ridges surrounding them.

"We can't stay here any longer," he told Shannon. "You got the flex litter?"

They began unfolding a long piece of black fabric with handles. A person could lie on it like a hammock and be carried by two others.

"Corelli," Black said weakly.

"What?"

"Corelli," he croaked again. "Blockhouse."

"What blockhouse?"

His memories were fuzzy and running together.

"Signal," he heard himself say hoarsely. "Mountain."

Shannon jerked around to look at Black. Merrick shook his head impatiently.

"What are you talking about, Lieutenant?"

Black's hazy thoughts focused. He tried to swallow.

"Telegraph." Deep breath. "Station."

"What the hell is he doing up there?"

"Prisoner," he gasped, followed by a fit of painful coughing.

"What!?"

He needed to stop trying to talk. He needed to rest.

"Girl."

"What girl?"

Merrick was coming into and out of focus.

"Shot me . . ." Black mumbled.

Merrick looked at him without comprehension, trying to decide if Black was simply out of his head. Black gestured weakly at Shannon.

"Meadows."

Shannon just scowled at him, then turned to Merrick.

"I don't know what he's talking about."

C'mon, Shannon.

"Caine . . ." Black wheezed.

He realized he was getting ready to pass out again.

"Kill Corelli."

"What?!"

Shannon, who'd been looking at the ground and muttering to himself, swore and looked up at Merrick.

"Yeah, he's probably right," he said tersely.

Black saw a fuzzy Merrick turn to look at Shannon questioningly.

"I think Caine knows where Corelli's at," Shannon said. "Shit."

"Get him . . ." Black murmured.

Thunder crashed through the ridges. Merrick had no time to press Shannon.

"We've gotta move," he declared.

He pointed at Black.

"Take him," he ordered Shannon. "Can you make it back?"

Shannon turned his disdainful gaze down on the crumpled Black.

"Yeah, I can make it back," he grunted.

Thunder, closer. It wasn't thunder.

"What's happening?" Black wheezed.

"It's all going to shit, that's what's happening," said Merrick, reaching for his rifle and assault pack.

"They're coming," Black said in barely a whisper.

"No, they're not," Merrick replied, shucking his pack over his shoulders. "They're here."

Shannon approached Black.

"Get him back to the COP," Merrick directed.

"End of the world," Black murmured.

"Go," Merrick said, looking down at Black's limp form.

"Roger."

He turned to go, then turned back.

"Shannon."

The big soldier, looming over Black's wilted form, turned.

"Sergeant Caine does not leave the COP for any purpose."

Shannon nodded his surly assent and turned back to Black. Merrick disappeared into the woods.

Another booming crash shook the ground around them. Closer.

"This," grunted Shannon as he squatted next to Black, "is gonna hurt, sir."

It did.

Shannon moved powerfully uphill. Black, draped around the corporal's massive shoulders like a sack, his own shoulder and side screaming profanities at him, managed three words before he passed out.

"You didn't tell."

The Talib sipped his tea placidly and watched the chill wind move the trees.

It had been an odd morning. But she was an odd little girl indeed.

And from an odd people. He'd heard of their females shearing their hair in mourning. These valley people and their ways. But in this case the confluence of tradition and ruse was perfect.

Admirable, even.

He saw it clearly now, of course. The strange girl who'd come to him all alone, many weeks ago, desperate to fight the infidel. Apparently an American had killed her father and brother at their home. She was wild for revenge.

This actually had been quite useful information to have. Not because the death of a sinful poppy grower and his son among these godforsaken lands was of intrinsic interest in itself. But because the chief of Darreh Sin, that buffoon, had told him nothing of this.

He claims to want, pretends to accept, my help. And yet he tells me nothing when an American soldier, an officer even, executes one of his growers like a dog.

The fact of the not telling told the Talib everything he needed to know about the chief and his loyalties. And knowing the deep grief, the rage of the chief's people, these backward, proud, emotional people—this had also been useful to him, regardless of what their chief wished. Very useful.

Then I must think, God, that you guided the girl to me for this purpose. She was, for a moment, your vessel.

Imagine that. God's mysteries abound.

She had been spirited indeed. He remembered the fire in her eyes. Oh, she had been very unhappy when he'd sent her back to her mother. He had generously overlooked her insolence as a product of her understandable grief.

Now he saw it, though. The resemblance. The simplicity of the disguise. The even stranger boy who had come to him that night not long after, calling himself Tajumal. Always wearing the headband, always pestering him in the dark, always coming in his rain hood whatever the weather. So earnest and humorless. As eager as the girl had been to fight.

The Talib chuckled, now that he knew.

He was younger than they usually came, but he'd had talents. Well, *she'd* had talents. Or luck, and a talent for deception.

Knocking out the radio equipment had been impressive and bold. He'd give him—her—that. But the piece of clothing with the officer's rank, and the prisoner, *if* this was true about the prisoner . . .

Here the girl had not yet learned how to stretch the truth convincingly.

Shot the officer and bound the soldier! An eleven-year-old girl!

The only thing interesting about this preposterous falsehood was to imagine what real story might lie behind the scene she had come upon. What had caused Americans to bind and shoot one another, up in the old English tower?

These things we will never know about one another. Our peoples' secrets.

I bring you another prize, she had said somberly, with such portent, after she revealed her true self. Then begged once again to fight the infidel. *I am the guardian of this valley,* she declared, or something equally silly and bombastic.

He shook his head and sipped his tea. Youth.

The prisoner—well, prisoners are always useful, as far as they go. If this part of her story turned out to be true. He would know soon enough.

One of many revelations this cold day will bring.

He had felt the tiniest bit sorry for her as he sent her back to her mother yet again. A bold girl. But she really ought to be whipped for lying like this.

38

Bootfalls echoing on tile. He lay on his back in darkness, on a jouncing, traveling litter.

He cracked his eyelids and saw stone above him. Stone to his left. Light and air to his right. Too bright.

Cold.

The dark of a stone column passed through his vision. The courtyard.

Before losing consciousness again, he noted with mild and detached interest the great tumult and shouting all about him, the whumping force of concussion waves pressing down upon his chest, and the tremendous volume of rocket and automatic weapons fire that rained down on Vega from every direction above.

When he came awake next it was with a start.

His right hand, moving like a rubber fish, fumbled uselessly about his pistol holster. There was no pistol there anyway.

He opened his eyes and lurched upward onto his elbows, his head punishing him mercilessly for it. He twisted left and right, panicked. Bright lights spun and stabbed at him. Somewhere nearby was a powerful, muffled rumbling.

"Whoa, there, L.T.," said a voice. "Easy."

He flinched away from a hand on his shoulder, pressing him down.

"Easy, sir. Easy."

Two hands now, firmer, pressing harder.

"Lay back, sir. You're okay."

A shape close in his squinted vision. Other shapes farther throughout the room. Some standing, some horizontal. The whole room seemed to vibrate every few seconds.

Explosions. Outside. He was indoors.

"Where's Sergeant Caine?" he demanded, trying to crane his head to look behind him.

"You're at the aid station, sir," came the reply, in the cool tones of an Army medic. "You're good."

A single, searing explosion of light, inches from his face, washed out his vision. He wrenched away from it, grunting, squeezing his eyes as tight as they would go.

"Whoops," said the voice. "Sorry, sir. Penlight. Here, try this."

He opened his eyes reluctantly and followed the young medic's index finger left, right, up and down. The effort of doing so made the cot shift beneath him. He grasped its sides queasily.

The kid pulled his eyelids wide and examined his pupils, nodding to himself.

"Dizzy, sir?"

He lay on a cot in a corner of the stone-walled room. Several casualties occupied other cots and litters. The nearest was awake, staring at Black silently as he held a soaked bandage to his upper arm.

Two medics stood crowded close around another, lying motionless and making weak wheezing sounds. A third medic lay on an exam table nearby, a red tube running from his arm to a transfusion bag slowly filling with blood.

Beyond that, a door, through which he thought he could see a portion of the courtyard. It was very, very noisy outside.

"Yeah, I'm dizzy," Black answered impatiently. "Where's Sergeant Caine?"

The young medic, coming into focus now, shook his head.

"Don't know, sir. How dizzy would you say you're feeling right n—"

"He hasn't been through here to check on your casualties?"

"No, sir, haven't seen him," the kid answered in clipped tones. "But it's pretty crazy outside right now, so everyone's a little bit busy. Now, how—"

"What about Sergeant Merrick? Where's he?"

"Sir," the kid answered impatiently, "I don't know where anybody is at except who's in here right now in front of me. Now stop trying to sit up and lay back so I can check you out."

He pressed Black firmly back to the cot and completed his exam in about thirty seconds, satisfying himself that Black was lucid and cogent, then rolling him gingerly to peek under the bandage on the back side of his shoulder. Black felt like he was going to keep rolling right off the cot.

The medic rolled him back again.

"What day is it?" Black asked, closing his eyes while the dizziness cleared.

"Sunday."

"What time?"

The medic checked his watch.

"About fifteen thirty."

He stood and turned to go.

It occurred to Black that he had no idea what time he'd arrived at the aid station. Nor for that matter what time it had been when Merrick and Shannon had found him.

"Hey, how long have I . . ."

But the medic was gone, back to his other casualties.

Black stared up at the stone ceiling, his mind racing. His head throbbed from his earlier effort at lifting himself, though his shoulder, and much of the rest of him, was now happily numb.

He turned his head gingerly and looked around at the other casualties.

No one had seen Merrick. No one had seen Caine.

They don't know.

An enormous crash outdoors sent another wave of vibrations through the aid station. Guys cursed.

"That one was fucking close," one of the medics spat, annoyed.

Get with it.

Grasping the cot rails with both hands, Black pushed himself fully upright. Angry sparkles filled his vision and his head felt as though all the liters of blood in his body were filling it. He put his boots on the hard floor and stood, knowing it was a mistake. The room careened wildly.

Willing the floor to right itself, his legs stiff as planks, he began to walk toward the door. He heard his soles scraping the tile but couldn't feel his feet. He figured he must have looked like the Frankenstein monster.

His right arm was trailing behind him. Someone was tugging on his wrist, squeezing it hard with their fingernails. He yanked it away roughly and scuffed onward.

The metallic crash behind him made him turn. He looked dumbly down at the intravenous line running from where it was taped to his wrist in a taut diagonal back to where it was now dragging the bag stand across the floor.

He had only an instant to register blurry annoyance before realizing, as the room went sideways entirely and he saw the wall rising up to meet him, that turning around had been a mistake.

It smacked him, hard and cold. His cheek scraped along its surface.

"What the fuck, L.T.?"

The same medic, easing him sideways toward another wall. No, the floor. Floor was good.

"What're you doing, sir?"

"Take me to the C.P."

Why did his own voice sound so slurry?

"What?"

"I need to go the C.P."

"C'mon, sir, let me help you up."

The kid squatted next to him, trying to figure out how best to haul him up without injuring him.

"I need to go now."

"C'mon, sir, we got other hurt guys here. Come get back in the cot."

"I need to talk on the radio."

The kid paused a half second.

"Right, sir," he said, adopting the placating tones medics used on casualties who weren't in their right minds. "The radio. Come back to the cot first."

Black, slumped along the bottom of the wall, grabbed him roughly by the forearm.

"I need to talk on the radio *now.*"

The kid startled, wrenching his arm free.

"No, sir, you don't," he answered, urgency and annoyance in his voice. "You need to get back in your cot and stop fucking up my triage."

His voice went cool again.

"Now, c'mon."

He attempted to sit Black fully upright. Black pushed back against his efforts.

"It's important," he pressed.

The kid was agitated now, looking over his shoulder at the rest of the room.

"Shit," he said, throwing his hands up. "Fine, sir, if you get back in your cot you can use my radio, okay?"

He reached into a little holster on the back of his equipment belt and produced his walkie-talkie, holding it up before Black's face.

"Now let's go."

Black shook his head, regretting it immediately.

"Not that one," he said, squeezing his eyes shut. "The *radio.* The battalion net in the C.P."

The kid shook his head.

"Let the dudes in the C.P. take care of that shit, sir."

"There's no one there."

The kid's brow furrowed in confusion.

"Negative, sir, there's dudes in the C.P. right n—"

"They don't know what I know."

"What?"

"I need to tell them."

"Tell them what, sir?"

"Take me there."

"What?"

"I can't walk."

The medic looked at him like he was crazy.

"No *way,* sir! It's off the *chain* out there."

He sent a thumb over his shoulder toward the direction of the noise.

"And you're concussed as fuck and you lost a shit-ton of blood," he finished. "I can't take you outside."

Taking too long.

Black grabbed the young soldier by both arms this time, tugging the kid's body down toward his own until they were face-to-face.

"Do you wanna die here today?" he nearly shouted.

The medic looked at him blankly.

"Am I altered?" he demanded. "I'm talking to you, right? I can talk on a damned radio!"

He saw that he finally had the kid's attention.

"I *need* to talk to Battalion!"

Had finally tapped the black reservoir of fear capped off below the surface.

"I'll lie down on the cot in the C.P., but I need you to *take* me there, *now!*"

The wide-eyed medic searched his face. Something in him clicked over, or broke.

"Fuck," he said.

Black released his arms and slumped back to the floor, exhausted.

The medic looked back over his shoulder at the room full of medics and soldiers. The wheezing casualty was now bellowing incoherently at someone or something imaginary, and no one was paying them any attention.

"Don't tell," Black muttered at the ceiling. "Just go."

The kid turned back and squatted, muttering curses to himself. He worked Black into a sitting position, casting glances toward the chaos in the rest of the aid station.

Black assisted as best he could, which was hardly at all, and allowed himself to be slumped across the medic's shoulders. He watched his view of the aid station go upside down, sending a wave of dizzy nausea through him. He groaned.

"You gonna hurl, sir?"

"No," he said, thinking he just might.

The medic struggled to his feet. It was the same fireman's carry Shannon had used, but this guy was about half Shannon's size.

"Gonna be loud out there, sir."

It was loud inside already.

"Got it."

The kid did a little hop in place to shuck Black's limp form higher on his shoulders, then he leaned forward and bounded through the doorway in a stomping half run.

"God-daaaaaammmmnniiiit!" he bellowed as the sound and light hit them.

Goddamn lieutenant.

He crashed upward through the dry leaves, gloving narrow tree trunks hand over hand in the steep parts, hauling himself forward, higher, closer.

Yawning mountaintops hung above him silently, the scatterfall of dried brush and cast-off tree limbs slanting away below and behind, hearing no sound but his feet and his breathing.

This ridge, then down the far side—no way around that draw—through the creek, then up one more and cut across the front. Good cover there, and fastest.

Too far.

One stomping foot in front of the other, legs pumping. Skinny branches snapping as he pushed through them. Brittle ground cover cracking. So much sound.

"Never catch a damn thing making all that noise, Rodney."

It was like home, really. The dim mornings hunting with his dad and his brothers. He couldn't get enough of it, the woods and the mountains. It was half the reason he joined the infantry. Truth was, this was damned beautiful country when you got down to it.

Damn Corelli. Damn dumb kid.

His heaving breaths made fog before his eyes. The other sound returned to him.

It came from behind, past descending ridges, the thump and thud, the unending cacophony echoing dull off mountainsides, chasing him all the way from where he was supposed to be, where he needed to be right now, over the peaks to find him and torment him here where he actually was.

Told him, told all of them, don't listen to a stupid officer who thinks he knows something.

He couldn't say whether it burned him more that he was going to die amidst this beauty, or that the stupid officer had thought right.

All this on me.

Panting and swearing, Merrick drove higher into the mountains.

39

He felt as though he'd been hurled naked and flailing into a heaving ocean made of sound. The medic wasn't kidding.

The fire was so thick and continuous that Black could hardly tell one sound from the other, incoming or outgoing, rocket, mortar, or machine gun. It all just ran together in a shrieking continuum.

"OURS OR THEIRS?" he shouted as the medic pounded up the breezeway that skirted the courtyard.

"EVERYONE'S," the kid shouted back.

Soldiers stomped past them the other way, slugging heavy ammo cans. Everyone they passed was yelling something at everyone else, or at them.

An impacting mortar round in the far corner of the courtyard heaved a truckbed's worth of earth into the sky. Black's hearing momentarily washed out. The medic staggered from the shock but didn't drop him.

"Hold on, sir!" he cried.

It's cold out here, Black thought as the kid reached the entry he'd been headed for.

They stumped along through a corridor of blast walls and beneath a heavily sandbagged opening.

"Make a hole!" the medic shouted at the gaggle of people in front of them. "Look out!"

They were in a narrow barracks bay that Black hadn't been to before. Several soldiers were in there, sweating and pointing and shouting at one another, clutching overheated weapons and jabbing fingers in every direction and unsuccessfully carrying on seven urgent, high-volume conversations at once.

"—wer Two needs fifty-cal ammo NOW."

"—at the mortar pit, but I don't kn—"

"No, fuck that! We need to—"

"—get there from here. You gotta go around!"

The medic pushed his way through, soldiers turning in the midst of their shouting to see who was being carried past.

An upside-down sergeant who Black recognized entered the far door ahead of them. One of Merrick's junior guys. Thick built, low to the ground, commanding. An afro that was way out of regulation.

He surveyed the ineffective scene before him.

"SHUT THE FUCK UP," he bellowed hoarsely, bringing the room to silence.

The soldiers all turned as he stomped toward them, sniffing their panic with contempt.

"We're gonna figure out who needs wh—"

He saw Black and his chauffeur approaching.

"Where's he going?" he demanded.

"Says he's gotta get to the C.P. to use the radio," the medic panted.

"Hell," the sergeant grunted, "he can't fuck it up any worse than it already is."

He stomped past toward the group of soldiers, looking dubiously over his shoulder at Black. Black gave a downward thumbs-up as the medic carried him out the door and down the corridor.

"How you doing, sir?" the medic puffed.

They were passing through a stone passageway now, the thunder outside momentarily dulled to a heavy rumble.

"Goopy."

"Yeah, I bet."

"What'd you give me?"

"Ain't the drugs, sir. It's the concussion."

"Oh."

They turned a corner. The noise was building again ahead of them.

"But I gave you a shitload of morphine."

"Oh."

The medic turned again and a square of light appeared in front of them.

"Gonna be loud again, sir."

Cold air hit them as they burst into a narrow outdoor channel between two buildings. Hessco baskets lined each side of the passage, but they were barely head high. Noise filled the universe.

"WAIT," Black shouted. "STOP."

The medic complied. With nothing else obstructing the sightlines, Black momentarily had an upside-down, nearly three-hundred-sixty-degree view of Vega's surroundings.

"GOTTA MOVE, SIR."

He looked up. Or down. Down past the medic, and saw.

They clung to the vertex of a great cavern, its walls studded with inverted trees, its floor a gray roil of clouds, all the air within it echoing with awful sound.

He saw what lay in every mountainslope sliding away beneath them in every direction. Saw what was brought upon Vega, and understood what was intended. He'd never seen or heard anything like it in his life.

Not even that day.

He felt certain in that moment that if he let go he would fall past those slopes and tumble among those clouds.

Not even on that mountain.

"SIR!" the medic urged.

"KEEP GOING," Black yelled.

They pushed on through the next entrance, cutting left at the first intersection. They were on the same route Caine had taken with him his first night at Vega.

"They don't know what, sir?" the medic panted.

"What?"

"What was it you said you know . . ."

He gasped and ran.

". . . that the C.P. guys don't know?"

Slung across the kid's shoulders, Black considered how to answer that question succinctly.

That you're facing more fighters than you or your headquarters ever imagined because your lieutenant murdered a kid and the Army built a wall and I thought I knew what I was doing and all of us together managed to accomplish what no one has accomplished in thousands of years, which is unite everyone in this valley in a single purpose.

They were close to the CP.

And we don't have a chance of holding this post unless everyone they've got in the province comes to help us.

"Just keep going."

The medic stomped around the final corner. The CP was just up the corridor.

"Thank you," Black muttered woozily.

"Right."

They'd arrived at the little door to the radio room.

"If it helps," Black said, "I ordered you to take me here."

"Aw, fuck your orders, sir."

The medic kicked the door open with a boot and squatted sideways through the low frame, barely managing to squeeze himself and Black through it.

He stopped short. Black turned his head upward at the upended scene before them.

Despite the outpost being under what the tactics manual would call a complex attack from a superior and determined force preparing the battlefield for ground assault, there was only one frantic, red-faced person on duty in the command post to direct its defenses.

Standing among the racks of radios, a taut telephone-style cord circling his body and stretching to a handset tucked under his chin, another handset in one hand, a walkie-talkie in the other hand, and a raft of maps sprawled across one another and spilling from the desktop, stood the cool kid. The freckled, T-shirted punk who'd been at the desk every time Black had been to the CP before. There was nothing cool about him right now.

"*Where the fuck is everybody?*" he screamed at them hysterically.

40

The radio nets were a cacophony of traffic, everyone from every corner of the outpost talking on top of everyone else, crosstalk clashing in the speakers, all of which appeared to have been turned on at once.

The panicked kid had been in the CP by himself for who knows how long, trying to juggle it all. He'd been expected to monitor the radios and read his book during the quiet times, and step out of the way for his platoon leader or platoon sergeant when something real was happening. From the look of the brick-size paperback lying on the floor next to the cot, that's exactly what he had been doing. He hadn't been expected to do this.

"Yeah, I know!" the kid shouted into a handset. "I'm getting it!"

He was trying to secure ammunition for one of the guard towers that was nearly out. Every other radio was clamoring for his attention simultaneously.

"Take them to Two!" he yelled at one walkie-talkie, shoving another under his arm.

The medic squatted and tried without success to place his cargo carefully on the cot. Black sloughed off his shoulders and tumbled heavily onto the rack. The room upended itself and he clung to the cot rails, stomach turning, head filled to bursting.

"Ohhhhh," he groaned, squeezing his eyes shut.

The medic stood, stretching his back, and surveyed the situation dubiously.

"What the fuck, sir?" the frazzled sentinel cried between transmissions.

He snatched up the walkie again.

"No, take them to *Two!*"

"Go," Black said to the medic, pinching the bridge of his nose. "Get back and do your thing."

"You sure, sir?"

"Yeah," Black replied, though he wasn't.

"Just stay still and rest, sir," he said. "I'll be back to check on you, whenever I can."

"Don't do that."

"Right, sir."

Someone hurled profanities at someone else over the nets. The medic gave a last skeptical look at the two of them and disappeared.

Black opened his eyes, blinking hard to clear the splotches in his vision. It was hardly quieter in here than it had been in the open air. The dissonant chorus of individual sounds outside was just buffed or dulled to sharper or rounder edges.

The kid was shouting into his radios.

"Where's Sergeant Caine?" Black asked the ceiling.

"What?"

He juggled handsets.

"No, to *Two!* I don't fucking know, sir!"

"Where did you last see him?"

"I don't know! Hours ago."

"So he's still gone."

"He's *what?*"

"What about Sergeant Merrick?"

"You tell me, sir!"

"He hasn't been by here or checked in?"

"No, he hasn't fucking been *by* here!" the kid shrieked at him. "Nobody's been by here!"

He craned to answer a different call.

"Two-forty ammo, not fifty cal!"

He tossed the handset.

"I've been here by myself the whole fucking time! I don't know where *anybody* is!"

"Has there been any traffic on the patrol net?"

"The *patrol* net?"

The radio channel used by personnel when they left Vega on foot.

"Yeah, the patrol net!"

"I'm not monitoring the patrol net! Why would I be monitoring the—"

Black cut him off.

"What is Battalion headquarters saying about getting us help?"

The kid looked at him like he was crazy.

"Battalion ain't saying shit, sir!"

"Why not?"

"The retrans!"

The retrans.

A pit opened in Black's stomach.

"We're not talking to anybody!" the kid hollered. "We're just talking to ourselves!"

He'd forgotten. The antenna hadn't been repaired yet.

"mIRC chat!" he countered.

"They put a rocket in the fucking dish!"

Their attackers had done their homework.

"The sat phone!"

"I told you, sir, it don't work down here!"

"That was *true?!*" Black exclaimed, flabbergasted.

"*Yeah,* it was true! Sat phone doesn't do shit!"

Black closed his eyes.

"Where the hell is Sergeant Merrick?" the kid cried desperately.

Battalion didn't even know they were under attack.

"Somebody," the soldier spat as he snatched up a handset, "needs to get him the he—"

"Sergeant Caine and Sergeant Merrick are not on the COP."

The kid gawked at him slackly. The radios, jabbering for his attention, went unanswered.

"What?" he cried. "Where the hell are they?"

"It doesn't matter," Black said urgently. "You need to check the patr—"

"Well, who the hell is in charge of this place?"

"You are."

"What?!"

In the noise and chaos of the fight, probably no one had figured out that both senior sergeants, one of whom would be expected to fill in for Lieutenant Pistone, were absent and the kid was in the CP all by himself.

"Stay cool," Black replied unconvincingly.

Or things had just been too desperate for anyone to stop what they were doing and go help him.

"Oh, we're fucked," the kid declared.

All the radios clamored at once.

"Oh, shit," he said, ramping up. "Nobody knows."

Black tried to sit up. The room promptly went sideways. Back down.

"Answer your radios," he directed, eyes pinched shut against the nausea.

"Nobody knows! Nobody's gonna come!"

"Answer your radios!"

The kid snatched another of his handsets suddenly.

"No, don't try to go to the mortar p—"

Someone stepped on his transmission. He cursed.

"I said *don't* go to the mortar pit!" the kid hollered, kicking the desk.

"Calm down."

"Fuck that, sir!" the kid yelled, his voice going shrill. "What are we gonna fucking *do?*"

"Calm down."

"*You* calm down, L.T.! I'm trying to—"

He lowered the handset and crammed the walkie-talkie full against his mouth.

"Just *hold on!* I'm almost with you guys!"

A blast nearby shook the room.

"God*damn* it!" the kid yelled as the radio speakers doused him in feedback.

"CALM. DOWN," Black shouted, his voice painfully loud in his head.

The kid threw all the handsets and walkies down onto the desktop at once. Black twisted to his side and pawed the big paperback off the floor. The kid made fists and hollered at him goggle-eyed.

"STOP TELLING ME TO CALM D—"

Black threw overhand. The book went splaying through the air in a straight line and made square contact with the middle of the kid's face.

He staggered backward, hands treading air, and gawked at Black wide-eyed.

"*What the FUCK!*" he screeched.

Black collapsed back onto the cot, dizzy from the effort of throwing.

"What's your name?" he asked the ceiling through squinched eyes.

He'd never seen the kid wearing his actual coat with his name tape on it. Just a T-shirt.

"What?"

"*What's your name?*" Black shouted, causing the kid to flinch.

"Hubbard!" he shrieked.

Black exhaled. The racket outside was unreal.

"Hubbard," he said, holding the cot rails. "Look at me."

His eyes were still closed against the dizziness.

"Are you looking at me?"

"Yes!" Hubbard retorted with all the petulance of a grounded teenager.

"Your compound is getting breached tonight."

He heard the kid among his maps and radios, panting.

"You gotta calm down and hold this place until help gets here."

"*What* help?" Hubbard shouted. "There's no help! No one even knows we're—"

"The convoy."

"What?"

He opened his eyes and looked at Hubbard.

"The convoy," he repeated. "It's Sunday."

It was a day for forgetting the obvious.

"Shit!" Hubbard exclaimed in wonder. "The convoy!"

"Yeah, the convoy. Now get your radios up and put the patrol net on the speaker."

Hubbard looked at his watch.

"That's not for, like, six hours!"

"Don't worry about the time. Just get on the radios."

Hubbard kept staring until Black gave him a *Well, come on!* with both hands. He turned to the squalling radio racks, fumbling with a speaker cable and blowing out a long breath.

Black lay on his back on the cot, listening to the cacophony.

"Oh, Jesus," Hubbard muttered, shaking his head as he fiddled with the radio. "Oh, we're fucked."

"Probably."

"Screw you, L.T."

"One thing at a time."

The speaker clicked on, its static joining the throng.

"Try to raise Sergeant Merrick."

Hubbard took up a fresh handset. He seemed to be calming.

"Vega Seven, this is Vega X-Ray, over."

They waited, Hubbard shifting his weight back and forth between his feet.

"Vega Seven, this is Vega X-Ray, how copy, over."

Clear static was all that returned. Hubbard looked at the radio expectantly.

"Leave it," Black directed. "Can you raise the O.P. without the retrans?"

Hubbard froze in place. His jaw went limp as he turned slowly to Black, a look of dawning horror in his eyes.

Black covered his face with his hands.

"Oh, shit!" Hubbard shouted, color leaving his face.

He twisted a handset cable free from one radio box, cramming it frantically onto the stubby output plug of another box sitting dormant at the bottom of the stack.

"Shit! Shit!"

Fucking lieutenant.

He splashed through a running creek at the bottom of a broad ravine and started upward through the pines on the far side.

Fucking Corelli.

He would have been cold had he not been working so hard.

Goddamn pussy God freak. I told him and told him that I'd take care of him.

The rumble over the mountains behind him continued unabated, calling him back to where the rest of his soldiers were trying to not die.

Brought this all on myself.

Not only himself.

What I get for doing the right thing.

It would all be over now, whatever happened today.

Sorry, Traynor.

He was getting closer.

Wanted to come get you, buddy.

Caine drove higher into the mountains.

41

I forgot! I forgot! Goddamn it!"

Hubbard nearly knocked over the radio stack wrestling with it.

"I'm sorry, sir!" he stammered, fumbling cables. "I just . . ."

A vibration ran through the room. Something impacting the grounds nearby.

"Everything's been happening all at once, I just . . ."

"You don't need the retrans?" Black cut in.

"They're on a different retrans tower!" Hubbard replied, stabbing at numbers on the keypad. "On one of the peaks between there and here!"

He shook his head as though to clear it and punched up more numbers.

"What?" Black demanded.

Hubbard cursed, jamming the buttons.

"God*damn* it!"

He stopped, glaring at the radio.

"*What?*" Black repeated.

"The frequency!"

"What about it?"

Hubbard looked at him helplessly.

"I don't remember the goddamn frequency!"

Black was flabbergasted.

"It's not already in the radio?"

"We're not allowed to keep it in the radio!" Hubbard shouted. "We have to clear it any time we use it to talk to the O.P.!"

He punched more numbers then cleared them, muttering combinations and profanities one after the other.

"Which is like one time since I've been here!"

"Well, *get* it!"

Paper was strewn all about Hubbard's station.

"Where's it written down?"

"We're not *allowed* to write it down! Sergeant Caine won't let us!"

Black resisted the urge to punch the wall. Hubbard cursed and jabbed.

"Wait," Black said suddenly. "Who's 'we'?"

Something Caine had said came to him in a rush, and he answered his own question.

"Oswalt," he declared.

Hubbard finally tuned in.

"What?"

"Oswalt's the other guy! That's allowed to talk to the O.P.!"

Hubbard smacked his head.

"Right! Oswalt! Wait, how'd you know th—"

"*Get* him!"

Hubbard scrabbled through the mess for his walkie-talkie, pinching the little dial on top and turning it several clicks.

"Yo, Oswalt! Oswalt, it's Hubbard!"

The radio crackled back without delay.

"Oswalt."

It was very noisy wherever he was.

"Where are you at right now?"

"Taking ammo to Tower Three."

"I need you to come to the C.P. right now."

Black, lying on his back, threw up his hands.

"Just tell him to *tell* it!"

The classification level of the frequency was hardly top priority at the moment.

"Hey, buddy," Hubbard said, lowering his voice. "I need the freek."

"The what?" came the staticky reply.

"The FREEK," Hubbard said, full volume.

"The freek?"

"Yeah, man, the *freek* freek. I need it right now. I can't remember it."

"We're not allowed to—"

"Give it," Black ordered.

Hubbard tossed the radio across the room. Black barely caught it using both hands.

"Oswalt, it's Lieutenant Black," he said briskly. "It's okay, I'm authorizing it, but we need it right now."

"Four-oh-six," came the instant reply.

Hubbard smacked his head again and started punching numbers. Black keyed the mic.

"I also need you to go to Sergeant Merrick's quarters right now and check to see if the satellite phone is in there."

"Roger," came the unquestioning reply through the chaos.

"I *told* you, sir!" Hubbard cut in. "The phone doesn't work here!"

"Take the master key," Black continued, ignoring him. "Bring the phone here as fast as you can."

"Roger."

He keyed off. Hubbard was yanking a connector out of one speaker and cramming a different one into it.

"What was that?" Black asked.

He could have sworn while he was talking to Oswalt he'd heard someone call his name over one of Hubbard's radio nets.

"Got it!" Hubbard shouted, not hearing him. "Hopefully these fuckers out there didn't take out the retrans already, or we won't be able to talk for sh—"

An earsplitting splash of static and reverb washed out the speaker, causing them both to jump.

An agitated voice cut midsentence through the noise.

"—p the goddamn radio one of these days!"

Hill.

"I say *again*," Hill went on, voice all annoyance. "Vega X-Ray, this is Traynor X-Ray, how about a damn acknowledgment!"

The chatter of automatic weapons was clearly audible through his words.

Hubbard snatched up the handset.

"Traynor X-Ray, this is—"

He was holding it upside down.

"Hill, it's me, Hubb!" he cried, righting it. "It's Hubb, man! We're here!"

Hill came back through the din, angry.

"Nice-a' you to answer the goddamn phone!"

"What's your situation?"

"There's a fucking fuck lotta fighters out here, that's our situation!"

Black heard urgency in Hill's voice, but he couldn't hear panic.

"Casualties?" Hubbard asked.

"Chen's K.I.A. and Snoop's K.I.A," Hill rattled off, Hubbard cursing after each name. "Everyone's pretty much shot one way or the other but we're still fi—"

An explosion on Hill's end overloaded the speaker.

"Fightin'," he finished tersely.

He left the mic open as he lowered the handset to yell something at someone. Black and Hubbard could hear the horrible patchsmack din.

"But we, uh," Hill continued, bringing the handset back up, "we could use some help in a hurry if it ain't too much trouble down there."

"Roger," Hubbard sent back. "We're in some heavy shit down here too, but we're, we're trying to figure—"

"Tell him stand by," Black cut in.

"The L.T. says stand by," Hubbard transmitted.

There was a long moment's pause.

"Uh, roger that," Hill came back. "But there ain't a lotta 'by' to be standin' on right now, if you get the picture."

"Roger, we're working it."

Hubbard keyed off and turned to Black.

"What're we gonna do, sir?"

Black was already on the walkie, calling Oswalt.

"Oswalt," came the reply.

"Status."

"I'm in Sergeant Merrick's now, sir. I'm not seeing it here."

"Sir," Hubbard said urgently, "I'm telling you the sat phone doesn't work down here."

"How do you know?"

"Whatta you mean, how do I know?"

"How do you know?"

"Sergeant Merrick said so!"

"Have you ever tried it yourself?"

Hubbard hesitated.

"No, I . . . I just . . ."

"Tear the place up," Black said to Oswalt over the radio. "Hurry."

"Roger."

He keyed off.

"Sir," Hubbard pressed, "even if the sat phone works, which I'm telling you it ain't gonna work, it'll take ages to get birds up here! We gotta do something for those guys *now!*"

He hopped from foot to foot.

"We gotta send a squad or something!"

Black looked at the kid and stated the obvious.

"There's no squad."

"Well, goddamm it, sir! What?"

It was madness. Units kept backups upon backups of every form of communication possible. Communication was life. You could always improvise *something.* Hell, an American officer in Grenada had used a calling card and pay phone when everything else failed, to route a call through his unit and get air strikes.

There was no pay phone in the Valley.

Wasting time.

Whoever was attacking COP Vega had come prepared, systematically taking out any long-range communications capability that . . .

Son of a bitch.

"Oswalt!" he called into the walkie.

"Here."

"Forget Sergeant Merrick's hootch! Go to Danny's!"

"What?" Hubbard cut in, confused.

Black jabbed a finger impatiently at Hubbard's radios, which clamored relentlessly. Hubbard grabbed them up.

"Go to Danny's," Black repeated into the walkie. "Look in there!"

"Roger."

Black heard it again. Someone calling his name on one of the nets.

"What was that?" he asked Hubbard.

Hubbard, drowning in crosstalk, cocked his head uncomprehendingly.

"What was what?" he called over the din.

"Someone was calling m—"

"Yo, Vega X-Ray," Hill cut back in on the big speaker. "I get ya that it's hot down there, but if y'all can maybe divert some of your air over here, that could, uh . . ."

He trailed off a moment, the sound of weapons filling the space.

"That could make a difference."

Hubbard looked helplessly at Black, who waved him to go ahead. Hubbard took up the handset, lips pursed.

"Uh," he transmitted. "We don't got no air support down here right now, Hill."

Several seconds went by.

"Roger that," Hill came back through hails of noise.

He keyed off and keyed on again.

"Standing by, over."

Hubbard lowered his handset and looked at Black somberly.

"Sir," he said in a low voice. "We need to do *something* to hel—"

WHUMP.

Something very large and powerful exploded within the compound, shaking the walls of the CP and setting the radio stacks buzzing. Black felt the air in the windowless room compress all around him, sending light washing through his vision.

He cried out and clutched his head, which felt as though two cars had run into it from opposite directions.

"What the *fuck* was *that*?" Hubbard shouted, grabbing at the radio stacks to steady himself.

Black was doubled in a situp crunch, forearms clutching his head.

"Recoilless rifle!" he heard himself shout through his hands.

It was only a guess, but the blast had been different from the others. Someone was trying to break through the walls.

"They're supposed to be suppressing that shit!" Hubbard cried, rooting among his handsets.

Hubbard's other radios were all squawking at him at once again. He'd been neglecting the rest of the outpost while they'd been hailing the O.P. A junior sergeant hurled curses and epithets at the CP through his walkie.

No one had been calling Black's name. One of the guard posts had been frantically reporting "black" on machine gun ammo—meaning, they were out—for the past couple minutes. While Hubbard and Black had been talking to Hill, fighters from that direction had been able to move a mobile artillery tube into position unmolested and get it online.

It had just blasted a hole somewhere in one of the compound's stone walls, and the sergeant was letting them know all this in the most colorful terms imaginable.

Black knew how it would go. That kind of lapse would only build on itself if not stopped. That's what the forces surrounding the COP were counting on. Death by a thousand huge cuts.

Hubbard worked the radios and verified that guys were already en route to the tower with fresh ammo. When he finished he tossed the handset and kicked the little desk chair, sending it spinning to the corner.

"Goddamn it!" he shouted.

Lying on his back again, palm across his forehead, Black held out a hand toward Hubbard.

"Give me Hill."

Hubbard stopped his venting and looked at Black's outstretched hand in silence.

"C'mon!" Black spat sharply.

Hubbard stretched the black telephone cable of the handset across the desk and put it in Black's hand. It barely reached.

Black took the hard plastic handset and pulled it to his throbbing head, one hand covering his eyes. He hoped there wouldn't be more blasts like that one.

Hurts.

He keyed the rubberized transmit button, waiting for the signature *beep* of encrypted radio communication.

"Hill, it's Lieutenant Black."

Nothing.

"Hill, you there?"

Static.

"Hey there, L.T., watcha got?" came Hill's drawling voice at last through the ongoing torrent.

Black swallowed.

"Listen, man," he began. "We're doing everything we can here to get some birds up to you guys. Break."

You didn't want to let an important transmission run longer than a few seconds. The signal tended to drift, especially on a poor connection. He keyed the radio afresh. Beep.

"You will be ahead of the COP in order of priority as soon as we get air on station. Break."

Hubbard closed his eyes.

"But I cannot tell you when I can get you help. Break."

Hubbard crossed his arms and lowered his head. He kicked the desk again, hard.

"Probably not soon," Black finished. "How copy?"

Nothing came back for several seconds. Hubbard raised his head and looked at Black.

When Hill opened the mic, all they heard at first was the merciless cacophony from his end.

"Roger that, bud," came the breezy reply, as though he'd just been told the week's mail would be an hour late. "I gotcha. Keep us posted."

"Do the same."

"Out."

Black let the handset snake back along its taut cable, clattering against the metal side of the desk. Hubbard didn't retrieve it.

"Oh, man," he moaned, arms still crossed.

"Get the radios back up."

"Oh, Jesus, we're just leaving all those guys to die, aren't we?"

"No we're not."

"Yes we are!" Hubbard wailed, rocking back and forth and hugging himself. "Aw, fuck, they're all gonna die!"

"Focus on now," Black told the ceiling.

"Oh, God."

He looked very pale.

"Get on your nets!"

Hubbard lurched and bent sideways, falling to his knees and vomiting explosively into the wastebasket that sat next to his desk.

"Stay with me," Black muttered, his own voice sloshing around in his head.

Hubbard hung his head over the wastebasket, panting, eyes closed, hands clutching its sides.

"Oh, Jesus," he murmured.

The volume of unanswered radio traffic pressed and seethed at them like a barely contained mob.

"C'mon, Hubbard," Black urged woozily. "C'mon, stay on your radios and forget everything else."

Nothing.

"You're doing good, Hubbard, but you gotta stay on it. You gotta keep on the nets and get a picture of what's happening all over so you can guide the defense."

He could hear his own voice growing taut and desperate.

"C'mon, man, they need you to do it."

Hubbard just shook his head.

"We're dead."

"We're not dead. We just gotta hold this place until the convoy gets here."

Hubbard screamed at him.

"How the fuck are we supposed to h—"

WHUMP.

Another concussion, as powerful as the one before, shook the walls visibly and crushed the air in the room. Hubbard ducked, shielding himself with his arms.

Black clutched his head and yowled in pain, curling to the side. His skull felt like it was going to collapse in on itself.

"Goddamn it!" Hubbard's distant voice shouted from behind the desk.

Subdividing phosphorescent blotches filled Black's vision.

Ohh, hurts.

He nearly rolled off the cot.

"Find out," he heard himself yelling from somewhere, "where that ca—"

"CHARLIE IN THE WIRE!"

The single transmitting voice cut through the rest of the clamor. Black opened his eyes in time to see the splotchy image of Hubbard's head pop above the desk, uncomprehending.

The rest of the radio traffic fell away.

"I mean, enemy in the wire!" came the same voice. "ENEMY IN THE WIRE!"

Hubbard leaped for his radios as the report was passed throughout the COP, cascading across the nets.

Charlie in the wire, Black repeated dumbly as Hubbard hollered into his handsets. Some kid had Vietnam on the brain.

They were breached.

Qadir burst ahead, sandals pounding dirt downhill. He felt the group surging forward on either side of him. Felt his long legs fly, his feet glide across the slope like he was made of air.

No, water. A droplet in the wave of red justice that would break upon the walls and rage through the openings, course through every rotten vessel and dark space inside. Wash it clean.

He stomped ahead of the older men and the younger boys, crisp air filling his lungs, the far hillsides of his stolen home rising above the looming compound. He would be first.

Welling tears bent his vision and he understood. Understood that if only for this moment alone it was worthwhile to have drawn his first breath, to have walked on this Earth.

Thank you.

He bounded over the scattered rubble and leaped through the ragged gap in the wall, his heaving breath in his ears, eyes adjusting instantly to the dim light. The racket of weapons was deafening in here. He turned to face it, raising his rifle without aiming, and shot the first wide-eyed American he saw in the face. Qadir saw nothing after.

42

You good, sir?"

The voice cut through the noise. He didn't recognize it. No, he did. Whose?

His.

"You good, sir?"

No, Hubbard's. Shouting at him through the racket.

Black's palms pressed on something cold and hard. His knees throbbed.

Concrete. He was on his hands and knees on the floor. Had he fallen out of the cot?

He thought maybe he'd lunged for the radio, when he'd heard something.

The breach.

"No, I know about that one!" Hubbard was calling into his radio. "Where's the other?"

"South wall!" someone came back. "There's at least six guys inside the backyard near Bay One!"

"Roger, roger!" Hubbard called, switching to his walkie-talkie. "Schupe, can you get anybody close to there?"

How much time had passed? Had he lost consciousness?

"Negative!" came the return call, punctuated with nearby gunfire. "No way right now! Check with Pilar!"

There was no more talking over the radio nets now. Only yelling.

"What about the guys in the mortar pit?" someone else called in.

"Do not go there!" Hubbard shouted back, then keyed a different radio handset. "Stand by!"

He returned to the first radio.

"Do not attempt that!" Hubbard repeated into the walkie. "Willis, take whoever you got and get to Bay Two. There's five or ten guys on foot right out the back door."

"Got it."

"Wright, come in!"

Another channel cut in.

"X-Ray, aid station!"

Black pushed himself backward into a sitting position, his back resting against the cot rail.

"Aid station, stand by! Stand by!"

A cloudy vision of Hubbard danced among the radios trying to wrangle a squad together to push the intruders back at the most recent breach point.

How many were there?

"X-ray!" someone squawked in. "Tower Three!"

"X-ray!" Hubbard shot back.

"We're black on ammo and there's guys inside the wall like thirty meters from us!"

Hubbard keyed the mic immediately.

"What if I can get you . . ."

He trailed off as he realized the guard tower had stepped on his transmission.

"We're outta here, man," they called in. "We're pulling back into the building."

Black and Hubbard exchanged looks. Hubbard punched the desktop.

"Shit!"

They were losing the initiative.

We have to regain it.

Hubbard squeezed the handset angrily, shaking his head in helpless exasperation.

"Roger!"

Or these guys are all going to die.

"We're pulling back through the backyard near the generators," the tower called back in. "Just don't let anyone fucking shoot us on the way!"

Hubbard threw up his arms.

"Do my best!" he shouted unconvincingly into the radio.

There were at least three different breach points, as far as Black could tell, with ground forces now making a concerted effort to push through the gaps. In at least two places they'd succeeded, and were now clashing with the barely organized resistance in the compound's makeshift passages and haphazard spaces.

The aid station cut back in.

"We still need some hands, man!" they pressed. "We need 'em now!"

"I *know!*" Hubbard shot back, frazzled. "I'm tryi—"

WHUMP.

The room shook violently, sending Hubbard under the desk again.

Black's head filled with high-pitched screeching. He doubled forward, clutching his temples, and tipped over to the hard floor.

"Damn it!" Hubbard shouted, grabbing his walkie-talkie. "Where was that? Where was that?"

"East wall!" someone shot back. "Near the connexes! Bay Two!"

The CP door burst open, smacking against the cinderblock wall. Hubbard jumped. Black flinched against the sharp noise.

A boot stomped through, followed by the rest of Shannon, ducking his armor-laden frame and pushing through the opening.

"Goddamn it, guy!" he boomed, "You gotta—"

He stopped short, seeing that it was only Hubbard running the CP.

"What the fuck?"

He saw Black on the floor holding his forehead.

"Jesus," he declared.

He stomped across to Hubbard's desk, peering down at Black as he went.

"Your fucking ears, Lieutenant."

Black touched his hands to the sides of his head.

"Show me where," Shannon told Hubbard.

Black held his fingers in front of his face and saw blood on all the tips.

Shannon listened as Hubbard jabbed fingers at a map of the compound, showing him where the most serious incursions had taken place.

"All right," Shannon said, pointing at the map. "I need a machine gun for cover *here* by the time we get to the yard. Can you get one there?"

"Yeah."

Shannon stubbed a huge finger into Hubbard's chest.

"*That's* your priority right now, Hubbard. You got it?"

He swept aside the riot of noise from Hubbard's radio stacks.

"None of this other bullshit, you understand?"

"Yeah. How many guys you got?"

Shannon glanced down at Black, their eyes meeting for a moment.

"Five."

"Shit."

"Just get it there."

He turned and headed for the door.

"Couldn't catch Caine in time," he told Black as he passed.

"Where are you going?"

"To take this bitch back," Shannon answered and was gone.

"Come on," Black heard him say to unseen soldiers in the hallway.

Hubbard leaped on his radios, trying desperately to cut into the furious crosstraffic now crowding all the nets.

"Brand!" he cried. "Pilar, you there?"

Everyone shouted at everyone else, trying to get a picture of what was happening where.

"Pilar!"

"Here."

"You gotta take the two-forty from the courtyard and move it to behind the Taj Mahal right now!"

"What? Negative! We can't move from here!"

"You gotta! Shannon needs it right now!"

Every person Hubbard spoke to was locked in his own pitched fight just to avoid losing further ground to the intruding forces.

"—moving west in the yard."

"No, I said *six* guys!"

"—nyone still inside that bay?"

"Gonna hit the generator if they—"

"X-RAY."

Shannon's voice cut through the din. Hubbard snatched up the radio.

"X-ray!"

"How 'bout it, Hubbard, you wanna get us the *god*damn machine gun or what?"

"I'm trying!" Hubbard hollered at him. "No one can get there!"

He stamped his boots on the ground in frustration.

"You're *trying?*" Shannon came back, incredulous. "Motherfucker, you gotta GET someone to—"

The aid station cut in.

"Hubbard, we can't wait on those guys!"

"I DON'T GOT ANY GUYS!"

He swung around to the walkie-talkie.

"Oswalt, get your ass back here now!"

"Roger," came Oswalt's drawling reply.

"No, wait!" Black called. "He needs to—"

The room bucked as something exploded outside, very close to the CP. Black howled and clung to the sideways floor.

His head was filled with concrete. No, his cheek was pressed against the cold concrete of the floor. He heard no sound.

Please stop. No more.

He opened his eyes and then realized they were already open.

The room was in darkness.

"Shit!" Hubbard was shouting. "The generator!"

The generator. Any interior part of the COP would now be in darkness.

Black heard the desk door slide open, something metallic thunking against its side. Radios squawked, voices thick with panic. No one indoors could see anything.

Something plunked down hard on the desktop. Pale white light made shadows around Black. Electric lantern.

The radio nets were now chaos as everyone tried to account for everyone else and for the location of the enemy. Black tried to pull himself to his hands and knees.

Please let me stop.

"Damn it!" Hubbard cried, slapping a battery pack into the back of a radio that didn't have one. "Damn it! Damn it!"

I mean let it stop.

"X-ray, aid station! We got no juice here, man! We're dark!"

Shannon cut in again.

"Hubbard," he growled, his voice colored with rage. "You *listen* to me. I don't care about the fucking gener—"

The door smacked open again. Who was that talking?

YOU GOOD, SIR?

Not him. Not possible.

"You good, sir?"

Oswalt's voice, above him.

"Oswalt!" he heard Hubbard cry. "Come here, man. I need you!"

"What's wrong with the lieut—"

"Don't worry about that! I need you to get the two-forty from the courtyard post and take it to Shannon right now!"

"Okay."

"You gotta haul ass, man, you understand? They need you bad."

Forehead to the floor, Black begged his world to stop spinning.

HAUL ASS.

"Here, look at the map," Hubbard was saying to Oswalt. "Let me show you where."

"Hubbard!" Shannon's voice roared through the radio. "Come in, goddamn it!"

"Okay, do you understand, Oswalt?" Hubbard was asking.

"Got it."

"Two-six Romeo."

Two-six Romeo? Who was that talking on the radio?

"Go there now, man. Don't stop."

"Don't stop."

It wasn't Two-Six Romeo.

"Tiger Zero-Zero."

"Shannon!" Hubbard was shouting at the walkie. "Oswalt's coming now!"

"Quiet!" Black shouted into the concrete. "Stop!"

"Vega Command, this is Tiger Zero-Zero inbound, over."

Hubbard and Oswalt fell silent at the new voice on the radio.

"Say again, Vega Command, this is Tiger Zero-Zero inbound, how copy?"

"Holy shit!"

Hubbard leaped and snatched up the handset.

"This is Vega!" he cried. "Vega X-Ray!"

"Roger, Vega X-Ray," came the cool, detached voice of the helicopter pilot. "We're two minutes out, approaching from your south."

Hubbard emitted a sound somewhere between a single laugh and a gasping sob.

"Somebody told 'em, sir!" he shouted at Black's prostrate form.

"What's your status, Vega X-Ray?" the pilot called down from somewhere among the angels.

Hubbard keyed back, cupping the handset to his mouth like a flowing spigot of life.

"Uh, we got dismounts on foot inside the compound, we got . . . many casualties, and we got no generator power."

"Good copy, X-Ray," came the pilot's soothing tones, as though hearing this kind of information pleased him. "I'm seeing your smoke up ahead. We're gonna lay down some fire for you, but visibility's gonna be pretty bad."

"Okay," Hubbard responded. "Yeah."

He shook his head to clear it.

"Yeah, we got no front line trace."

"Roger that, X-Ray," the pilot answered, unflappable. "Are you guys able to paint some targets for us?"

"Yeah, we can try to . . ."

Hubbard trailed off as he saw Oswalt still standing there.

"Oswalt, *go,* man!"

Don't stop.

"Oswalt!" Black shouted into the floor, his voice booming inside his own skull.

He pushed against the floor and rolled himself onto his back, a wave of phosphenes cresting across his eyes. Oswalt's dim form loomed behind them.

"Hey, sir," he said calmly. "There wasn't any satellite phone in Danny's room."

Danny's room.

"But his ham radio thingy was talking."

He'd sent Oswalt to Danny's room.

"Saying a bunch of numbers in Pashto."

He looked stupidly up at Oswalt, towering and spinning above him.

Don't stop.

"At least they sounded like numbers. Like off the phrase card."

Numbers. Black squeezed his eyes shut against the wavering vision of the big soldier.

Get there.

Pain was bringing clarity.

"What are the coordinates to the O.P.?" he demanded.

Oswalt rattled them off.

"Write 'em, Hubbard!" Black called, his voice bouncing in a thousand directions in his head.

Hubbard scrambled for a pen. Black opened his eyes and pushed himself to his elbows, feeling like he were on a raft in an ocean storm. He rattled questions off tersely.

"What direction is Darreh Sin from here?"

"That's northeast, sir," Oswalt answered, as though it were the most natural question to be asked at that moment in time.

"How far is it from right here to Tower Three?"

Oswalt shrugged.

"About a hundred fifty meters, sir."

"I need you to take a radio and go to the roof."

"Whoa, whoa!" Hubbard yelped.

"And do what, sir?"

Black's temples felt as though a skewer ran from one to the other.

Let me rest.

"Talk to the Apache and direct his fire."

"Sir, I'm not trained to—"

"You don't need to be," Black interrupted. "You just talk to the guys like you're having a conversation, just distance and direction and they'll do the rest."

Oswalt blinked once, but before Black could say anything else he stepped to the far corner of the CP and gathered one of the portable "manpack" radio sets.

"Sir," Hubbard protested, "Shannon used to be an F.O."

Forward observer.

"Let me call him and have him handle th—"

"Shannon's busy," Black stated flatly.

Oswalt returned with the radio.

"Find some cover up there," Black admonished. "You may need to keep moving around."

His vision was too mottled for him to keep his eyes open without getting dizzy. He stretched an arm across his face.

"Hubbard, give him the freek."

Hubbard gave it.

"They're waiting to talk to you," he continued. "Just tell 'em where the bad guys are breaking through and where their biggest guns are shooting from."

"Roger, sir."

Black heard Oswalt sling the pack.

"You got this, Oswalt," Hubbard said without conviction.

Black moved his arm and looked up at the big soldier through bright spangles. An explosion echoed from the far side of the compound.

"You're not scared of a damned thing," he said.

Oswalt turned to go. Black collapsed back onto the hard floor, which wouldn't still itself anymore.

"Get there, Oswalt," he called weakly as Oswalt disappeared into the noise and chaos.

Hubbard was on the radio now, passing coordinates of O.P. Traynor to the helicopters.

"We got a squad of guys in trouble there right now," he was telling the pilot.

The floor was so cold.

Get there.

"Fuck you, Hubbard!" came Shannon's snarling voice through the walkie-talkie. "We're going without it, you fucker!"

"No!" Hubbard called back. "Don't do that! We've got air on sta—"

"WE'RE ON FIRE!" someone cut in on another net.

"Say again!" Hubbard shouted into the handset, finger in one ear. "What about fire?"

"In the yard!" the voice came back. "The generator started a fire in the yard! The fucking building's on fire near the chow hall!"

Fire. Of course it was fire.

"GodDAMN IT!" Hubbard was hollering, pounding the desktop over and over with his fist.

Fire would spread.

Black squeezed his throbbing eyes against the steady spinning and heaving of the room.

"You're doing good," he mumbled at Hubbard, who was shouting uselessly into his radios.

Don't stop.

"We're gonna hold it," he lied.

The exchange of gunfire echoed sharp in the stone corridors.

"Yo, Hill!" Hubbard's distant voice was calling into the Traynor net. "We got an Apache on the way to you right now. Hill, you there?"

The firefight in the halls sounded closer than Hubbard's voice.

Behind it rose the sound of a helicopter.

"Hill, come in, man!"

His last thought, as every molecule in his universe converted itself simultaneously to pure sound and the force of the blast poured cement and stone through the roof of the CP, was that at least he was already on the floor.

He did not dream, but saw.

A rough hand grasped the handle on the back of his body armor and hauled him to his feet.

His platoon sergeant. Brennan. Bleeding from a gash on his face. His mouth shouted without sound.

YOU GOOD, SIR?

Black's head rang with the noiseless echo of the blast that had knocked him to the ground.

He nodded. They clawed their way upward. The boulders were close.

Fultz, his radioman, climbed with them through the chaos. Ten more meters of tall, tan grass and the three of them tumbled panting behind the rocks.

The sounds of the fight were cutting back through the haze, returning to Black's hearing. The rattle and clatter of automatic weapons, punctuated with rocket impacts against the mountainside.

In twos and threes across the steep slope, a tatter of soldiers scrambled and clawed, dragging themselves and their buddies upward in tandem. Up from the doomed vehicles.

"X-Ray, this is Two-Six Romeo!" Fultz was shouting into his radio. "I have Two-Six Actual here."

That was him. Two-Six. The "six" element of second platoon. Romeo was the radioman. Actual was the guy. The person in charge. The person responsible.

"X-Ray, how copy?"

Get out of the kill zone. First rule of getting ambushed, right after Return fire. They couldn't get out of the kill zone.

Most of the platoon was climbing up, up where they could get cover, get angles. Someone was dragging Zeke, the 'terp, along.

Zeke had told him. You go through that place with half a platoon, you all die, he'd said. Your commander is an idiot, he'd said.

So now they were all in it together.

"X-Ray, Two-Six Romeo!"

No one answered.

The volume of fire raining around them on the slopes was tremendous. Guys dove behind rocks and just curled there, until their buddies kicked them in the seat of the pants and made them go.

Black peered around the boulder at the ugly straggle on the dry mountainside. Momentum. Keep the initiative. They had lost all initiative from the moment it began.

We have to regain it or these guys are all going to die.

Brennan's shouting brought him back.

"COULD YOU GET COMMS FROM YOUR TRUCK?"

Black shook his head.

"NO."

"ME NEITHER."

Black pointed up.

"FULTZ AND I HAVE TO GO HIGHER."

If they climbed to the ridgeline and cleared the level of the opposite mountain they could maybe hit the retrans with Fultz's radio.

Helicopters. Jets. Artillery. All the glories and pleasures of life were carried in Fultz's pack. Black would direct them all like a maestro.

A blast sent them ducking to the hillside.

Brennan came back up and nodded.

"I'LL CONSOLIDATE HERE," he shouted, pointing at the steeply sloping ground beneath his boots. "THIS IS HIGH ENOUGH."

Black nodded back and turned to Fultz, who gave a somber thumbs-up. Brennan grabbed Fultz and immediately began yanking ammo magazines, grenades, the side plates on his body armor, anything else of any weight off of his person. The long-range radio pack with all its batteries was gonna be heavy enough on the way up.

When he reached for Fultz's rifle the kid finally resisted. Brennan tugged it away.

"YOU AIN'T GONNA NEED IT IF YOU DON'T HAUL ASS THE WHOLE WAY."

The rifle weighed only eight pounds loaded, but the difference between running with your hands free and with a rifle in them was huge. Black slung his own behind his back.

Brennan clapped Fultz on the shoulder hard enough to almost knock him over, and turned to Black.

"I GOT THIS," he hollered. "GO, SIR."

Black went to a crouch on his boot-toes and peeked around the boulders. There was no sense waiting for a break in the fire. There was none, and there would be none.

Moving target. They're not gonna hit a moving target.

"SIR," Brennan shouted from behind him.

Black turned his head. Brennan was shaking his.

"DON'T STOP."

Black launched himself from behind the rocks and turned uphill.

The riot of sound was unreal. Explosions mingled with urgent shouts across the hillside. The bullets made a horrible soft thumping noise when they impacted the dirt close to him and Fultz. They clawed upward through the hail.

The first mistake he made was to raise his head and look ahead of him. A scrubby tan carpet of dry grass blades stretched steeply above them an impossible distance, dotted with stones and boulder outcroppings all the way to the horizon, where the grass met the sky.

They climbed past a tumble of boulders in which soldiers had taken up multilevel residence, rifles answering the fire from the slopes across the canyon. The nearest guy gawked at Black and Fultz clambering madly by, then understood.

"Go, guys, go!" he screamed wildly. "Get there!"

Black had had months to acclimate to the altitude. He was fit. But this climb was inhuman. He needed to rest.

Their attackers on the opposite side of the canyon were smart enough to figure out what was going on. Once they did, they let it be known.

Only the distance between the two sides of the canyon and the sure knowledge that stopping or slowing would mean death kept the two alive, kept them moving upward against their burning lungs and revolting legs. That and the fire peppering the ground near them.

They pressed on, panting and gasping.

The sounds of the main fight faded beneath them, overtaken by their own hoarse breaths. Black didn't look up ahead of them anymore. He saw only the dry earth before his eyes, and kept moving.

He realized that none of the contrived, enforced sufferings he'd endured through all of his training were anything at all.

Please, just one moment's rest.

An explosion opened the earth not far beneath them.

There were no rocks here big enough to duck behind. Only the open grass, burned in the sun.

Don't stop.

He'd had a roommate back at the FOB, another young officer whom Black hadn't liked much. The guy had cut out and posted a small square of paper near his bunk, from something someone back home had sent. In bold print at the top it read "A Lieutenant's Prayer."

Black had found the title irritating before he'd even read what was below. The prayer itself he had found no less exasperating and precious. The words returned to him from nowhere as he scrabbled at the slope and crushed a foot-trail through the dead grass.

> *Please God*
> *Do not take any of my guys*
> *I cannot handle that.*

As he climbed now he could think of nothing but those words.

Someone on the other side of the canyon was still giving it a go. Rounds thudded into the earth nearby. His legs felt like they had been poured with lava.

Please God let me stop.

43

Six Actual.

Dark.

". . . Six Actual."

Someone nearby was talking.

This was something important, he told himself. He found it hard to maintain interest.

You should listen.

He listened. It was gone.

Someone else was talking. That wasn't the voice.

". . . near the connexes by the north wall of the compound."

Oswalt.

"There are three or four there and on the far side, and no friendlies."

Over a radio speaker. He proceeded as blandly and methodically as if he were reading off serial numbers in the arms room.

That's good. Oswalt will take care of everything.

"Roger that," came the pilot's easy reply. "Coming around."

It troubled him that he couldn't hear the other thing. He felt sure it was important.

Well, he would rest a moment instead then.

". . . Six Actual, how copy?"

Oh, it was coming back. Good.

"Vega X-Ray, this is Vega Six Actual, how copy?"

This was something he knew.

"Vega X-Ray, this is Vega Six Actual, Cyclone Mobile is three minutes out, how copy?"

Now he understood.

"Vega X-Ray, how copy?"

It was odd. He was sure he had been lying on his back.

He seemed to be standing now, though he wasn't certain he could feel his feet. Moving past piles of stone intermingled with disheveled radio equipment.

"Sorry," he heard himself mumble to the motionless form behind what was left of Hubbard's desk, "but I had to throw the book at you."

Hubbard didn't laugh.

Nobody gets my jokes.

It was tough going, climbing over the rubble between him and the door.

". . . X-Ray, how copy?"

The sound faded behind him as he crossed the threshold.

He was vaguely aware, as he traveled the corridor, of the air vibrating, throbbing around him. He could feel it on his face, pulsing, returning, but the sounds seemed distant. Mostly he heard his boots scuffing along the floor.

Brennan ran up to him.

Not Brennan. A soldier, mouthing words at him that he knew he could hear. He just couldn't muster the interest in what the kid was saying.

There was smoke ahead. Probably from the door he was heading toward.

He passed through an open space between two buildings, noting the great flames soaring above him to his left as he went. To his right he was sure there had been a wing of the building where now there was empty air. Maybe there hadn't been. Maybe it had always been rubble.

He thought he might be coughing. He passed indoors again and was pleased to see Fultz pressing on at his side.

Not Fultz. A soldier passing by, screaming something to him. Neat trick, Fultz.

It would be right down this passage, then through another open area. That's the way. Then there would be one more tunnel.

He felt air on his face again. Cold air. Then heat. Cinders washed across his vision in an artificial wind.

It was dim. Nearly the end of twilight. He saw light and looked up mutely to the black mountainside looming above the compound's buildings.

A lateral scrum of orange sunbursts rolled side by side, descending its face. There must have been dozens, all at once, a carpet of fire unfurling.

Someone invited bombers. It looked as though the mountain were crumbling down on top of them in flames.

He scuffled forward. The cinders stung his face. No, they weren't hot.

Cold.

Not cinders. Cold pinpricks. Frozen.

Snow.

It fell silently through the pressing din around him as he dragged his booted feet through the dirt yard. An early snow.

He loved the snow.

The tunnel approached, pressed in close and dark, but he kept moving. Almost there.

He hadn't passed half its length before he saw it, framed by the rectangled opening ahead. Right there beyond the end of the tunnel, like sighting the promised harbor in a spyglass. Like it was meant to be.

Six Actual.

Corelli raised his bare head in the shadows and watched the first flakes fall past the door.

Christmastime soon, back home.

He shifted his weight against the stone. It helped to move sometimes, let a different part go numb. Ease the pressure from the bindings on his hands.

The snow was barely visible in the deep pale of the gloaming sky. He thought he could hear the sound it made as it fell, even over the distant rumble of violence from beyond the mountain passes. From where his friends were.

Weighed in the balances.

He felt himself shiver beneath his uniform. The chill from the stone. He lowered his head and sang quietly to himself while he awaited what he deserved.

44

The end of the tunnel loomed. He was there, not twenty meters away in the flashing dark, standing square in the middle of the courtyard, a row of rumbling gun trucks behind him, orange slashes arcing upward from all their turrets.

Tumult all about him, soldiers slugging ammo cans from the trucks, medics bearing litters toward them. But he stood there amidst it a picture of calm, his rifle hanging idly at his side, gazing upward at the inferno in the hillsides with the bearing of a man who has stepped out to the veranda to enjoy a Fourth of July display on the next field over.

At the end of the tunnel a medic squatted under the breezeway, hunched over a pair of prostrate legs, back turned. Black saw the medic's form bouncing and rushing at him with startling speed.

His confusion passed when he realized he was running at the medic. Of course.

Yes.

He pulled the startled kid entirely off balance doing it, nearly spilling himself, but the pistol tugged free in his grasp, free of the medic's holster. He completed a stumbling three-sixty, feeling like he'd barely broken stride, and felt his stomping boots smack on mud. Felt the cold air again. Saw the face, which had turned now and was looking over Black's head to the mountains.

It was a forgettable one, angular and unhandsome, taut with years of underestimation and underappreciation. But the burn in Pistone's coal-dark eyes as he soaked in the spectacle above them was all Black needed to see. A half second's glance to feel certain as he stamped ahead, bootsoles skidding beneath him, and squared the pistol in the air before his face.

The force of the medic's running tackle spun him from behind, sending the two of them tangled together to the ground. They smacked hard and slid, cutting a black trough across the slick surface now speckled in soft gray.

A single shot cracked into the dark as they struck. Black's sole contribution of violence to the day.

"Goddamn it, sir!"

The voice was so far.

"What the hell!?"

He felt himself pressed into the moist earth as the medic sat on him with all his weight. Felt the pistol pulled easily from his reaching hands. Felt the cold seeping through his uniform layers to his skin.

Heard another voice shouting at the medic, the voice of a sergeant to his soldier. Something about Black being altered and to stop fucking around and stick him already.

And his own voice, someplace distant, screaming upward at the spectacled face that stood looking down at him now, splashed in shifting orange light. At the same coal eyes. Screaming at those eyes that They were your guys.

The needle didn't hurt as it entered his injured arm. He felt nothing as its contents coursed through him. Pulled him downward.

Illuminated flakes fell gently into his vision, drifting between him and those eyes. He saw but did not hear the words that were spoken down to him in return. He understood them, though, and knew he would not forget them.

But the speaker turned away, and Black lost them as his straining limbs slackened and he sank lower, let them swirl away as particles of smoke before his waving hand. Let them free of his grasp and found his dark rest in ashes and snow.

He'd never been a good singer. Hardly could carry a tune. His sister made fun of him for it. But he'd never cared much.

Mostly he sang alone anyway. He'd sung through all his albums during the dark Land Nav nights in training. Sung himself all the way over the mountains and up here when the lieutenant told him to go. Sang when he was farthest from safety.

The rumbling surged in the distance. Corelli sang on, barely above a whisper, in a quavering boy's voice.

See him in a manger laid

Whom the angels praise above

It must have been thunderous where they were. He listened to the awful far tumult and sang to the stone floor as the snow outside settled to the ground.

While we raise our hearts in love

Glooooo-oooooo-ooooria

In excelsis deo

The shape filled the doorway, framed black against the early evening.

Only what I have earned.

"Sir!"

He turned his head. Fultz, rasping and clawing beside him, pointed upward.

He looked. The ridgeline, barely twenty feet further.

As they stomped and struggled upward through the last steps, he heard a new sound growing above and behind him.

They staggered and fell to earth at the crest, out of sight.

He collapsed in a heap just over the top, the noise rising stronger and more steady behind them. He rolled to his back, heaving gasps raking in and out of him, a fresh panorama of height and depth filling his vision. His body, ravenous for air, gorged at the meager feast up here.

Fultz lay on his face beside him, sucking in the mountaintop soil, one arm thrust out toward him holding the handset.

The noise resolved itself and roared over his face, faceless and unknowing. Heavy-lift cargo helicopters, on their way someplace in some other godforsaken valley, with twenty-foot concrete blast barriers hanging beneath them.

45

A hazy, brutal shape loomed before his vision, haloed in snowglare. He moved his hand, which had been holding his head, and squinted upward.

Shannon. Just looking down at him. Smeared in grime and sweat.

Behind him the courtyard and its walls were covered in a gentle inch of snow, which now threw the morning sun in Black's eyes. The Humvees were gone, muddy ruts and bootprints the only sign of their former presence. He tasted multiple flavors of smoke.

Someone had propped him in a folding camp chair in the breezeway and put a field jacket on him. A fresh IV line snaked out from beneath the coat. His head pounded like a dozen hangovers. He realized he was shivering.

"Found your pack," Shannon grunted.

Black lowered his head and saw his assault pack, which he had left in Pistone's hootch two days before, hanging by its straps in the corporal's huge hand. It sloughed to the stone in a slumping heap of canvas by Shannon's feet. Black heard two dull objects move against each other inside it.

Black stared at the pack dumbly. His jaw felt slack, as though his mouth were hanging open.

He raised his head and looked up again. Shannon was looking away.

"Might need that," he said to the breezeway wall.

Black looked past him at the silent hills, now mottled in gray. The side of his face throbbed.

"Corel—" he began, and erupted in a fit of coughing.

When he finished he saw Shannon looking down at him again in distaste, brow curled as though trying to solve a problem in his head. He produced a dirt-stained, half-drunk water bottle from a cargo pocket and held it out silently. Black took it and drank, water running down the sides of his mouth.

When he looked up Shannon's hands were shoved in his pockets and he was looking away again.

"Empty pair of flex-cuffs," he muttered.

Behind him the wind on the slopes raised white swirls from dusted tree limbs. Soldiers and medics hustled to and from the courtyard. Most carried ammunition and M.R.E. cases, which they stacked against the breezeway walls.

Black tried to remember how long he'd been watching them. How long he'd been conscious.

"Oswalt," he croaked.

"He's cool."

"O.P."

Shannon turned and eyeballed the soldiers coming and going before he spoke.

"Ain't no O.P."

Black looked past Shannon at the snow-powdered hills.

A medic sergeant appeared, the same one from the night before, informing him that his MEDEVAC flight would be arriving in a few minutes. His tone made it clear that there would be no dicking around and Black *would* be getting on the bird.

The sergeant stomped away, barking at his junior medics.

It took Black a moment to realize that Shannon was still standing there. He'd momentarily forgotten.

He noticed for the first time that Shannon's body armor and weapon were stacked against the breezeway wall nearby. He looked up at the hulking soldier, who stared intently down the breezeway, hands in his pockets again.

Soldiers came by with cots and cases of medical supplies. Everything in the outpost was being assembled close to the courtyard.

"I didn't—" Shannon blurted out suddenly.

Black looked up. Shannon, looking out at the hills, shook his head and exhaled in muscular exasperation.

"I didn't know Sergeant Merrick was fucking investigating anything," he said in an angry gush of words, "until he told you out there yesterday."

He crossed his bulging forearms.

"I didn't know who knew what or who wanted to know what."

He glared at the soldiers hustling about the courtyard and shoved his hands back into his pockets.

Black watched the soldiers too.

"Bullshit," he sighed wearily.

Shannon uncrossed his arms and looked down at Black a long time before he spoke.

From above, in daylight, it looked so ordinary. A valley like all the rest. Mountains like any others. From up here they could've been the mountains back home. Like with his dad and brother.

They flew just below the level of the ridges, hazy sunshafts winking, flashing across into his eyes. He watched out the chopper door as the coils of black smoke receded, its origin shrinking to a dot in the crook of the snow-dusted valley sides.

Did Brydon go with Caine, when he went out to do his business?

He had dreaded asking the question.

Naw. That wasn't the dick Caine fucked him with.

Black looked around the interior of the helicopter. There were other soldiers there, strapped into the narrow seats. Lesser wounded like himself. After the criticals and the bodies.

One of them, caked in ash and dried blood, saw Black looking at him. He smiled and gave a flip of the chin. Black looked away.

What was Caine doing outside the COP?

You know what he was doing.

Where is he now?

Shannon had told him, watching Black's reaction coolly. When he spoke it was without triumph and without pity.

I told you the day I met you, Lieutenant. You fuck with this valley and it will fuck you back.

"HEARD WHAT YOU DID, SIR," the soldier in the bird called over the rotors and wind.

Black turned his head and looked at the kid blankly.

"HEARD WHAT YOU DID."

What he did.

How did Caine know where to go looking for Corelli?

He hadn't expected Shannon to know.

That was probably me.

Shannon's big brows curled at him.

Thought you were a paperwork bubba.

Long story.

The soldier in the helicopter nodded at Black enthusiastically.

"FUCK YEAH, L.T.!"

They'd gotten below the snow line. Scrubby slopes sped past the open doors.

What were you gonna be, Lieutenant? Before you ran away from it to be in the Army?

It was the second time that week someone had asked him that. He said so.

Yeah, well, whatever it was, you might want to just go do that. Army ain't for you.

The medic sergeant had come back then, and told Black his ride was almost there.

See you later then.

But Black called to Shannon, over the rising noise of the approaching helicopter.

Why did you refuse the order that night?

It was the only thing he'd really wanted to know from him.

When Caine told you to go after the girl?

Shannon had got a distant look in his eyes.

Didn't know if it was a girl or boy.

Black told him. Shannon's assessment was succinct.

Goddamn.

Two medics had come up the breezeway, ready to help Black aboard. Shannon bent to gather his gear.

Yeah, well, anyway, I don't give a fuck about no hajji kid.

That Black believed.

But Caine was an asshole.

He shouldered his load.

And so are you.

And he'd turned and stumped away down the breezeway, a hulking, moving island of calm in the blowing snow.

Mountainsides fell away. The broad plain opened below them. The chopper banked and adjusted course, bound for home.

Clear of the valleys, they picked up speed. The sound of the wind and the engines was deafening in the open compartment. But all Black could hear was what Shannon had told him. About Caine.

Sergeant Merrick found him.

Where?

The big corporal looked steadily into his eyes.

Like Parsons.

Like who?

Their altitude was appreciably dropping, the air warming.

They crucified his ass.

Black looked out the door and saw Omaha in the distance.

46

He thumbed through the stack of bills then tossed them back onto the cot with the rest. A chilling breeze blew through the gaps and sent them swirling past the open trunk, brown rectangles lined up in its mouth. He'd only seen heroin bricks in person one other time.

He took a last look around Caine's hootch and strode out, climbing over rubble and picking his way through the remains of the disemboweled outpost.

His lieutenant was waiting, silently. Everyone else was on board already. The two of them checked the timer and set the detonators together. Strode out to the hulking, crouching bird, rotors turning, whining, ready to claw upward.

They stopped at the base of the ramp. The lieutenant looked at him expectantly.

He knew it would come to this nonsense. He should let it go. Remember what Shannon said.

Goddamned Shannon.

Just let it go. Don't let on.

No goddamned way.

He turned and looked in the lieutenant's dark eyes.

"Get on the fucking helicopter, sir."

The lieutenant looked back at him, long and probingly, before turning and stumping up into the troop compartment.

Shaking off the feeling of sudden nakedness, he turned back and looked at it. All of it. Looked up to the empty hills and mountainsides, which had taken all of them.

Not empty.

The crew gunner hollered at him through the rotor wash. He had the kid by several ranks, but helicopter crews, like medics, honor no courtesies and respect no rank. They respect the bird. It's what keeps them in the sky.

Merrick turned away and put one boot heavily on the ramp, then the other, its sole scuffing a little cloud of dirt behind it as he stepped up.

He didn't look out as they rose away. He looked at the ID card in his hand.

47

The recovery section of Charlie Med was subdivided with plywood and sheets into individual curtained bays for convalescing soldiers. Black wanted to rest at his hootch, but the doctors told him no way.

He'd lost a significant amount of blood in the twenty-four hours between being shot and his first contact with the medics at Vega. The bullet had made a lucky pass-through, but his wound was fairly messed up from lack of prompt treatment and inadvisable physical activity. He had been severely dehydrated when found by Shannon, and the doctors told him he had suffered multiple significant concussions. He rated a bed in the hospital for a few days.

When they began asking questions about how he'd suffered his injuries, he kept his answers as perfunctory as possible. What information he did provide was so bizarre and confounding that they invariably shook their heads and waved him off, leaving him for the inevitable investigators to talk to.

Never mind, I don't even want to know. U.S. nine-millimeter pistol wound, got it. Banged your head falling onto a stone floor, got it. Wandered in the woods with no water, got it.

Then they would leave, which was fine with him. By the end of the first morning he was tired of the place.

"Goddamn, L.T., I thought I told you!"

The violinmaker.

"Sorry," he replied, grinning.

She'd just shown up for a shift, with a pack slung over her shoulder. She'd seen his name on the incoming roster the night before.

She grabbed a stool and peppered him with gruff questions about the aid he'd received from the medics in the field and the treatment he'd gotten once he'd made it to Charlie Med. Since he didn't remember much about the first part, those questions were easy to answer.

When she'd satisfied herself that his care was not being neglected, she sat back against the plywood partition and looked at him, brow furrowed.

"What the hell, man? What happened out there?"

He looked down at his sheets, saying nothing and shaking his head.

She eyed him another moment then shrugged, letting it go.

"Anyway, I brought you some stuff," she said, digging in the pack. "Continue the classical portion of your woeful musical education."

Out came a portable CD player with an expensive-looking pair of headphones and a stack of discs. She handed them over and Black commenced thumbing through them.

"Charles Ives . . . ?" he mumbled.

The violinmaker rolled her eyes.

"American," she said. "Everyone knows about him now, so you should know about him."

He kept flipping.

He held up a disc reproachfully.

"I know who Beethoven is," he complained.

"You've heard his Fifth Symphony?"

"C'mon," he said. "Da-da-da-DUM."

"Hey, I don't know, man. There are some serious holes in your music."

Black looked away.

"We were sheltered."

She eyed him sidelong, waiting for more, but he offered no more.

"I bet," she said, shaking her head. "Anyway, no, you *haven't* heard it. Not till you hear *that* recording."

She pointed at the CD in his hand.

"Wiener Philharmoniker?" he read. "Carlos Kleiber?"

"*Veener,* not *Weener,*" she corrected, exasperated. "Vienna Philharmonic. 1975."

She pointed at the headphones.

"Put it on in the dark with those on. You'll see."

"Thanks."

"No sweat," she said, rising to go. "I'll check on you during my shifts. And if you decide you wanna tell me what the hell happened, I'm around."

"Cool."

"Cool."

She went. She came by daily to check on him and break his balls about one thing or another, but she didn't ask about the Valley.

She must have told Kourash he was at Charlie Med. He made his way over from the Green Beans Coffee the next day, fretting over Black like a doting parent and generally wringing his hands at the threadbare condition of his young friend.

"I am sorry, my brother," he told Black sadly. "I wished that you do not go in this war."

Sergeant Cousins came by to visit, which was good of him. Smoke Toma didn't show, which was probably for the best.

Late on the third day, the person Black had most hoped for and most dreaded walked in.

He appeared unannounced and lingered in the doorway a long time. His arm was bandaged but he didn't look bad physically. When he lowered his angular frame into a chair, Black saw the dark circles under his eyes and the ashen pallor of his skin. He wondered if he looked that bad himself.

He sat in the chair with his elbows on his knees, glaring at a far point on the floor. When he finally spoke it was in a voice so hollow and gray it startled Black. He hardly recognized it.

"What the hell," Merrick said, eyes unmoving, "is the end of the world?"

Black felt very tired.

He pointed at the wheelchair in the corner.

"Give me that thing."

48

They got their coffees from Kourash, who fussed over Black and gushed hospitality all over the startled, surly sergeant.

"A friend of *Breedman* Will is my brother," he said graciously.

"I'm not— I'm . . ." Merrick stammered.

"Can we have the deck for a bit?" Black asked his friend, thumbing over his shoulder toward the back door.

Kourash palmed his chest.

"Yours, my brother."

Merrick pushed Black's chair through the door, which Kourash latched behind them, and out onto the empty deck. The air was chill, but the snow in the mountains hadn't made it down this far.

They situated themselves at a metal table in a corner. Merrick lowered himself into a plastic deck chair and squinted out at a bleak amber horizon.

The late afternoon sun hung above the mountains, sending long shadows across the plain toward Omaha and inching across the wood planks where they sat.

Black looked at the tall sergeant folded awkwardly into the small chair, legs out straight before him, boots crossed at the ankles, eyes to the mountains.

"Where'd you hear that?" he asked Merrick.

"The people in the Meadows."

"Oh."

Merrick turned to him.

"And you said it."

He eyed Black closely.

"Laying on your ass in the woods."

He said nothing more. Just looked.

Black dropped his gaze and told him about the wall.

He told Merrick how the soldiers at Xanadu, whoever they were, had obviously been tolerating the growers while they tried to stop foreign fighters coming in. Until someone somewhere got tired of all the hassle, of being unable to control a critical piece of geography, and came up with the idea of the wall.

Told how the growers were cut off right along with the fighters and all the other growers in the Valley. How the growers flipped sides. How they massed forces with the Taliban and obliterated Xanadu.

And how the wall stayed. How no one could punch through it. How the growers of the Valley must have made a new deal with their new allies to move their product.

But someone else in the Valley found out about the wall. About Xanadu.

"How?"

Black looked away.

"I don't know."

Caine knew the growers' predicament, but he couldn't have known about their new arrangement. He was the reason the growers in the Meadow burned their fields that night.

"To get out from under his shakedown," Merrick said flatly.

The Darreh Sin growers were getting double-shook down, by an American and by the Americans' enemies. The American didn't know it, and the growers couldn't tell him. Their backs were against the wall, and their chief's back was against the wall.

And then Pistone. The last thing that nobody could take, on top of every other thing.

Merrick sat in silence, his cup sending tendrils of steam into the cool air. Finally he shook his head.

"No," he said flatly. "The whole Valley, all those freaking tribes with their feuds and all their bullshit, they don't all team up to take us out just because some nobody and his son get shot somewhere."

Black watched the coils rise from his own coffee.

"The boy," he said, "was the thing that made it all come apart."

They slurped somberly at their warm cups and shivered in the breeze spilling out of the passes and across the plain and chilling them where they sat.

Merrick watched the disc of the sun creep downward toward the mountaintops.

"Who the hell comes up with a fucking wall across a valley?"

Black watched it too.

"People very high up the food chain."

He cradled his coffee against the breeze.

"In more than one country."

Merrick scowled and sipped and set his cup on the tabletop, planting his feet flat on the deck beneath him and crossing his arms.

Black eyed him.

"That's why you kept the O.P. guys in lockdown when they came back to the FOB."

Merrick nodded gruffly.

"No Americans east of Darreh Sin."

Officially.

Soldiers trudged past in both directions, going about their business, alone and in pairs, rifles slung over their backs as they made for the chow hall or the M.W.R. or the gym or their hootches. The day rhythm of the FOB was turning to night.

Merrick uncrooked an arm and took a sip of coffee. He set it back down and extended his long legs in front of him, recrossing his arms against the chill. His eyes fell to a distant universe floating in the air over the ends of his boots.

"Pistone . . ." he murmured.

He looked out at the mountains, then looked down again. When he spoke his voice was run through with bitterness.

"Made an asshole of me," he said. "Both of them."

Black sipped at his own coffee and set it down. The sun hung just above the line of the ridges.

"I didn't suspect Pistone either," he said finally. "Until Corelli told me."

Merrick turned on him sharply.

"Yeah, well, you didn't work with Pistone every day," he spat. "Guy walked around right in front of me and I didn't know jack."

He shook his head in disgust.

"The people even tried to tell me."

"What?"

"The fucking civilians. In the Meadows."

He drifted into memory.

"Said the Devil isn't gonna take any more of their babies."

They both considered that.

A Humvee rumbled by on a dirt road behind the market. Its noise faded, leaving the two of them staring at their cups.

"Fucking nothing was right since that night," Merrick muttered. "I knew it, but nobody would say dick."

Black waited for more, but Merrick didn't offer it.

"That's why you tried to scare me off," he said finally.

Merrick scowled at the deck, his gaze boring a hole in the wood before his feet. When he finally spoke it was as though to himself, with defiance.

"I was *working* it."

He exhaled heavily and shook his head, eyes to the deck.

"Never even found out who he had helping him move his shit down the Valley."

Black looked away and studied the contours of his cup. Merrick seemed distracted and didn't notice.

Black had realized something, though he doubted Merrick wanted to hear it. He said it anyway.

"I would've done stuff the same way."

"Well, then you'd be an idiot," Merrick shot back angrily. "I let my senior squad leader *and* my lieutenant make a fool of me. I didn't know what was going on in *my* fucking platoon."

He stood and stalked across to the railing at the edge of the deck, hands crammed in his pockets. He glared at the mountains and watched as the entire disc of the sun dipped below the ridges.

It seemed to grow instantly colder as the sun disappeared. Black wished he'd brought something thicker to wear.

Merrick spoke, facing the mountains.

"None of them came to me."

Black looked up.

"Not one."

He looked down at his half cup of chalky coffee and decided to tell the truth.

"They respected you."

Merrick turned around, eyes narrow, the sunset panorama framed behind him.

"Screw off."

"Shannon said you didn't need to be burdened with knowing about the Meadows or any of the rest of it."

"That's fucking stupid," Merrick said bitterly. "Fucking Shannon."

"Shannon worships you."

"Shannon's dead."

He went out by himself, Merrick said, to cut Caine down from the tree.

"Against my orders," he added.

He came back and slumped into his chair, dark clouds roiling his brow.

He took up his coffee roughly, sipped it, frowned, and set it back down. Black tasted his own, which was also cold.

People passed by in the fading light. Merrick's eyes drifted again, to the same invisible point. A minute passed in silence.

When Merrick spoke it was in a growl, through nearly clenched teeth.

"I tried to beat that fucker."

Black looked up. Merrick, his bitter gaze fixed in the distance, shook his head in disgust.

"I tried my hardest to beat his ass."

Black's brow furrowed.

"You did beat him."

Someone else just . . .

Merrick looked up at him, scowling. He shook his head.

Black didn't understand.

"Caine didn't get killed on the way to the station," Merrick stated flatly. "He got killed on the way *back* from it."

Black asked him how he knew that. Merrick told him. There was little else to say.

They drained the last of their gray coffees and rapped on the door. Kourash let them through, and Merrick wheeled Black back through the gravel and along the dirt pathways, back to Charlie Med.

Black climbed onto his bed. Merrick watched him silently, hands in his pockets.

"The thing that happened with your last platoon," he said finally.

Black looked up in surprise. Merrick looked at the floor.

"The way it was in the papers and stuff. Was that how it went down?"

"Yeah."

Merrick opened his mouth to speak, then closed it. He crossed his arms then shoved his hands in his pockets again. When he finally spoke it was in a voice with little comfort.

"Maybe stuff in life balances out in the end."

Black said nothing and looked down at his sheets.

Merrick turned to go, then stopped as though remembering something. He turned around and looked at Black.

"They found Doc Brydon's body in the Taj Mahal while you were out running around the Valley."

Black watched his own hands smooth the sheets.

"Shot himself in the face. You know anything about that?"

"No."

Merrick left. Black reached into his pocket and removed Jason Traynor's ID card. He sat staring at it.

49

Only one other visitor came in the days before Black was discharged from Charlie Med.

He came in wordlessly and sat down on a stool, facing Black. He put his hands in his lap and smiled at Black serenely, onyx eyes shining behind his spectacles.

He sat like that a full minute, just looking.

Finally Black let out an exasperated breath.

"What is this?" he asked. "You're gonna put the whammy on me?"

His visitor said nothing.

"Okay, fine. Don't talk. You don't have to. You can sit there smiling and listen."

His visitor just kept smiling.

"You screwed up," Black said, to no discernible reaction.

He waited a moment and went on.

"You left me your signed confession."

His visitor blinked once but otherwise sat rock still.

"I know why you carried it with you," Black pressed. "It's your goddamned talisman."

"I want it."

The soft voice startled him. It made his skin crawl.

"Fuck you," Black said sharply. "You won't have it, and you won't find it."

He looked at the pale hands, clasped gently in his visitor's lap. Then up at his eyes.

"I know who you are," Black said. "You're a damned legend in the Valley."

The eyes beamed and burned, examining Black.

Black leaned forward.

"I know you by name."

The smile was gone, giving way to an unnameable expression. His visitor leaned forward as well, his face close to Black's, his eyes searching the air as though he were listening very closely for something, and spoke a single word, hardly more than a whisper.

"Try."

He sat back, and the beatific smile returned. He rose, placing a small metal object on the side table, shining eyes on Black.

Pistone left quietly, without another word.

Black picked it up. It was a metal dog tag reading WILLIAM BRYDON.

50

There were camps for when you were going in, and camps for when you were coming out. You'd go through one at the beginning of a deployment, the other at the end of one.

They were basically the same place. Sprawling tracts of land in the Kuwaiti desert, cordoned off with walls, inside each one a momentary city of tents and temporary buildings and trailer-sized mock-ups of fast-food joints and prefab Americana, with gravel poured among the spaces.

The difference was that one type of camp was filled with people contemplating their mortality while they waited for word that it was their unit's turn to move forward to Iraq or Afghanistan. The other was filled with people enjoying the pleasant surprise of being still alive and wondering what to do with the rest of their lives.

This one was the camp for people coming out. It was a place to spend a couple days eating free chow, showering, visiting the telephone bank or Internet café, and staring out at the desert as you waited to be called for the flight home. Most of the people on this camp were on their way from Iraq, which suited him just fine.

Few paid him much notice. This was a place of jostling anonymity where many traveled alone, and where as a rule no one's business was anyone's business. No one except the proprietors of this particular camp's Green Beans Coffee trailer noticed that he had been roaming its avenues and byways for three weeks and change, which was much longer than the usual stay.

He hung a towel over the bar of his bunk, the lower one at the far end of a long row. It was one of the standard grab-a-rack units they sent you to when you arrived at the camp.

The morning sun was already high as he emerged. He padded along in loafers, backpack slung over one shoulder, across the gravel toward what he thought of as the town square.

Up the steps to the coffee trailer, hello to the Green Beans guys, this crew from Bangladesh, then back out again with a steaming cup and across the way to the U.S.O. tent. He pulled open the door and paused just inside, as he always did, to give his eyes time to adjust to the dark. No boots or shoes allowed; you left them in cubbies just inside the entrance and went in your socks.

On the outside the Camp Alabama U.S.O. tent was your usual stark-white half-pipe semi-permanent FOB tent, maybe fifty feet high and a hundred long. On the inside was a bit of dimly lit deployment genius.

Table lamps sprawled next to leather couches across the carpeted floor. Soft cubby areas and carpeted platforms were built against the walls; soldiers snored away. In the center a raised platform housed a self-serve café with coffee and water, ringed by a black iron railing with streetlamps casting pools of light on the tables.

One far corner of the building was cordoned off with cubicle walls creating a miniature movie theater. Another contained banks of computer terminals. He took his coffee and headed for these.

He found a terminal situated such that his back would be to the corner and slumped down into the chair, dropping his pack to the floor by his feet and cracking his coffee lid open to take some of the scald off of it. He logged in and waited for his e-mail to bring him that morning's entry in a running correspondence.

Re: RE: re: re: re: re: Stuff

Why didn't you tell Sergeant Merrick about Billy?

He put the lid back on his cup and typed.

Billy didn't deserve that.

He sipped his coffee and stared at the screen.

He knew what it was to be a ghost. Let his ghost rest where it belongs.

He sent the message and cracked his knuckles. He knew his correspondent was waiting, on the other side of the planet and many hours away, for his message and would write back. While he waited he reached into his backpack and came out with a paperback novel about a part-time Israeli assassin with too much baggage who just wants to quit and spend his time restoring the paintings of Christian Renaissance masters.

The reply came back a couple minutes later.

You don't believe in ghosts. At least you don't think you do.

Do you really think it's your place to decide whether his parents deserve the truth? Didn't you tell me once that *you* deserved the truth regardless of what it was? Isn't that what you said to Dad?

His little sister had stopped seeming so little a long time ago. He stared at the screen deciding what to say in response when a follow-up message came in.

Sorry. Don't answer that.

[Hold on, getting more coffee.]

Following her lead, he went and warmed up his own coffee at the streetlamp café and came back to see what else she had sent.

Do you really think Private Corelli might still be alive?

He hit REPLY and typed one sentence.

I will find out.

He hit SEND and went back to his book. In this installment of the Israeli spy's adventures, he had managed to befriend a pope.

The mail flashed a reply.

Try to rest first, okay BB? The people who can look are looking.

"BB" stood for "big brother." He hit REPLY.

I sent him out there.

He didn't know what else to say, so he sent it. The reply came quickly.

Okay, BB, signing off for tonight. I wish you would talk to somebody else (I know, not my business) but I'm glad you're telling me at least.

Are you sure you should be talking about this stuff over email?

—LS

"Little sister." He punched a quick response.

No one's listening. Have a good night.

—BB

He closed his e-mail and sat staring out at the dimly humming tent. In the movie theater enclosure next door a high-performance motorcycle screamed through the fourth or fifth installment of an action series featuring endless road chases and improbable kung fu.

He closed the novel and tossed it back into his backpack. He rose and took several steps toward the door before stopping, shaking his head at himself irritably.

His baby sister, he decided, not for the first time, was too wise for her own good.

He trudged back to the terminal, pack sloughing to the floor again, and went back online to his e-mail folder.

The old message was still in his inbox. The one from before he ever went to Vega.

He stared at the message for a long time before opening the folder where he kept his saved e-mail drafts. When he was recuperating at Charlie Med, he'd had Cousins wheel him to the S-1 shop so he could get on the computer and cancel the e-mail he'd set to automatically send if he hadn't returned from COP Vega in ten days. The draft was still in the folder.

He read it over, then took the mouse and highlighted most of it. He hit DELETE and started typing from scratch.

> I did get your note. I am safe. I've been away, but I should have told you before I went.

He punched a couple of ENTERs and typed

> There is a lot to tell.

Then deleted it. Instead he typed

> Don't read too much into dreams.

He hit SEND, logged off, and slung his backpack.

He fetched his shoes and trudged across the camp to the chow hall. After he ate, he went back to the Green Beans for a fresh coffee and settled in for an afternoon with his book on the deck outside.

He was only a few pages in when he heard the puckish voice behind him.

"Mediocrates, I presume."

It was the name his friend from Officer Candidate School had called him in the e-mail before he left Omaha for the Valley. The smartass. Camp Alabama was the last place on Earth Black would have expected to hear his voice. For a moment he thought he must be mistaken.

But when he turned and saw the figure of the Monk, clean-shaven and grinning wryly in civilian clothes, he knew he hadn't been mistaken at all.

Danny stood with him, looking sheepish.

51

They both had coffees in their hands. Black gawked. His friend looked at him expectantly.

"So?" he said, holding palm and cup to the sky. "May we?"

His actual name, Black knew, was Pyne. He hadn't used it much since O.C.S.

Pyne put on a horrible French accent.

"Mais oui?"

He went back to his own voice.

"Or what?"

Dumbfounded, Black nodded. The two men stepped forward, Danny cradling his cup as he shrank into the seat farthest from Black.

"Hello, L.T.," he mumbled, eyes to the floor.

"Nice one, by the way, in the e-mail," Pyne cracked as he toed a metal chair out for himself. "'Lord of the Files.' I get it. Well played, you."

He made himself comfortable.

"So, how long you planning to hide out from the world?"

He looked around the gravel concourse with its lash-up shops and low-rent vendors.

"I mean, this is some fine living," he said appreciatively. "Don't get me wrong. But seriously."

He sipped his coffee and burned his lips.

"Corelli," Black stated flatly.

This sobered his friend, who shook his head grimly.

Black stared at the tabletop.

"I'm on it," Pyne said quietly.

Black watched the steam rise from his coffee.

"You know I would have been there in a heartbeat," Pyne said, "if . . ."

"Yeah."

Black said nothing else. Pyne shrugged off the moment, taking up his scalding coffee and changing the subject.

"Thanks for not blowing my cover," he said brightly. "That was smooth."

Black nodded glumly.

"And for not shooting me," Pyne went on, blowing over the top of his cup. "Not so smooth."

"I *did* shoot you. My rifle didn't shoot you."

They sat in silence for a minute.

"How'd you rig it for yourself to hide out here anyway?" Pyne asked, appraising their surroundings.

"'On my way home,'" Black said, making morose quotes in the air.

Pyne, squinching his face over his coffee, looked up and cocked his head.

"One of the benefits of being a paper-pusher," Black said. "How'd you find me here?"

"One of the benefits of being me," his friend said from behind his cup, eyebrows raised mischievously.

Black waited to see if there was anything more forthcoming, but Pyne just shook his head.

"You don't want to see the sausages get made."

He took a careful sip and opened his mouth to speak. Black held up a finger and turned to Danny, who seemed to think his coffee cup was big enough to hide all of him.

"Danny," he said. "I know."

Danny hung his head miserably.

"I am shame, L.T. I swear it I don't know Sergeant Caine's . . . business was . . . was the middle of this."

Pyne nodded quietly and sipped.

"I only translate for him one time," Danny went on. "He takes me to the main grower, big guy, and has me make the business, for him to tell the others. After that Caine never told me nothing and I don't see it."

"What did he say he'd do if you didn't help?"

"Kill."

Black nodded.

"It wasn't your fault, Danny. You saved my life."

"A-*hem,*" Pyne said.

Black looked at him quizzically.

"You're welcome," Pyne said generously. "Saving your ass on another Land Nav course again."

Black squinted at the two of them.

"Danny, so you're . . ."

He drifted off.

"Nah," Pyne cut in. "Not formally."

He swirled his cup.

"Danny helped me keep tabs on what those eleven-bravo boneheads were up to in my valley."

Eleven-Bravo was the Army's job classification for an infantryman. "*My*" was Pyne's classification for anyplace he saw fit to ply his wares.

"It was Danny that told me something was going on at the COP. I mean, something besides your Sergeant Caine's amateur drug lord impersonation."

Black's eyes widened.

"Yeah, I knew about that nonsense," his friend said blandly. "I let that play out for a bit."

Black goggled.

"You let it *play out?*"

Pyne shrugged.

"He was making himself part of the natural food chain of the valley, and for a time it was . . ."

He circled a hand in the air.

"Nondisruptive to my activities."

Black just gawked, speechless.

"And then, later on," Pyne went on casually, "things were, uh . . ."

He swirled his cup again.

"Disrupted."

He sat back and shook his head, remembering.

"First time I felt like people genuinely hated me there," he said distantly.

Everyone considered that.

"After the night of that fire I was freaking radioactive. Even Merak shut me down."

"Merak?"

"Darreh Sin chief."

"That's his name?"

"You didn't know his name?"

"Caine never told me."

Pyne shook his head contemptuously.

"You were working him?" Black asked.

"Duh," Pyne replied. "Obviously."

"Did you tell him about the wall?"

Pyne looked to Danny for signs of recognition.

"Why?" he said blankly.

"After I showed him the heroin brick—"

Pyne rolled his eyes.

"—he said he would kill us all to the end of the world."

"Damn," his friend said sarcastically. "Stone-cold."

He swigged eagerly, finally happy with the temperature.

"Anyway," he said. "Yeah, after the fire that place went straight sideways on me."

He eyed Black.

"That's when I knew Americans fucked something up and somebody had to figure out what."

Black nodded and sipped his own.

"Yeah," he murmured. "I can see . . ."

He caught the meaning in Pyne's casual words.

"Wait, what's that supposed to mean?"

Pyne smiled into his cup.

"Hey, Danny," he said. "Wanna meet me back at the hootch before chow?"

Danny nodded and turned to Black.

"I see you, L.T."

He rose and left. Black turned to his friend.

"You initiated the investigation."

Pyne shook his head.

"I just reached out to, uh, some friends in the Civil Affairs community."

"The water project."

Pyne shrugged.

"Maybe Merak opens up a little."

"Which he did."

Pyne pinched the air in his fingers.

"Teeny little crack. But somebody needed to blow it open."

"You made the fifteen-six happen."

Pyne shook his head again.

"Not the fifteen-six itself," he said, appreciating the beauty of the thing. "That happened all on its own after Merak complained about the freaking goats."

Black stared at him.

"You got me put on it!"

His friend looked off at the horizon with an innocent-cherub expression.

Black gawked.

"You think this is funny?" he blurted out, too loudly. "People are dead!"

Pyne looked left and right to see if Black had drawn anyone's attention. He leaned across the table, turning serious.

"No," he said tersely. "I don't think it's funny. I'm not a fan of closet psycho freaks going for a little free play in my own geostrategically significant piece of backyard. I needed that unfucked."

"So you just *picked* me?"

Pyne leaned back and shrugged again.

"I knew you were located at FOB Omaha. Who did you want me to pick?"

"Anybody!"

Pyne looked insulted.

"Yeah, right," he scoffed.

"It's supposed to be random!"

"*'It's supposed to be random!'*" Pyne mocked. "The siren song of Army mediocrity."

"So you *hacked* it?"

Pyne smiled, sipping.

"We've got good hackers," he said with evident pride.

"You had no right!"

Pyne grew annoyed, leaning in again.

"Don't wuss out on me," he said sharply, jabbing the tabletop with a finger. "Have you noticed you're a soldier in a war? Soldiers get picked arbitrarily for shitty missions all the time, including missions where people get killed. Including missions where people are *guaranteed* to get killed."

He leaned back in his chair, calming.

"This shitty mission happened to be yours."

Black realized his jaw was literally hanging open.

"You're not in my chain of command!" he practically shouted.

Pyne rolled his eyes.

"Oh, *that's* your objection?" he said languidly. "That your arbitrary assignment didn't come from your Colonel Goldenhair? Excuse me, but when you swore your commissioning oath there wasn't anything in there about you being guaranteed not to get random assignments from God-knows-who."

Black just spluttered, speechless. Pyne frowned at him dismissively.

"I mean, it's not like I sent you out there all alone," he said, exasperated. "You *knew* I had my eye on you the whole time."

"What? No I didn't!"

Pyne crinkled his brow.

"What'd you think the note with the coordinates and the freek was for?"

"I didn't open that note until after Danny disappeared and Caine was trying to kill me!"

Pyne was flabbergasted.

"Why not?!"

"I thought it was a love note like you said!"

His friend's mouth hung open, then closed. Then formed itself into a pinched, suppressed smile.

"When was the last time I had a girl?" he said, trying not to laugh.

"I don't know!" Black shot back. "I never see you!"

"When I *do* have a girl, since when do I write her love notes with freaking *hearts* on them?"

Black stewed.

"Speaking of which," his friend added. "You talk about way too much stuff on your personal e-mail."

Black looked up in surprise, then reddened. Pyne waved him off.

"There's more interesting dirt on the ground outside this coffee shop."

Black scowled and sulked.

"I'm sorry, man," his friend said, still grinning but softening. "I just thought when you saw me at Vega my cryptic-handshake-and-significant-look routine made it pretty obvious."

Black sighed, deflated.

"You know I wouldn't leave you out there flapping," Pyne said, mildly wounded. "That's why I had people keeping an eye on you."

"What?"

"Well, Danny had your back as much as he could . . ."

Black realized.

"Bosch."

The graffiti. Taking the heat on himself when Shannon threw the grenade.

Pyne nodded.

"Seemed like a good kid, for certain purposes," he said, growing somber. "We might've been interested in him."

Black looked at him but nothing more was offered. He sank back into memory.

Bosch. All the guys at the O.P.

Something occurred to him. He looked at Pyne narrow-eyed.

"What do you know about Traynor?"

"O.P. or guy?"

"Guy."

"Still working on him too."

"Still *working* on him?"

"Yeah, of course. You think I was going to leave it to your Sergeant Caine to try to . . ."

He trailed off as he saw the look of incomprehension on Black's face.

"Never mind."

"What?" Black pressed.

"Don't worry about it," his friend said blankly. "This part's sort of out of your lane."

Black fished in his pocket and slapped Jason Traynor's ID on the table.

"Screw my lane."

Pyne eyed the card and looked around furtively. He crossed his arms, sighed, and pointed at the table.

"*They* gave me that."

"Who?"

"Duh. The people who took Jason."

"*Took* him?"

"Yeah."

"He's alive."

"Not officially."

Black screwed up his brow.

"What people?"

"Complicated."

"Was Caine there?"

Pyne shrugged.

"Don't know about that. I didn't meet that dude until I found out he was kinda double-working me."

"Double-*working* you?"

"Yeah, like, working all the growers and all his other contacts to try to find out what happened to Traynor and get him back."

Black's jaw was hanging open again.

"Anyway," Pyne went on casually. "*That* was disruptive to my activities."

Black's head spun.

"What did you do?"

Pyne took up his cooling cup.

"Went and met him and gave him the I.D. card and told him his boy was alive, and we're working on it, and stop making so much noise."

He peered down into it.

"I don't think he did stop, though. He was pretty shook up about the kid."

He sipped and reflected.

"Think that's why he was stockpiling cash," he mused. "Trying to get a big enough bounty stacked up that Valley dudes would have an incentive—"

His tilted cup hovered in front of his face.

"—I mean a *real* incentive, like, fuck-your-daughter-murder-your-cousin incentive, to find out where Traynor was."

He shook his head sadly and downed the last of his coffee.

"Dude was desperate."

Black could only think of one thing to say.

"Who the hell *are* you guys?"

The Monk looked around the town square, milling with people.

"We should walk."

They loped along an empty dirt road near the edge of the camp, Pyne trying without success to mollify his sullen friend.

"I picked you because this was important and you are excellent. You can talk to people, and you can handle people."

"Yeah, like I handled the chief."

Pyne chuckled.

"Sounds like you were handling him pretty good until you whipped your brick out," he cracked, smiling at his own pun.

Black sulked. Pyne sighed.

"Don't sell yourself short, dude. You put that whole thing together in a week's time. That's no joke."

"I got people killed."

"Don't be dramatic," Pyne scoffed. "The war got people killed. A bad sergeant and a bad lieutenant got people killed. Shitty leaders at echelons above—"

He swirled a finger up to heaven.

"—who left that stupid COP in place long after it had outlived its reason for being got people killed."

He pointed at Black.

"*You* got the truth."

Black wondered if there was anything his friend didn't have an answer for. His friend, as always, read his mind.

"I needed to know what was going on in the Valley," Pyne said sharply. "And I preferred seeing you assigned to it than some randomly selected twenty-three-year-old douchebro wearing a lieutenant's bar."

He drove on unapologetically.

"You want—what's your friend's name? Derr? You want *him* trying to crack COP Vega? I decided you had as good a shot as anyone of getting it done. And I obviously was right."

Black shook his head wearily. They walked.

"Why not just get me alone and tell me what you knew?"

"Not so simple."

"You talked to Danny and Bosch."

"Bosch, I just passed a note to in the courtyard," Pyne admonished. "Danny was, uh, easier to communicate with. You, that's tricky without blowing my cover."

"You passed *me* a note."

Pyne hemmed and hawed.

"Fair enough," he allowed. "But I kinda had to see how it played out."

"What's that mean?"

"You asked who the hell we are."

"Yeah?"

The Monk looked off at the horizon.

"To the extent we have a name, we mostly call ourselves The Activity."

DEMONS

Recalled with fondness and annoyance in equal measure by generations of Forward Observer and officer trainees, the imposing presence of Signal Mountain dominates the "no-man's land" of Fort Sill's firing ranges and impact areas. A lone sentinel at the southeastern end of the Wichita Mountains, so named for General Sheridan's emplacement of a heliograph signal station at its summit during the Indian Wars (and having been put to similar use by the Indian peoples themselves, via smoke signal, for uncounted ages before that time), Signal Mountain now serves as a primary impact point for the numerous area-fire weapon systems trained upon it at the Fort.

Among its notable features are slopes of gently increasing gradient and a single-story stone blockhouse at the summit, dating to 1871, which housed the signalling activity. Though never fired on directly, it has seen many decades' use as a convenient aiming reference point by Observer trainees as they hone their craft, sending shells and bombs at the many hulks and target vehicles dotting the mountain's flanks, *e.g.*: "From the Blockhouse, Signal Mountain: Left five-zero, down two hundred, fire for effect," *&c.* Though they may never enter the impact area and approach it, the Blockhouse is as a second home for these trainees, and once seen is never forgotten; one might say almost venerated, in the way that those vexing and mundane particulars of military training come to be viewed in an entirely different aspect in the light of fond recollection. Memories of the Blockhouse are the badge of the Observer; and for those officers and enlisted men who spent their hours and days sweating in the Oklahoma heat, squinting up at its shadow as it looked down on them from its untouched height, its radio designator rolls from the tongue even many years later like the old familiar name of an old familiar friend, with whom one may have squabbled in youth but who is by now practically family.

From *Rogers' History of the Field Artillery,*
The Fort Sill Museum Press, 1972

The professor frowned at the leatherbound journal in his hands. Its cover was embossed with Celtic scrollwork.

"This is evidence," he said disapprovingly.

His guest ignored him. The professor undid the leather band around the book and turned it warily in his hands, holding it up to catch the light of his floor lamp. As always in the evenings, his cavernous office was sparsely lit. Shadows cowered in its vaulted ceilings.

He was not old, though it would be an unkindness to youth to call him young. While his long face was yet unlined, the silver at the temples and above the ears was making a real encroachment into the jet-black now, and the winner of this contest was no longer really in doubt.

He opened the journal's cover and thumbed to its final entries.

2 November—

Danny has been acting so shady since the thing. When I asked him about SFC Merrick I thought he was going to jump out of his skin.

A 15-6 investigator is coming next week, probably about whatever all

He turned a page.

of this is, and hopefully everything can get sorted out. I told Merrick about the investigator, to see how he would react. He was pissed like he always is, so I couldn't really tell anything from that. But he told me not to tell SSG Caine about it, which is totally shady too.

I don't know if all of this has to do with Caine's drug thing or what, but I'm pretty sure one of them's got Danny working for him. I told Caine he needs to knock it off but he doesn't listen to me. I'm just going to tell the investigator whatever I know. I hate this place, but it's my responsibility to try to make things right in my platoon.

"You shouldn't be showing me this or telling me this," he admonished, scanning the pages with dark, close-set eyes. "If you want to talk to me, you should talk to me about you."

He closed the journal and looked up at Black, frowning again. Black slumped, arms crossed, in an easy chair and waited out the older man.

The professor sighed.

"If Private Corelli's account was true—" he began tentatively.

"It's true," Black cut in sharply.

"*Then,*" the professor continued with some annoyance, "this is, once again, evidence you are holding in your possession, which I am certain you are not authorized to possess."

"Potential evidence."

"Semantics."

Black shook his head.

"It's bullshit written for my benefit."

The professor cringed visibly at the mouth on his guest.

"It's worthless," Black said, "unless Corelli is found."

"And you think he's alive because . . . ?"

"Because Sergeant Caine had his I.D. and dog tags on his person when he was found."

The professor put his fingers to his temples and looked pained.

"Which sounds to me," he said, hesitating, "rather like . . . like—"

"Only Corelli knows everything," Black stated flatly.

The professor shook his head and stubbed a finger to the center of the journal's cover.

"This isn't yours to keep," he stated flatly.

"Shannon didn't trust anyone else with it."

"Which is relevant *how?*"

"Shannon saved my life."

"Will . . ."

Black pointed defiantly at the journal.

"If I gave that to the investigators," he said, "they would just read those entries and chase down Danny and Sergeant Merrick and give them even more grief than they already have."

He held the professor's gaze until the older man looked away.

The professor examined the words again purse-lipped.

"I take it you wish me to safeguard this for you?"

Black shook his head.

"I got it covered."

He retrieved the journal and stuffed it back in his pack. The professor regarded him unhappily.

"Aren't you worried about a psychopath knowing that you have his diary?"

Black's eyes blazed.

"I *want* him to know I've got it."

The professor looked unimpressed.

"Your bluster is beneath your years."

Black reddened and looked down at the carpet. The professor said nothing else. Black knew he was already admonishing himself for embarrassing his young friend.

"Pistone's not a psychopath," Black said finally.

He sank back in the deep chair, ruminating.

"That's too easy on him."

His gaze traced the tendrils of the tree-of-life design as its paisleyed buds danced along the curve of the carpet's medallion.

"I don't care," he murmured, "if anybody finds out I was there when Billy died."

"Yet you *do* care if people know *why* he died."

Black watched woodland creatures leap beneath willow fronds.

"And you believe that that is your judgment to make."

Black said nothing. The professor softened, but pressed.

"You don't think his family deserves to know the truth about their son?"

Black frowned.

"That's what my sister said."

"Wise sister."

A page of ancient parchment sat in a heavy oaken frame on the far wall. On its carefully preserved surface was a passage from the Vulgate, Saint Jerome's Latin translation of the Bible, inscribed in Gothic black-letter, illuminated in gold leaf and crimson.

Black's eyes moved down the text.

IN PRINCIPIO ERAT
VERBUM : ET VER
BUM ERAT APUD
DEUM : ET DEUS
ERAT VERBUM :

The professor broke the silence.

"Do you . . ."

He hesitated, clearing his throat and studying his hands.

"Do you still talk to your brother?"

Black turned a scowl toward the older man and glared flaming daggers. The professor put his palms up in surrender and rose from his chair. He crossed to a side table, where he poured them each a drink.

"You know it's my job to ask," he murmured, his back to Black.

He brought the glasses to a large window and waited. Black rose and watched his own reflection approach as he moved from the pool of lamplight, the pinpoints of a far city emerging through his apparition.

The professor handed Black his drink.

"Is it all gone now?"

Black nodded, taking the glass and turning to the window. They drank silently, looking across at the distant city.

The professor glanced sidelong at his young friend.

"My son," he said. "Am I really the only one you came here to see?"

Black only scowled. The professor smiled.

"For goodness' sake, you fool," he said, shaking his head.

"That's what my sister says."

"Wise sister."

Black left through the ground-floor exit beneath sneering stone gargoyles and crossed the shadowed campus grounds, the great building with its parapets and buttresses receding behind him. Moonlight shafted onto him as his feet found the path through the trees, to the wooded neighborhood where he sat for a long time behind the wheel of another rental car, keys in the ignition, watching the darkened house as it slept before him.

Four days later he sat in the same car on a tree-lined by-road in the American Midwest. The houses were sparse along here. Large unfenced properties opening to gentle swells of grassland and wood. It was gorgeous, at least what he could make out at night.

He slept, and when he woke he confirmed that it was indeed beautiful land.

As he had done many times over the past weeks, he replayed in his head the conversation he'd had with Pyne as they roamed the outskirts of the transit camp in the Kuwaiti desert.

You're saying that I have "people skills."

He'd said it in the most drab and incredulous tone he could muster.

You have a specific ability to learn things from people. That's valuable.

I'm not a cog.

No. You are anything but a cog.

Black had stopped and looked his friend in the eye.

What's that supposed to mean?

He reached into his pocket and drew out his tiny leatherbound notebook. He unlaced it and stared at the page, counting the scratches, then put it away.

"See you," he murmured.

Looking through the car's windows at the well-groomed home behind the trees, he realized that he needed to go clean himself up before he went and knocked. He could drive into town and find a motel or someplace where he could shower. Then he would come back.

And he would come back, he told himself. He was not going to lose his nerve.

He took a last look at the mailbox before he pulled away. The name on it was BRYDON.

ACKNOWLEDGMENTS

I hope military readers will excuse my simplifications of rank, gear, terminology, uniforms, and tactics; it's a story for civilians too, guys. Readers familiar with Nuristan and its peoples, languages, and geography will similarly recognize the points where *this* Nuristan departs from the actual, which I have never visited. The work of Richard Strand and Eric Newby, among others, was especially useful on this score, though any errors are of course my own. There are many valleys in Nuristan, but there is no Valley, and the places depicted there aren't real. Most importantly, while this story took inspiration from many places and events, and many honorable people, nothing in it is meant to stand in for their actual stories, which only they can tell truthfully.

I am indebted to Alex London, whose generosity got me on the road. My agent, Robert Guinsler, is a gentleman and a force; he stuck with me, improved my work, and made it happen so smoothly. Bryan Fyffe is an extraordinary illustrator who managed to do a war book cover like no other. Geddy, Alex, and Neil: We've never met but if you see this, please accept a fan's humble offering. Finally, I am deeply fortunate to have worked with my editor, Ben Sevier, whose talents are formidable, and his team at Penguin, especially Stephanie Kelly and Nancy Resnick. Ben saw just what needed to be done and showed the way.

I am grateful to any reader who has made it this far. Mostly, to the Bravo guys: I wouldn't know anything about real soldiers if you hadn't shown me.

John Renehan served in the Army's Third Infantry Division as a field artillery officer in Iraq. He previously worked as an attorney in New York City. He lives with his family in Virginia. This is his first novel.

THE VALLEY

JOHN RENEHAN

A Conversation with the Author

DUTTON
est. 1852

A Conversation with the Author

What inspired you to write the book?

I had it mind for a long time to write fiction, but when I was younger, I just couldn't put it all together and cross that gap between the potential of ideas and the specifics of words on the page. I am impressed with people who can write good novels when they're twenty-four. That was not me. The way your mind works really does change as you cross from your twenties to your thirties and then forty, and for me it took that long to sort out how I would approach fiction.

I did some magazine and newspaper writing on the side while I was still in the military, and then I finally tried a book-length manuscript that was meant to be a sort of memoir or travel journal of my platoon's time in Iraq (as though we needed one more of *those*). I never sold that book, but writing it turned out to be the best training for fiction—having to take a big, finite pile of factual vignettes that are more and less related to one another, and present them together in a way that remains true but is also coherent as a single story. I remember thinking it would be so much easier to write fiction because I could write whatever I wanted to. Turns out, it's *harder* to write fiction, precisely because you can write whatever you want to and that infinity of choices can be overwhelming. But practicing the disciplines of finding the story buried in all that material and shaping it in a compelling way—that was priceless.

As for *The Valley*, after our first child was born I started reading detective and spy fiction for the first time, just for something to keep the pages turning during those early years when you're so tired all the time. Having been in the Army, I knew the difficult history of the remote outposts we'd established in Afghanistan, and I came across some good journalism about military investigations in the Afghanistan and Iraq wars. And that got me thinking about some of the routine—just really mundane and bureaucratic—investigations I'd had to do as a lieutenant in Iraq.

So all of that was percolating, and I was walking to work one day and got an idea for a scene—a moment, really (a naive, distraught Corelli-like soldier sobbing, "Why would the lieutenant *do* that, sir?")—and it all gelled into the basic setup for *The Valley*, this notion of transplanting a traditional detective-procedural story to a remote war setting with strictly military characters and a stand-in amateur in the detective role. There was nothing particularly original about the premise (a friend called it "*Shutter Island* meets *Restrepo*," and I had to admit that wasn't bad), but I knew it was a good premise that I could work with. I think I spent another year and a half developing it in my head, letting the universe grow in there before I tried to write anything. And then, of course, it changed vastly as I wrote it. But at its heart it really just started as a mystery story before it grew into something that you could read either as a thriller or as a war novel.

Tell us a little bit about your service in the Army.

I came to the Army late. I'd been an attorney working in New York City for a few years before I applied to go to Officer Candidate School (OCS), which is how you get commissioned if you've already graduated from college and didn't do ROTC or one of the military academies. OCS is an interesting place during wartime; it draws a lot of professional people who had never really considered the military when they were younger, which in turn affects the demographics of the officer corps. In a counterinsurgency campaign demanding maturity, cultural competency, and creativity in leadership, I think this is a good thing.

I was thirty-two with a career already when I went in. Most of my fellow lieutenants were in the twenty-two to twenty-six age range and had gone straight from college to the Army. It's definitely different. When you're used to being treated like a professional it's harder to tuck your head and soak up all the indignities of military life. But the little dramas and frustrations don't get to you as much and it's easier to manage all the "personalities" you get in the Army. I would not have wanted to do the job of a lieutenant as my twenty-three-year-old self.

I was commissioned as a field artillery officer and was

stationed at Fort Stewart, right outside Savannah, Georgia. We went to Iraq in 2007 for one of the long fifteen-month deployments during "the surge," and I spent most of that deployment in and around Ramadi, which is the capital of Anbar Province. We spent a lot of our time living in Iraqi outposts in and around the city, working to stand up the Iraqi security forces and help them to claim and secure their own city. That was surreal, working side by side with men some of whom a year before had been trying to kill Americans but who were now our allies; but it was a gratifying time, watching the city go from being one of the most dangerous in Iraq to one of the safer ones before our eyes. Sadly, with the rise of the Islamic State, Ramadi is a dangerous place again.

Why did you decide to set *The Valley* in Afghanistan even though you served in Iraq? What challenges did this present to writing the story?

Honestly, it never crossed my mind to set it anywhere but the Afghanistan theater. It needed a kind of geographic isolation that you just don't have in Iraq, even though Iraq is big and there are a lot of remote parts of it. *The Valley* was just a mountain story from the beginning.

Setting it in Afghanistan didn't really seem like an additional challenge at the time. I think the main thing I brought to the table from my own experience was just knowing how military people walk and talk, what the life is like, what Army people are like generally. I'm not trying to tell the story of the Afghanistan war writ large, so it was the people that were the focus and the driver of the story and they were the thing I was most concerned with getting right. Beyond that, mostly it was the normal business of setting a book someplace you've never been—researching your locales as best you can and apologizing for what you get wrong. Fortunately, there is rich, if limited, travel and ethnographic literature on the Nuristan province, where the story takes place. It's a place unlike any other in Afghanistan, with an ethnically and culturally distinct people, and it has been an object of fascination to Westerners for centuries.

Lots of early reviews have compared *The Valley* to Joseph Conrad's *Heart of Darkness.* Was this something you had in mind from the beginning?

Call me dense and unlettered but this one hit me out of left field. I had never read Conrad or knew the story in any detail until an early reader said, "I like the *Heart of Darkness* thing you've got going here!" and I panicked and ran out and got a copy. Okay, so now I get it: spooky, evocative geographic feature, check. Protagonist leaves safety and proceeds farther into geographic feature, check. Beyond that, honestly I have a hard time seeing it. Conrad's book is this famously allegorical attempt to get to the root of a historical era. *The Valley* has no such ambitions. No one should have such ambitions for his first novel. It's a character story about people's secrets and baggage and Black's growing personal obsession. And not for nothing, to get to the Valley you don't need to look to a literary river—or any further than the very historical and nonliterary mountains that were every bit as remote as the Valley; or the outposts, every bit as godforsaken as COP Vega, where nonfictional young Americans were engaged in knock-down-drag-out slugfests every bit as desperate as what is depicted in the book. *That's* the source material. I'm just not sure how much of that side of the Afghanistan war has made it into the common consciousness.

End of rant. As the reader will have surmised, this all drove me a little bonkers for a while. People would call it an "homage" to Conrad and I'd grind my teeth. Here I had taken this big loose bucket full of Kipling and Coleridge and Tim O'Brien and Dennis Lehane and John le Carré and the First Anglo-Afghan War and early British expeditions to Nuristan and crime novels and old art-rock lyrics and a bunch of other Easter eggs that I'm still telling myself someone will find, and dumped it all into the mix and rolled it out—*ta-DAA!*—into this big lumpy story with everything still sticking out of the dough, and what people took from all that was . . . Conrad. Arrgh. Didn't people see that if it's an homage to anything it's an homage to Kipling's *The Man Who Would Be King* (about Westerners meddling in Nuristan)? Couldn't they read my mind and see what a major influence O'Brien's *Going After Cacciato* was?

Et cetera. My wife, who heard versions of all this whining (and who gave Will Black his last name, by the way), gently reminded me that people mostly were just trying to be complimentary. I'm calm now, and I realize that (a) these are good "problems" to have, and (b) once you publish a story it's really not yours anymore, and that's really the point of writing.

***The Valley*'s Lieutenant Black is frustrated with the Army and already has one foot out the door when the novel begins. Does this mirror your own experience?**

As boring as it must sound, I had a good experience in the Army, tough times and all. I made lifelong friends, which is something you aren't really expecting to happen anymore once you're all grown up; and I got to work with soldiers, who are some of the finest, most inspiring, and also, most exasperating young people you will meet. They can be some of the smartest kids around, and then they'll do the dumbest things that will drive you crazy, and then they'll surprise and impress you again. (Any military person reading this knows I say this with love.)

All that said, the Army is a big, bureaucratic organization with a lot on its plate. If you're conscientious, if you want your unit to be excellent and want to take care of your soldiers, there will be frustrations. You get orders that don't make sense; you have higher-ups who won't hear what they need to hear or have forgotten what it's like to be a private; you have to tell your soldiers to do things you don't want to have to tell them to do. Sometimes you truly don't have the big picture from where you're standing, but anyone who cares kicks some trash cans. It's just part of it.

Black is just more of an extreme case. He doesn't hate the Army, in his heart. He loved it once. But he's been wronged by the Army. He did his best yet is disgraced, and now he carries a giant chip on his shoulder made of disillusionment and guilt. Same for the other characters; being frustrated by the Army is just part of being in the Army, even if you love it.

What do you hope readers take away from your novel?

Above all else, a good read: a story that will catch them and carry them someplace unexpected and that doesn't feel narrowly like a "war book" as they're reading it. Having early readers tell me that they couldn't put the book down (or berate me for costing them X nights of sleep) is really gratifying, but more so when it comes from readers who don't consider themselves "war novel people."

Also, I hope the book shows readers military people as they actually are—ordinary people who wear a costume to work—not in the caricatured ways they're usually portrayed, even in admiring works. Young soldiers have unique jobs and carry unique burdens, but at the end of the day they are nineteen-year-old, twenty-first-century American kids. I worked hard to show them as I knew them.

Finally, I hope readers take away a feel for the role that the concept of responsibility, of blame, plays in military life. Military fiction deals a lot with certain traditional themes—comradeship, sacrifice, loss of buddies—but not a lot with the awful weight of responsibility, of blameworthiness, that all military leaders carry at all times, whether they are in charge of five people or five thousand. It's something you're not really prepared for when you join the military—this idea that everything everyone beneath you does or fails to do is your responsibility, and everything that goes wrong is your fault, even if it's not. You internalize that accountability from the beginning, and you understand why it is absolutely necessary, but it never leaves you alone. It's an itch you can never scratch; there is never a moment when you sit back and say that you've done all you can do for your soldiers. There is always more you can do, to train them, to protect them, to get them what they need, and you feel like you have failed them a dozen times every day. When things go wrong, as they will, when people are hurt and lost, this sense of accountability and shame can crush leaders. At best, they are never the same. At worst, they are broken as people; they don't know how to set down that burden. I can truthfully say that I am more relieved that I never lost a soldier than I am that I came home unharmed—not because I'm so selfless a person, but because I don't know how I could handle that.

At one point, Merrick tries to comfort Black, who carries more weight on his shoulders than anyone ought to, and all he can offer is to say, lamely, that "maybe stuff in life balances out in the end." Meaning: maybe there is something good ahead for you that will make up for all the bad. It's pretty hollow comfort, because as he looks to the future Merrick knows that Black, like he himself, will never be able to set down that weight. This is the most prominent military theme in the story, and at one level this is what *The Valley* is about. Every military person in the book, even the ones who emerge as "bad guys," in some way believes that everything that happens is his own fault.

But more than anything, what I hope readers take away is a reading experience that leaves them feeling they've been on a journey someplace they weren't expecting to go. It's a dark story, but it's meant to be enjoyed. As odd as it must sound, I hope for readers to take the same joy in reading the book that I did in writing it, despite the fact that the themes and subject matter are far from happy ones.

There seem to be some loose ends at the conclusion of the story. Was that intentional?

Definitely! You have to work hard to put together everything that's happened, but there *is* an explanation for everything. Nothing in there is just the "fog of war." *The Valley* also opens some storylines that are left unresolved at the end, to be taken up in future books. Hopefully this is more tantalizing than frustrating for the reader. . . .

Is *The Valley* meant to be a real place in Afghanistan? Is it the Korangal Valley? Is Combat Outpost Vega meant to be COP Keating, the real-life outpost detailed in Jake Tapper's *The Outpost* and elsewhere?

No. There are a lot of mountains and valleys in Nuristan, but there's no Valley. (The Korangal Valley is in Kunar Province.) Same for COP Vega; I had been fascinated by the real-life COP Keating ever since I'd seen the Army's after-action review of the events there in 2009, and my COP Vega is definitely "that kind of place" (though I really went to town as far as the physical scale and complexity of the outpost itself). But *The Valley* is not about those real places. Mostly I just drew on them for setting. So while readers familiar with COP Keating or with Jake Tapper's riveting book will recognize some details, *The Valley* is not meant to be the story of those men, or inspired by it, or a reimagining of it, or a symbolic-allegorical . . . you get the point. I'm just telling a story. Only they can tell their stories.

Is all the Chuck Norris graffiti a real thing?

One hundred percent. You can't walk into a Porta-Potty overseas without reading it.